The Mayhem in the Masquerade

A Cozy Mystery

L.L. Gray

Heroic Rose Publishing

For anyone who's ever felt lost, out of place, and still held on to hope—
May you always find stories that feel like home.
Thank you for coming back to Havenwood.

Contents

Grab your FREE novella now!

Want a free book?

Of course you do, what madness could possess someone to **not** want free books?
There's no catch - you do sign-up for my mailing list but you can unsubscribe at any time.
There's also no spam.
Ever.
Sign up here to get your free book!
https://www.subscribepage.io/havenwood

Invitations and Incantations

I LEANED AROUND MR. Wigglesworth's cat apartment, stretching to press the final piece of tape on the corner of the gold and deep purple flyer in Spellbooks' front window. Outside, the early March wind swept the last of winter's chill through Havenwood's darkened streets. This was the fourth time I'd redone the window display this month. Maybe it was nerves. Maybe perfectionism. Or maybe it was the fact that I'd never hosted such a big event at Spellbooks before. Honestly, it was probably a mix of all three. But I knew in my bones that I *needed* this to be absolutely perfect.

"There. All done," I said, dusting off my hands and stepping back to admire the display. "What do you think, Spellbooks?" An approving vibration ran along the floorboards of the cozy shop, making me smile. Seven months ago, if you had told me I'd be talking to a shop and it talked back, I wouldn't have believed you. Now? Well, now, it was a completely different story. Spellbooks and I were business partners, and this event on the flyer was my best shot at drawing in more customers before—

Luna, my great-granny's familiar, interrupted my train of thought as she hopped over to inspect my work. Her snow-white fur nearly blended in with the lingering patches of frost on the ground outside the window, save for the twitch of her long ears. She surveyed the display with a critical eye, deciding whether it met her impossibly high standards. As she thoughtfully took it all in, I glanced down Arcadia Avenue. The evening stretched, quiet beneath an indigo sky caught between seasons. Thin starlight broke through the darkness, sparkling off the edges of rooftops still dusted with ice. March in Connecticut was a contradiction, teetering between winter's stubborn hold and spring's tentative arrival. Soon, the first real thaw would draw people back to the streets, eager for fresh air and the promise of new beginnings. In my opinion, it couldn't come soon enough.

"I have to admit, Harper," Luna said, her voice carrying that familiar hint of reluctant approval, "the display looks good."

I glanced down at her, a smirk tugging at my lips. "Fluff and furballs! Did I hear a compliment, or are my ears playing tricks on me?"

Luna's nose twitched, and she shot me a sidelong glare. "Don't get sassy, or I might just take it back," she replied with a sniff.

I chuckled, the sound carrying in the quiet air of the shop. "I'll take it. You know," I continued, glancing back at the flyer, which proclaimed Garrett Grimshaw's upcoming signing, "this event couldn't have come at a better time."

Luna peered out at the empty street, her ears flicking as a distant wind chime clinked. "Business hasn't exactly been bustling, has it?"

My stomach clenched. It was a simple question, but hearing it aloud made the feelings I'd been trying to ignore and shove to a little corner in the back of my mind feel more real. A slump after the holidays was normal, but this? This was something else. If things didn't pick up soon, I'd have to start making actual cuts which I wasn't ready to admit out loud. To be honest, I didn't even like admitting it to myself. My thoughts skittered away from the notion and every day I hoped against hope that this would be the day things would take a turn.

And every day, they didn't.

"Harper?" Luna asked. "Fluff and furballs, you look like you forgot to put coffee in the pot and just got a big swig of hot water. What's on your mind?"

I pasted on a breezy smile. "Oh, you know how it is. It must be winter lulls or something." I waved a hand dismissively, as if my dwindling sales were as natural as the snow melting outside. It sure didn't feel that way, but I wasn't about to say that to Luna. "Anyway, let's see how those flyers look from the outside."

Before Luna could press the issue, I grabbed my jacket from the hook and headed for the door.

Luna followed me out onto Arcadia Avenue, the chill of the March evening nipping at my nose. I pulled my jacket tighter, the scent of distant wood smoke mixing with the elusive promise of a thaw. Even in the off-season, Havenwood held onto its charm. Quaint shops lined the street, with their whimsical signs and cozy interiors, each offering a touch of magic. But today, the charm felt a little overshadowed by the emptiness.

"What if no one shows up?" I murmured, my breath fogging in the cold. "What if this event is a complete flop?"

Luna waved a tiny paw at the flyer plastered on the glass. "Since when have you known Garrett Grimshaw to do anything that was a flop?"

"His last book wasn't well-received," I pointed out.

Luna's whiskers twitched. "Which only resulted in more sales for him, or didn't you do your homework?"

"What about that recent movie adaptation?" I asked.

Luna sniffed disdainfully. "Doesn't count. They changed the ending of the book to make it more palatable for Hollywood audiences. If they'd stuck with the original, it would've been better—and a lot more controversial."

I grinned. "Not everything has to be controversial to be entertaining, Luna."

Luna flicked her ears in my direction. "Maybe, but it does create more of a buzz. And isn't that what we're going for here by inviting a best-selling author to do a book signing at Spellbooks?"

The wind picked up again, and I hitched the collar of my coat higher. "Garrett Grimshaw visiting Spellbooks for a book launch is a big opportunity," I said, glancing at the poster once more. Its bold lettering seemed to pop against the colorful background, promising an afternoon with the famous author and a chance to get his newest book signed.

"That's right. Keep your eyes on the prize," Luna replied, thumping her back foot for emphasis. "Who knows? Maybe this could spark something bigger. You could become a recognized stop on the literary map. The shop where all the greats come to sign their books."

I snorted, sticking my hands deep into my pockets as my fingers started to tingle with the cold. "Let's focus on getting past this event first."

"Don't you mean smashing it out of the park?" Luna asked.

"That's the goal, but I'm so nervous I'd settle for surviving," I admitted with a shrug. "I'm not sure I could handle more literary greats. Have you seen the email with the list of requirements his publicist sent me?"

Luna's ears twitched, and she rolled her eyes. "How could I miss it? I think the printer's still recovering from the length of that thing."

I nodded. "I swear, it's about ten pages long and gives minute-by-minute details on what his itinerary will look like, the specific temperature of the room, the refreshments, additional snacks for Garrett Grimshaw, the fact he's given up alcohol so no champagne, the list goes on! It even specifies what kind of tea he likes—English Breakfast with exactly one spoonful of honey and a generous splash of milk."

Luna shrugged. "Take your shot, kid. It's the best any of us can do."

"I suppose," I murmured, tipping my head to consider the display. Was the flyer perfectly square? The right side might be ever so slightly higher. I should fix that.

Luna interrupted my thoughts. "Speaking of tea, I'm off to see Agatha. We're finalizing plans for our *Bridgerton* marathon."

I blinked. "Wait. *That's* what you and Agatha are dressing up for? Not the masquerade ball the Silverthornes are hosting for Garrett Grimshaw's book launch?"

Luna scoffed. "Please. Why would I want to spend an evening surrounded by non-magical folks who can't appreciate my impeccable fashion sense?" She flicked her ears dramatically. "Imagine the scandal if I arrived in full regalia! How would the humans handle a rabbit in an evening gown?"

I grinned, already imagining the scene. "I think it could be great. Maybe Garrett Grimshaw would write you into his next book."

Luna waved a paw. "Please. I don't need to inspire any more artists. Been there, done that."

"Whaaa—" My brain stalled out as I tried to recall a piece of literature or artwork featuring a white rabbit. Of course, there was the White Rabbit from *Alice's Adventures in Wonderland* by Lewis Carroll, but beyond that I was stumped.

She winked at me. "However, if you know where to walk in London, you might just find a picture of little old me."

"Where?" I demanded.

"Wouldn't you like to know?" she asked archly, running a paw along her whiskers.

I rolled my eyes and shook my head. "You know, I bet I could get Gabriel to illusion a painting to look like this supposed masterpiece in London. If you come to the masquerade ball, you could have all of Havenwood wondering if a famous artist's best muse lives right here in Connecticut."

Luna flicked her ears dismissively. "Please. As if I'd waste an evening among folks who wouldn't recognize true artistry if it bit them. And before you say it, no. I'm not going to bite anyone to prove a point." She put a paw to her chin and tipped her head to the side. "Unless they have radishes. Then I might. Maybe. But only if I was in dire need."

"I don't think there'll be radishes at the ball, but Gabriel could always illusion you into something that wouldn't raise eyebrows if you change your mind. Oh! I know! You could go as Agatha's emotional support rabbit."

Luna gave me a look so flat it could shatter glass. "Harper, *no one* is up to that job. Agatha doesn't even like snickerdoodles. That's a clear sign of incurable emotional instability if ever I've heard one."

"That's a...point," I said before rushing on. "But I wouldn't want you to miss out. A masquerade ball sounds like fun!"

"Hmph. I have plenty of balls to view and don't have to get sweaty hopping around to what your young folks have the audacity to call music." She flicked her tail. "Enjoy your *boring* ball. I'll be indulging in tea, pajamas, and all the snickerdoodles I can eat."

And with that, she strutted down the street with all the regal grace of the diamond of the season.

The bell above the door tinkled as I stepped back inside. The sound echoed in the much-too-quiet shop, amplifying the stillness inside. I wished I could throw myself into a Bridgerton marathon and pretend my biggest concern was whether or not Daphne would end up with the Duke. Instead, I was stuck here, staring at a flyer and wondering if this book signing was enough to turn things around.

I sighed, worry creeping back in. Spellbooks had always been my refuge, even when I was a child visiting Great-Granny Bea. But lately, that refuge had started to feel like an isolation chamber. The nearly empty sales log on the counter was a glaring reminder of how bad things had become.

Granny Bea would've known how to draw people in, even in these slow months. What if I couldn't live up to her legacy? What if I couldn't afford to keep Spellbooks open? No, I shouldn't think like that. Business would pick up. It had to.

Busying myself, I adjusted the front table display for the third time this morning, trying to channel some of Granny Bea's charm. A neat stack of Garrett Grimshaw's previous bestseller, *Shadows of the Unseen*, sat front and center, its striking cover featuring a cloaked figure lurking in the glow of a streetlight. The book was the first installment of his long-running Rhett Ryder series full of spies, disguises, and daring escapes. Kind of like James Bond meets MacGyver, if Bond ever had to build an explosive out of a pocket watch and chewing gum.

It was always a solid seller, even before Grimshaw announced the location of his launch at Spellbooks, but even die-hard fans admitted the last few books in the series had lost some of their edge. The intrigue was still there, the action-packed espionage sequences thrilling as ever, but they lacked the punch of Grimshaw's earlier work.

Until now.

The buzz around the newest book, *Masks of Deception*, was different. Early reviews promised it was Grimshaw's best in years with a twist no one would see coming. I could barely wait to dive in myself.

I glanced behind the counter, where several sealed boxes sat untouched, boldly stamped with: **DO NOT OPEN UNTIL RELEASE DATE.** Grimshaw's newest novel, dripping with Mardi Gras charm, was safely secured under layers of packing tape, just waiting for the official go-ahead from Valerie St. James, his publicist.

I ran a finger along the edge of one of the boxes, fighting the urge to peel back the tape. Just one peek wouldn't hurt, right? It wasn't like I was going to sell them early.

Still, I pulled my hand back and exhaled. Better to make a show of it once Garrett Grimshaw and his publicity team arrived. I imagined unveiling the books with a dramatic flourish when the time was right. If I was going to sell this signing as an event worth attending, I needed to make sure everything was picture perfect because, with a celebrity author of Grimshaw's renown, there would definitely be cameras capturing every detail of the event.

I tapped the box and stepped back. Almost. I needed to do this right. For Spellbooks.

Despite everything being set for tomorrow, I still had to pinch myself. Submitting Spellbooks to a social media competition had been a last-ditch effort to drum up business, and to be honest, something I never expected to amount to anything. When Garrett Grimshaw's team reached out, I thought I was dreaming. Now, with the day nearly here, excitement and nervous energy twisted inside me, making me feel like I was on an emotional rollercoaster.

I turned toward the window, absently smoothing a stray ribbon on the nearby display as I peered out onto Arcadia Avenue. The street had felt abandoned for months, winter clinging to Havenwood like an unwelcome guest. Tomorrow, though, would be different.

There'd be people. Grimshaw fans. Customers in Spellbooks again.

Not just the occasional passerby bundled in scarves, hurrying from one destination to the next, but an actual crowd right here in Spellbooks.

My best friend, Bella, had mentioned her family's B&B, the Enchanted Oasis, was fully booked for the first time since New Year's, with more guests set to arrive tomorrow. If her reports were anything to go by, Grimshaw's fans had already begun descending on Havenwood, eager to be here for the book's launch day and the exclusive masquerade ball that had been planned as part of the festivities.

I still wasn't sure how a simple book signing had turned into a town-wide event, but once the inns began filling up, Gabriel and his family had seized the opportunity. The masquerade ball they were hosting in Grimshaw's honor would help celebrate the book and, if I had to guess, quietly boost Havenwood's economy. The Silverthornes never missed a chance to ensure the entire town benefited when they threw an event.

But all of this was because of Spellbooks and me.

A flicker of something settled in my chest, an unfamiliar but welcome warmth. Pride, maybe. Or possibly even hope.

Even with the nerves buzzing through me and the quiet worries I hadn't voiced to anyone, one thing was certain—tomorrow, Spellbooks would be filled with people again.

Anxious energy crept back in, and I pulled out my laptop, scanning Valerie's itinerary and the extensive notes I'd taken since the signing had been confirmed. Valerie and Garrett had a complicated history. They'd enjoyed a whirlwind romance followed by a messy divorce, and yet somehow, still manage to develop a professional partnership that had everyone scratching their heads. Tomorrow, they'd be arriving with his entire entourage, including his new fiancée, Savannah Chase, and the inevitable media circus that followed him everywhere.

Satisfied that I knew the schedule, I flitted around the shop, fixing the last of the decorations and tweaking the display table one more time. Rows of chairs filled the main area of the shop which Spellbooks had helped me clear, giving it an expectant air.

"Hey, Spellbooks," I called out softly, placing my hand on the wall. The wood warmed beneath my touch, a gentle acknowledgment from the spirit that lived within these walls. "Don't forget Garrett Grimshaw is coming tomorrow. It would be really nice if things could go smoothly. We both need this to go well."

The floorboards gave a little rumble beneath my feet, and I couldn't tell if it was agreement or laughter.

I patted the wall affectionately. "Let's aim for a relatively normal day tomorrow. *Normal* normal, not Havenwood normal. No imps escaping from stone spells, no spontaneous tea parties popping up, and definitely no talking books, okay?"

Spellbooks gave another gentle rumble, and the chalkboard behind the counter scratched out a message:

DON'T WORRY, HARPER. BEST BEHAVIOR.

I sighed, relief mixing with a flicker of hope. "Thank you. I want to make this an event to remember."

With one last glance around, I locked up the shop and headed upstairs to my apartment. As I passed the window, my reflection caught my eye. What I saw startled me. A tired face looked back at me surrounded by wind-tousled hair and deep shadows under my eyes from too many restless nights.

I took a deep breath as I pushed my hair back into some semblance of order, reminding myself that this event was a chance. Maybe, with a little luck and a lot of effort, it could be the kick start both Spellbooks and I so desperately needed.

Spellbooks in the Spotlight

THE NEXT MORNING DAWNED with a brilliant blue, cloud-dappled sky, just as I'd hoped. Maybe I shouldn't have been surprised. My best friend Bella's boyfriend, Alex, had a minor magical knack for reading the weather. Even though he was in Vegas on an exclusive chef-in-training residency, he'd checked Havenwood's weather forecast and confirmed that sunshine and only a few fluffy clouds were in our immediate future.

Relieved, I took in the way the morning light streamed through Spellbooks' front windows, bathing the shop in warm, golden hues. Dust motes floated lazily through the air, drifting in that peaceful, timeless way that only seemed to happen in old, quiet places. I swirled my coffee in its cup and let out a long, steadying breath, enjoying the moment of calm before the excitement of the day.

My phone buzzed, interrupting my thoughts. I glanced down to see Bella's name and answered immediately, "Hey, Bella! Got everything?"

"Absolutely," she chirped, sounding as bright as the day outside. "Mama's been up since dawn baking."

"Oh dear, I hope she didn't go to too much trouble," I replied, feeling a pang of guilt. "I didn't mean to make her wake up early."

"Harper, please." Bella laughed, the sound light and familiar. "You know she loves any excuse to make more food. As long as you're putting our flyers out with the treats, she's happy. Besides, we *all* want to see Havenwood and Spellbooks packed as much as you do."

"Well, if you're sure."

Bella tsked. "Don't be silly. It's already working. You got Grimshaw's team to stay at the Oasis, which means more business for my parents as well as for Spellbooks. This is amazing! You're amazing!"

I consciously relaxed my shoulders, forcing the anxiety in my stomach to settle. Maybe Bella was right. Maybe, even before the book signing started, the mere promise of Garrett Grimshaw's presence was already making a difference. Not just for Spellbooks, but for the rest of the community.

I *needed* that to be true.

"Thank you," I said, my voice steady, even if my thoughts weren't. "I really hope this event does some good."

For a moment, I almost added more. Almost admitted that I wasn't just hoping this event would help. I was depending on it. But I bit the words back. The last thing I wanted was for her to worry about me when her plate was already full running the Oasis with her parents.

This *had* to work.

Bella seemed to read my mind despite my attempt to hide my anxiety from her. "Don't worry about a thing. It's going to be better than good. It's going to be awesome. Look, the weather's perfect, and Garrett Grimshaw's got a huge following, right? This is going to be exactly the boost all of us in Havenwood need this time of year, trust me. Just keep doing what you're doing." She paused before adding, "But I do have a van full of food, so I could use a hand unloading it all. You won't believe how much Mama baked!"

I laughed, picturing Honey in a whirlwind of flour and rolling pins. "I can't wait. Thank you again, Bella. And make sure to thank your mom for me."

After we hung up, I gave myself a quick once-over in the mirror. Instead of my usual waves, I'd swept my hair into a sleek bun in an attempt at looking polished, professional.

The outfit had taken forever to settle on, but I'd finally landed on black trousers, a crisp white shirt, and a new blazer. It was the kind of thing a real business owner would wear. Someone who had everything under control. Someone who wasn't secretly wondering if they'd still have a business in six months.

If Thaddeus, my odious cousin, had inherited the shop, would he have let things get this bad?

I swallowed hard and forced a steadying breath. No one else knew how close I was to the edge. As long as I looked the part, maybe—just maybe—I could convince them, and myself, that I still had a grip on things.

Today, at least, I could pretend. Today, I looked like someone who deserved to stand behind the counter of Sullivan's Spellbooks, welcoming literary royalty and hosting an event that would hopefully keep us afloat.

As I clattered down the stairs, the subtle scent of aged paper, ink, and the faintest hint of lavender from the small satchets tucked among the books filled the air. The shelves shifted subtly, almost like Spellbooks was trying to steady me. I took a moment to give myself a mental pep talk.

You've got this. Bella's right. Everything is planned, and it's going to be a great event.

Because it was a special day, I set an extra bowl of treats outside Mr. Wigglesworth's cat apartment. Maybe that would keep him occupied and—hopefully—off my lap. Orange fur would definitely clash with my ensemble. As I waited for Bella, I hurried around the shop, straightening already perfectly aligned books and swiping invisible dust from shelves.

Luna hopped onto the counter beside me, her whiskers twitching with her usual wry amusement. "Fluff and furballs, I've seen less anxiety in a mouse surrounded by foxes."

"When have you ever been in a fox den?" I teased, brushing a hand over the wall's polished wood.

She gave me a lofty look. "Someone had to rescue the mouse," she quipped, smirking.

"Naturally," I replied with a soft laugh.

"Those foxes were terrified the second they saw my ninja headband," Luna said.

"Hey, speaking of your headband, could we put a pause on any ninja behavior today? I don't think these important book people can handle a ninja rabbit."

"No one can handle a ninja rabbit," Luna said with a haughty sniff, and then she relented. "But you make a valid point. I will masquerade as a plain, boring rabbit as long as there are people in the shop."

"Thanks Luna," I said with a sigh. I skimmed my hand along the wall's smooth surface, and it pulsed lightly under my fingertips. "That goes for you too, Spellbooks. Remember, we're keeping things entirely mundane today, okay?"

The shop was surprisingly still.

"Spellbooks? Did you hear me?" I asked, gently tapping the wall.

Luna snorted. "Spellbooks is just doing what you asked," she said, thumping her foot.

I could feel a faint, warm hum beneath my fingers, like a whispered promise. I chuckled, giving the wall a final pat. "Thanks, Spellbooks. That means a lot."

With the shop on board, I felt a bit more at ease. The shelves sat tall and proud, brimming with books arranged in neat rows, and the glass-fronted cabinets gleamed. This place had been Granny Bea's legacy, and now it was mine. With Spellbooks as my partner, I just hoped I could make it as successful as she had.

About ten minutes later, Bella pulled up in the Enchanted Oasis' van, honking as she arrived. I hurried out to help her, and when she slid open the van door, my jaw dropped. Inside was a riot of Mardi Gras colors, each box radiating warmth and delicious scents that had my mouth watering.

"Oh wow, Bella...this is...!"

She rolled her eyes, smiling. "It's a lot, I know. You know how Mama gets when she's in the zone."

The van was stacked with boxes brimming with Honey's Mardi Gras magic. I lifted one cover, revealing her signature beignets, still warm and dusted generously with powdered sugar that clung to the pastries like delicate snowflakes. Beside them lay a tray of mini king cakes, each intricately iced in purple, green, and gold, crowned with tiny fleur-de-lis sprinkles and a dusting of edible glitter that shimmered in the morning light. Beyond the tray was a veritable mountain of boxes.

"Bella, I can't afford all this! It's so much more than what we talked about!" I exclaimed.

She waved away my protest, handing me another box. "Don't worry about it. Mama's thrilled you asked, and honestly? This event is already doing wonders for Havenwood. The Oasis is booked solid, Hocus Mochas sold out of chocolate before noon yesterday, if you can believe that! Even the Hobbit Hole and the Dragon's Den are scrambling to keep up. A *ton* of people are coming to town just for this signing."

I forced a smile, even as my stomach twisted. From the outside, it looked like a win. The town was buzzing. The event would hopefully go smoothly. Normally, that would've been enough to keep me going. A happy Havenwood meant I was doing something right. But no one seemed to suspect just how frayed I felt inside.

Spellbooks was still wobbling on uneven footing, and no amount of smiling faces could fix the tight coil of worry that had taken up permanent residence in my chest. I wanted this event to matter. For Havenwood, of course, but also for me. For Spellbooks. For the strange little corner of magic I'd built my life around.

And that was the part I didn't want to admit aloud. The part I kept tucked behind every smile and cheerful comment. Because what kind of person thinks about their business first, when so much more is at stake?

Bella winked, oblivious to my spiraling thoughts. "Oh, and wait until you see these." She opened another box, revealing rows of golden crab cakes, flecked with green onions and what looked like red Cajun spices, garnished with fresh parsley and a thin slice of lemon.

The sight distracted me from my thoughts and my mouth watered. "I hope taste testing is allowed," I said hopefully.

"Allowed? It's encouraged. But only after we set up the buffet," Bella said, hefting an armful carefully and heading towards the door.

Inside, we placed trays of finger food on tables around the shop. On the large table along the back wall, Bella and I worked on creating a sumptuous buffet made of all the Mardi Gras-themed treats Honey sent over. The centerpiece was Honey's pièce de résistance: a towering bread pudding, warm and gooey, studded with raisins and pecans, all bathed in a creamy, spiced bourbon sauce. Around it, we arranged clusters of brightly colored pralines, their sugary shells catching the light. Crab cakes, beignets, and king cakes filled out the rest of the table. It was a feast of flavors and colors, each bite offering a little bit of Mardi Gras magic.

"What are these?" I asked, lifting up two cardboard coffee containers, complete with little spouts.

"Oh, you've got to try this," Bella said, setting the disposable coffee containers on the end of the table and grabbing a purple and gold paper cup for me. She grinned as she filled it and passed it to me. I inhaled deeply, the rich scent of coffee and a hint of something *more* filling my lungs.

"What is it?" I asked curiously.

"Chicory coffee. It's a special blend from Mama's fae friend, Kenzie, who owns a café down in New Orleans."

"Wow!" I said, burying my nose in the paper cup and inhaling gratefully. "This really is a special treat."

Bella smiled as she arranged the rest of the paper cups beside the coffee dispensers. "Mama thought it'd add a bit of *je ne sais quoi* to your event. Her words, not mine. You already know what you want the *quoi* to be today. In a word: incredible."

"Absolutely," I said, sticking out my fist.

Bella knocked her knuckles against mine, turning up her smile to full brilliance. I couldn't help but grin back. My best friend could read me like a book, no pun intended. She must've sensed my anxiety and was offering her unwavering support. Bella was the best.

I glanced around the shop. With the food and décor matching the Mardi Gras theme of the book with deep purples, rich greens, and brilliant golds, Spellbooks looked ready for a party. Everything felt so festive and professional that my nerves began to fade, replaced by a warm hum of excitement.

A knock sounded at the front door. I glanced out the window to see two familiar faces—Isadora, radiating restless energy like the crackling of a fire that refused to be contained, and Gabriel, whose smile sent a quiet warmth blooming through my chest, steadying me. I opened the door, and they stepped in.

"Hey Harper! Hi Bella! Goodness, this is incredible!" Isadora gushed with her usual enthusiasm. She bounced over to the buffet table, exclaiming over the food as Bella smiled.

Gabriel pulled me into a gentle hug before pressing a kiss to my temple. "She's right. Everything looks amazing," he murmured. His gaze lingered on me, warm and encouraging. "You've really outdone yourself, Harper."

"Thanks." I couldn't help but smile. He always seemed to know just how to settle my nerves.

Gabriel shot me a wink as he slid out of his jacket, revealing a crisp blue shirt under a stylish navy blazer. My heart did a little flutter at the sight of him. I was a lucky girl.

I hadn't always been so sure about him, about us. Back in February, we'd found ourselves tangled in a puzzle surrounding the missing heart of the magical heartwood tree, but it turned out that solving the conundrum of my own heart had been the biggest mystery of all. Over the past few weeks, our relationship, while still new, had only grown. Gabriel never wavered. He was always there with quiet support, steady as ever.

The *second* he heard about the possibility of a Garrett Grimshaw signing, he threw himself into plans, making sure I had everything I needed before I even thought to ask. The masquerade ball was mostly his brainchild. His way of making the event feel even bigger. And Isadora had, of course, insisted on coming back from her magic academy to help with the execution of the party.

I glanced at him again, warmth blooming in my heart. Whatever happened today, I wasn't facing it alone.

But even as the thought settled, a pang of guilt crept in. He had no idea how much I was keeping from him. None of them did.

Isadora bounced over, her eyes bright as she took in the spread. "Harper, this place is magical! I mean, look at all this food. I can't believe Honey did all of this! And the decorations? Perfection!" She gave a chef's kiss, throwing her hand up into the air dramatically.

I glanced around, taking it all in as if through her eyes. The brightly colored treats, the polished wood shelves, the cozy glow from the morning sun filtering in through the windows. On the surface, Spellbooks looked like it was ready to start an adventure.

So why did I still feel like I was about to trip over the first page?

I smoothed my hands over my blazer, hoping the shop's warmth would settle the jittery feeling in my chest.

Gabriel reached for my hand, giving it a gentle squeeze. "This is going to be a magnificent event," he said, his voice full of quiet confidence. "For you, for Spellbooks, and for Havenwood. Getting Garrett Grimshaw to do a book signing here? You astound me. What a fantastic accomplishment."

I forced a laugh, rolling my eyes. "You're biased."

He leaned closer, eyes twinkling. "Maybe, but I'm also right."

Gabriel stayed by my side as I fussed over the last-minute touches. He was there with a steadying hand on my shoulder or a small nod of encouragement, always seeming to know what I needed, even when I didn't. Just before people began to arrive, he stepped in front of me, brushing a stray wisp of hair back into place.

"After this, you deserve a night to just enjoy the masquerade ball at the manor," he said, holding my gaze with a sincerity that made my heart skip a beat. "When you wrap up this event, I'm making it my mission to ensure you get to relax and have some fun."

"Your mission? Are you a spy like Rhett Ryder now?" I teased.

"A promise, then," He smiled, leaning in for a soft kiss, then straightened, giving my hand one last squeeze.

"Have you told her about the surprise?" Isadora asked, practically vibrating with excitement.

Gabriel shot her a look that could have melted ice. She clasped her hands over her mouth, eyes widening in guilty realization.

"No, I thought I'd keep it a *surprise*. I should've known better than to tell you about it," he said, his tone good natured even though his expression was mildly exasperated.

Isadora put her hands on her hips, refusing to be cowed by her big brother. "You wouldn't have pulled it off without me."

I inserted myself between them and held up a hand, laughing. "Don't worry, I'll act surprised when I see it, whatever 'it' is."

I was grateful for the distraction. It gave me something to latch onto besides the tight coil of nerves I was barely keeping in check. If I could focus on their antics, I wouldn't have to think about whether this event would actually save my shop.

Before Gabriel could respond, Luna thumped her foot on the floor, drawing our attention toward the window.

"Surprises and all that fluff will have to wait," she said, pointing an ear towards the road outside. "They're here."

"They're here?" I gasped, rushing toward the window.

Luna nodded and hopped down to the floor. "And that's my cue to leave. No offense, but I have no interest in getting trampled by a mob of excitable book lovers."

I snorted. "You could stay, you know. Lend some moral support."

She scoffed. "And risk getting mistaken for a *mascot*? No, thank you. Agatha and I have far more sophisticated plans for those of us who don't wish to mingle with your little literary circus."

I narrowed my eyes. "You mean going to Agatha's for a Bridgerton tea, don't you?"

Luna fluffed up her fur. "I don't see how that's relevant."

"You do know that show is based on a series of books, don't you?"

She flicked an ear. "Yes, but the show has orchestral pop covers and dramatically smoldering eye contact, so really, it's a completely different experience."

I chuckled. "Fine, go enjoy your scandalous Regency drama. Just try not to start a turf war between the Ton and the book lovers."

"No promises," she quipped, before making her way to the door like a queen mildly inconvenienced by her court.

Man of the Hour

WE CRANED OUR NECKS toward the window, curiosity drawing us in like moths to a flame. Outside, three glossy black sedans, windows tinted so dark it was impossible to see inside, pulled up in perfect formation.

The drivers exited in near unison, their crisp black suits, gleaming gold buttons, and neatly tied ties evoking a sense of purpose and order. But it was the lone security guard who commanded my attention.

The tall, no-nonsense man stepped out of the lead car, his movements efficient, assessing the area with a sharp, practiced gaze. His tailored suit barely concealing the tension in his posture. I could tell by his stance and alertness that he wasn't just for show. This was someone who had training and took his job seriously.

A few passersby slowed, throwing curious glances at the procession, their expressions ranging from mild interest to wide-eyed surprise. Across the street, a teenager held up his phone, snapping a quick photo, while an older woman whispered to her companion, gesturing toward the sleek black cars. The guard took it all in, his sharp gaze scanning the area, completely unfazed by the attention.

"Interesting," Isadora murmured, watching as the passengers emerged.

I hummed in agreement, but a flicker of unease stirred in my gut. I told myself it was just the excitement of the event, nothing more.

"That seems like a lot," Bella whispered. "Do all authors come with their own bodyguard?"

"This is *Garrett Grimshaw* we're talking about," Isadora murmured back. "This guy is basically a rockstar in the book world, isn't he?"

"Something like that," I said as I grabbed my coat, slipping it on so I could greet my guests properly.

"Is that him?" Bella whispered, gripping my arm.

Our eyes locked onto the first figure stepping out of the lead car. I shook my head as I recognized her from my research.

"No, I think that's his publicist, Valerie St. James," I whispered back.

The woman radiated sophistication in a way that made me want to shrink back and check for lint on my blazer. She wore a long, emerald green wool coat over a stylish black sheath dress. Her shoes were impossibly high and matched her purse perfectly. Her sleek, chin-length bob was razor sharp, every strand in place as though she'd just stepped off a magazine cover. Every detail of her appearance was sleek and meticulously polished.

I slipped out of the shop and smiled warmly as she cast a quick, appraising glance in my direction. She gave an approving nod before checking on the rest of the entourage, exuding authority with every click of her high heels.

Trailing behind her was a mousy-looking younger woman juggling two coffees, a stack of books, and two overstuffed bags. In contrast to Ms. St. James, her appearance looked more thrown together, almost like my everyday style, and she seemed to be a moment away from toppling over. She pushed her oversized glasses up her nose with the back of her hand, but they kept slipping down every time she attempted to balance her load. Even from where I stood, her awe at her boss was unmistakable.

I knew that look. I'd seen it plenty of times when my dad was stationed overseas. It was the same way junior officers snapped to attention when the commanding officer walked into the room. Cool and competent on the surface, but the second their superior turned away, their nerves slipped through the cracks.

And sure enough, as soon as Ms. St. James turned her head, a flicker of uncertainty crossed the assistant's face before she smoothed it away.

Funny. I'd thought I was the only one faking confidence today.

"Who's that?" Bella whispered from beside me.

"That's Mindy Hart," I whispered back. "Valerie's assistant."

"She looks terrified," Bella observed.

"I would be too if I worked for Valerie St. James," Isadora breathed, joining our hushed conversation. "The woman is a *legend* in the publishing world. She can sell anything between two covers."

I nodded, but kept my eyes fixed on the second car as another set of doors swung open. Out stepped a young man, stiffly adjusting the collar of his crisp blue shirt. His blond hair looked stylishly tousled, in a precisely carefree manner that probably took him hours to get just right. He had that polished, almost preppy vibe, though his gaze was fixed on his phone in a way that hinted at disinterest, or possibly even disdain.

Beside him stood a striking older woman with blond hair swept up into an elegant twist, her large diamond earrings catching the light. With a practiced touch, she reached up to brush a lock of hair off the young man's face, her perfectly manicured nails just grazing his cheek before he flicked his head impatiently, causing the hair to fall right back.

"I don't recognize them. Who are they?" I asked, feeling anxiety blossom in my chest. Valerie hadn't said anyone besides Garrett and his fiancée would be attending, and I didn't recognize either of these people.

"That's Tiffany Moncrief-Grimshaw," Isadora whispered excitedly. "Garrett's second wife and their son, Nate. When they split, it was huge news. All over the tabloids for what seemed like an age."

"Oh," I breathed, watching the three women standing within arm's reach of each other and exchanging sidelong glances that could curdle cream. "This is going to be...interesting."

"No, don't worry about a thing. They're on good terms now," Isadora reassured me.

Nate shot an icy glare toward the third car, and his mother caught his elbow, turning him away with a plastic smile frozen on her beautiful face.

"Are you sure about that?" I asked softly.

Before anyone could answer, the man of the hour stepped out of his car. Garrett Grimshaw. He wore a black silk button-down under a snazzy, ebony blazer over dark wash jeans and somehow managed to exude a chilled, nonchalant air. He reflexively ran a hand through his long, light brown hair as he scanned the area. The movement was practiced yet effortless, as though he'd mastered the art of looking perfectly windswept.

A ripple of excitement passed through the onlookers gathering on Arcadia Avenue. A few people along the sidewalk fumbled for their phones, while others elbowed companions and whispered excitedly. Someone called out his name, and Garrett, ever the professional, flashed a grin and lifted a hand in an easy wave. A camera shutter clicked, then another.

Nodding in approval at the turnout, he spun back to the car, offering his hand to the woman still inside. As she exited the vehicle, I recognized her immediately from Valerie's detailed information. It was Savannah Chase, the social media darling, and Garrett's fiancée.

She was influencer perfection, every inch of her curated for the camera lens. Her long blonde hair fell in sleek, beachy waves, and her white dress, tailored to emphasize every angle, shimmered subtly under the late-morning sun. An oversized gold necklace rested across her collarbones, positioned just-so to catch the light, while her makeup was meticulously contoured and coordinated, giving her an almost flawless, filter-smooth look.

She draped her coat loosely over her shoulders, more for aesthetic flair than warmth, despite the chill in the air. More cameras clicked. A group of early arrivals huddled nearby, phones lifted, snapping photos and whispering excitedly. Her polished smile never faltered, but something about it seemed fixed in place, a careful mask of effortless charm. Even as heads turned in her direction, I caught the flicker of something in her eyes. Was that mild boredom or perhaps the exhaustion of someone always being watched?

"Is that Savannah Chase? The Instagram influencer?" Bella breathed.

"And Garrett's new fiancée," I confirmed, taking in the glint of the oversized diamond on her ring finger.

"Of course. Isadora," Gabriel muttered, giving Isadora a nudge as she leaned in, eyes wide. Isadora glanced at him and then stood straight, putting on what I'd come to term her "perfectly poised for the tourists" face. It was the joyful, welcoming expression she used at all the town events, and, all things considered, this was a pretty big event, even by Havenwood standards. I was glad she, Gabriel, and Bella were all by my side as Garrett's team headed in our direction.

Valerie St. James paused in front of us, her dark eyes flicking across each of our faces. I had to resist the urge to squirm. Finally, she nodded, addressing me. "Harper Sullivan, I presume?"

I dipped my head, already knowing she wasn't a fan of physical contact. "Yes, it's so nice to meet you in person, Ms. St. James."

Valerie nodded as she took in Spellbooks. "Call me Valerie, please. I must say, I'm pleased to see that the pictures don't do your adorable shop justice. You can't always trust social media these days to be sure what you see is what you get."

"It can be tricky," I admitted, "but Sullivan's Spellbooks has been an institution in Havenwood for decades."

Valerie nodded, and I thought I caught a hint of a smile at the corners of her mouth. "I can see that. It's absolutely perfect for what I had in mind for Garrett today." She stepped back and gestured behind her. "Speaking of, please allow me to introduce the man of the hour, Garrett Grimshaw."

Garrett flashed a charming, practiced smile as he extended his hand. "Miss Sullivan, thank you so much for hosting us," he said, pumping my hand with the easy confidence of someone who had done this a hundred times before. "It's a pleasure to be here. I can't think of a better place to kick off my book tour than in such a delightful shop. My book and your charming store are the perfect match, don't you think?"

More camera shutters clicked, and I managed a polite nod, though my thoughts tumbled over each other like an overturned stack of books. Launch day. Tour kickoff. So many people watching. I needed to stay sharp, to make this look effortless. I could *not* afford to mess this up.

Calm, composed, collected. That's how a successful business owner should look, right?

Garrett turned to the group, flashing that grin like it came with its own spotlight. "And who else is part of our welcoming committee?" he asked.

The question jolted me. I should've already made introductions.

"Yes! Right, of course," I said, my voice a touch too bright. "This is Gabriel Silverthorne. His family is hosting the masquerade ball in your honor this evening. And here is Bella DeLuca. Her family catered this event. I can't wait for you to see the food. And this is Isadora, Gabriel's sister."

Garrett lifted Isadora's hand, lightly brushing her knuckles with an airy kiss. "Charmed, I'm sure."

Isadora blushed a pretty pink that nearly was a perfect match for her hair.

Savannah swept up beside Garrett, clutching his arm. He blinked and dropped Isadora's hand. Savannah ignored Isadora and held out her hand to me. The way she held it, I wasn't sure if I was meant to kiss it or shake it. I opted for shaking and her nails sparkled in the sun. Savannah's nails were a bubblegum pink, perfectly matching her lip gloss. Tiny crystals adorned each one, catching the sunlight

"This is such a cute little shop," she cooed, flashing a too-bright smile. She slid her fingers along his biceps, letting her diamond ring catch the light with practiced precision. "Garrett has been just dying to visit. It's all he's talked about. Getting out of the city and meeting some real fans." She glanced over her shoulder, giving a coy little finger wave at the gathered onlookers. The sound of cameras snapping intensified.

"Savannah, darling," Garrett interrupted, laughing slightly. "We're *all* thrilled to be here." He tossed back his hair again as he shot his fiancée a look.

"Of course," Savannah said, looking up and down Arcadia Avenue. "I love a quaint little town. There's always so many kitschy things around. And it's a great change of pace for my audience. I bet I'll find some cute places to photograph my new perfume for its launch next month." With practiced efficiency, she whipped out a small glass bottle from her purse. Its shape mimicked the diamond on her ring, and it contained a pretty pink solution. She spritzed it in the air. "*Savannah* by Savannah Chase. Pre-order your bottle now."

The scent hit me a moment later. It was an overpowering blend of sugary vanilla and sharp citrus, with an unexpected burst of peppery spice that crept to the back of my nose and made me want to sneeze. It was the kind of scent that overwhelmed the senses, leaving you wondering if it was meant to entice or confuse.

Garrett laughed a little too loudly, patting her hand. "That's my Savannah, always hard at work."

A clipped, refined voice cut in. "Yes, well, we're *all* hard at work, but today is about you, Garrett," Valerie said, stepping forward.

"Always there to keep me on track," Garrett said, his smile not faltering an iota. "This is your show, Valerie. Just tell us where we should go so we can take our places and smile for the cameras." Both he and Savannah turned to the onlookers and struck a pose so obviously practiced that it elicited a soft snort of amusement from Bella.

A new voice broke in. "Are you going to make introductions, Valerie, or force us to stand out in the cold all day?"

My gaze shifted to the pair waiting impatiently behind Garrett and Savannah. The elegant blonde woman swept past Valerie, her heels clicking sharply against the sidewalk. Her eyes, cool and calculating, flicked over the shop before landing on Savannah with a faintly raised brow that spoke volumes.

She extended her hand with effortless grace, the buttery leather of her designer bag shifting slightly in the crook of her arm. I blinked, recognition hitting me a second too late. That was a Birkin. A real one.

I'd never seen one in person before. The closest I'd gotten to one of the famous bags was in magazines or in the kind of TV shows where people bought handbags that cost more than a car. How much did those go for? Twenty grand? More? That bag alone could probably pay off my bills, restock Spellbooks, and still leave me enough to buy a used car.

"Tiffany Moncrief...," she said, her tone crisp, before pausing just long enough to add, "Grimshaw," the name dropping like a gauntlet as she cast a fleeting glance toward Savannah.

Then, just as smoothly, she returned her attention to me. Her smile was impeccably polite. "Charming little shop you have here."

"Thank you," I murmured, resisting the urge to smooth the front of my blouse. My hands felt clammy as my brain scrambled to process what was unfolding. One ex-wife I'd braced myself for. Two? Plus a new fiancée? That was an entirely different battlefield.

Tiffany stepped aside with the grace of a queen yielding space, inclining her head toward the young man at her shoulder. "And this is my son, Nathan Grimshaw."

"Nate," he corrected, his handshake brisk and perfunctory, his eyes never quite meeting mine. Instead, his gaze pulled magnetically to Savannah, lingering just a moment too long. Something sharp flickered in his expression for a moment before a mask of cool indifference slid into place, but I was sure of what I'd seen. What had happened between Garrett's son and his fiancée to result in such a look?

I hesitated, my mind catching up a second too late. Wait. How old was Nate again? Mid-to-late twenties? Savannah couldn't be much older. She was closer to his age than Garrett's.

That explained the tension. His new stepmother-to-be was practically his peer. I can't imagine that made family dinners very easy.

Savannah, for her part, tossed her hair with a flick of practiced indifference, angling her chin as though Nate wasn't worth her notice. But the way her lips twitched into a faint, knowing smirk suggested she noticed plenty.

Tiffany's gaze cut between them, cool and assessing, before her lips pressed into a thin line.

"Shall we go inside, darling?" Savannah said suddenly, her tone syrupy as she looked up at Garrett, slipping an arm through his. "These photos will look just amazing with the books in the background." She pulled out her phone, tilting it for a quick selfie with Garrett, who offered an obliging smile, his practiced charm effortlessly defusing the undercurrent of tension swirling around him.

Valerie sighed softly, the sound just audible above the click of Savannah's phone. "Garrett," she said, her voice polished and professional, "let's keep the focus on the book, shall we? The fewer distractions, the better." Her gaze swept briefly to his hair. "And there's still time for a trim before the ball today. A fresh cut always photographs well."

Garrett raked a hand through his hair in an exaggerated gesture, his grin flashing with just enough defiance to hint at his amusement. "I like it long, Valerie. I think it adds some mystery, don't you?"

"Well, it's wonderful to meet all of you," I said quickly, forcing a bright smile. "But it's too chilly to be standing outside on the sidewalk all day. Please, come inside and warm up. We have refreshments waiting." I moved to open the door for everyone.

"Fabulous," Savannah exclaimed, brushing past me. "You don't happen to have champagne this early, do you?"

Tiffany's lips thinned. "It's a bit early for drinking, don't you think?" she asked snidely.

Before Savannah could respond, Valerie stepped in smoothly. "Please remember this is a dry event," she said, her polished tone carrying an edge. "Garrett's made some wonderful choices for his health recently, and we should all be supportive." Her pointed glance at Savannah left little room for argument. Turning to me, she added, "You have the beignets as requested?"

I nodded quickly. "Made fresh this morning, courtesy of Bella's mother. She's a whiz with pastries."

Garrett laughed, the sound a little too loud but warm, nonetheless. "I can't wait to try them. After my research trip to New Orleans for *Masks of Deception*, I can't get enough of beignets. I may have replaced one vice with another, but hey, what's life without a little indulgence?"

Bella spoke up, her calm voice soothing the brewing tension. "Exactly what my mother always says. She'd love to hear your thoughts on the beignets, and she sent over some chicory coffee straight from New Orleans which will be the perfect pairing."

"Incredible!" Garrett exclaimed, his enthusiasm infectious. "I can't wait."

I held the door as everyone filed into Spellbooks, with Valerie's assistant bringing up the rear. A notebook slipped out of one of the overstuffed bags as she struggled with her load, and I swooped to pick it up for her.

"Here, I've got that," I said.

"Thanks," the assistant murmured, shoving her glasses up the bridge of her nose. They immediately slid back down. "I'm Mindy Hart, by the way. The one behind all those emails?"

"Nice to meet you face to face. I'm Harper Sullivan," I said. "Can I help you?" I gestured to the precarious load she was carrying.

Mindy gratefully passed me the coffees and then hitched the bags higher. "I know. I recognize you from the contest. I have to say, your shop is delightful. It's gorgeous! I'm glad Valerie picked Spellbooks. I was really rooting for you."

"That's so kind of you. To be honest, I almost didn't enter. I wasn't sure Spellbooks could compete with some of those giant bookstores in New York."

"Don't doubt yourself," Mindy said sincerely. "From the start, Valerie was very clear about wanting something outside the city. She's an absolute genius when it comes to book launches, so your shop must've been perfect in her eyes."

"You sound like you enjoy working for her," I said as we stepped inside.

"Enjoy? That might be pushing it," Mindy said with a little chuckle. "But I know I'm lucky to learn from someone with her experience. Assistants who last at least a year with her always go on to incredible careers. It's like she has the golden touch—everything around her sparkles." Despite her obvious admiration, the exhaustion in her eyes was hard to miss.

"Well, I'm glad you're both here. It's lovely to meet you, Mindy," I said warmly, hoping my own smile didn't look as strained as it felt.

As I handed off the coffees, my gaze swept the shop, taking in the scene unfolding before me. Tiffany and Nate stood near the counter. Their stiff postures and sharp glances at Savannah betrayed their shared disdain. Savannah, oblivious to, or perhaps ignoring, the tension was taking selfies with Garrett, who dutifully posed beside her, beignet in hand. Bella hovered nearby, attempting to direct attention back to the refreshments, while Gabriel and Isadora guided Valerie through the shelves with an air of professional charm that seemed effortless for both Silverthorne siblings.

I forced a steadying breath. Soon, the shop would be full, lively with excited book lovers, exactly as I had hoped. This was what Spellbooks needed. A full house. Big names. Buzz.

So why did I still feel like I was holding my breath, waiting for the other shoe to drop?

I curled my fingers around my cup, the warmth of the coffee seeping into my soul. This had to work. I had put everything into making this event a success, and if today didn't change things for Spellbooks, I wasn't sure what would.

Pasting on a smile, I squared my shoulders and joined in the excitement of the final preparations before we opened Spellbooks to the public for the largest event we'd ever hosted.

masks of Deception

THE SHOP BRIMMED WITH people, far more than I'd anticipated. Every seat was taken, with more attendees lining the walls and spilling into every available space. Spellbooks shifted subtly to help, widening the aisles and clearing corners, but it wasn't enough. As I darted around to make room, even the staircase became prime real estate for a few determined onlookers craning their necks for a better view. After the recent lull in business, it was thrilling to have this many people in the shop, but it was also overwhelming.

Somehow, we managed to fit everyone in, although it was more than a little squished. Once everyone was settled, Garrett took his place at the front to much applause. He grinned, flicking his hair back and posing for the audience to snap photos before he began to read from his latest novel, his deep voice and theatrical pauses drawing the crowd in. When he reached the cliffhanger ending of the selected chapter, he snapped the book shut with a practiced flourish, tossing his hair back with an expert flick.

"If that doesn't whet your appetite," he said, flashing a charming smile, "I don't know what will. And lucky for you, I'll be here all afternoon, signing books and answering your questions...well, the ones I can, anyway."

He leaned in with a conspiratorial wink that sent a wave of giggles through the crowd. Then, as if suddenly struck by inspiration, he clapped his hands together.

"You know, since tonight's the big masquerade ball up at the Silverthorne estate—" he let the name drop with just enough casual arrogance to make it seem exclusive "—I think it's only fair that some of my biggest fans get a chance to join in the fun."

A ripple of excited whispers swept through the audience. I could almost feel the energy shift as people leaned forward, eager, hopeful. Not everyone was excited, though. Valerie, standing off to the side near me, stiffened.

"Let's do a drawing!" Garrett announced, his enthusiasm feeding theirs. "Write your name and number down, and I'll pick a few lucky winners to be my special guests."

He turned toward Valerie, all charm. "Val, be a dear and fetch me some paper and a bowl, will you?"

Valerie's expression barely flickered. She smiled, smooth and polished, every bit the professional. "That's a wonderful idea, Garrett," she said brightly.

She turned ever so slightly, leaning over to whisper to Mindy, but I was close enough to overhear, "And it's *so* nice when he tells me about these things *before* he does them. Mindy, make it happen."

Mindy shot me a desperate look as Valerie stepped away, still smiling for the audience like this had been part of the plan all along.

Next to me, Gabriel leaned forward and murmured to the assistant. "Don't worry about a thing. We've got plenty of space at my family's estate to accommodate some late invitees."

"And I've got a bowl and some paper in the back," I offered.

Mindy's shoulders relaxed, and a relieved smile graced her lips. She shoved her glasses back up into place. "Really? You two are heroes. Thank you so much." I gave her a reassuring smile before hurrying off to find the items for Garrett's drawing.

By the time I returned, a line had formed, winding its way between shelves and halfway up the stairs. I set the bowl and paper on the table at the front before moving through the shop, trying to keep an eye on everything at once.

I caught sight of the stack of *Masks of Deception* that I'd neatly arranged early this morning on Garrett's signing table. Just for a second, I froze. I'd spent so long staring at that sealed box and building the moment up in my mind over the past week. Now here it was. The glossy covers of the new release gleaming under the lights, casually on display like they belonged here. And Garrett Grimshaw, literary legend and international bestseller, was right here in Spellbooks. Signing his novels.

A quiet swell of pride crept up my spine, and a flush of excitement heated my cheeks. Not because of anything *I'd* done, necessarily, but because this odd little bookshop I loved so fiercely had somehow become the kind of place where moments like this could happen.

Then someone called my name from across the room, and just like that, I was swept back into the fray.

Honey's Mardi Gras-themed treats disappeared quickly, but Bella kept the trays filled, chatting with guests as she handed out pastries and drinks. Gabriel manned the register so I could play host, and from the steady ding of sales, he was clearly taking his temporary title of "cashier-in-chief" very seriously. Isadora handled the crowd, keeping the line moving, refilling displays, and redirecting eager fans when they lingered too long. I floated between them, filling in where needed—checking on sales, answering questions, and making sure Garrett's signing table was stocked with fresh pens and books. Although I was busy running around, I couldn't help but notice the tension simmering from Garrett's entourage.

Valerie stood near the front of the room, eyeing Savannah at the back, who was snapping pictures of her perfume bottle in various locations, nudging customers out of the way as she angled her phone for the perfect shot. Savannah's tight dress and over-the-top jewelry screamed for attention, glittering under the overhead lights as she struck another exaggerated pose. She tilted her phone, lips pursed in a practiced pout, oblivious to the growing frustration around her.

Valerie's lips thinned as her gaze flickered between the self-absorbed fiancée and the increasingly impatient crowd, who were too polite to say anything but not polite enough to hide their annoyance. The phone's flash went off again—twice.

With a dramatic sigh, Savannah flipped her hair over one shoulder and examined the photo. "Ugh. Bad angle. One more." She didn't even glance at the people she nudged out of the way as she shifted to get a better shot.

Valerie let out an audible exhale, shooting a glare at Mindy before tipping her head toward the oblivious influencer in a silent command. Mindy sprang into action, weaving through the crowd toward the middle of the room, where Savannah had staked out a clear space for her mini photoshoot near the romance display.

Savannah extended one long leg, tilted her head just so, and snapped another photo. "Hashtag bestselling fiancée," she announced loudly, beaming at her screen.

"Excuse me, Miss Chase," Mindy chirped with a practiced smile. "So sorry to interrupt, but a couple of guests mentioned the scent might be a bit strong for the space and we all want today to go smoothly for Mr. Grimshaw, don't we?" She gently plucked the perfume bottle from Savannah's hand before the influencer could respond.

Savannah blinked. "Wait...what?"

"I just want to make sure everyone's breathing easy while they wait!" Mindy added with another sunny smile.

Savannah huffed and spun on her heel, marching past the line of guests toward the coat rack near the back wall where Valerie, Nate, and Tiffany had claimed a corner for themselves. She yanked her bag off the hook with enough force to make the coats beside it sway. Mindy leapt forward, steadying them before any could fall.

Nearby, Tiffany took a long, deliberate sip of her coffee. "You could always take a photo with your fiancé instead," she said, voice smooth and just a little too pleasant. "After all, the crowd is here because it's *his* name on the cover, not yours."

Savannah whirled on her, mouth gaping in outrage and giving a surprisingly accurate impression of a furious fish.

Valerie's professional smile didn't budge, but her tone cooled a degree as she raised an eyebrow fractionally at Savannah. "And we wouldn't want to overshadow the author, would we?"

Nate gave a soft snort. "Not that it's stopped her before."

Tiffany's lips twitched behind her cup, and she offered an airy, "Fifteen minutes of fame *is* still technically fame, dear."

The blonde influencer bristled, and her head snapped towards the trio. For a heartbeat, she stood frozen with her bag clutched in one hand as she glared daggers at them. Then, just as suddenly, her expression smoothed into something camera-ready. She flipped her silky hair over her shoulder and flounced toward the front of the room.

Valerie's brow twitched, though she quickly masked the reaction with a practiced smile. She flicked her fingers at Mindy who pursued Savannah. However, she wasn't quite fast enough as Savannah cut a swath through the gathered crowd. In no time, the blonde influencer was at Garrett's side, slipping her arm through his with a well-timed pout.

"Garrett, darling," she cooed, pitching her voice just loud enough to carry. "When can we grab a drink? I want to toast your success."

Mindy stepped forward, a professional smile in place. "Perhaps later, Miss Chase. We do have a schedule to keep."

Savannah rolled her eyes with exaggerated annoyance. "But in New York, they'd have already brought out the champagne to toast Garrett's latest masterpiece," she said, her tone dripping with disdain. Her gaze slid to Tiffany and her fingers clenched on Garrett's arm before she plastered on an even more dazzling smile for the crowd. With practiced ease, she leaned into Garrett for another photo.

Garrett stiffened for half a second, but then, with the grace of a practiced performer, he pulled Savannah in closer. "You know me," he said smoothly, dropping a kiss to her temple, "I'm trying to make better choices these days."

Savannah let out a light laugh, tilting her head up at him. "Oh, is that what we're calling it? I seem to remember champagne at your birthday party last month."

Garrett's jaw tensed, but the moment passed in an instant. He grinned, tossing a wink to the audience. "Everyone falls off the wagon now and then. But the doctor says I need to be healthier, and I'm determined to be the best I can in all things." He leaned in and kissed her cheek. "Especially for you."

Nate scowled from his seat, his arms crossed tightly over his chest. "Unbelievable," he muttered, glaring at Savannah with an expression that practically curdled the air around him. Tiffany gave a soft sigh, her gaze never leaving Garrett, who chuckled and shifted slightly under Savannah's perfect pout.

The crowd continued to buzz around them, oblivious to the quiet tensions rippling beneath the surface. For my part, I just kept moving, determined to hold things together as best I could. But as I glanced back at the fractures forming in Garrett's entourage with Tiffany and Nate bristling on one side, and Savannah circling Garrett like a glittering hawk on the other, I couldn't shake the sinking feeling that the real chaos hadn't even started yet.

Little did I know how right I was.

A familiar, nasally voice pricked my ear, reminding me that there was no such thing as a quiet moment in Havenwood. I glanced over to see Hortense and Oswald Puddleton huddled by the door, their distinctive voices loud enough to carry over the noise of the excited crowd.

"How did she snag Garrett Grimshaw for her little shop?" Hortense complained, narrowing her eyes at me as if I'd somehow managed the impossible.

Oswald huffed, patting his pockets in a distracted manner. "Silent partner, I'll bet. No other explanation for it." He glanced around as if trying to catch sight of some wealthy benefactor lurking behind the shelves, pulling my strings.

Coming from the Puddletons, the words shouldn't have stung, but they did. Because that's how people saw me, wasn't it? A placeholder, a lucky fluke, a girl stumbling into something she couldn't possibly have built on her own. The thought burrowed deep, worming its way past my carefully maintained sense of confidence and sinking into something raw. I forced myself not to react, but it was hard not to storm over and give the Puddletons a piece of my mind. I'd worked for this. Fought for Spellbooks and my life in Havenwood. It wasn't dumb luck or charity. But no matter what I did, people like the Puddletons would always find a way to chip away at it.

I swallowed down the knot in my throat just as Valerie appeared at my side, her voice quiet but steely. "Who are they?" she asked, her sharp gaze on the Puddletons.

I cupped a hand around my mouth, lowering my voice. "They run the other bookshop in town. We...don't exactly see eye to eye. They're probably not thrilled Garrett chose to do his book signing here."

Valerie's lips tightened, and she snapped her fingers without taking her gaze off the Puddletons. "Mindy," she called, her voice soft but commanding.

Mindy hurried over, her expression tense but eager to please. "Yes, Ms. St. James?"

Valerie nodded toward the Puddletons. "Make sure they're attended to, won't you? The special treatment? And then encourage them to leave if they're not here to buy." Mindy's nod was quick, and she was off to charm the Puddletons before I could blink.

"Hi there! Big fans of Mr. Grimshaw, I presume?" Mindy asked them with forced cheer, gently nudging them toward the line. "Why don't I get you in line for a signature?"

Hortense opened her mouth, likely to protest, but Oswald prodded her forward, grumbling as he went. "Fine, but we pre-ordered our own copy so don't expect us to purchase one here," he muttered, shooting me a baleful glare as they finally joined the line.

"Are you excited about meeting Mr. Grimshaw?" Mindy asked, her voice sweet as syrup while she settled in beside them, cheerfully distracting them from further complaints.

"Smoothly done," I murmured, more than a little impressed.

Valerie nodded approvingly as she watched Mindy work. "This isn't our first signing, Miss Sullivan. I like things to go without a hitch."

I gave her a small nod. "We feel the same in Havenwood. We'll make sure this event shines."

"Hm." Valerie arched a brow, eyeing the room again. She lifted a finger to inspect it for any speck of dust, looking around with the faintest hint of approval.

Her gaze shifted to Savannah, who was adjusting her coat and reaching into her bag only to pull out a second identical perfume bottle. Of course she had a backup.

Savannah angled her phone, tapping on the screen with her thumb as she held it out. "Okay, savvy babes," she purred into the camera, "tell me this isn't the perfect launch-day glam." She struck a pouty pose next to the bottle, glancing at the light like she was auditioning for her own skincare brand.

Valerie's lips thinned. With practiced grace, she made her way to Savannah and lowered herself into the seat beside her with such precise control that even Savannah straightened instinctively.

Valerie leaned over slightly, whispering something with a quiet, biting tone. Savannah's jaw tightened, but she sat up properly, finally tucking her phone away. After a long pause, she got to her feet and walked over to Garrett, perching on the arm of his chair and brushing a hand through his hair in a way that was almost territorial.

"My darling," she cooed, loud enough for half the shop to hear, "I'm going to get the largest coffee I can find. The long trip from New York is catching up to me."

Garrett flashed his trademark grin, looking for all the world like he belonged in a fashion magazine spread rather than a book signing. "Of course. Enjoy."

Savannah placed a lingering kiss on his cheek, her fingers trailing along his jawline in a way that made Tiffany sniff and Nate roll his eyes. Then, with a dramatic sigh, she adjusted her coat over her shoulders and turned to the security guard.

"Come with me," she said, looping her arm through his without waiting for an answer. "You never know who might be lurking around."

The guard hesitated, glancing toward Garrett, who nodded slightly at the man. I was impressed the stoic security guard didn't roll his eyes as Savannah tightened her grip and sauntered away with a sway in her step. He did however free himself from her grip, walking a few reluctant paces behind the influencer as she stepped out onto Arcadia Avenue.

The crowd murmured, watching her go. Garrett smiled, looking after her with an indulgent sigh before turning back to his fans, his polished grin firmly in place. As the line shifted forward, his hand lingered for a moment on the table, flexing subtly before picking up the pen again.

Tiffany, seated beside Nate with her posture ramrod straight, let out a faint sound of disapproval. She looked carved from ice as her gaze flicked from Garrett to the retreating Savannah. Nate tipped his head back, exhaling sharply through his nose before shaking his head.

"She just doesn't appreciate what's at stake," Tiffany murmured, her voice tight with tension.

Nate remained silent but cast another withering glance in the direction where Savannah had disappeared before whirling on his heel and storming towards the sunroom and out the back of the shop.

The line was moving, but just slowly enough to encourage dramatic sighs, pointed glances, and the occasional purse shuffle loud enough to be considered a protest. Naturally, to make matters worse, the Puddletons were still here, hovering near the middle of the queue like the world owed them front-row access and a warm scone.

Eventually, the pace began to take its toll on Garrett and it was clear he was starting to flag. His smile was still charming, but the sparkle had dulled just a bit, and he was lingering between signatures like he needed a second to reset. Valerie, ever vigilant, clocked it immediately. She tapped Mindy on the arm and pressed a napkin-wrapped beignet into her hand.

"Take this to Mr. Grimshaw," she said, her voice low but firm. "He's looking a bit worn, and you know how his blood sugar can dip."

"Great idea!" Mindy said with a bright smile, grabbing a second beignet for good measure. "He loves these, and he's signed books straight through lunch. I'm not surprised he's tired." She wove her way through the crowd, focused on Garrett, who was still charming his way through yet another photo op with an eager fan.

And then, of course, it happened.

Just as Mindy reached the front table, Hortense Puddleton, clutching her oversized purse, stepped to the side, craning to get a better look and colliding into Mindy with a bump.

"Oh! Watch where you're going," Hortense sniffed, not bothering to apologize as Mindy stumbled, the beignets flying from her hands.

I watched, helpless, as the first one spiraled in slow motion, a perfect, golden puff arcing through the air like a frosted comet and hit Garrett squarely in the chest.

A soft *whump* sounded, followed by an explosion of powdered sugar that billowed into the air like an overly festive snow globe. Gasps rippled through the line. Hortense recoiled with an offended huff, brushing a hand down her sensible cardigan as if powdered sugar were contagious.

"Well, that's what happens when people don't watch where they're going," she sniffed loudly, casting a withering look at Mindy like she'd committed a personal affront.

Garrett stared down at the white blotch blooming across his black silk shirt.

Mindy froze, one hand over her mouth, eyes wide with horror.

"Well," Tiffany murmured in the sudden stillness, her voice impressively dry. "That will photograph beautifully."

"Oh, no! Mr. Grimshaw, I'm so sorry!" Mindy gasped, scrambling for napkins as Garrett rose, brushing at his shirt in vain. The more she tried to salvage the fabric, the worse it got. The fine sugar spread across the material in an uneven, powdery smear.

Garrett's polite smile stretched taut as he forced a chuckle for the audience's benefit. "It's...quite alright, really," he said through clenched teeth, nudging Mindy aside and patting at his shirt, which only served to push the sugar deeper into the fabric instead of the opposite.

Mindy's face turned pale with panic. "I—I'll go grab the spare outfit from the car," she stammered, already backing toward the exit, nearly colliding with Oswald this time.

Garrett threw out a hand. "No. I'll go." He took a deep breath, composing himself before turning back to the crowd with his well-practiced, contrite smile. "Apologies, everyone! I think a quick costume change is in order. The rumpled writer aesthetic is charming in theory, but let's face it. No one wants a picture with one covered in sugar."

A ripple of laughter spread through the crowd, easing the tension as Garrett waved and started toward the door. "Don't worry, I'll be back in just a few minutes," he added smoothly, the audience parting to let him pass.

Valerie's brows furrowed as her sharp gaze darted around the room. "Someone should go with him," she said, her tone low and tight, scanning for the security guard, obviously forgetting that Savannah had dragged him away and neither had yet to return.

Tiffany scoffed, folding her arms. "Oh, come now, Valerie. We're in a small town. What could possibly happen? He's not about to be mobbed by overzealous fans here like he would in New York. Why, this event only looks crowded because the ridiculous shop is so small."

My jaw tightened, heat rising to my cheeks. Spellbooks was more than just a shop—it was my home, my livelihood, and the heart of everything I was working to protect. I refused to let anyone speak poorly of it, no matter who they were.

Before I could respond, Valerie's frown deepened. "Why do we have security if they aren't around to do the job?'

I glanced at Gabriel, who was already shrugging off his jacket. "I'll go after him," he offered, tucking the blazer over his arm. "If nothing else, he might need this to cover up the mess. We're about the same size."

I nodded quickly. "I'll go too. Maybe we can get that shirt dry-cleaned straightaway."

As we stepped outside, a sharp gust of wind carried away the warmth of the bookshop. I shivered, rubbing at my arms.

At the curb, a sleek black sedan idled with its trunk open. Shadows pooled in the recess, making it impossible to see inside, but something was back there. Perhaps a heap of fabric, or maybe luggage. Or maybe—

Before I could fully process what I was looking at, a man in a dark uniform with a hat pulled down low over his eyes slammed the trunk down hard. Or, at least, tried to, but it bounced back with a thud, like it had hit something solid.

For the briefest second, I saw…something. A movement half hidden by the edge of the car. Was that a hand? An arm perhaps?

The air froze in my lungs. A sick, rolling wave of dread churned through my gut. My knees locked, my shoes rooted to the pavement. I couldn't believe what was happening right before my eyes.

The driver didn't stop. He wrenched the trunk open again, shoved something inside, and this time, it latched firmly shut. He spun toward the driver's seat, his boots slapping hard against the pavement. Then, without missing a beat, he threw himself into the driver's seat, yanked the door closed, and hit the gas.

The engine roared to life as the tires screeched against the pavement. The car lurched forward, leaving fresh black streaks on the asphalt as it shot down Arcadia Avenue and disappeared around the corner.

My fingertips went numb. I staggered back, gasping, reaching blindly until my hand found Gabriel's arm. I gripped hard, too hard.

My stomach plummeted. My pulse hammered.

"Wait—" Gabriel started.

"That was him!" My voice came out too loud, too ragged. "That was Garrett!"

My heart pounded against my ribs.

"They just stuffed him in the trunk! They're kidnapping Garrett Grimshaw!"

Gabriel exhaled sharply, pulling out his phone. His fingers hovered over the screen for half a second before he dialed. "We don't know that for sure."

"Are you kidding me?" My voice pitched higher. I felt like I was coming untethered. "You saw what I saw! They threw him in the trunk like a bag of laundry and sped off!"

Gabriel squeezed his eyes shut for the briefest moment, then snapped back into action. "We don't know that for sure," he repeated, firmer this time.

I threw out my arms. "Then where is he? Today's his big launch. He wouldn't just wander off. So, where'd he go?"

Gabriel's grip tightened around his phone. "I don't know. But I'm calling the sheriff." His voice was clipped, controlled, but beneath it, I could hear the tension straining at his usually calm, composed nature.

I bit my lip, hands shaking. My pulse was erratic, my stomach twisting itself into knots. "What about everyone inside? They're going to notice he's gone any second."

Gabriel's gaze flicked toward the shop, and the blurred shapes of people through the windows. His jaw tensed. "We can't let this get out. If word spreads, this turns into a media circus. Havenwood's entire reputation, including that of Spellbooks, could take a hit it might never recover from."

I clenched my jaw, panic tightening my throat. "But—"

Gabriel exhaled sharply. For the first time, his carefully composed mask cracked, just a little. "Harper, think. If word spreads now, it's over. The second people start whispering 'kidnapping,' the press will descend like vultures. And if we're wrong? If there's another explanation?" His voice dropped, quieter but no less intense. "Then we'll have destroyed Havenwood's reputation for nothing."

I swallowed hard. Not just Havenwood's.

My gaze flicked toward the shelves and displays I'd fussed over for weeks. Spellbooks would never recover from something like this. The thought hit fast and sharp. Then the guilt chased in right behind it. I shouldn't be focused on me and my problems. Not at a time like this.

"But what if we're *not* wrong?" I asked, voice barely above a whisper.

Gabriel hesitated, his jaw tightening as he ran a hand through his hair. His eyes flicked to the shop windows, then down to his phone, like he was hoping it might offer a better answer. The silence stretched, thick and expectant, as if even the air was holding its breath.

"We handle it, but quietly," he said at last, the words slow, like he didn't quite want to say them. "Just until we know more. If the press catches wind of a disappearance, it could spiral out of control. And if we're wrong..." He didn't finish the sentence. He didn't need to.

He paused again. His gaze dropped, and when he spoke again, it was lower. Almost reluctant. "Maybe we say Garrett felt unwell."

The words landed like a stone in my chest.

My brain scrambled for something—anything—to say next, but every possible excuse sounded ridiculous. My heart pounded faster. I wasn't built for this. I could barely bluff my way through a board game. How was I supposed to lie to a room full of people who trusted me?

They were going to ask questions. They were going to look at me.

And I was going to crack wide open.

I stared at him, stomach churning. "Lie to them?" I whispered. "Gabriel, I'm not sure I can pull that off."

Gabriel met my gaze, and I could still see the tension pulling at his features. "I know," he said softly. "I hate it too, but we're not lying to them forever. Panicking that room won't help Garrett. But buying ourselves time to find him might."

He was right. I took a shaky breath before swallowing hard and forcing a nod. "Alright. I'll do what I can, but you'd better find him fast."

Gabriel gave my shoulder a reassuring squeeze. "We will. Just stall them."

Taking a deep breath, I turned back to the shop, every step feeling heavier than the last. Gabriel was right. If this turned into a media spectacle, it wouldn't just be my shop on the line. It would be the town's entire reputation. My stomach twisted. I hated this. But Gabriel was right.

If I walked in there and told them what I'd just witnessed, it wouldn't help Garrett.

But a well-placed lie might buy him the time he needed to be found before any harm could be done.

As I reached the door, I could already see curious faces pressed against the windows, craning to see what was happening. The buzz of conversation inside swirled with anticipation, but no one seemed to realize the gravity of the situation yet.

I paused for a moment, gripping the door handle, my mind racing for the right words. The weight of responsibility pressed down on me, my stomach churning with a mix of guilt and determination.

This couldn't be happening. Garrett Grimshaw—*the* Garrett Grimshaw—was gone, whisked away from under my nose. This was beyond disastrous. Every hope I'd pinned on this event, the business-saving publicity, the potential of Spellbooks as a literary destination was gone in an instant. And I was about to walk into a room full of people and try to convince them that everything was fine.

I pushed open the door, my forced smile already plastered in place. Valerie's sharp gaze locked onto me, her expression expectant and concerned. The hum of conversation faltered, eyes turning toward me like a spotlight. My palms grew clammy, and my heart pounded so hard it was a miracle no one could hear it. As the seconds stretched, the knot in my stomach tightened. This was the hardest thing I'd ever done. But somehow, I had to make them believe the lie. At least long enough for Gabriel and the sheriff to bring Garrett back.

One wrong word, one crack in my facade, and it would all come crumbling down.

There would be no coming back from this.

A Gathering Storm

I STEPPED IN FRONT of the table where Garrett had been signing books mere moments before, forcing a bright smile that didn't feel remotely genuine. The hum of conversation faltered as dozens of curious faces turned toward me. Valerie's sharp gaze locked onto mine, her expression brimming with unspoken questions. I was hyperaware of the eyes that were on me, and my already shallow breathing started to come faster. The only thing keeping my composure from cracking completely was the knowledge that Gabriel, Spellbooks, and all of Havenwood were counting on me.

"Ladies and gentlemen," I began, projecting my voice with what I hoped sounded like warmth and confidence, "thank you all so much for coming out today. Mr. Grimshaw has been absolutely thrilled with the turnout, but unfortunately, he's not feeling well." I paused, gauging the reaction of the crowd. A ripple of murmurs spread through the shop, equal parts curiosity and concern.

I continued. "I think we could all tell he was putting up a good front for us, but he's taken a turn for the worse. He's asked me to pass on his apologies to you for the inconvenience. However, I'm sure we all wish him a speedy recovery."

My eyes darted to the back of the room. Valerie's lips pressed into a thin line, her expression hovering somewhere between worry and disbelief. Beside her, Tiffany's perfectly arched brow lifted in skepticism, while Nate folded his arms tightly, his sharp gaze fixed on me like he was analyzing every syllable I spoke. None of them looked convinced, and the realization sent a fresh wave of anxiety crawling up my spine.

Movement in the crowd caught my attention, and relief washed over me as Gabriel made his way forward. His steady presence seemed to radiate calm, though I could see the tension in the set of his jaw. He reached my side and gave a small nod to the room, his voice cutting smoothly through the hum of speculation.

"We understand that this is unfortunate, and Mr. Grimshaw feels terrible about the inconvenience to you," he said, his tone even and reassuring. "However, I know he cares about his fans and wouldn't want to leave anyone empty-handed. For those of you who missed your chance, we'll be arranging signed books to be delivered to you. Please leave your name and contact details with Miss Mindy Hart at the back. She's the lady with the glasses who's waving now."

I glanced at Mindy, who looked surprised, but raised her hand above her head and waved with a tentative smile. I marveled at Gabriel's composure under pressure, especially the clever way he went about getting a list of the current attendees without raising any suspicions. The murmurs rose again, this time tinged with excitement.

He paused just long enough to let the murmurs settle before continuing, "Additionally, we're increasing the number of guests drawn from the special lottery for tonight's event at Silverthorne Manor. We want to include as many of you as possible. And we're keeping our fingers crossed that Mr. Grimshaw will be well enough to make an appearance."

A sharp sniff sliced through the air. "Oh, how convenient," Hortense Puddleton announced, crossing her arms. "A mysterious illness? I bet it was the crab cakes. Who serves seafood at a book signing? Only someone without experience. In fact, I bet that's what made Mr. Grimshaw ill." She tsked dramatically.

A few people turned toward me, their expressions hesitant. A handful looked intrigued, maybe even suspicious, but most seemed caught between curiosity and frustration.

Heat crawled up my neck. I could not let the Puddletons twist this into a win for them. My business was already struggling. I didn't need rumors of food poisoning making it worse. I flicked my gaze toward Bella, whose face had gone from slightly annoyed to volcanic. Oh no. That wasn't just frustration. That was full-blown, insulted-on-my-mother's-behalf rage.

Bella stepped forward, her cheeks bright pink. I could tell she was seconds away from launching into a tirade, likely about how Hortense wouldn't know good food if it leapt off the page of a cookbook and slapped her across the face with a well-buttered scone. I didn't need any more drama today, especially not between my best friend and the odious rivals down the street, so I quickly spoke up, raising my voice in what I hoped was a confident manner.

"I can personally vouch for the food," I said, offering a calm smile, "but of course, we all want to be cautious when someone isn't feeling well. That's why we've already contacted the professionals to see that Garrett Grimshaw is getting the best care possible." I swallowed. It wasn't exactly a lie, but I was certainly walking a fine line. Knowing that I wasn't the greatest liar by a long shot, I hurriedly went on. "And, to show my appreciation, anyone here today can bring their receipt back to Spellbooks for a special discount on their next purchase." I'd have to look at my books to see what I could afford, but if it got people in the door, the extra discount would be worth it.

Instead of skepticism, the crowd's mood brightened with interest. A few people murmured their approval, and someone near the back actually cheered. Hortense's mouth pinched as the energy in the room shifted.

Gabriel, ever composed, stepped in smoothly. "A generous offer," he said with an easy smile. "I'm sure we all wish Mr. Grimshaw a speedy recovery, and we will be reaching out to the winners of the drawing soon. If you need assistance with your costumes for the masquerade ball, I can personally vouch for Elliott Ashford over at the Silver Needle. His clothes are incredible!"

The murmurs rose again, this time tinged with excitement. I could feel the shift as anticipation for an elegant evening overtook any lingering frustration. Some fans were already whispering to each other about costumes and imagining the grandeur of a ball at Silverthorne Manor.

"Is he alright?" someone called from the back. The fan clutching a well-worn paperback of one of Garrett's early works looked particularly distressed.

I nodded quickly. "He's fine, just a little under the weather. One of his terrible migraines caught up with him, I'm afraid. I'm sure we can all empathize. A little rest and some quiet should have him back on his feet by tonight."

Gabriel offered a sympathetic nod and pressed a hand lightly to his temple in a silent gesture of understanding. If I hadn't known better, I would've believed it myself. As it was, it took all of my concentration to keep a serene yet concerned expression on my face as people started to file out of Spellbooks. The murmurs turned to animated chatter as fans began discussing the ball, excitement lighting up their faces.

My shoulders slumped with relief, but before I could fully relax, Gabriel leaned close, his breath brushing my ear as he murmured, "Don't relax just yet. We've got some more damage control to do." His subtle nod toward Valerie, Tiffany, and Nate was all I needed to snap back into focus.

Just as I turned toward the trio, Hortense Puddleton's grating voice sliced through the buzz of departing fans.

"Drama seems to follow Harper Sullivan wherever she goes, doesn't it?" Her tone was sugary sweet, but her words dripped with venom. She sniffed loudly, crossing her arms and leaning toward Oswald. "Honestly, this whole fiasco could have been avoided with a little foresight."

Oswald gave a pompous harrumph, patting his round belly. "Exactly. A seasoned business owner would know better than to serve messy foods at a book signing. Beignets? Seafood? Amateurs always overreach. If she'd known better, Grimshaw would still be here, signing books."

"Which is why they should've picked the Dusty Tome for this event," Hortense added shrilly, her voice grating like nails on a chalkboard. "At least *we* know how to run things properly. Isn't that right, Oswald?"

"Absolutely!" Oswald crowed.

My jaw clenched so tightly it was a miracle my teeth didn't crack. My nails bit into my palms as I fought the urge to snap back. However, I didn't want to make more of a scene here. I was determined to live up to my idea of a competent business owner despite the recent slump. So, instead of giving a sharp retort to my unpleasant neighbors, I forced a pleasant, unbothered smile as Bella strode over with storm clouds on her face.

"I appreciate your feedback, Hortense," I said smoothly, keeping my tone light. "It's always...enlightening to hear your thoughts." For just a moment, I was proud of how composed I sounded and that I didn't rise to the bait.

Bella, however, had no such reservations. She crossed her arms and tilted her head. Her smile was just a little too sharp.

"I'm sure you'll enjoy the refreshments at the ball this evening if you win the drawing," she said sweetly. Then she gasped, eyes widening in mock realization. "Oh, wait. That's right. Didn't Vivienne Silverthorne *explicitly* ban you from events at the manor after the despicable way you behaved at the Christmas Eve Ball?" She pressed a hand to her chest as if the thought pained her. "What a loss."

I had to bite the inside of my cheek to keep from laughing. When it came to dealing with the Puddletons today, Bella was brutal, and I loved her for it.

Hortense's smirk faltered, and Oswald huffed in indignation, but Bella wasn't finished. She sighed dramatically, all exaggerated sympathy. "Such a shame, really. The Silverthorne chefs are legendary. They're experts at catering events for refined palates." She let the words hang before adding, "Much like my mother, who, incidentally, catered *this* event." Bella clasped her hands together, the picture of innocent delight. "Isn't it funny how you both managed to enjoy them without complaint...until now?"

I coughed into my fist, barely hiding a smile.

Hortense's face twisted like she'd just bitten into a lemon, and Oswald's harrumph turned into a strangled cough. Oswald opened his mouth, likely to retort, but Bella looped her arm through mine, tugging me in the opposite direction. I turned away before he could get a word in, plastering my polite smile back on as more Grimshaw fans continued to shuffle out. The Puddletons looked around at the lack of a supportive audience listening to their snide comments and beat a hasty retreat.

Bella: a million. Puddletons: zero.

As the room finally emptied, I exhaled a breath I hadn't realized I'd been holding. The Puddletons were the least of my worries. We had to find Garrett Grimshaw. A sudden thought occurred to me, and I took a breath, reaching out with my magic toward the ley lines thrumming beneath Havenwood. Just a few weeks ago, through a series of unexpected turns, I'd become the guardian of the heartwood tree, or rather heartwood trees, plural, since the treant Jeremiah helped to grow several saplings. The magical trees acted as gateways to the three ley lines that converged here in Havenwood. This unique connection helped to keep Havenwood hidden, blending the magic of the town with the Silverthorne family's spells. Our magical community lived in peace, shielded from the outside world's prying eyes.

Focusing on the connection to the heartwood, I sent my thoughts toward it. *"Heartwood?"*

Almost immediately, a warm, calm voice replied, echoing through my mind. *"Yes, Harper?"*

I explained the situation quickly, hoping for some magical way to locate Garrett. *"Is there any way to track a black sedan moving through town?"*

A silence stretched between us, then I felt it, like a breath of wind that wasn't wind at all. A shift in the air like the exhale of something ancient and sorrowful.

"I would if I could, but there are two obstacles. First, neither Garrett Grimshaw nor the person with him seem to have any magical connection. That makes them...well, hard to locate."

"Hard to locate?" I thought at the tree.

"Imagine paranormals as little beacons, bright lights in the dark. Humans, by comparison, are more like shadows. Easily lost in the background."

Frustration welled up. *"Is there anything you can do to counteract that?"*

"The second problem, the heartwood continued, *is their surroundings. Presumably, they're on a paved road in a car, surrounded by town infrastructure. Without nature around them—a tree, even a flower—there's nothing for me to use as a connection point."*

I released a frustrated breath. *"What about the saplings we planted in the woods around town?"*

I hadn't enjoyed the process, but we'd gotten them in the ground. Eventually. Between Vivienne's magic, my connection to the trees, and Jeremiah's meticulous planning, we'd managed to push through despite the frozen soil. It had been slow, backbreaking work, but it was done. And thank goodness it was. Maybe, just maybe, those saplings could help us now.

"Ah...," the heartwood's tone lifted a bit. *"If they pass one of the saplings, there's a slim chance I could recognize Garrett from your description. But I wouldn't place all your hope on that. Saplings are young and inexperienced with humans. They sense magic far more easily than mundane life."*

I hesitated. *"But...you're a sapling too, right?"*

"Technically," it said, it's voice a little wry. *"But I was planted near the old heartwood. I soaked up the remnants of the ancient magic. That doesn't make me better, but it does make me...different."*

A question popped to the front of my mind. *"If that's the case, is it even possible for the others to find him?"*

There was a beat of silence. *"We won't know until we try,"* the heartwood finally said.

I sent a mental image of Garrett: his wavy brown hair, dark jeans, blazer, and powdered sugar stains on his shirt. *"Please. Do your best. It's important."*

"I'll see what I can find and alert you at once if the saplings detect anything," the heartwood said.

"Thanks. We need to find him ASAP."

"You've got it. Branches crossed," the heartwood replied.

The entire exchange took less time than speaking the conversation would have, but it consumed my entire attention. When I broke off the communication, I blinked back into awareness, only to find Gabriel standing slightly closer than before, his stance casual but deliberate.

Had he intentionally stepped in front of me? Just enough to shield me from view? Warmth curled through me. He was so thoughtful. Subtle, too. With him there, any casual observer would've missed the magic entirely.

Unfortunately, Valerie was anything but. She stood a few feet away, her sharp eyes darting between Gabriel and me like a hawk circling its prey.

"What is going on?" Valerie hissed through a clenched jaw and a forced smile that looked more like a grimace as I stepped towards Gabriel and shook my head.

Tiffany hovered nearby. "I don't believe for one minute that Garrett is sick. Even when he had the flu, that couldn't keep him away from his adoring fans. What's really going on?"

Behind her, Bella shot me a questioning look, but I couldn't answer her right now. Not when I had to think of something to say.

Gabriel didn't miss a beat, his calm demeanor belying the tension that rolled off him. "We need to gather everyone," he said quietly, though his words carried the expectant tone of authority. He directed his gaze toward Valerie. "Anyone from Garrett's team—drivers, security, everyone. Get them here now, please."

Valerie snapped her fingers at Mindy without looking. The assistant immediately scurried off to round everyone up. Valerie's sharp eyes narrowed. "What exactly is going on?"

Gabriel met her gaze evenly. "Harper and I think we saw Garrett leaving in a car."

I swallowed hard, forcing myself to nod along, even though every instinct screamed that this wasn't some diva disappearing act. *He didn't just leave. He was taken.* But now wasn't the time to fight that battle. Not yet.

Valerie's expression twisted in disbelief, her perfectly polished exterior cracking. "That's not possible. He knew how big of a deal this event was. He wouldn't just vanish. I'm calling him," she said flatly, pulling her phone from her pocket. She tapped Garrett's contact info and held it to her ear. Moments later, her frown deepened. "Straight to voicemail," she muttered. Her gaze flicked between us, her irritation giving way to a flicker of unease.

"That doesn't mean—" Tiffany interjected, her arms crossed tightly. "It could just be a dead battery."

"Not Dad," Nate said, his jaw tight. "He's glued to that thing whenever he's not in front of his fans and always brings an extra charger with him just in case. If it's off, something's wrong."

Valerie's lips thinned further, the air around her brimming with suppressed frustration. "This makes no sense," she snapped, pacing a few steps as if motion might bring clarity. "Why would he leave by himself without telling anyone?"

"He didn't leave alone. He was, um, with someone," I added hesitantly, choosing my words carefully. "Whoever it was wore a driver's uniform."

Before Valerie could respond, Mindy reappeared, breathless but efficient. Behind her, the three drivers filtered into the room, exchanging uneasy glances. The tension in the air had clearly reached them as well.

Valerie wasted no time, spinning to address the group. "I want to know exactly where everyone has been. Who saw Mr. Grimshaw leave? Who went with him? Where's his bodyguard? Where are the drivers?"

The tallest of the drivers stepped forward. "We've all been here, ma'am," he said, his tone firm but polite. "All three of us. None of us left with Mr. Grimshaw."

Valerie's sharp gaze flicked to Mindy. "What about his security?"

Mindy winced, holding up her phone. "I just checked. Dirk is still with Miss Chase." She hesitated before adding, "She hasn't come back yet."

A muscle twitched in Valerie's jaw. "You mean to tell me that *no one* was with Garrett?"

A heavy silence fell over the room.

Valerie pinched the bridge of her nose, muttering something that was probably not fit for polite company. Then she snapped her fingers at Mindy. "Get them back here. *Now.*"

Mindy jumped, fumbling her phone from her pocket, and nearly dropping it in her hurry to make the call.

Valerie turned back to the group, her expression cold and cutting. "You're telling me that Garrett was completely alone when it happened?" No one spoke. No one needed to. The answer was already clear. Valerie started pacing. "How did this happen? We need to get him back. Immediately! What will people say when they find out he disappeared from his own book launch? This is a catastrophe!"

Gabriel's jaw tightened. "I agree," he said grimly. "I've already contacted the police, but I'll see if they have an update." Without waiting for a response, he stepped aside, his phone already pressed to his ear as he walked toward the window, his voice low but urgent.

I exhaled slowly, trying to suppress the chill of anxiety creeping up my spine. This event was supposed to help fix things. A packed shop, a high-profile signing, a chance to remind people that Spellbooks was still worth their time and money. Instead, Garrett Grimshaw had vanished, and the only thing people would remember about today was the chaos. My business had already been struggling. This would only make it worse!

I glanced around the room, my gaze landing on Bella. Concern etched into the lines of her face. The moment our eyes met she gave me a small, reassuring smile. No words, just quiet support, but it helped.

Isadora, meanwhile, was already on her phone, her fingers flying across the screen. Probably checking in with her family or pulling in whatever magical resources she could. She didn't look up, but the tight set of her jaw told me she was just as focused on solving this as the rest of us.

I swallowed hard and straightened my shoulders. Whatever happened next, I could handle it. Because I wasn't in this alone. Among the four of us, surely, we could figure out what happened to Garrett and get him back. It wouldn't be the first time we'd solved a mystery. We could crack this one too.

Tiffany crossed her arms tightly over her chest, drawing my attention back. Her polished composure cracked as worry seeped into her voice. "We *have* to find him. We don't have time to sit around waiting."

Nate gave a sharp nod, his voice taut. "Exactly. The longer we wait, the harder it'll be to trace him. We need to act fast."

"By doing what, exactly?" Valerie snapped. Her hands balled into fists, her usual poise cracking under the strain. "None of us have any idea who took him or why."

I glanced between them, the rising tension in the room wrapping around me like a vise. My chest tightened, my heart racing as their voices clashed, each argument louder than the last. It felt like the room was shrinking with every second Garrett remained missing.

"Stop," I said, my voice firmer than I expected. It silenced the room like a snapped string. I straightened my spine, forcing confidence I didn't entirely feel. "Arguing isn't going to help. Gabriel's updating the police. That's the first step. Once we know more, we can figure out what to do next."

Nate huffed, pulling out his phone. "We should be calling someone. The press. His agent. Someone with contacts."

"Good idea," Tiffany said, reaching for her purse. "I have the mayor's number, and I should be able to—"

"No," I said, more sharply this time. "The sheriff asked us not to say anything yet. If word gets out before we know what's actually happening, it could make things worse."

Valerie crossed her arms, her expression tight. "So, we do nothing? That's your plan?"

I met her gaze head-on. "We don't make it worse. That's the plan." I took a breath, then pushed forward, voice trembling with frustration. "Do you want to be responsible for Garrett getting hurt? Because if we send up a flare right now, if we panic and make this public without facts, we could drive whoever took him underground...or worse."

Tiffany paused, her fingers tightening around her purse strap. Nate exchanged a look with her. She sighed and glared at me.

"Fine," she snapped. "We'll leave it to the professionals."

"Thank you," I said, relieved.

"For now," she finished darkly.

Valerie's sharp gaze locked onto mine, her lips pressing into a thin line, but she didn't say anything else. Instead, she spun on her heel, heading toward Gabriel, who was still deep in conversation, pacing near the front window.

"I told him to stay in New York," Tiffany huffed. "At least there, we know people. We could organize a search party."

I took a breath, meeting her eyes and forcing steel into my spine. "Havenwood isn't exactly a sprawling metropolis," I said, keeping my tone calm and in control, just like I'd seen my dad do countless times in his job as a Master Sergeant. "But a small town is a benefit in this situation. It's a lot harder to slip through the cracks. I'm sure the police are doing everything they can." I crossed my fingers behind my back and out of sight, hoping against hope that the police would find him and soon.

A sharp look flickered across Valerie's face, and I braced for impact, expecting her to call me out or take over the conversation entirely. But instead, her gaze shuttered, a mask dropping into place as her eyes landed squarely on Tiffany. Despite her unreadable expression, I had the distinct feeling she was unimpressed with the other woman's behavior.

Tiffany seemed to feel it too, and she caught herself. She pressed her lips together and folded her arms, clearly trying to bite back her next complaint.

I swallowed hard and glanced around the room. The atmosphere felt tight, stretched thin like old book pages on the verge of tearing. Garrett was gone, and the longer he stayed missing, the harder it would be to bring him back.

I sucked in a breath and forced myself to focus. We had to find him. Somehow, some way, we would. But as the room fell into a tense, uneasy silence, I couldn't shake the nagging doubt that whispered in the back of my mind.

What if we were already too late?

I Know What I Saw

THE TENSION IN THE room was suffocating. Valerie paced, her heels clicking against the floor, while Tiffany and Nate whispered heatedly nearby. I glanced at Bella and Isadora, who stood near the door, watching the scene unfold with worried expressions.

Steeling myself, I addressed the group. "I know the police are on the case, but is there anything that you can think of that might help them in this situation?"

Tiffany let out a disdainful sniff, obviously recovered from the nonverbal cowing from Valerie. She folded her arms across her chest. "The police? In a town like this?" she muttered, loud enough for everyone to hear. "What's the most action they've ever seen? A missing cat?"

Isadora's gaze narrowed, however her tone was calm but firm. "You'd be surprised what Sheriff Jackson, and his team, are capable of. This isn't their first time dealing with a crisis."

Tiffany opened her mouth to respond, but I interrupted before things escalated. "She's right." I grabbed a notebook and pen from the counter. "You all know Garrett better than anyone. You'd be the best people to provide insight into why he might've been taken. And if we can figure out the why, we're that much closer to figuring out who might be behind his disappearance and where he is." I turned to Valerie first, hoping for a lead. "Has Garrett mentioned any enemies recently? Rivals who might want to see him fail?"

Valerie rolled her eyes. "Rival authors? Of *Garrett Grimshaw*? Of course. The real question is who *isn't* envious of Garrett. They may put on a supportive front, but privately, they're jealous of anyone else's success. However, authors are all talk, no action. The real threats are always from outside." She flicked a quick glance at Tiffany. "Though some would argue family can be just as troublesome."

Tiffany sniffed, her eyes narrowing. "I hardly think the problem here is Garrett's support system, Valerie. The real issue is his publicist dragging him all over the country to squeeze every penny from him year after year. He's exhausted. Why, I wouldn't be surprised if..." she trailed off.

Valerie's eyes narrowed, and her voice was edged with ice. "If *what*, Tiffany?"

Tiffany threw her hands in the air. "Well, how do we know he was taken?" she demanded. "Maybe he just needed an escape from all the pressure. People who are put under an immense amount of stress sometimes snap, don't they?"

My stomach twisted. I didn't want to consider it, but the way Tiffany said it, like it was an entirely plausible scenario, made me wonder. *Could* Garrett really have staged this himself?

No.

The thought barely had time to take root before I crushed it. I knew what I'd seen. The trunk. The movement. Someone *was* inside. Garrett hadn't run. He'd been taken. End of story.

Valerie's expression sharpened. "Escape?" she echoed, her voice like a knife's edge. "You think he ran? That he abandoned a sold-out event, his fans, his obligations—because he was *stressed*?"

Tiffany lifted her chin, defiant. "Why not? You've wrung him dry, and now, poof, he's vanished. Maybe he finally realized what I've been saying for months. That he needed a break."

Valerie took a slow, measured breath, as if barely restraining herself. "Garrett is not reckless. He understands commitment."

"That's rich, coming from you," Tiffany shot back, her tone dripping with venom.

Valerie's eyes narrowed dangerously. "Just because our marriage didn't work, doesn't mean I'm not committed to his success. I've been by his side throughout his career, and I never hear you complain when he's cashing those royalty checks that help to fund your extravagant lifestyle."

Tiffany took a step closer, her hands balled into fists at her sides. "Don't insinuate that I was a gold-digger. We both know who *that* title belongs to."

"Don't confuse my business acumen with your greed," Valerie snapped back.

Tiffany's lips curled. "Please. You're just bitter because he might've finally outgrown your control. You don't own him, Valerie."

Valerie arched a brow. "And you do?" She gave a humorless laugh. "You spent fifteen years complaining about how much he worked, and now, suddenly, you care?"

Nate's hand tightened into a fist, his voice tense as he stepped closer to Valerie. "Don't talk to my mother like that."

Valerie barely spared him a glance. "Ah, the prodigal son finds a spine at last. How noble." Her gaze flicked back to Tiffany. "Although, you both should be thanking me. I've kept Garrett on top of the charts for years. On multiple continents, I might add. And he told me what your alimony settlement was, Tiffany." She gave a mocking little bow. "You're welcome."

I caught my breath at the vitriol in her tone, willing the headache forming behind my eyes to back off. This was *not* how today was supposed to go. This event was meant to help Spellbooks, not turn it into the setting for a reality TV showdown for the ex-wives of Garrett Grimshaw. For half a second, I debated stepping in, but before I could, Tiffany scoffed, throwing gasoline on the fire.

"How can you claim you're so good for him when you let that Chase girl into his life? Now there's a divorce waiting to happen. Although I shouldn't really be surprised," Tiffany shot back, her cold smile barely masking her fury. "You wouldn't know the sacrifices it takes to make a marriage work if they stared you straight in the face. Maybe that's the real reason why he left you."

Valerie's face flushed, her knuckles whitening as her nails dug into her palms. Her voice remained eerily calm, each word coming out clipped and precise. "As I recall, *I* left *him*. And if you want to bask in the glory of your fifteen-year marriage, by all means, enjoy it. You didn't contribute anything except that brooding excuse for a son who does little more than drain Garrett's accounts."

"Watch your tone," Nate warned, his voice low.

Valerie spun on him, her words cutting like knives. "And *you!* You're what? Twenty-two? Twenty-three? When are you going to get a job and stop living off your father's name?"

"You little—" Nate took a threatening step forward.

Oh no.

Before I could think better of it, I quickly inserted myself between them, planting a hand on his chest with enough force behind it to let him know I meant business.

"That's *enough.*" My voice rang with authority as I channeled my father's command voice. "Stand. Down."

The room went still. I held Nate's gaze first, unflinching, until his jaw tightened, and he looked away, stepping back with a muttered curse. Tiffany's lips parted like she wanted to argue, but when I turned my attention to her, she snapped her mouth shut, crossing her arms tightly. Valerie was the last to break, her icy glare locked onto mine in a silent challenge. But even she caved, exhaling sharply and folding her arms, her expression unreadable.

I let a beat pass before I spoke again, my voice steady and calm despite my racing heart. "I get it. There're issues to be resolved here. Perhaps we could do that after we find Garrett?"

Silence.

Nate ran a hand through his hair, tense but no longer looking ready to take a swing. Tiffany pressed her lips into a thin line, gaze darting away. Valerie stayed perfectly still, her eyes locked on Tiffany and her expression unreadable, but at least she wasn't launching more verbal daggers.

Good enough. For now.

I nodded, taking a step back so I could keep an eye on each of them. "Alright then. Let's focus. Did Garrett mention receiving any threats recently?"

Valerie's expression darkened. "He's had his share of jealous rivals and obsessive fans. But threats? Not that I know of." She glanced at Mindy. "Check the fan correspondence immediately. Is there anything suspicious?"

Mindy fumbled with her tablet, her fingers flying over the screen. "There are a few fans who've been...overly persistent. I'll flag the names and prepare a file for the police."

I quickly added "crazed fan" to the top of a blank page with a question mark beside it.

"And in his personal life?" I pressed. "Any conflicts? Arguments? A fight with his fiancée perhaps? Maybe he was jealous of someone else in her life, and it escalated?"

Valerie shook her head. "As much as I dislike Garrett becoming involved with someone half his age from an optics point of view, I doubt Miss Chase would do anything to jeopardize her relationship with him."

My pen hovered above my page. "Because they were madly in love?"

Nate snorted. "Because she's a gold digger, and he's her meal ticket. He just can't see that, even if the rest of us can."

Tiffany exhaled sharply, shaking her head. "Maybe he realized he didn't want to marry her. Maybe he finally saw her for what she is and got cold feet." She tilted her head, eyes glinting. "Or maybe there was another woman."

Valerie gave an elegant snort. "Please. If Garrett had a wandering eye, Savannah would be the last to know. I, on the other hand, would hear about it first." She shot Tiffany a look. "And let's just say, it wouldn't be the first time."

Tiffany's expression hardened, but she refused to meet Valerie's gaze. "It would certainly fit with his pattern of behavior from when we were together."

A flicker of something—hurt, maybe—crossed Nate's face before he masked it with a humorless scoff. "Right. Because out of all the people Dad's burned, someone finally decided to kidnap him over a cheating scandal."

Silence settled over the group. No one jumped in to argue, no further accusations were hurled. For a moment, I waited, half-expecting someone to elaborate, to take the bait Nate had thrown out. But when no one did, I shifted my focus back to the paper in my hands.

I jotted down Savannah's name on the list with a small asterisk beside it, then added Nate's as well. There was something about his bitterness that nagged at me. Especially when it came to Savannah. There was definitely more to his story than he was letting on, and I intended to get to the bottom of it.

"Anyone else who might bear a grudge against Garrett?" I asked, looking around the room to gauge their reactions.

Tiffany tilted her head, considering the question. "His editor, Albus Robinson, might be worth a look," she said slowly. "They've been at odds over the direction of the Rhett Ryder series. Garrett's been threatening to leave him for years, which would have been the end of Albus's career."

Valerie frowned. "Albus has a temper, but I can't imagine him resorting to...this. Besides, he has other clients, even if none are as successful as Garrett."

I added Albus's name on my growing list. "Anyone else?" I prompted, watching their faces carefully.

Nate ran a hand through his tousled hair. It was a gesture so reminiscent of Garrett that it caught me off guard. "Dad has no shortage of people who'd want a slice of his fame."

"Or his fortune," Valerie added darkly.

Tiffany spoke up. "Take your pick: disgruntled fans, jealous rivals, spurned ex-lovers." She cast a pointed glance at Valerie. "Sound familiar?"

Valerie didn't rise to the bait, though her narrowed gaze spoke volumes. "We should still consider the possibility of a fan whose obsession crossed the line," she said, glancing at Mindy. "Any names from your list that you recognized here today?"

Mindy, still scanning her tablet, lifted a shoulder hesitantly. "Perhaps? Not everyone in this file has a photograph so it might take me some more time to say for sure."

I tapped the pen against my notebook thoughtfully. The list was growing, but so were the questions. Garrett's circle seemed full of potential suspects or at least people harboring enough resentment to make them worth investigating.

Before I could ask more, Gabriel approached, his expression grave but controlled. "Any news?" I asked, hoping for some glimmer of progress.

He nodded. "Sheriff Jackson's already tracking the sedan. He's brought Bill in on the case, too."

I caught Gabriel's warning look, but I didn't need the reminder. Officer Bill, a centaur with a knack for tracking, was an excellent choice. Unless, of course, Sheriff Jackson decided to shift into his wolf form. I couldn't help the fleeting thought: in a footrace, who would win—a centaur or a werewolf? Only in Havenwood did questions like that even cross your mind.

Gabriel's voice broke through my wandering thoughts. "Officer Reggie is on his way here now. And I've looped in my mother. She has contacts all over the state. Don't worry," he added, his voice steady. "We'll find him."

Just then, the shop door swung open, and Officer Reggie strode in. Well, more like shuffled in, adjusting his belt with one hand while balancing a notepad in the other. His boyish face held the same eager determination as always, but the moment he took in the simmering hostilities in the room, his expression faltered.

"Good afternoon, folks. Lovely day, isn't it?" he said, clearing his throat as he fumbled with his notepad. "I've been, uh, fully briefed on the situation. Time is of the essence, so I'm gonna need to ask some, uh... pertinent questions." He adjusted his belt again before glancing at his notes, his lips moving slightly as he reread whatever he'd written.

I barely resisted the urge to sigh. Reggie was a good guy. Exactly the type of neighbor you'd invite to the block party barbeque, but, as far as detective work went, he was about as sharp as a butter knife. If he was leading these interviews, it just meant one thing: I needed to keep my eyes and ears open.

Officer Reggie blinked up from his notes and straightened his shoulders. "Ms. St. James, Mr. Grimshaw, Mrs. Moncrief-Grimshaw," he said, attempting an authoritative tone that didn't quite land. "I'll need to speak with each of you individually." Then he turned to me with an uncertain smile. "Uh, Harper, you got somewhere private we can use?"

I forced a reassuring nod. "Of course," I said, gesturing toward the back of the shop. "The sunroom is available."

"Great! Great." He nodded, flipping a page in his notebook. "If the rest of you don't mind waiting here, I'll start with, uh..." He squinted at his notes. "Oh! Ms. St. James."

Tiffany and Nate exchanged exasperated glances, their whispered complaints barely audible as they sank into nearby chairs. Valerie, clutching her phone like a lifeline, followed Reggie toward the sunroom, her heels clicking sharply against the hardwood floor.

I exhaled a shaky breath. Reggie meant well, but if he was our best shot at unraveling the truth, I was going to have to work twice as hard to stay ahead.

Bella sidled up beside me, her hand brushing against mine. "Are you doing okay?" she murmured, her voice low.

"Not really," I admitted. "This is not how I anticipated this day going. Garrett is missing, the stakes couldn't be higher, and now I'm juggling a room full of suspects who all seem ready to bite each other's heads off. I'm just waiting for someone to blame me outright."

Isadora came closer and squeezed my arm. "No one's blaming you, Harper. And even if they try, we've got your back."

Bella nodded, her calm presence a balm to my frayed nerves. "Isa's right. Gabriel's already looped in the sheriff, and Officer Reggie is, well... trying his best. And as for these three? Well, their issues have nothing to do with you. Don't let them get under your skin."

I smiled faintly, grateful for their support. "Thanks, both of you. That helps."

Isadora arched a perfectly shaped brow, her voice taking on a teasing lilt. "Besides, I'd love to see someone try to take you on with Bella in the room. She was ready to lay a WWE smackdown on that Nate guy if he hadn't backed down."

Bella grinned, raising a fist. "That's right. Nobody messes with my best friend."

The moment of levity was fleeting but much needed, and I felt a little of the tension ease. Then I spotted Mindy slipping toward the wall opposite Nate and his mother, her shoulders sagging with what looked like relief. I caught up with her, lowering my voice as I called out. "Mindy, wait a second."

She paused, glancing over her shoulder. "Yes?"

"You look like you just dodged a bullet," I said, keeping my tone casual. "Something wrong?"

Mindy hesitated, her gaze darting toward the sunroom before leaning in closer. "It's just...tense. It always is when Garrett's ex-wives are in the same room."

I raised an eyebrow, silently encouraging her to continue.

She sighed, lowering her voice further. "It's especially bad this time, with everything riding on this tour."

I frowned. "What do you mean?"

She hesitated, then leaned in. "It's not public yet, but early reactions to Garrett's new book haven't been great," she admitted. "Valerie's been working overtime to manage the fallout."

"What kind of fallout?" I pressed.

Mindy gestured toward the stack of Garrett's novels on display. "Have you read it?"

I hesitated. "Not yet," I admitted. I hurriedly added, "It's on my list though."

Mindy bit her lip. "Then you don't know."

A slow unease crept over me. "Know what?"

She lowered her voice. "Garrett finally did it. He's been threatening to do it for ages, but he finally pulled the trigger."

"What do you mean?" I asked.

Mindy glanced around and then whispered. "He killed off Rhett Ryder."

My stomach dropped. "What? But that's—"

"A disaster." Mindy nodded grimly. "His fans are already furious. Valerie is doing everything she can to convince him to walk it back."

I blinked. "Walk it back? But the book's already out."

"Yes, but this tour isn't just about sales—it's about spinning the narrative. Valerie's pushing for an official announcement: that the death isn't real. That Rhett's only in a coma and he's coming back."

I stared at her. "So, she's hoping Garrett will go along with this story?"

Mindy nodded. "But he isn't budging, which is why she pushed for a launch outside of New York. She's hoping that the backlash from fans here will encourage him to reconsider so when they head to larger venues, he'll go along with her narrative. But Garrett..." she trailed off and shook her head.

I filled in the blank. "Garrett won't budge."

She nodded. "He's convinced the controversy will drive sales. And honestly? I don't think it's just about that. I think he's done."

That gave me pause. "Done? With what?"

Mindy hesitated, then glanced over her shoulder. "He wants out of this series. Out of all of it. He's sick of Rhett Ryder, sick of writing the same thing over and over. And, well..." she dropped her voice even lower, "Savannah's been pushing him to start something new. Something about their relationship. A fresh start, no baggage."

I let that sink in. Garrett wasn't just killing off a character. He was burning bridges. Walking away from his entire literary legacy to chase something new. Maybe Tiffany had a point. Had I misread what I'd seen on the street? Could Garrett and Savannah have planned this together? Not as some dramatic industry statement, but as an escape? A chance to ditch the tour, the pressure, the spotlight and vanish on their own terms?

The thought barely had time to take root before my mind snapped back to what I witnessed outside Spellbooks. The car. The trunk. Someone had been inside; I was sure of it. Garrett hadn't run. He hadn't staged this as a dramatic farewell tour. He'd been taken.

Besides, Valerie needed him here. If he didn't personally walk back Rhett Ryder's death, it was over. For the series, for his fans, and possibly for his entire career. His disappearance certainly wouldn't do her any favors.

But that didn't mean it wasn't helping someone else.

I tapped my fingers against my notebook, letting my mind spin through the possibilities.

If Garrett was breaking away from his past, that meant breaking away from Tiffany and Nate, too. Was it possible Nate had finally had enough? I glanced toward him. He was stiff in his chair, his jaw tight. He'd been quick to dismiss his father's love life, but something about his tone had felt...off.

And Tiffany? She clearly wasn't convinced this was a kidnapping. Her theory? He'd run. Maybe with another woman. Or maybe he'd just left to get away from them all. But was she pushing this idea because she truly believed it—or because she wanted everyone else to?

And then there was Savannah. His biggest cheerleader, the one whispering in his ear to ditch everything and start fresh. But how far would she go to make sure that happened? And where was she? Was it merely coincidence that she'd vanished just before he had, or was there something more sinister at play here?

Before I could say more, Valerie's sharp voice rang out from the sunroom. "Mindy!"

Mindy jumped, clutching her folders to her chest. "Yes, Ms. St. James!" she stammered, hurrying toward the back.

I watched her retreat, my gut tightening. At the moment, I was confident about three things.

Garrett Grimshaw hadn't simply vanished.

Someone had taken him.

And if we didn't find him soon, we might not like what we found.

Not the Day I Planned

GABRIEL STOOD BY THE front counter, his phone pressed to his ear as he paced back and forth, his expression tense. I assumed he was either talking to his mother or to the sheriff. Nearby, Isadora mirrored his movements, her own phone glued to her ear as she stepped briskly between displays of books.

Bella sidled over to me, carrying a tray full of snacks. I shook my head and pressed a hand to my roiling stomach. "Thanks, but I couldn't eat a thing."

"These aren't for you. They were for them," she said, tipping her head toward the three men in driver's uniforms standing in the corner munching on beignets. "People are always chattier when they feel comfortable. I figured one of them might've seen something, so I brought snacks and struck up a conversation."

"Bella! You're brilliant!"

"I know," she said with a smirk.

"Did you find anything out?" I asked.

Her smirk faded almost instantly. "Apparently, they were supposed to stay with the cars all day. However, they thought snack breaks were more important. One even admitted to leaving the keys in the car because, and I quote, 'in a small town like this, you just don't expect nothing to happen. Ain't like this is New York.'"

"Seriously?" I asked.

Bella nodded. "I know, right? I mean, Havenwood is generally a safe place and normally, I wouldn't fault his logic, but today?"

"Today, nothing is going the way it's supposed to," I muttered.

The door to Spellbooks swung open, sending the bell above it jangling. I glanced up to see a tall, broad-shouldered man in a severe black suit had just stormed in. His sharp gaze scanned the shop like a hawk searching for prey. His shoulders were squared, his jaw locked tight. I recognized him instantly as the security guard Garrett had sent away with Savannah, so why was he returning alone?

I hurried over as the man stormed inside.

"Where is he?" the man barked, his voice cutting through the hum of conversation. Heads turned. The energy in the room shifted.

I stepped forward cautiously. "Wh—"

"Grimshaw," he snapped, rounding on me. "Where is he? Mindy Hart said he disappeared. That they think he was kidnapped."

I straightened my spine, forcing calm into my voice. "That's what we're trying to find out."

"What do we know? Fill me in immediately," he demanded.

"Not much," I admitted. "We saw someone throw him in the back of a car and drive off. Beyond that, we don't have much to go on at the moment, I'm afraid."

His sharp gaze flicked to me, recognition sparking in his eyes. "You're Harper Sullivan. You're the one running this disaster of an event."

I bristled. "I wouldn't call it a disaster—"

"Oh, wouldn't you?" he shot back. "Because from where I'm standing, the man I'm supposed to be protecting is missing, and no one seems to have any answers."

Bella moved beside me, her presence a steadying force. "And who do you think you are to go around talking to people like that?"

"Dirk Steele," the man said, his tone clipped. "Grimshaw's head of security. Or at least, I would be if anyone had let me do my job properly instead of babysitting a spoiled twenty-something-year-old."

Bella crossed her arms. "Speaking of, where is Savannah Chase?"

Dirk's expression darkened. "If I knew, I'd be dragging her back here myself."

I exchanged a glance with Bella. "You lost her?"

Dirk glared at me. "No, I didn't lose her. She ditched me."

My stomach twisted. Savannah disappeared right around the same time Garrett had. That wasn't suspicious at all.

"What happened?" Bella asked.

"That's what I'm trying to find out," Dirk snapped.

I held up my hands, palms outward. "Whoa. Slow down. We're all on the same team here. We just want answers, same as you."

Dirk exhaled sharply, visibly forcing himself to rein in his frustration. "Grimshaw asked me to keep an eye on her while she went to get coffee. It's not unusual for him to make a request like that, especially when we're in a new place. I figured it would be ten minutes, fifteen tops and he was safe enough here, so I followed. But when I told her it was time to return, she threw a fit." He crossed his arms. "Said I wasn't her babysitter, and she'd come back when she was good and ready."

Bella narrowed her eyes. "And you just...let her wander off?"

Dirk's expression tightened. "You wanted me to physically drag her back?"

I opened my mouth, then shut it. He had a point. Savannah Chase was a grown woman. If she'd made a scene and refused to come back, Dirk couldn't exactly handcuff her and throw her over his shoulder.

Dirk's jaw ticked. "I got the call from Mindy and overheard some people talking about Grimshaw coming down with something as I was on my way back here." He exhaled sharply. "By the time I got the news, it was too late."

Something about his tone nagged at me. "You didn't know about any threats against him?"

Dirk hesitated. "Not that I was made aware of." His expression darkened. "But I should have been. If I'd had my team—"

I picked up on that instantly. "Your team?" I studied him. His frustration seemed real, but that didn't mean he wasn't hiding something. "You were the only security he had today?"

Dirk let out a harsh breath. "Not by choice. I wanted a full team. I *should* have had a full team." His jaw clenched. "But someone thought it was unnecessary. Said it wasn't in the budget. Now look where we are."

I exchanged a glance with Bella. "And who was that?" I asked.

"Not a clue." Dirk exhaled sharply. "If I ever find out who made that stupid decision, I'm going to give them a piece of my mind. I told them we needed more guys, but would they listen? No." He squeezed his large hands into fists, his knuckles cracking loudly. He looked at me suddenly. "You said someone drove him away? Give me the details. What did the car look like? Can you give me a description of the driver?"

I hesitated, but there wasn't a reason not to share what I'd seen. "Whoever it was took one of the black sedans you arrived in. I couldn't get a clear look in the trunk, but I saw something crumpled inside. The driver couldn't shut the trunk on the first try and what looked like an arm blocked it. He tried again and then dashed around to the front of the car and peeled down the street."

"And the driver, what did he look like?" Dirk pressed immediately.

I frowned, closing my eyes and trying to remember every detail. "He wore a cap, pulled down low over his eyes. Black jacket, tall guy."

"Anything else? Hair color, eyes?" Dirk demanded.

I shook my head slowly. "I didn't get a clear look at him. It all happened so fast."

Dirk sighed and rubbed at the back of his neck. "It's not much to go on. I assume someone's checked the drivers."

Bella gestured to the side of the room where the three men huddled, with their heads close together. "All three of them are accounted for," she said.

A deep furrow creased Dirk's brow. "If they are all here, how did someone get the keys?"

Bella sighed. "One of the drivers said that he left the keys in the car. They didn't expect anything like this to happen in such a small town."

Dirk's scowl deepened, and he muttered something under his breath that sounded suspiciously like, "Amateurs."

I kept my focus on Dirk. "So, if all three drivers were here, who was behind the wheel of the car that took Garrett?"

His mouth thinned. "Someone who shouldn't have been." He exhaled sharply. "What I *do* know is that I should've been there when it happened, not babysitting some prissy princess."

Before I could push further, Officer Reggie emerged from the back, flipping through his notepad with a confused look on his face. His gaze landed on Dirk, and his eyes lit up.

"Who are you?" the police officer asked.

The security guard stepped forward, hand outstretched. "Dirk Steele, Mr. Grimshaw's security detail. Please, let me know if there's anything I can do, Officer."

"Security, you say?" Reggie asked. "Oh, well. Right. I should probably talk to you. If you're security, you'll know stuff."

"Stuff?" Dirk repeated, raking Reggie with a speculative look. I didn't need to be a mind reader to realize he was reevaluating his initial opinion of the police officer.

Reggie nodded sagely. "Yep. If you are security that means you probably know *lots* of important stuff." He motioned toward the sunroom. "I'd love to pick your brain about a gig in security."

"What about Grimshaw's disappearance?" Dirk demanded.

"Oh yeah. That too," Officer Reggie said with a bright smile.

Dirk's mouth twitched like he was debating whether to say something, but in the end, he exhaled sharply and followed Reggie toward the sunroom.

As soon as the door shut behind them, Gabriel was at my side. His voice was quiet, but urgent. "Harper, can we talk for a moment?" He tipped his head slightly toward Valerie, who had just returned to the main room.

I hesitated, my gaze flicking toward Bella. She caught my look and gave me an encouraging nod before turning back to the drivers with her usual effortless charm.

I followed Gabriel to a quieter corner of the shop, my pulse quickening. "What is it?" I asked as soon as we were out of earshot. "Has the sheriff found anything?"

Gabriel shook his head, his jaw tightening. "Nothing yet."

I exhaled slowly, adjusting to the lack of information as my hopes for a quick resolution dimmed. "So, what now?"

"Lucas is reinforcing the town wards, hoping to attune them to Garrett," Gabriel explained. "If Garrett crosses any of the boundaries, he should get a magical alert."

"Can that even work?" I asked.

"It's unorthodox, but Lucas can be...creative with his magic." He hesitated, then lowered his voice. "Speaking of creative, earlier you spaced out for a second. Were you connecting to the heartwood? Can it help?"

I hesitated, rubbing the back of my neck. "Yes, I tried reaching out to the heartwood earlier, but it didn't give me anything useful. To be honest, it didn't seem like the spirit trusted the saplings very much. The impression I got was that they were very green, no pun intended."

"Maybe proximity would help," he suggested, his expression earnest. "The closer you are to him—or at least the forest itself—the stronger the connection might become."

I frowned, doubt gnawing at me. "I don't know, Gabriel, but I guess it's worth a shot. I've barely scratched the surface of what it means to be the heartwood's guardian. What if I mess it up? What if I don't feel anything at all?"

Gabriel didn't answer right away, and for a second, I regretted letting the words slip out. I was used to keeping my insecurities wrapped up tight where no one could poke at them. But Gabriel had this way of seeing past the surface I displayed to the world, of looking at me like I was more capable than I felt.

His voice, when it came, was steady. "Then you try again."

I let out a short, humorless laugh. "That easy, huh?"

"It doesn't have to be easy," he said. "Just possible."

He stepped closer, his voice steady and sure. "You know more than you think, Harper. When Lysandra Wraithmoor came for us, you didn't stop to think—you acted. You reached out to the heartwood instinctively and look how that turned out. You can do this."

I swallowed, staring down at my hands. A part of me wanted to believe him. Another part of me—the part that had spent years hiding my magic from the world—wasn't sure I could.

But Garrett was missing. And if there was even a chance I could find him...

I took a slow breath, nodding. "Okay. I'll try," I said, the uncertainty thick in my voice. "But I might need you to hold my hand along the way."

Gabriel smiled, lifting my hand to his lips and pressing a firm kiss to my knuckles. "Always."

We moved quickly through the shop, filling in Isadora and Bella on our plans.

"Would you mind staying behind until Officer Reggie is done taking statements and then closing up?" I asked Bella, lowering my voice. "I don't want to leave Spellbooks unattended with all this chaos, but if I can do something to help find Garrett, I need to try."

Bella nodded, already seeming to anticipate the request. "Of course. I'll make sure everything is locked up tight. No worries," she said confidently. She glanced at Isadora. "Are you sticking around too?"

Isadora crossed her arms, arching a brow at the sunroom. "Oh, absolutely. Someone has to make sure Reggie doesn't get distracted by a shiny object mid-interview."

I exhaled, relieved. "Thanks, both of you."

Bella waved me off. "Go. Find Garrett. We've got this."

I gave them a grateful look before turning toward Gabriel. "Let's go."

With that, we grabbed our coats and headed out the front door. The crisp air bit at my cheeks as we crossed to Gabriel's car, its dark frame gleaming in the afternoon sun. He unlocked the doors, and I slid into the passenger seat, my hands twisting in my lap as the engine hummed to life.

This was supposed to be a fun day. Meet a famous author, snap a few pictures, maybe geek out over his latest book. Instead, I was about to dive headfirst into the unknown, relying on a bond I barely understood to find someone who might already be in serious danger.

I just hoped my connection to the heartwood was enough to find Garrett before his disappearance irreversibly tainted both Spellbooks and Havenwood.

Perfume and Peril

THE FOREST STRETCHED ENDLESSLY around us. Every step we took crunched against dry leaves. Stray branches snagged my sleek updo and scratched my cheeks, but I barely noticed. The ley lines bolstered my energy as I tapped into the heartwood, yet the effort felt like shouting into an empty void. The tree's connection to the forest wasn't as all-encompassing as I'd hoped. It could sense magic, but the problem was Garrett wasn't magical. He was just a regular, human author.

We weren't dressed in sensible hiking clothes either. Yet, given the urgency of the situation, neither of us had taken the time to change. So, we did the best we could to cover as much ground as possible. Eventually, Gabriel suggested returning to the car and cruising slowly along the roads running through the forest. If I could maintain my connection with the heartwood, it might speed up our search.

It took all of my concentration to focus on my link with the heartwood as we drove, scanning the surrounding area for signs of life. The effort was draining, mentally and emotionally, even with the heartwood's connection to the magic in the ley lines. Each time I reached out, it felt like grasping at smoke.

If I weren't so focused on finding Garrett, I might have been fascinated by the flashes of hidden life the heartwood revealed. A fox darted through the underbrush, birds twittered in the branches and, beneath it all, I could sense with my magic the quiet hum of ancient roots reaching towards the ley lines. But I couldn't afford distractions. Time was slipping through our fingers.

After what felt like an eternity, though it had only been an hour, I slumped against the seat, frustration winding tighter inside me. "He's not here," I said quietly. "At least...if he is, I can't sense him."

Gabriel placed a hand on my shoulder, his calm anchoring me. "You tried. That's what matters. If you're up for it, let's try the next road, see if we can pick up a signal."

I sighed, leaning my head from side to side. The *crack-crack-crack* of releasing tension gave me a momentary reprieve. "I'll do everything in my power to help. I just wish we had more to go on, but I can't seem to make any progress with the heartwood. Having trees as my eyes and ears is cool, but also surprisingly limiting."

Gabriel gave a small, understanding smile. "You're doing more than anyone else could. The fact that you can even try this at all is incredible. Don't downplay it."

Just then, his phone buzzed, and the screen on the console lit up, displaying Sheriff Jackson's name.

The fatigue tugging at me evaporated in a rush of adrenaline as Gabriel answered the call.

"Sheriff? Gabriel here. I've got you on speaker with Harper."

"Good. We've found the car," Sheriff Jackson's deep voice crackled through the speaker. "It's abandoned on Willow Creek Road, but we could use some magical backup. Lucas is tied up on the other side of town, and he said you might be closer. How fast can you get here?"

Gabriel exchanged a glance with me before responding, "We're not far. Ten minutes tops."

"Good," Jackson said. "Bill and I have secured the perimeter, but we could use an extra set of eyes—and senses."

"On our way," Gabriel confirmed, disconnecting the call.

I tightened my seatbelt as he shifted the car into gear. The roads blurred past as we sped toward Willow Creek Road, urgency buzzing in the air between us. I pressed my hands together, reaching for a steadiness that felt increasingly elusive. Was Garrett there? But if he was, why hadn't the sheriff said as much? What would we find when we got to Willow Creek Road?

Sheriff Jackson's head snapped up as Gabriel eased his car onto the shoulder behind the police cruiser. The sheriff's expression was as unyielding as ever, his sharp eyes scanning us as he approached.

"Silverthorne," he greeted Gabriel, extending a hand. His gravelly voice carried the weight of authority and gravitas.

"Sheriff," Gabriel returned, shaking his hand.

The sheriff's gaze flicked to me, a single brow arching in question. His expression held a flicker of curiosity. I could almost read his mind. Gabriel wouldn't have just brought his girlfriend along for a police investigation. But whatever question was forming behind those sharp eyes, he let it go.

"Miss Sullivan," he greeted me, his tone formal but not unkind.

Before I could respond, the rhythmic clip-clop of hooves echoed down the road. At first, it seemed like a mounted officer was approaching, but I knew better. The shimmer of glamour surrounding him faded as he drew closer, revealing Officer Bill in his true form—a powerful centaur, his muscular horse's legs moving with the practiced grace of a seasoned police officer. His jacket flapped slightly in the breeze, his disheveled hair suggesting he'd been searching tirelessly.

"Any luck?" Sheriff Jackson asked as Bill trotted up.

Bill shook his head, his somber expression reflecting the gravity of the situation. "No tracks, Sheriff. Whoever did this knew what they were doing. No marks on either side of the road."

The sheriff muttered under his breath, then looked back at Gabriel and me. "Give me a moment while I catch them up," he said to Bill, who nodded and moved to the far side of the road to resume his search.

"What can we do to help?" Gabriel asked, his tone calm but direct.

Sheriff Jackson gestured toward the black sedan parked haphazardly on the shoulder. "Bill spotted this car during his sweep. It's an exact match for the one Grimshaw disappeared in. He called it in right away."

Gabriel's gaze fixed on the vehicle, its tinted windows nearly black, and doors firmly shut. "And it was left just like this?"

Jackson nodded, his expression hard. "Untouched, as far as we can tell. No wildlife's been near it yet, so it hasn't been here long. The problem is getting inside. We could break a window, but that risks compromising the scene, and the locksmith is at least forty-five minutes out." He paused, glancing meaningfully at Gabriel. "I was hoping you could lend a hand."

Gabriel exchanged a quick glance with me. I didn't need him to spell it out to understand immediately what he was thinking. "We'll take a look, Sheriff," Gabriel said.

"There's more," the sheriff added. "I need you to check for any magical residue. Look for illusions, spells, anything that might give us a lead. We found a few footprints leading to what we assume was another car that must've been waiting here. Looks like they transferred Grimshaw to a different vehicle and vanished without leaving so much as a tire tread. If you can pick up anything, it'd be invaluable."

As the sheriff spoke, I drew on my magic. The heartwood's power surged within me, amplifying my connection to the metal of the car. With this much energy, I didn't need to touch the locks to manipulate them. Gabriel, catching the faintest shift in my expression, gave me a barely perceptible nod. A silent acknowledgment. A go-ahead. He knew about my magic, but Sheriff Jackson didn't. Gabriel also knew I preferred to keep it that way. Ever supportive, he played along seamlessly. He rested his hand on the car's door, masking my work as the locks gave a sharp click and popped open.

"All yours, Sheriff," Gabriel said smoothly, stepping back.

Jackson gave a satisfied nod, his sharp gaze shifting between us. "Let's see what secrets this thing is hiding." He pulled out a pair of latex gloves, snapping them on easily.

"Can we help, Sheriff?" Gabriel asked.

After a moment's pause, Sheriff Jackson pulled two more pairs of latex gloves from his pocket and handed one to me and one to Gabriel. "We're bending protocol a bit here, but as of now, both of you are acting as consultants for the Havenwood Police Department in an official capacity," he said gruffly.

Gabriel and I nodded in unison, slipping on the gloves. The weight of his words settled over me, adding to the mounting pressure.

"Do you see anything noteworthy, Sheriff?" I asked, keeping my voice steady despite the nerves twisting in my stomach.

Sheriff Jackson sighed, inspecting the car. "Minor scuff marks on the door, but no blood." He paused, inhaling deeply, then grimaced. "No scent, either. Except for perfume. Something strong and floral, with a sharp spice."

I stiffened. "Savannah Chase."

The sheriff's gaze sharpened. "Who's that?"

"Grimshaw's fiancée. She's launching a signature scent. It matches what you're picking up," I explained.

Gabriel frowned. "If Grimshaw and Savannah shared this car, her scent makes sense. Doesn't mean she was involved."

"Unless she wasn't with him willingly," I countered. "No one's seen her since she went to get coffee. Dirk said she refused to come back." I hesitated, a new thought clicking into place. "Or maybe she didn't want to be found."

The sheriff's mouth flattened. "Either way, this complicates things." He exhaled sharply, rubbing at his nose and taking a step back from the car. "And it gets worse." He gestured toward the cracked perfume bottle lying near the driver's seat. "That stuff's completely saturated the area. It's strong enough that I can't pick up any other scent. No trace of Grimshaw, the kidnapper, or anything else. That stuff is too overpowering."

"That's not good," I murmured.

"What's our next move, then Sheriff?" Gabriel asked.

The sheriff held up a finger and then sneezed three times in quick succession. He took another step back, away from the car and its overwhelming scent as he wiped at his watering eyes. "We need to finish processing the scene and then track down this Savannah Chase as soon as possible."

Gabriel crouched, inspecting under the car. "I don't see her orchestrating a kidnapping, though."

"She'd probably post a selfie with the victim," I muttered.

The sheriff snorted, pulling out the floor mats to sniff them. "One of those? Doesn't scream mastermind to me. Perhaps you're right and she's a victim too. Perfume like that isn't exactly subtle."

Gabriel straightened, his tone serious. "If this was planned by professionals, they wouldn't have left anything behind that could link them to the crime. There's no way someone rode in this car and didn't have some of the scent transfer to them. Not saying that they'd know our sheriff is a werewolf or anything, but this feels...careless."

"Or deliberate," I suggested, wiping my gloved hands on my pants. "A setup to frame Savannah and throw us off the trail."

The sheriff's jaw tightened. "Either way, she needs to answer some questions. However, I'm not going to chase after some random lead before I've completed a thorough inspection of this vehicle. The kidnappers might have been sloppy, but we can't afford to be."

"Agreed," Gabriel said.

We moved as a team, each taking a section of the vehicle to inspect. I knelt by the passenger seat, running my fingers along the upholstery, but turned up nothing useful. Gabriel leaned in over my shoulder, his sharp eyes scanning the floor.

"There's something under the seat." He reached carefully, pulling out a small object. Gabriel carefully held up a shattered piece of glass that glinted faintly in the fading sunlight. "This has to be part of that broken perfume bottle, right?"

Sheriff Jackson took it, his nose wrinkling. "Definitely the same perfume. No doubt about it. She was in this car. But if she was involved, why leave all this behind?"

Gabriel frowned, carefully turning the glass over in his palm. "If this was meant to be clean, the car never would have been left here at all. I'm leaning toward the hypothesis that this wasn't a professional job."

Sheriff Jackson slipped the shard into an evidence bag, his expression unreadable. "Maybe, but this isn't helping her case. Do you think she'd kidnap her own fiancé?"

I hesitated, images of Savannah's endless selfies and public displays of affection swirling in my mind. "Honestly, it seems out of character. She's more interested in social media fame than crime. But..." I trailed off, a seed of doubt still growing.

The sheriff raised a hand. "Either she was desperate for money, or it's just residual from the broken bottle. Still, worth looking into."

I frowned, something nagging at the back of my mind. Savannah had been carrying that perfume bottle with her throughout the entire signing, spritzing herself every chance she got. Until Mindy had taken it and she pulled out her spare. That much was true. But according to Dirk, she'd gone to get coffee, yet she'd never returned.

So how did her perfume end up shattered inside the car?

My stomach twisted. Either Savannah carried at least three bottles of her unreleased scent which seemed over the top, even for her, or she had been with Garrett when he was taken.

Nearby, Bill called out from the trees, interrupting my thoughts. Sheriff Jackson went to investigate what his officer had found. Gabriel glanced between me and the car. "I'm going to cast some tracking spells to see if I can detect any residual magic just to make sure we're covering all of our bases. Are you okay for a couple minutes?"

I nodded, and he moved a few steps away. He closed his eyes, his lips moving silently. Grateful for the brief solitude, I stretched out with my metal magic, feeling for any abnormalities within the car's metallic landscape. The interior's metal pieces—the buckles, frame, engine—all hummed in my mind, a chaotic mosaic of parts. Slowly, I sorted through them, looking for anything that didn't fit.

Something small and round under the driver's seat caught my attention. My heart leaped as I called out, "Sheriff, I think there's something under the seat!"

He returned swiftly, crouching beside me. "What am I looking for?"

"Something small, round, about the size of a quarter. It's under the driver's seat."

Using a flashlight, he retrieved a small gold disc pinched between his gloved fingers.

He held it up to the light. "What's this? A button?"

"That's weird," I murmured. "It must've fallen off. Do you think it was it from one of Garrett's party? Like a driver? Or maybe the kidnapper wore it?"

Sheriff Jackson turned it over. "A bit flashy for a driver, don't you think? But I don't see a kidnapper dressing in theme to match the event of the day." He was right. The elaborate design of an open book was stamped on the button.

"Yeah," I agreed, frowning. "Definitely weird though." I turned the image over in my mind, committing the design to memory. "I'll keep an eye out, see if anything matches."

The sheriff rolled the button between his gloved fingers, contemplating. "Could it have been torn off during a struggle?"

"Hard to say," I said. "Maybe it was loose and fell off... or maybe someone was where they weren't supposed to be."

A moment of silence passed as we all considered the strange button. Then Gabriel spoke, his voice low. "If that button didn't belong to one of the staff, then someone wanted to look like they did."

The sheriff's eyes narrowed. "Which means someone used the chaos to blend in."

"Exactly," I said. "They knew the timing. The layout. How to disappear in plain sight." A chill crept down my spine. "This wasn't random. It was planned."

The sheriff's jaw set. "Then whoever did this had help or access they shouldn't have."

Gabriel nodded, tension radiating from him. "And if that's true, we're not just dealing with a kidnapping. We're dealing with a setup."

The sheriff's phone buzzed in his pocket as he slid the button into an evidence bag. He pulled the phone out, glancing at the screen. "Officer Reggie," he said, waving the phone at me. "I'd better take this. I need to see if he found this Chase woman yet." He stepped away to answer the phone.

Taking the opportunity, I found the button that opened the trunk and moved to the back of the car. The lid popped with a soft *thunk*, and I hesitated for a moment before lifting it fully, my heartbeat thundering loudly in my ears.

Inside, nothing but darkness and the faint, sterile scent of new carpet and rubber greeted me. I swept my gaze over the space. Garment bags lay neatly along one side. A lone briefcase sat beside them, tilted at an odd angle, as if it had been shoved in hastily.

I frowned, stepping closer. My gloved fingers skimmed the briefcase, and a quick pulse of metal magic told me the locks were engaged. No scrapes. No dents. No signs of a struggle.

Huh.

If I'd been shoved into the trunk of a car, I'd have done everything in my power to escape. Kicking, thrashing, anything. The result would've been chaos. The garment bags would be crumpled, the briefcase banged and damaged.

Had Garrett been knocked unconscious?

That would explain the relatively neat state of the trunk. If he had been knocked unconscious, maybe by the force of the trunk slamming shut, then we had even more reason to find him now. He could have a head injury. Maybe even a concussion or possibly something worse. I doubted kidnappers factored medical attention into their plans. Right now, Garrett could be out there, bleeding, unconscious—

I swallowed against the rising urgency. There had to be a clue here, and, if there was, I was determined to find it. Ignoring the garment bags, I carefully opened the briefcase, brushing it with just enough metal magic to avoid smudging any prints left behind.

Inside, I found an embossed folder with the distinguished monogram: *Property of Garrett Grimshaw.*

Curious, I opened it, revealing what looked like legal papers. But as I flipped through the pages, my breath hitched.

These weren't just any legal documents.

They were copies of Garrett's last will and testament. From what I could tell, there was both the original and an unsigned, amended version.

My pulse quickened as my eyes scanned the amendments.

The changes were staggering. Garrett was cutting Nate out of the inheritance entirely. Where Nate had once been listed as the recipient of half the estate, the new document gave a full 75% to Savannah. The remaining 25% would be split between his ex-wives, leaving Nate with nothing.

I swallowed, my hands shaking slightly as I processed the revelations. Had Nate discovered these changes? Could he have been desperate enough to stop them?

And then a darker thought surfaced. Could Savannah be behind this? With her as the prime beneficiary, maybe she had a different kind of plan for securing the estate. The kind of plan that didn't include Garrett at all. But if that were true, why leave these papers in the car? Especially if they were unsigned.

Lost in thought, I barely noticed Sheriff Jackson reappear beside me, his gaze sharp. "Something interesting, Miss Sullivan?"

Flustered, I nodded and handed him the documents. "Garrett was making some serious changes to his estate."

The sheriff whistled, his expression darkening as he scanned the papers. "Savannah inherits almost everything, and Nate's cut out entirely. That's motive for both of them."

"If Savannah wanted Garrett gone, she wouldn't need to marry him," I pointed out. "She'd inherit it all if he died."

"Only if it's signed," Sheriff Jackson said grimly. "I suppose it's one way to avoid paying for a wedding. She gets him to sign it and then offs him. Or maybe this Nate fella wants to stop the amendments to the will going through. Either way, this is shaping up to be more than just a kidnapping."

Gabriel jogged over, his brow furrowed. "No clear trace of magic," he said.

I turned to him sharply. "No trace at all?"

He hesitated, rubbing his jaw. "Not exactly. There's something lingering. It's too faint for me to get a clear reading. It could be spellwork from the kidnappers or just residual energy from Lucas reinforcing the town wards. It's hard to tell."

"We can't say for certain there's no magic involved which means I'm not calling the feds," the sheriff said grimly.

"Really? Wouldn't they be as susceptible to the magic spells surrounding Havenwood as the tourists?" I asked.

The sheriff shook his head. "Not at all. First and foremost, the feds would be here on a job, looking for clues. The magic isn't designed to combat a trained investigator, just to smooth out the edges of a family on vacation who happens to see a vampire flash too much fang. Secondly, if there is magic involved, how are we going to explain away a troll grabbing Mr. Grimshaw? Or a chimera?"

"But it was a human driving. I saw that with my own eyes," I insisted.

The sheriff arched a bushy brow. "My point still stands. Just replace the troll with a wizard. If the feds come in, guns drawn, the hypothetical wizard will respond to the threat in kind. Given that law enforcement officers all wear body cams these days, we'd be handing the feds irrefutable evidence of the supernatural world. Then what do you think would happen? There'd be no way to contain it."

"But what if it's a normal human?" I asked. "Isn't that a possibility still? Gabriel said his scan for magic was inconclusive."

The sheriff thought for just a moment and then shook his head. "Right now, that's not a risk we can take. Revealing the supernatural world wouldn't just compromise Havenwood and everyone who lives in it, it would compromise every supernatural on the planet. If there was video evidence of a wizard casting spells against law enforcement, it would spread like wildfire. There'd be no turning back."

Gabriel spoke up. "He's right, Harper. We can't afford to risk it. There's too much at stake."

I wanted to argue. To insist that Grimshaw's life was more important than secrecy. But was it?

What about Honey and Antonio, who had built the Enchanted Oasis as a safe place for both humans and supernatural visitors alike? Or Jeremiah, the old treant who tended to the botanical gardens and his nephew, Jeremy? Then there was Martha, Luna, and a whole host of other people I'd met here. My eyes snapped to Gabriel, but he was already watching me, his expression tight. What about the Silverthornes? Gabriel's family had spent decades protecting Havenwood, careful not to draw the wrong kind of attention.

What would happen to all of them if the wrong people found out? If the world saw a witch shielding herself from bullets or a vampire moving faster than the eye could track? If the feds confirmed what they'd only ever whispered about in conspiracy theories or plots for fantasy TV shows?

Everything would change.

Everything would burn.

And it would've started here.

I exhaled slowly, wrapping my arms around myself. So much for this event being a career boost. Instead, my shop was ground zero for a scandal, my reputation was at risk, my already fragile financial situation felt like it was crumbling beneath me, and now I might be responsible for revealing the supernatural world.

And I had no clue how to fix any of it.

A swell of a sob I barely suppressed clogged my throat. I sucked in a sharp breath, but it barely helped. I wasn't ready for this. Any of it.

I wasn't ready to be the heartwood's guardian. I wasn't ready to carry the future of Spellbooks on my shoulders. I wasn't ready to stand between a town full of magic and a world that wouldn't understand.

Granny Bea's voice suddenly echoed in my mind, steady and certain, the way it always had been when I was younger and scared of something I couldn't avoid or hide from.

"The world doesn't wait for you to be ready, Harper. It moves, with or without you. The only question is—are you going to move with it?"

I swallowed hard, the strength in her words settling deep into my bones. I squared my shoulders, forcing myself to take a steadying breath. Later. I could break down later. Right now, I needed to focus on what I could control. Find Grimshaw. Protect Havenwood. Keep the world from learning that magic wasn't just in fairy tales.

I took another deep breath and nodded. "Okay, what's our next move?"

"Wait for the kidnappers to contact us," the sheriff replied bluntly. "If this is a ransom situation, time is critical. If they mean to harm him..." He paused, his jaw tightening. "Well, let's just say we need to act fast. Keeping everyone close ensures we don't miss anything."

Gabriel crossed his arms. "And if we don't hear from the kidnappers?"

"Then we keep pushing. Follow every lead, chase down every possibility," the sheriff said firmly. "No way am I letting a famous author disappear in Havenwood on my watch."

A chill prickled at the back of my neck. He was right, but this wasn't just about finding Garrett Grimshaw anymore. If we failed, Havenwood—the town built on secrets and hidden in plain sight—would be at the center of a scandal no magic could erase.

And if Havenwood fell under media scrutiny, how long before everything else about the supernatural world unraveled?

Shadows and Schemes

THE DRIVE TO THE Silverthorne manor stretched in silence, the kind that left the faint hum of the car engine feeling too loud. Outside, the early March sun dipped lower, painting the road in elongated shadows that danced with each curve. Frost clung to the roadside in a stubborn veil, catching the light with a quiet, brittle gleam. A chill seeped into the car, clinging to the edges of our coats despite the heater's best efforts.

Ahead, the sheriff's cruiser led the way, its lights casting brief, rhythmic flashes across the tree trunks that lined the road. Each flicker felt like a beacon, steady and unrelenting, as if urging us forward.

The manor came into view around the final bend, its silhouette rising like a sentinel against the sky. Light played across the ivy-clad stone walls, but the windows remained dark, giving nothing away. As the car slowed and the gravel of the drive crunched beneath the tires, an uneasy stillness settled over me.

This was the first time I'd been back since the Christmas Eve Ball. My eyes drifted toward the garage where everything had unraveled that night. The memory tightened in my chest before I could stop it. The audacious jewel theft that had almost ended with me being the victim of a kidnapping. I still remembered the feel of being forced into the trunk of the Silverthorne's car, knowing that if that trunk lid shut on me, it might be the last time I saw my friends and family.

Was this what Garrett felt today?

I pulled in a slow breath, but it hitched in my throat, frost-laced and sharp.

Beside me, Gabriel shifted. I hadn't said anything, but somehow, he knew. Without a word, his fingers brushed against mine before curling around them, warm and solid. An anchor.

I let out the breath I'd been holding, grounding myself in the present. The manor stood before me now, unchanged, indifferent to what had happened the last time I was here.

I wasn't the same person who had walked into that ball.

I squeezed Gabriel's hand once before stepping out of the car, the crunch of gravel beneath my boots pulling me fully back to the moment. There were bigger things to focus on now.

Garrett Grimshaw was still missing. And it was time to get some answers.

Gabriel led us briskly through the grand foyer and into the ballroom. Staff were already bustling about, adorning the space with gold and purple streamers, flickering candle lanterns, and towering posters for *Masks of Deception*. The room's opulence couldn't entirely dispel the undercurrent of unease. My gaze lingered on the decorations, wondering if Garrett would ever get to see the party meant to honor him.

No! I shoved the thought aside. *We would find him. We* had *to.*

Vivienne appeared, her calm presence as commanding as ever. She moved through the chaos of the ballroom like a queen surveying her court, regal and severe. "Sheriff, Gabriel, Harper," she greeted each of us with a curt nod. "Follow me, please."

She led us into the library, its mahogany shelves and deep shadows a stark contrast to the bright chaos of the ballroom. The Silverthorne crest loomed above the fireplace, and the scent of old books and polished wood filled the air. Vivienne closed the heavy door behind us, shutting out the noise of the party preparations.

"Now," she said, her piercing gaze settling on Sheriff Jackson, "tell me what you know."

The sheriff recounted the situation with precise efficiency, outlining the limited evidence we'd discovered at the scene. Gabriel and I also added our observations and suppositions based on the evidence uncovered. Vivienne listened intently, her fingers tapping lightly on the arm of her chair.

When the sheriff finished, she leaned back, her expression unreadable. "I agree with you. Someone close to Garrett very well might have orchestrated this. Or perhaps it was someone else entirely. The fan theory bears a closer examination. Either way, without a ransom demand, the motive remains ambiguous, giving us no clear insight into who the perpetrator might be."

The sheriff waved his phone. "I've been following up with my team, but we need time to dig deeper. Unfortunately, if this goes public too soon, it could create a frenzy. One wrong word or someone leaking this to the press could make a bad situation infinitely worse."

I crossed my arms. "What about Savannah? Has she finally turned up?"

The sheriff exhaled sharply. "She's back. My deputy found her strutting through town like nothing was wrong. She claimed she 'lost track of time' shopping and 'couldn't possibly be expected to deal with all this stress' without a little retail therapy." His voice dripped with disdain. "Said she didn't even know Garrett was missing until we told her."

Gabriel muttered, "That's convenient."

I frowned, tapping my fingers against my sleeve. I agreed with Gabriel. Something about that didn't sit right. But another realization crowded in. Havenwood was only so big. It wasn't New York City, where someone could vanish into the crowd easily and without a trace. If Garrett was still in town, we should have found him by now.

"I won't allow that to happen," Vivienne said crisply, clearly responding to something I'd half missed while lost in thought.

She folded her arms. "Everyone who might have an inkling of the truth has been brought here under the guise of Silverthorne hospitality and their devices have been collected."

I blinked. "Collected? Why?"

The sheriff waved a hand. "We told them we needed to install tracking and monitoring software in case the kidnappers try to contact them instead of the police."

I blinked. "You *have* that kind of software? That sounds really advanced."

The sheriff let out a short laugh. "Not a chance. Not that I understand most of that gobbledygook anyway." He crossed his arms. "No, Lucas put a spell on the devices."

"A spell?" I repeated, my stomach twisting.

Vivienne nodded. "It's necessary. We don't want any outgoing messages in case the kidnappers try to lure someone away—then we'd have two kidnappings on our hands instead of one. Instead, Lucas is rerouting all communications through the command center we've set up here. Any messages they try to send will appear to have gone through on their end, but they won't actually be delivered."

Gabriel let out a low whistle. "That's a significant piece of magic and a lot to sustain. Does Lucas need help?"

"I think he's nearly done," Vivienne said, her tone clipped. "But you're right. It's a lot of magic to expend. When he finishes, he'll need to eat and rest. Hopefully, he'll recover his energy soon."

"Do you think we should cancel the masquerade?" Gabriel asked, his tone measured.

The sheriff glanced at Vivienne. "We were just discussing that on the phone. I'm leaning towards canceling," the sheriff said.

"Whereas I think there are significant benefits to keeping to the plan. Both for Havenwood and for Mr. Grimshaw," Vivienne said.

I nodded, my mind racing through the possibilities. "If we go ahead as planned, sticking to the schedule might force the kidnapper's hand. They could panic, make a mistake. One we might be able to use to our advantage."

The sheriff rubbed his chin thoughtfully. "I must admit that I do like the idea of that."

Beside him, Vivienne turned sharply to look at me. A flicker of something—was that approval?—crossed her face. "My thoughts exactly," she said, her voice measured but intrigued.

I swallowed, surprised by the unexpected agreement. Vivienne Silverthorne intimidated me. She had ever since I moved to Havenwood. She was sharp, calculating, always three steps ahead. But for the first time, it felt like she was really *seeing* me. At least, the confident, decisive person I strove to be.

"Additionally," Vivienne continued, "I refuse to let some outsider dictate how *my* town operates. We do not bend to threats. If anything, we use them to our advantage."

Gabriel nodded and opened his mouth, but before he could respond, the door burst open, and Valerie St. James stormed in. Her usual polished composure was replaced with frantic energy, her sharp eyes darting around the room. "What are you doing about this?" she demanded, her voice high-pitched with urgency. "Garrett's missing, and you're all just standing around talking? We should be calling every media outlet, raising alarms, making sure the world knows he's gone!"

"Ms. St. James," Vivienne said, her tone calm but firm, "we're handling the situation. A media blitz would only complicate matters."

"Complicate matters?" Valerie's voice rose. "This is a national crisis! Garrett Grimshaw, the author of the New York Times best-selling Rhett Ryder series, vanishing in the middle of his tour? Do you know what this could do to his career? To mine?" She caught herself, then added quickly, "To his family? His fans? The longer he's missing, the worse this looks for everyone."

"Ms. St. James," Vivienne interjected smoothly, her tone icy, "a public spectacle would do more harm than good. We have no ransom demand, no credible leads, and no reason to believe the kidnappers want publicity. Until we know more, discretion is our best weapon."

Valerie glared, her chest rising and falling with barely contained frustration. "Am I hearing you right? Your plan is to do nothing? Sit here and hope he miraculously turns up?"

"We're far from doing nothing," Sheriff Jackson said calmly.

"Indeed," Vivienne added. "In fact, after finding Garrett's car abandoned, it's safe to assume foul play. As Harper shrewdly pointed out, acting in a manner contrary to what the kidnappers believe we will do might force them to make a mistake."

If it hadn't been for the rising tension in the room, I might've beamed with pride at Vivienne's words. However, I kept my face schooled in a look of engaged concern. Now was definitely not the time for celebration, despite the fact Vivienne had just given me public credit for a good idea.

"So, you're certain now?" Valerie asked, folding her arms. "It *was* a kidnapping. That took you long enough. And even more reason to *do* something, to make some sort of announcement, to get help!"

Sheriff Jackson exhaled slowly. "Certain? No. But it's looking more likely." He met Valerie's gaze. "And right now, every second we waste arguing is a second we're not using to get ahead of whoever *does* know exactly what happened."

Vivienne lifted her chin. "We stay the course. We proceed as if nothing is wrong because that, more than anything, will unsettle them."

Valerie scoffed. "You want to continue the launch? The masquerade? What an utterly idiotic idea! Everyone will know immediately that something is wrong when Garrett doesn't make an appearance. No, what we need to do is contact every news agency out there. I would've done so already if you would just give me my phone. Then I—"

Vivienne interrupted smoothly. "We've already thought of that. In fact, we've found quite a convincing double to stand in for Mr. Grimshaw. Isn't that right, Gabriel?" She raised an eyebrow in her son's direction.

He immediately nodded, obviously reading his mother's intentions. "Absolutely. We've been quite lucky on that front. The double is nearly identical and will, in my opinion, fool everyone but those closest to Mr. Grimshaw." He gestured at Valerie. "The support of you, Mrs. Moncrief-Grimshaw, and the others would further cement the story in the eyes of the public."

The sheriff spoke up, obviously following Vivienne's train of thought that Gabriel could illusion himself to look like Garrett Grimshaw without it needing to be spelled out for him. "Exactly. A double should quell any rumors and maintain the appearance of normalcy," the sheriff said firmly. "And that's what we want right now until we hear from whoever is behind this."

"Normalcy?" Valerie hissed. "None of this is normal! You're more worried about saving face, about your precious town, and your reputations, than you are about Garrett. He's out there, alone and scared, and you're talking about appearances?" Her voice rose, raw with frustration. "Who knows what's happening to him? We should be organizing a search party, contacting the news, getting more eyes on this. Maybe someone will see him and report it!"

"And what happens if the kidnappers see it first and they think we're getting too close?" Sheriff Jackson countered, folding his arms. "If they think we're calling in the cavalry, what do you think they'll do? Keep him comfortable? Or get rid of the evidence before they're caught?"

Valerie's jaw tightened, but she wasn't backing down yet. "This is idiotic! We won't find him by sitting here and doing nothing."

"We *are* doing something," Vivienne said sharply. "We're keeping control of the narrative. If you want to help, the best thing you can do is keep this from turning into a media circus."

"Control the narrative?" Valerie scoffed. "I don't care about narratives anymore. I care about Garrett."

I stepped forward. "We all do. But think about it. If the kidnappers are watching, and suddenly the entire country is looking for Garrett Grimshaw, the kidnappers could panic. Maybe they'll run. Maybe they'll do something worse." I took a breath, forcing myself to meet her eyes. "I know you want to *do* something. I do too. But what if we act rashly and make this worse? Would you be able to live with that?"

She flinched, but covered it quickly with another scowl. "So, what, we just sit here and hope?"

"No," I pressed on. "We use the masquerade to our advantage. Right now, whoever did this thinks they have the upper hand. But if we go on as planned and act like *we're* the ones in control, it throws them off. Maybe they panic. Maybe they make a mistake we can use."

Sheriff Jackson nodded. "They've played their hand. Now we let them think we're playing ours."

Valerie's shoulders rose and fell with quick, shallow breaths, her frustration still simmering. "And if this plan of yours *doesn't* work? If Garrett—" Her voice caught, just slightly, before she forced the words out. "If he gets hurt because we waited?"

Vivienne's gaze was cool and unwavering. "We're doing our best to make sure that doesn't happen. You have my personal guarantee that every resource I possess will be used to rectify the situation."

Silence stretched between them, thick and heavy.

Finally, Valerie exhaled sharply and looked away, breaking eye contact first. "Fine. But if you're wrong, *none* of you will hear the end of it." Her gaze flicked back to me, unreadable, before she turned on her heel and stormed out, slamming the door behind her.

Vivienne arched an eyebrow. "Well, that was dramatic."

"Understandable, though," I said, surprising myself by speaking up. Where had this sudden burst of confidence come from? "She's scared. Garrett's not just her client—he's her ex and her colleague. Maybe even her friend, in a way. They've known each other for decades. If I were in her position, I'd probably be out of my mind with worry."

Sheriff Jackson grunted. "Scared or not, she's pushing for a media frenzy that would only hinder the investigation. Even with Lucas' charm, I'd recommend keeping a close eye on her. Desperate people do desperate things."

Gabriel exhaled sharply. "She's not going to like being cut off from her contacts."

"She doesn't have a choice," the sheriff said. "If there's a ransom, it'll likely come to her phone. We need to be ready. That's why Lucas is working on the tracking spell now so we don't lose a crucial lead."

"And if she pushes back?" Gabriel asked.

Sheriff Jackson's mouth thinned. "Then we remind her that if Grimshaw's kidnappers try to reach her and she fumbles it, *she* could be the reason we don't get him back."

Vivienne nodded thoughtfully. "Agreed. Harper, you have more of a connection with her than any of us. Perhaps you could speak with her later. See if you can calm her down even more and keep her from doing anything rash."

"I'll try," I said, thinking of how I might approach her.

"Good," Vivienne said briskly. "Now, Sheriff, as I was saying, we'll proceed with the masquerade. Gabriel's illusion magic will keep the rumors at bay, and the event will give us a chance to disrupt the kidnapper's agenda."

The sheriff nodded, though his expression remained wary. "Fine. But we need to watch everyone closely. If there's so much as a whisper about Garrett's whereabouts or there's a ransom call, we act."

Vivienne's lips curved into a faint, steely smile. "Agreed. Let the show begin."

Where in Havenwood is Garrett Grimshaw?

Vivienne and Sheriff Jackson swept out of the room, heads together in an intense conversation.

Gabriel touched my arm, pulling my attention back to him. "I've got to work on this illusion spell. Crafting something that mimics another person I don't know very well is difficult, even more so when he's as high profile as Garrett Grimshaw. This needs to be perfect. I can't afford any suspicion, so I need to do as much research as possible to get all of his mannerisms right."

I nodded. "What can I do to help?"

Gabriel lifted his shoulder. "Not much, to be honest. However, if you can dig up any information, you know, useful tidbits or affectations that I could use, that would be good. I know you have a knack for solving mysteries, and right now, I could use all the help I can get."

I bit my lip and nodded, thinking of what this might mean for me, for Spellbooks, and for Havenwood if it got out that Garrett Grimshaw was kidnapped from my bookshop. But I kept that to myself. Gabriel gave my hand an encouraging squeeze, brushing my cheek with a kiss before hurrying away.

I felt a bit lost in the massive Silverthorne mansion, but before I could move, Gabriel popped his head back in. "Oh, before I forget, I've arranged a surprise for you in the study. With the masquerade ball still on, it might be the perfect time for you to check it out."

"Don't you want to come?" I asked.

"I'd love to, but I really do need to focus on this research. However, that doesn't mean you shouldn't take a moment to enjoy it," Gabriel said.

"Well, I'll wait, then. I'd rather see it with you. But maybe I can find Isadora. She and I can bring some snacks for the other guests. Giving people food always has a way of getting them talking," I said, my mind flashing back to Bella.

Gabriel nodded. "Perfect. I'll see you soon." He gave me a kiss on the cheek before hurrying off.

The tension in the room had settled like a fog, but it still clung to me as I stepped out, letting the heavy doors close behind me. I wasn't ready to face the collection of tense guests yet, so I wandered down the hall instead, finding a quiet alcove near a set of tall windows.

I pulled out my phone, messaging Bella to check in on her. I should really let her know I was here. Hopefully, she was on her way soon.

Hey, you good? Did Mr. W give you any trouble while locking up? Thanks again for handling everything at Spellbooks. We're already at the Silverthorne's. Let me know when you're on your way.

As the text whooshed away, I pulled up Isadora's number and sent her a quick message to let her know where I was. I wasn't familiar enough with the Silverthorne mansion to go wandering around alone, and I wasn't sure Vivienne would appreciate any unwanted intrusion into her family's home, especially with everyone so on edge.

I tapped my fingers on the phone screen, impatience simmering within me. Each second without a response from Isadora felt like a tick closer to unraveling everything I was trying to keep from falling apart. Garrett Grimshaw had vanished without a trace, and now, the dark shadow of suspicion was starting to settle over Havenwood...and Spellbooks. Valerie's words from earlier lingered in the back of my mind, needling their way into my thoughts. Was I really doing this for Garrett? Or was I just terrified of what would happen to Havenwood, to my shop, to *me*, if everything fell apart? I swallowed hard, but the question didn't go away.

The silence on my phone was deafening, though the room around me buzzed with noise and motion. Someone knocked over a tray of glassware near the refreshment table, the sharp clatter drawing a few startled gasps and a burst of nervous laughter. Across the room, volunteers scurried past in masks and glittering outfits, adjusting tablecloths, checking name cards, and arguing over the playlist for the third time. But despite the flurry of activity, the festive decorations still hung in place, blissfully unaware of the storm gathering beneath them.

My thoughts kept drifting back to Savannah and her connection to Garrett. How did an apparently self-obsessed influencer and a celebrity author meet and form a long-term relationship? Their age gap was an obvious difference, but the rest didn't quite fit either. Was there more to their relationship than met the eye, or was I just searching for fractures where there weren't any?

I didn't want to believe anyone close to Garrett was involved in his disappearance. But with every clue pointing in their direction, my resolve was starting to crack. Could Savannah really be behind this? Or Nate? Or Tiffany? Could one of them have pulled the strings while smiling in our faces?

I wrapped my arms around myself and exhaled slowly. The view outside was nothing but dark silhouettes of trees against the dimming sky, but my thoughts were miles away, circling the same questions over and over. Havenwood wasn't that big. So where was Garrett? And why did it feel more and more like we were playing into someone else's plan?

Somewhere in the background noise, a cheerful voice bubbled up over the din.

"Harper!"

A moment later, Isadora bounced into view, taking the stairs two at a time and practically vibrating with energy. Her pink hair swished with every step, and she had that bright-eyed look of someone who'd just finished three errands, solved a minor crisis, and still found time to compliment your earrings. She wove through the chaos of the ballroom, skirting a precarious dessert tower with practiced grace.

"Hey, Harper!" she said brightly, as if we weren't knee-deep in a crisis. "How are you?"

"Fine...I guess."

Isadora shot me a sympathetic look. "Mother filled me in on the plan. So, we're trying to figure out where Garrett Grimshaw is while throwing a wrench in the plans of the kidnappers? Count me in! What do you need?"

I nodded, my mind racing. "The sheriff found the abandoned car, but couldn't turn up much, except that there was what appeared to be a broken bottle of Savannah's signature perfume in the car, and there was a gold button under the seat. It might've been from one of the drivers or possibly the kidnapper himself."

Isadora twirled her hair, thinking. "Well, neither one of those are exactly hard evidence." She paused, her brow furrowed.

I agreed. "Both those things could have happened before Garrett's disappearance. But we need to dig deeper."

Isadora shifted her weight, concern flashing in her eyes. "But how?"

"Your mother is prepping for the masquerade, and Gabriel's trying to work out this illusion spell to make himself look like Garrett. But I think we need to talk to Garrett's inner circle, starting with the ones closest to him."

I hesitated for a moment, unsure if I was ready to face those who might be hiding secrets. "Do you really think one of them is behind this?" Isadora asked, her voice barely above a whisper.

I lifted a shoulder, my thoughts swirling. "Maybe. Maybe not. But it's the only lead we have right now. The sheriff and Vivienne are already covering the angle of outside threats—ransom, old enemies, people looking for leverage. But what if this wasn't a stranger? What if it was someone closer to him? Maybe not a traditional kidnapping, but something more personal. A grudge, a betrayal, maybe even a last-ditch effort to stop him from doing something."

Isadora frowned, considering. "So, you're thinking this wasn't just about money. That whoever took him had a personal stake in keeping him quiet or stopping him from deciding?"

I sighed, frustration creeping into my voice despite my best efforts. "Maybe. But then again, maybe not. All I know for sure is I don't have time to sit on my hands and wait. We need to discover what happened to him *before* anyone realizes something is wrong."

Isadora gave me a sympathetic look, stepping closer to pull me into a hug. "It'll be okay. We'll figure it out."

I swallowed hard, nodding against her shoulder. The comfort was welcome, but it wasn't enough to quiet the thoughts whirling in my mind.

I can't let this happen. I can't let Spellbooks become a crime scene. I can't fail. My fingers curled into the fabric of her sleeve before I forced myself to step back, shaking off the moment of vulnerability.

Isadora met my gaze, and the determined set of her jaw said plenty. She gave a single resolute nod. "Just tell me where to start," she said firmly.

"First, Savannah Chase. She was conveniently absent at exactly the same time that Garrett went missing." I said.

"Wasn't she getting a coffee?" Isadora asked.

"No one takes that long to get a coffee," I argued.

"Well, didn't she mention she might go shopping or something? Getting a coffee for me is only partially about the caffeine jolt. It's mostly about taking a break," Isadora said.

"That's a good point. Let's see what she was up to." I pulled up Savannah's social media profile, flipping through her most recent photos. They were all of her posing around town with her perfume bottle. Her last few posts were from Hocus Mochas, and I noticed the perfume bottle was conspicuously absent. Was that because the baristas at the café had protested her spraying her signature scent all over or because she stashed it in the car prior to kidnapping her fiancé?

I shook my head. Even though the circumstantial evidence pointed at Savannah, jumping to conclusions wouldn't get me anywhere. I focused back on the photos. The next one was a picture of a perfectly frothy cappuccino with a caption that read: "Fuel for a big day ahead!" Her final post of the day was a selfie of Savannah with an overly surprised face, hinting at some big news.

I turned the phone to show Isadora the photo. "What do you think this means?" I asked.

Isadora looked nonplussed. "That she had a surprise? That could be anything. You don't think she'd admit to kidnapping her famous fiancé on social media, do you?"

I blew out a breath, Isadora's logic deflating me a little. "I suppose not. But why was she gone so long?"

Isadora shrugged. "I'm not sure. But Officer Reggie interviewed her. From what I could tell, he didn't seem to think there was anything amiss in her story."

"Wait a second. *Reggie* interviewed her?" I asked, my voice edging on disbelief.

Isadora nodded. "Yeah. As soon as she turned up at Spellbooks. Why?"

I pinched the bridge of my nose. "Don't get me wrong, Reggie's got a heart of gold, but he's...not exactly Havenwood's top investigator."

Isadora snorted. "That's putting it mildly. He once arrested a scarecrow."

I blinked. "You're kidding."

"Nope," she said seriously. "He claimed it looked suspicious standing in the same spot all day."

I sighed. "Okay, well, that settles it. If Reggie was the one who talked to Savannah, we need to talk to her too. Maybe we'll uncover something he missed."

Isadora nodded. "Good idea. I know the sheriff will want to interview her himself eventually, but let's be honest, he can be intense. Maybe she'd be more open with us. You know, two girls her age just having a chit chat."

"Perfect," I agreed. "Especially if she's scared or hiding something. If we can put her at ease, she might tell us something she wouldn't say to a cop."

Isadora pointed at me in agreement. "People love to talk when they feel safe. And if she lets something slip? Even better."

"You know," I said, my mind whirling. "Maybe we should apply the same tactic to all of them—Tiffany, Nate, Valerie, and Mindy. Make them feel safe and see if they'll let something slip."

Isadora tilted her head. "You think one of them is involved?"

"It's possible," I admitted. "Even if they didn't have a hand in the kidnapping, they might've seen something without realizing its importance." I hesitated, doubt creeping in, but I pushed it aside. What other avenue did I have? Sitting back and waiting wasn't an option. "They're our best lead, and we can't afford to ignore the possibilities."

"Okay," Isadora said, linking her arm in mine. "To the kitchen, it is."

I followed her down the winding halls, my mind racing. The Silverthorne mansion, with its endless corridors and imposing walls, seemed to close in around me, a constant reminder of the stakes.

My thoughts churned with questions. What if Savannah knew more than she was letting on? Could the shattered perfume bottle and driver's button really be meaningless? Or were they breadcrumbs leading to a much darker truth?

"Harper," Isadora said softly, breaking into my spiraling thoughts. "We'll figure this out. We have to."

I nodded, trying to force a smile. "We will," I said, though it felt more like a promise I wasn't sure I could keep.

As we turned a corner, the faint hum of activity from the kitchen reached my ears. We stepped into the warm glow of the kitchen, the scent of freshly baked pastries wrapped around us, offering a fleeting sense of comfort. But the clock was ticking, and Garrett could be slipping further from our reach by the second.

Garrett was out there. Somewhere.

I took a deep breath, squaring my shoulders.

Whoever had taken him didn't know what they were up against. But I was about to make sure they found out.

who's got the button?

T HE KITCHEN BUZZED WITH life, a symphony of clattering pots, sizzling pans, and the hum of coordinated chatter. A surprisingly large team of staff moved with seamless precision, assembling what appeared to be a feast fit for royalty. My jaw dropped as I took in the scene.

"Is this normal for you guys?" I asked, genuinely taken aback.

Isadora let out a laugh, bouncing up onto her toes. "Oh, absolutely not. This is special-occasion chaos. Normally, it's just the four of us, and, let's be real, I'm at the academy most of the time, Gabriel would rather be doing his thing around town, and Lucas mostly survives on coffee and sheer stubbornness. But Mother refuses to under-cater. Ever. She'd rather have leftovers for a month than risk running out of hors d'oeuvres."

She turned to me mid-bounce, her grin faltering slightly. "Wait a sec...is this your first time back since Christmas Eve?"

I hesitated, adjusting my shirt self-consciously. I hadn't meant to avoid the manor, but now that she mentioned it, a dull weight settled in my chest. The last time I was here, the ballroom had been glittering with lights, music, and magic. It had been another festive, bustling occasion. However, I'd also nearly lost everything.

"Yeah," I admitted, keeping my voice light even as my stomach twisted. I hoped she wouldn't notice how frail my voice sounded.

Isadora's brow furrowed, but only for a second before she looped an arm through mine, tugging me toward the nearest counter. "Well, welcome back! And lucky you, you're here just in time for the best part—free food. C'mon, let's see if we can snag some taste tests before Mother notices."

I let out a small laugh, the tension in my shoulders easing just a little. "Now that's a plan I can get behind." I inhaled deeply, the air rich with tantalizing aromas. "Well, whatever they're making, it smells incredible."

One of the chefs glanced up from the stove, offering a quick, friendly nod and smile. "That's very kind of you to say, Miss," he said, his accent smooth and warm.

Isadora smiled, gesturing toward him. "This is Jacques. He's the maestro behind all of this. Nothing leaves this kitchen without his seal of approval."

"Everything smells amazing, Jacques," I said warmly, returning his smile. "I can't wait to taste everything tonight."

Jacques chuckled, his eyes sparkling with pride. "Why wait to enjoy it? Life's too short to delay good food, good wine, or good love."

Before I could reply, he turned and grabbed a pristine white plate, loading it with an enticing assortment from the nearby trays. With a flourish, he handed it to me. "Here. A little something to tide you over."

The plate was a vibrant array of Mardi Gras-inspired delights. Crispy golden shrimp po'boys nestled next to sliders brimming with spicy jambalaya. Warm, bite-sized beignets, dusted with powdered sugar, promised a sweet finish. Gleaming crab cakes with a golden crust sat beside a tangy remoulade sauce, their aroma mouthwatering. The pièce de résistance was a small bowl of gumbo, its rich, spiced broth concealing tender chicken, smoky andouille sausage, and the subtle earthiness of okra. On the side, hushpuppies gleamed, their crispy exterior hinting at a soft, savory center.

"This looks divine," I said, my mouth already watering.

Jacques gave a knowing grin. "Bon appétit, Miss. They are made to be savored."

Isadora picked a crab cake from the plate and popped it into her mouth, rolling her eyes with a soft moan of appreciation. "This is why you can never leave," she said, smiling at Jacques, who beamed at the compliment.

"Trust me, Miss Isadora, I don't intend to," Jacques said, his hands busy stirring a pot on the stove.

I grabbed a slider and indulged in a large bite. The flavors hit me a moment later, and I peered at the half in my hand in surprise, intrigued by how something so simple could pack so much flavor. The spiced jambalaya inside the soft, pillowy bun was rich, with just the right amount of heat, and the smoky sausage added depth to each bite. I couldn't help but nod in appreciation as I swallowed, my eyes wide. "This is incredible. You've got a gift."

Jacques smiled. "Thank you. If you'd like," he continued, lowering his voice slightly, "feel free to head over there to enjoy your snacks." He gestured toward a small sunroom just off the kitchen. "It's a lovely spot, especially with the view of the gardens."

"Actually," Isadora said, clearing her throat, "we were hoping you could put together a tray. Nothing fancy, really. We thought some of Mother's guests might appreciate a little something to eat. Oh, and maybe some tea, or possibly even some coffee?"

Jacques nodded immediately. "It's easy to do, Miss Isadora. Give me ten minutes, and I'll have something ready for you. You go enjoy your snacks; let me take care of the rest." He made a little shooing gesture with his hands.

I was about to offer to help when Isadora stopped me with a quick shake of her head. "Thank you, Jacques. We appreciate it." She linked her arm through mine and pulled me toward the door of the sunroom.

"I don't want to put him out," I whispered, glancing back at Jacques, who was already busy organizing trays.

Isadora shot me a mischievous smile. "Jacques has a very particular way of doing things. He'd probably be more upset if you offered to help than if you just let him do it his way. It's his pride, you see. Ten minutes, and then we're on our way."

I nodded tentatively. "Okay. Well, if you're certain."

"I am," she said as she opened the door wide, leading us into a sunroom that stretched almost the length of the kitchen. Cozy nook-like areas held several small tables and chairs. It felt far less grandiose than the rest of the mansion, almost homey in comparison.

"This is cute," I said, glancing around.

Isadora nodded, her eyes softening. "It's one of my favorite places in the house. It's a quiet escape for the staff when they need a break. I like to use it on weekends when they have their days off. The gardens are just gorgeous from here. You'll have to come back in the spring to see them in full bloom."

"I can't wait," I replied honestly. I meant it. This was the first real, quiet moment I'd had since Garrett Grimshaw and his team descended.

I turned to Isadora, gesturing to the snacks in her hand. "Where should we sit? Wait. Who's that?"

Isadora's gaze swept the room before her expression shifted as she noticed the three men sat huddled around a small table. They weren't exactly hiding, but their stiff postures and hushed conversation gave them the air of people trying not to be noticed.

"Whoever they are, they definitely aren't Silverthorne staff," she said.

"Are those...the drivers? The ones from Grimshaw's entourage?" I asked, lowering my voice.

Isadora squinted, then nodded slowly. "I think so. Hard to tell from here. Let's find out."

As we approached, their conversation cut off mid-sentence. Three pairs of wary eyes snapped to us, tracking our movements like they were expecting trouble.

They weren't as put-together as they had been earlier. Exhaustion had obviously left its mark. Their shirts were unbuttoned at the collar with sleeves rolled up and their posture was tense. The tallest of the group, a hulking man with close-cropped dark hair and a permanent scowl, folded his arms across his chest. His massive biceps strained against his sleeves. The second, wiry and restless, bounced one knee under the table, fingers tapping an uneven rhythm against his glass. The last man was stocky, with thinning hair. He attempted a half-smile as we walked up, but it didn't reach his eyes.

I tried to dredge up their names, but nothing came. Had I ever even heard them? My mind raced through the events of the day. I'd met and chatted with so many people, they all blurred together. It was possible we'd been introduced, but if so, their names had slipped through the cracks.

They, on the other hand, knew exactly who I was.

The scowling one, clearly the unofficial leader judging by his stance, grunted. "So. You're the bookshop girl."

Great. So much for a warm welcome.

Isadora, thankfully, was not one to be deterred. "Hello, I'm Isadora Silverthorne!" she said brightly, setting the plate of treats Jacques had prepared in the center of their table. "My chef said you were sitting back here. We thought you might like some snacks."

Her warm tone seemed to disarm them slightly, though they still exchanged uncertain glances. Isadora pulled up a chair, her movement smooth and confident, as though she'd been hosting guests her entire life. To be fair, she probably had. I followed her lead, sitting down beside her.

The drivers hesitated before nodding and mumbling their thanks, their movements stiff as they reached for the plate of food. A moment of uncomfortable silence stretched before one of them finally spoke.

"Real nice of ya, Miss," the nearest driver said, his voice a bit too fast, like he was trying to fill the silence. His wild-eyed look darted around the room, and he fidgeted nervously with the edge of his jacket.

That's when I saw it.

My eyes zeroed in on the jacket adorned with shiny gold buttons. One in particular caught the light as it shifted, and I felt a jolt of recognition.

There was a distinctive open book symbol stamped into the shiny gold.

It was the exact same design as the button I'd found in the car earlier. My pulse quickened. Either one of the drivers lost a button or they'd been a lot closer to Garrett's disappearance than they were letting on.

"Yeah, 'preciate it," the large man across from him added, startling me back to the moment. His voice rougher, more measured. He had the broad, solid build of someone used to hauling weights around with ease. A dark tattoo curled down his wrist under his cuffed shirt, and another peeked out above his collar.

The third, a wiry man with a shock of red hair, gave an easy grin. "We always got time for free food. Name's Frankie, by the way. That's Lenny," he nodded toward the nervous one, "and that's Vic." He gestured to the broad-shouldered man, who gave a slight nod of acknowledgment.

I smiled. "Nice to meet you all. I'm Harper."

Isadora gestured at the plate. "Well, don't just stare at it. You might as well dive in."

The men didn't need to be told twice. As they grabbed at the food, I let my gaze flick over their jackets. Vic's was slung over the back of his chair, but both Lenny and Frankie still wore theirs. The dark, lustrous fabric was accented with ornate gold buttons that gleamed under the light, each one etched with a detailed open book. They were elegant and clearly crafted with care.

What caught my attention most, though, was the inner lining. A glimpse of deep pink fabric peeked through whenever they moved, revealing a pattern of gilded spines and swirling pages. It certainly wasn't a style choice I'd have expected the three of them to pick for themselves. The jackets were flashy and undeniably custom. My mind flew back to the button I'd found in the abandoned car. Maybe there was a clue here, waiting to be discovered.

I tilted my head, letting curiosity color my tone. "I couldn't help but notice your jackets," I said lightly. "They're quite something. Very stylish."

Frankie perked up, flashing a grin as he brushed a crumb from his lapel. "Yeah, Miss Chase picked 'em out. Said we had to look the part for the tour. Valerie—uh, Ms. St. James—thought it was a waste, but once Miss Chase got Mr. Grimshaw to sign off on it, that was that. Not that I'm complainin'." He ran a hand down the front of his jacket, grinning. "Ain't never had a jacket this nice before."

I nodded, my mind racing. Maybe one of them was missing a button. Would that be enough to tie them to the kidnapping? Perhaps not, but maybe, just maybe, I could turn the circumstantial evidence into a real lead.

"Fascinating," I said, my voice barely concealing my excitement. "These are really intricate, and, as a bookshop owner, I love the bookish details. Do you mind if I take a closer look?"

"Go for it," Vic said. He handed it over with a casual shrug. "It's a nice jacket, and all, but it ain't like it can measure up to this." He gestured to the tray and popped another hushpuppy into his mouth.

While Lenny attacked a slider, devouring it in a single bite, I examined Vic's jacket. As I ran my fingers along the fabric, the buttons caught my attention again. The gold gleamed under the light, each one etched with the same intricate open book design, like tiny works of art. I caught my breath. There was no doubt. It was an exact match for the button we'd discovered in the abandoned car.

"Wow," I murmured, holding it open to show Isadora. "Even the buttons are works of art." I traced my fingers down the front and along the cuffs. Unfortunately, Vic wasn't missing a button from his jacket.

"Miss Chase don't do nothing halfway," Frankie said, leaning in to point at the buttons on his own jacket. "She had these made special. Said we had to look important. 'Memorable,' was her word, ya know? Ms. St. James thought the whole idea was 'tacky.' Her words, not mine. But hey,

Miss Chase wanted it, so we got 'em." He ran a hand along his jacket, striking a pose. I noticed he wasn't missing any of his buttons either.

"Memorable is right," I agreed, glancing back at Lenny's jacket. I could see the top button, but the rest were hidden by the table. Were they all there?

Isadora gave me a sideways look, but didn't call me out. She already knew about the button in the car.

I passed Vic's coat back. "Miss Chase has good taste."

"Yep," Vic grunted around a mouth full of crab cake.

Frankie, on the other hand, wasn't done talking. "She's got taste, yeah, but these musta cost a fortune. Bet Mr. Grimshaw didn't even blink. Gives her whatever she wants." He shook his head. "Had one made for each of us. Even had one for his kid, but the brat wouldn't wear it. Said it made him 'look like staff.'"

Lenny snorted, rolling his eyes. "Like we'd take style tips from him."

"Made him look like a real a…" Vic looked up guiltily at the two of us and finished, "a…real piece of work."

"Yeah, but that's just his face," Frankie sniggered. "Ain't no tailor in the world can patch up a bad personality."

Isadora nodded sympathetically. "You can buy style, but you can't buy class, am I right?"

A chuckle rippled around the table. Frankie pointed finger guns at her. "You got it, miss."

I leaned forward, keeping my voice easy. "So, these are all identical? No variations for, say, the different drivers? Like maybe a more demure one for Ms. Valerie St. James, with her publicist career, and a different one for the driver of Mr. Grimshaw's car?"

The men shook their heads in unison.

"Nope," Vic said. "All identical down to the lining." He stuffed another crab cake in his mouth, effectively ending any further comment.

Frankie leaned in, clearly as eager to talk as Vic was to eat. "I drove Mrs. Moncrief-Grimshaw's car," he said quickly, his words tumbling out as if he couldn't hold them back. "And I made the same suggestion, miss. We could have different colors, maybe, or something like that to signify which car we were meant to be driving. Even suggested matching the jacket color to the car color. But no, they wanted black—black, black, *black*. Boring, if you ask me."

"Absolutely," Isadora added with a dramatic sigh, fluffing her pink hair. "A little color never hurt anyone."

I barely heard them, my eyes flashing back to Lenny. Could he really be involved in the kidnapping? If so, what was his motive? I studied him carefully, looking for any tells. His whole body seemed keyed up whenever Savannah's name came up. He seemed awfully quick to defend her, like he had a personal stake in how she was perceived. Could there be something there? Maybe he thought Garrett was in the way. Maybe he figured if he got rid of him, Savannah would finally see him. Perhaps this kidnapping was really about Savannah, not Garrett.

If Lenny was guilty, he certainly was a cool customer, sitting here with the other drivers, eating and chatting like nothing was wrong. I wasn't sure I could pull that off.

But, then again, maybe he wasn't involved at all, and I was grasping at straws. There was a fourth matching jacket out there. The one belonging to Nate Grimshaw. Could the button in the car have come from Nate's jacket? If so, what was it doing in Garrett's car...unless he was part of the kidnapping? Now I really needed to get a better look at Lenny's jacket to see if any buttons were missing. But how could I get him to stand up?

As if on cue, Jacques stepped into the sunroom, wiping his hands on a towel. "Your tray is ready, Miss Silverthorne," he announced, his voice warm and cheerful.

Thinking fast, I hastily jumped to my feet, plastering on a smile. Isadora shot me a strange look as she rose to join me. "Thank you, Jacques. We'll take it from here."

I turned to the drivers, extending my hand to Lenny. "But before we go, it's been nice to talk to you. I hope that you enjoy the food."

Lenny hesitated for a moment, glancing at my outstretched hand. Tension coiled in my stomach. What if he didn't stand? I fought to keep my smile steady as my pulse quickened. After a long, taut moment, manners won out. He finally rose, shaking my hand with a surprisingly firm grip. My eyes darted to his jacket as he stood, scanning for any irregularities.

The buttons were all there.

If the button in the car didn't belong to any of the drivers, the only option left was Nate. But that wasn't possible because he had been in Spellbooks the entire event, hadn't he? I closed my eyes, scanning through my memories just in case.

The realization hit me like a punch to the gut, stealing the air from my lungs.

No. No, he hadn't.

Just after Savannah swept out of the shop, he stormed out the back. In the hustle and bustle, I just hadn't registered his petulance as important. What if it wasn't petulance, but a calculated scheme to get back at his father?

My mind scrambled to catch up with the implications. Nate. Garrett's own son. The button, the jacket, the will. He'd even stormed out of the shop just before Garrett was taken. It all lined up in a way that made my stomach twist. I fought to keep my expression neutral as I turned to Frankie and then Vic, shaking their hands in turn.

"Thank you again," I said smoothly, forcing a smile as I turned to Isadora. "Let's grab that tray and head to the drawing room," I said, my voice steadier than I felt.

Isadora nodded, though her brow furrowed briefly, before she turned to lead the way. I followed, but my thoughts churned.

A chill crawled down my spine, icy and insistent, like the creeping dread of standing too close to the edge of a cliff while the wind blew forcefully at my back. If Nate was behind this, it wasn't just an act of anger or rebellion. It was a calculated move, a son forcing his father's hand in the most brutal way possible. My heart thudded painfully in my chest as a darker possibility seized hold of me: What if this wasn't just a kidnapping? What if Nate wasn't looking to bring his father back, but to make sure Garrett never returned at all?

I stumbled slightly, catching myself as Isadora glanced back at me, her brow furrowed. "Are you okay?" she asked, her voice tinged with concern.

I nodded quickly, forcing a weak smile. "Yeah. Just...thinking."

Thinking. That was one word for the spiral of fear and adrenaline clawing its way through my chest. Garrett's life—his very existence—might be hanging by a thread, and I was walking into a room with the man who might be responsible.

No. Nate wouldn't do that to his dad. He *couldn't.* Could he?

But the possibility dug its claws into my frontal cortex and refused to let go. The button. The jacket. The will. It all pointed back to one undeniable fact: Nate Grimshaw had to be involved. But to what end? If he was mad because his father removed him from the will, a kidnapping wouldn't change that. Garrett would just be motivated to cut him out all the faster as soon as he was released. No, the only way to ensure the will wouldn't change...

My breath caught, and my vision tunneled. If Nate couldn't convince his father and the documents weren't finalized, then the one sure way to keep his inheritance was to make sure Garrett couldn't change it. Which meant making sure he didn't come back.

Ever.

Was this kidnapping about to become a murder? Or worse, what if it already had? That would explain the lack of ransom call.

My pulse quickened with every step as we walked down the corridor. The tea cart's wheels squeaked faintly, an almost rhythmic reminder of the ticking clock I felt so acutely. If I was right about Nate, then what waited for us behind that door wasn't just a chance at answers. It was a confrontation I couldn't avoid, even if I wasn't entirely sure I was ready for it. A man's life depended on it, and ready or not, I had to face what was on the other side.

Evasive Maneuvers

Isadora reached for the doorknob, pausing to glance at me again. "Ready?" she asked softly, her voice barely above a whisper.

No. I thought, but I nodded anyway. "Ready," I lied, swallowing hard as the door creaked open.

As we stepped into the drawing room, the atmosphere hit me like a wall, thick and tense. Mindy Hart and Valerie St. James were huddled together on one side of the room, their heads close in whispered conversation. From their body language alone, they might as well have erected a "no trespassing" sign. On the other side, Tiffany Moncrief-Grimshaw and Nate sat in frosty silence, but the set of their jaws and the stiffness in their postures spoke volumes. My eyes swept the room once more, but to my surprise, Savannah Chase was nowhere to be seen.

Where was she?

Isadora, ever the diplomat, broke the ice with her usual brightness. "We thought you could use some sustenance, so we liberated these treats from the kitchen. I do hope they're to your satisfaction," she announced enthusiastically.

Tiffany fanned herself as though the act of breathing in the same air as the rest of us required effort. "Very kind of you. After being interrogated by that gruff, grizzled man your town calls a sheriff, a stiff drink is just what I need. Thank you." Her tone carried the unmistakable edge of someone accustomed to complaining for sport.

Nate didn't bother with niceties. He was on his feet the moment the cart stopped rolling, grabbing a plate and piling it high with food as though it were his birthright. His movements were quick but pointedly sloppy, the way someone acts when they want you to know they don't care. He didn't spare a glance in our direction, let alone utter a word of gratitude, as though we were beneath his notice.

Isadora, unruffled, turned her attention to Tiffany, offering her a delicate porcelain teacup. "Would you like milk or sugar with your tea?"

Tiffany waved a dismissive hand, her diamonds flashing under the dim lighting. "Is that all you have? I'd much prefer champagne, darling, or maybe even a whiskey. I don't understand why Garrett deciding to go on this health kick and abstaining from alcohol means we all must. If any day calls for a bolstering of the nerves, it's today. However," she added, her voice dripping with condescension, "if tea is all that's on offer, I suppose I must *graciously* accept."

The way she said "graciously" made it clear she was doing us all a favor by deigning to sip tea in our presence. It was a testament to Isadora that she managed to serve the entitled woman without batting an eyelid.

Mindy and Valerie, meanwhile, were so engrossed in their whispered conversation they didn't even glance up. The world could have ended outside, and they likely wouldn't have noticed.

I grabbed a few items from the tray and moved to sit near Nate, trying to appear casual while my mind raced with questions as Isadora pushed the cart over towards Mindy and Valerie. His disinterest in everything around him only made him seem more suspicious.

"How are you doing?" I asked.

Nate's eyes flicked toward me, cold and sharp, before he took a deliberate bite of a po'boy.

"You know, with, um, everything?" I added in a rush.

Great interrogation technique, Harper, I chastised myself. *You're really asking the hard questions here.*

Nate chewed slowly, dragging out the silence until it was unbearable. Finally, he swallowed, leaning back in his chair with an air of entitled nonchalance. "When you've lived with a man like Garrett Grimshaw as long as I have, you get used to him disappearing. Always running off, doing his own thing." He shrugged, his lips curling into a smirk that didn't reach his eyes. "This, though? If I didn't know better, I'd say he was doing it just to get attention, except he's never been one to avoid the spotlight."

I stiffened. If Nate was really behind his father's disappearance, I needed to get him to reveal a clue. "That's...an interesting take," I said carefully, even as a knot of unease tightened in my stomach. "I'm getting the feeling there's some bad blood between the two of you," I ventured.

Nate snorted, his eyes hardening. "You can say that again. The old man cared about his books more than he ever cared about me. Oh, sure, he'd splash money in my direction when he forgot a birthday or graduation, but money can't replace a father's presence. You know what I'm saying?" He took another bite, chewing with deliberate slowness, as though the act gave him time to stew in his resentment.

I thought about my own father, about the love and warmth we shared even without wealth. It was something Nate probably wouldn't understand. Still, I couldn't help but feel a flicker of empathy, despite his entitled attitude. "That must have been hard," I said softly.

"Hard?" Nate repeated, not looking up. He gave a humorless chuckle. "No, I got used to it. Got used to him being a ghost in my life. But this?" He gestured vaguely, the movement sharp. "Dragging me along on tour, posing for cameras like we're some Hallmark family? It's just another way he gets to feel better about himself. It's not about me. It never is. It's about the story he's selling."

His voice cracked slightly on that last word, but he covered it with a scowl. "The doting father who brought his son along for the ride. Never mind that he forgot half my birthdays growing up." His words dripped with bitterness, each one hitting the air between us like a hammer blow.

I frowned. It didn't line up. Garrett Grimshaw didn't seem like the kind of man obsessed with playing the perfect parent. He made his living off murder and scandal and heavily leaned into his celebrity author status. In fact, I'd been surprised when I'd received the message from his publicist that the event was to be dry. He seemed to love parties, had a playboy reputation, and was on his third wife, who was half his age. So why the sudden image shift?

"Why do you think he suddenly cared about looking like Father of the Year?" I asked, unable to stop myself as my curiosity took over.

Nate scoffed, shaking his head. "Because perception is everything," he shot back. "It's not about *being* a great dad, it's about *looking* like a great dad. Playing the part in the moment. You know, when it benefits him the most. it's easier to pretend to care than to actually do the work. This whole trip has been about keeping things neat on paper. Like if he smiles enough and signs the right number of books, we'll forget the rest."

I studied him carefully. That made a certain kind of sense. But it still didn't explain one thing.

"If he just needed space," I said, "why vanish without saying anything? Why not quietly push the launch out a week or two and disappear for a weekend?"

Something flickered in Nate's expression. Guilt? Confusion? Frustration? He covered it with a shrug. "Maybe he finally wanted some peace and quiet," he muttered. "Or maybe he's just messing with us. Wouldn't be the first time."

Or maybe, I thought, *you know* exactly *why he's not picking up. Because you made sure he couldn't.*

I studied Nate for a moment longer. There was something almost theatrical about his resentment, as though he wanted the room to know just how wounded he was. "It must be exhausting," I ventured, my voice carefully neutral, "keeping up appearances, that is."

He looked up, his lips twisted into a faint sneer. "That's an understatement. Honestly, between him and Savannah? They deserve each other. She doesn't care about anything but her next wave of attention. This tour isn't about support. It's about staying in the spotlight long enough to sell her perfume and pick up a few new followers along the way."

The moment he mentioned Savannah, I opened my mouth, intending to ask about the jacket. Before I could pursue that line of questioning, Tiffany's voice cut into our conversation, smooth and polished but with an edge sharp enough to slice glass.

"Speaking of Miss Chase," Tiffany said, her tone saccharine, "it's interesting she's still with the sheriff, isn't it? Do you think that means they suspect her involvement?" She smiled at me, the kind of smile that made me feel like I'd just caught the attention of a predator who was now stalking through the jungle after me.

I returned the smile, working to keep it light and polite. "I'm sure the sheriff is being thorough. He's very good at his job."

Tiffany waved a manicured hand dismissively, her diamonds flashing in the light. "But one can never be sure in these situations, isn't that true? Besides, Savannah hasn't been in Garrett's life for very long. Who knows what she was up to before she sank her claws into my husband. Apologies, my *ex*-husband."

Nate shifted awkwardly, and my eyes flicked to him. What made him uncomfortable? That his mother still referred to his father as her husband? That would've made me uncomfortable. They'd been divorced for years. Or did his reaction have something to do with Savannah? But why?

"It seems you and Nate were deep in conversation," she remarked, her sharp gaze flitting between the two of us like a hawk assessing its prey. "Come now, I could do with a distraction. What has you young people so engaged?"

"Just discussing family," I said lightly, glancing at Nate, who was suddenly very focused on his food. "Actually, now that you mention Savannah, I was curious about those custom jackets she designed for the tour." Nate stiffened slightly, but didn't look up. I pressed on. "One of the drivers showed me his. Those details! I don't suppose—"

Tiffany swooped in, her voice cutting clean through the moment. "Savannah," she said with a sigh, shaking her head as though even the thought of the other woman was exhausting. "Everything with that girl has to be over the top, doesn't it? Those jackets, for example. She insisted on the most intense lining, the flashiest buttons. I said, 'Savannah, darling, no one's going to be looking at the help. Why bother? They're supposed to blend into the background anyway.' But you know her. She's always looking for a reason to spend other people's money." She paused, her lips curving into a smug smile. "It's quite ironic, really. She acts like she's this independent influencer, but we all know she wouldn't survive a day without Garrett's checkbook."

Nate muttered something under his breath, but I couldn't catch it. Tiffany, however, didn't seem to care. She was fully absorbed in her own monologue. "Still, I suppose we're stuck with her. She'll be part of the family soon enough."

Her words lingered in the air, and I caught the faintest flicker of something in her expression—triumph? Satisfaction? But that didn't fit. Whatever it was, it felt calculated, like everything else about her.

Across the room, Valerie St. James suddenly stood, her posture rigid. Mindy Hart followed quickly, clutching her notebook like a lifeline. Their whispered conversation had ended as abruptly, and their swift exit left the room feeling colder.

Refusing to be deterred, I shifted my attention back to Nate, determined to press my earlier question. "So, Nate, about the jackets Savannah had made. There's a button missing on one of them. Do you know if—"

"Fascinated by jackets, are you?" Tiffany interrupted, her laugh tinkling like broken glass. "If fashion is what interests you, dear, there are far better icons to emulate than Savannah Chase. She might be enjoying her fleeting moment in the spotlight, but believe me, it won't last. She's all flash and no substance. These influencer types thrive on drama, and the public eats it up. But when the show's over, who will remember her?"

I kept my smile fixed in place, even as frustration simmered beneath my calm façade. "Yes, but about the jackets. I heard there was one made for Nate. I'd love to get a closer look."

His grip on his fork tightened, his knuckles going white as he stabbed a crab cake with unnecessary force. The tines scraped against the plate, the sound sharp and grating. He stuffed it in his mouth and chewed methodically, as though forcing himself to focus on anything *but* me.

It was as though I hadn't spoken at all.

Tiffany didn't miss a beat, waving off my words as though they were insignificant. "Such a waste, really," she continued. "Those jackets cost an obscene amount of money, and for what? Garrett indulged Savannah's every whim, as usual. She batted her lashes, and he opened his wallet. No surprise there." Her voice was honeyed, but there was a razor-sharp edge underneath, a bitterness she couldn't fully conceal and didn't really bother to try.

Before I could respond, Isadora rejoined us, her bright energy cutting through the tension like sunlight through a storm cloud. "Everything all right here?" she asked, her gaze sweeping over Tiffany and Nate, then flicking to me as though she could sense the mounting unease.

I narrowed my eyes at Tiffany. Why was she so determined to shut down my line of questioning? Was she just being her usual attention-seeking self, or was she deliberately running interference? My eyes flicked back to Nate, still avoiding me, still chewing with that stiff, deliberate slowness.

Was she covering for him?

Or worse—was she the one pulling the strings?

"Absolutely," Tiffany replied to Isadora, her smile as smooth and polished as her tone. "We were just discussing Garrett's penchant for extravagance. It's remarkable, really, how one man can waste so much money on frivolities. Why I remember one time when..."

Her voice faded into the background as she launched into a story that sounded like equal parts braggadocio and Savannah-bashing. I forced a polite expression, nodding absently, but my focus was elsewhere. Nate sat stiffly, his jaw clenched, his fork absently stabbing at the remnants of his plate. He hadn't looked at me once since I brought up the jackets, and Tiffany's relentless commentary was only making it harder to press the issue. I clenched my jaw. If Tiffany kept dominating the conversation, I wasn't going to get anywhere.

If I wanted answers about Nate's jacket or anything else, I needed to get him alone. But with Tiffany practically glued to his side, ready to run interference at the first sign of trouble, that wasn't going to be easy.

I nodded along to her monologue, feigning interest while my thoughts spun. Someone here knew more than they were letting on. And if Nate was involved, at least being under watch meant he couldn't be actively hurting Garrett.

Unless he had help.

The thought hit like a gut punch. What if he'd used that tantrum in the shop to storm off, then slipped out and stashed Garrett somewhere before returning to play the concerned son? How long could someone survive without water? Hours? Days?

The ticking clock in my head got louder.

I clenched my fists. If there was even a chance Nate was behind this, I had to act fast. I just needed five minutes. No Tiffany. No distractions. Just Nate, and a few pointed questions.

But how, when his mother was stuck to his side like a chatty burr?

My eyes drifted to the half-open door at the far end of the room. The sheriff *had* been gone with Savannah for a long time. What could be taking so long? And what about Valerie and Mindy? Their abrupt exit replayed in my mind, each hurried step an echo that didn't sit right. Were they avoiding something, or possibly, someone?

A new idea struck. Before I could overthink it, I jumped to my feet.

All eyes turned to me, and I felt the heat creep up my neck. "I...umm...just remembered something," I said, fumbling for a plausible excuse. "Something from the shop. That's right. Mindy, umm, left something behind earlier, and I don't want her to forget it."

Tiffany arched a perfectly groomed brow, her skepticism sharp enough to cut. "How thoughtful of you," she said, her voice dripping with a sweetness that didn't match the sharp look in her eyes.

I forced a tight smile. "Excuse me," I muttered, pivoting before anyone could ask more questions. My sudden exit probably seemed rude, but I didn't have the luxury of polite subtlety. Every second mattered now.

I slipped into the hallway, my pulse hammering in my ears. Isadora, bless her, was still holding Tiffany's attention, but I knew it wouldn't last long. Nate wouldn't sit quietly forever, either. I had minutes—maybe less—to track down Mindy and convince her to help me. She might be the only person with the means to separate Tiffany from Nate, and I couldn't let this opportunity slip away.

But where was she?

The hallway stretched before me, dim and quiet, each step echoing like a countdown. The ticking clock in my head pounded louder with every passing moment, its rhythm relentless and unforgiving. Garrett's life depended on this—on me.

I quickened my pace, my hastily formed plan racing alongside the beat of my pulse. Find Mindy. Convince her to help. Do it before Tiffany or Nate made their move.

As I raced down the hall, hoping I'd picked the right direction, the clock in my head wasn't just ticking.

It was screaming.

A Shadow in the Hall

A MURMUR OF VOICES reached my ears, faint but distinct. I slowed, my breath catching as my instincts flared. Someone was up ahead. I hesitated, torn between urgency and caution, but the words became clearer as I neared. The timbre of the voices, a mix of hushed anger and strained control, sent a prickle of unease skittering up my spine. My pulse quickened, and instinctively, I pressed myself against the wall, trying to blend into the shadows as I crept forward.

My dad would have likely reprimanded me for eavesdropping, but then again, he hadn't ever had a celebrity author kidnapped right in front of his shop.

I listened closely. Valerie's sharp, cultured tones sliced through the stillness of the hall, brittle and fraying at the edges.

"I don't care," she snapped, her voice taut as a drawn bowstring. "We need to control this narrative before it spirals out of hand."

Mindy's nervous response followed, barely audible. "I...I don't know what to tell you. She must have missed the memo or ignored it."

"Well, what are we going to do about it?" Valerie's tone sharpened further, cracking like a vase fissuring under pressure. "We can't afford her running her mouth. Not now."

Mindy hesitated. "Maybe...maybe *we* could release a statement to the press?"

Valerie's response was immediate and cold. "No. The sheriff made it clear he doesn't want us fueling speculation. I'm not about to draw his ire or worse, escalate the situation."

There was a pause, and then Mindy spoke again, her voice trembling. "What about something vague? I mean, wouldn't more people looking for Garrett be a good thing?"

"And how?" Valerie sounded interested, but skeptical.

"Well..." Mindy ventured, her voice shaky. "Maybe a third party? Someone not connected to the firm. A vague statement might steer public opinion in the right direction. Just enough to get people curious and start asking questions themselves."

Valerie fell silent for a moment before exhaling sharply. "Interesting thought. But it can't come from me. If I publicly contradict the sheriff, I'll lose credibility. The leak will have to be you. Yes, an assistant acting out of concern would be forgiven." Her tone turned calculating. "Of course, I'll have to reprimand you in public, but...yes, it could work."

Mindy's voice dropped to a murmur. "I can't do anything until I get my devices back from the police, but once I do, I can make some calls."

"Good," Valerie muttered, her words clipped and venomous. "It's imperative we control the narrative—not that idiot child with a cellphone. Thank goodness the sheriff took her phone as well or this would already be all over social media."

She sighed heavily, her voice softening but losing none of its edge. "Do we know what the kidnappers want yet?"

"The sheriff still has our phones," Mindy said. "When I asked when we might get them back, he mentioned something about a software issue they're still working around. He didn't say anything about contact from the kidnappers, but I got the impression there hasn't been any."

Valerie's voice darkened further, taking on a chilling quality. "That doesn't make sense. Why haven't they...unless..." She trailed off, and I could almost hear the wheels turning in her mind.

"What are you thinking?" Mindy asked hesitantly.

A long silence followed, thick and suffocating. When Valerie finally spoke again, her voice was ice-cold, and all business. "I'm thinking we need action, not waiting for the next shoe to drop. Draft contingency plans for every scenario. I want them in my hands in twenty minutes."

Mindy hesitated. "Are you...are you okay? I mean, he was your husband, after all."

Another pause. The air felt heavy, and I strained to catch Valerie's response.

When she finally spoke, her tone was steel wrapped in silk. "I don't have the luxury of falling apart. Not now. Garrett would expect better from me. I have to focus on the business, on the outcome. Anything else is a distraction."

Her words rang hollowly, like she was trying to convince herself as much as Mindy. A sharp, desperate edge bled through her polished facade, making my stomach churn.

One thing was clear: Valerie was barely holding it together. And desperate people? They made desperate decisions. If Valerie decided to take matters into her own hands, this situation could spiral out of control faster than I could save it.

Footsteps clicked toward the door. I knew that if they saw me now, I'd be caught.

Acting fast, I pulled my phone from my pocket and pressed it to my ear, forcing my posture into something I hoped was casual enough to be dismissed. As Valerie swept into the hallway, I leaned against the wall, nodded absently, and muttered a fake, "Mmhmm, yeah, I understand."

Her sharp gaze flicked over me, clearly unimpressed. I offered her a polite, distracted wave, as if too engrossed in my "conversation" to notice her irritation.

She huffed but continued past me without another word, her heels clicking sharply against the floor.

I waited until the sound had completely faded before lowering my phone and exhaling.

That had been close.

Straightening, I glanced toward the room Valerie had just left. Mindy was still inside, rifling through a thick stack of papers, her shoulders tense.

Now was my chance.

I knocked lightly on the doorframe. "Hey, need a hand?"

Mindy startled, turning swiftly. The top few papers flew off the stack, drifting to the floor. "Oh! Harper. Hi. I—uh, I need to get these organized before Valerie sees."

I stepped inside. "No problem. I'm happy to help."

She shot me a grateful smile as she hefted the stack, attempting to crouch to collect the papers. "Thanks. I swear, sometimes I think she expects me to have six pairs of hands."

"Here, I've got those," I said as I hurried to collect the few sheets that had drifted to the floor. "You're definitely earning that recommendation."

Mindy gave a dry laugh. "Believe me, I'm trying. A reference from Valerie could open a lot of doors." She glanced toward the door as if expecting Valerie to reappear at any moment.

I nodded, but my attention snagged on a smaller, folded slip of paper among the documents. Unlike the crisp printouts, this was handwritten.

A slow, uneasy chill crawled up my spine as I unfolded it.

The words were scrawled in tight, slanted writing, the ink slightly smudged, as though written in a hurry.

You need to deliver it or else...

The words sent a chill down my spine. Before I could make sense of them, Mindy reached out and snatched the paper from my hand. Her fingers crumpled the scrap as she tucked it behind her back, her expression tightening into something unreadable.

"That's private!" she exclaimed.

"Sorry," I said instinctively.

"Right. Well. Thanks for the help," she said in a rush, shuffling the stack into her binder. Her fingers fumbled as she pushed her glasses up her nose. "I'd better go. Valerie's waiting."

"Mindy, wait—" I started, but she was already halfway down the hall, her pace quick and purposeful.

I thought back to the note, my pulse pounding. What did it mean?

My brain immediately leaped to the worst-case scenario. Was it a ransom demand? But that didn't make sense. Valerie had insisted there'd been no ransom, no contact from whoever took Garrett. So where had this come from?

My stomach twisted. If this was just about a publicity deadline, it was an oddly threatening way to phrase it. But if it wasn't...had someone found a way to reach Valerie despite their electronics being confiscated by the police? If that was the case, why hadn't either of them told the sheriff? Were they plotting behind the sheriff's back to hand over the ransom?

I exhaled sharply, glancing at where Mindy had disappeared. Wasn't this exactly how a single kidnapping turned into two? Or worse? If Valerie had received a ransom note and was keeping it quiet, things could go spectacularly wrong.

Should I tell the sheriff? Would he even take a hastily scribbled note I'd only seen for a second seriously? But could I ignore the possibilities?

I sighed, my shoulders sagging. So much for getting Mindy's help with Nate and Tiffany. Somehow, I'd ended up with more questions than answers.

Just as I turned to head back toward the drawing room, a flicker of movement caught my eye. I froze. At the end of the hallway, in the shadows of a darkened doorway, someone was standing there, watching me. My breath hitched.

"Hello?" I called out, forcing my voice to stay steady.

The figure didn't respond. They didn't move. They just stood there, silent and still, the shadows obscuring their face. A cold shiver crawled up my spine.

"Can I help you?" I asked, my voice trembling slightly.

Nothing. The hulking figure lingered for a heartbeat longer, then turned and disappeared into the darkness without a sound.

My heart pounded in my chest as I stared at the empty doorway. Had I imagined it? No, I was sure someone had been there. If it had been one of the Silverthorne employees, surely they would've answered me and stepped into the light. But whoever it was hadn't. So, who was it? And why had they been watching me?

Swallowing hard, I forced my feet to move, edging toward the half-open door at the end of the hallway. My pulse roared in my ears as I pushed it open. The room beyond was empty, dimly lit, and utterly still.

I lingered for a moment, the silence pressing in around me. The feeling of being watched hadn't faded. If anything, it felt stronger, clinging to me like a second skin. I shook my head, trying to dispel the unease crawling up my spine, but it refused to budge.

Lights, Camera, Interrogation

As soon as I walked through the door of the drawing room, Isadora graciously extricated herself from the one-sided conversation with Tiffany Moncrief-Grimshaw and hurried to my side.

"Come with me," she said under her breath, catching my elbow and steering me in the back out into the hall.

"What's going on?" I asked in a whisper.

"Mother wants everyone together to plan," she replied, her tone clipped but urgent. She held up her phone. "She said we should come as soon as possible."

"But...what about Nate? And Valerie?" I asked. "I haven't had a chance to talk to her yet."

Isadora shot me a pointed look. "Trust me, you don't want to keep Mother waiting when she's like this. Besides, they aren't going anywhere. The sheriff still has all their devices and Mother insisted on parking the cars in the garage out of 'hospitality' but really because she can lock them in. Trust me, they aren't leaving unless it's on foot."

I thought of Nate's angry, sullen demeanor and privately doubted that even the formidable Silverthorne manor could keep him contained if he decided to bolt. Still, the idea of delaying Vivienne Silverthorne to pursue my line of questioning wasn't exactly appealing.

Isadora led me through the twisting hallways of the manor with unerring accuracy, stopping at a door in a section of the house I hadn't seen before. She tapped lightly, and Vivienne herself promptly opened it.

Vivienne's expression was sharp and pinched, but it softened slightly when she saw her daughter. "Good, you're here," she said briskly, pulling the door wide. "Come in."

I slipped in after Isadora, and Vivienne shut the door firmly behind us. My eyes widened as I took in the room. A large table dominated the center, strewn with papers, maps, and an array of strange-looking equipment. The sheriff stood near one side, speaking in low tones on his phone, while Officer Reggie hovered awkwardly near the door. My gaze landed on Savannah Chase. She was slumped in a chair with her arms crossed. Her face a storm of frustration and fear.

Gone was the flawless influencer who always seemed poised for the perfect photo. Now, she looked small and deflated, her carefully curated confidence replaced with an unmistakable mix of annoyance and unease.

Vivienne moved toward the sheriff, waiting with the kind of commanding presence that made people instinctively clear a path.

"What's going on?" I whispered to Isadora.

She shrugged. "Mother said the kidnappers haven't made any contact yet, not even a ransom demand."

I opened my mouth to say something, but before I could, Isadora tilted her head, lowering her voice. "And before you ask, Lucas finished with the magical tracking on their phones, but the sheriff is hanging on to them as long as he can so he can keep control of the situation."

My shoulders slumped. That ruled out any secret messages coming through their confiscated devices.

Which meant one of two things: Either no demand had been sent at all, or someone had found another way to make contact. I frowned, my thoughts flicking back to the note I'd found among Mindy's papers.

You need to deliver it or else...

Was that connected to this whole mess? A ransom demand passed in secret. Or just another business-related threat in Garrett's world of publishing deals and high-stakes marketing? Should I say something or was this a product of my overactive imagination?

Before I could decide, Vivienne turned her attention to us, her gaze sharp and probing. "What have you learned?" she asked, her voice low but urgent.

Isadora shook her head regretfully. "Nothing."

Vivienne's focus shifted to me, pinning me in place. "Anything?" she demanded. "Have you heard or seen anything useful?"

I swallowed hard under her piercing scrutiny. "Not much," I admitted, "but there's something." I hesitated. Should I mention the note? Or the person I saw watching me? In a place this big, it could've been a staff member who didn't want to disturb me. I didn't really believe that, but the possibility lingered. While I was trying to make up my mind, Vivienne gestured impatiently for me to continue. I opted to report on the discoveries we made in the car. "There was a missing button found in the car. A gold one, custom-made for the drivers' jackets. It was found under the driver's seat of the abandoned car."

"Yes, I'm aware of that," Vivienne said sharply. "Go on."

I took a breath. "We checked the drivers' jackets, and none of them are missing a button. But there's a fourth jacket. One made for Nate Grimshaw. He refused to wear it."

Vivienne's eyes narrowed slightly. "Interesting."

I quickly recounted the rest of my findings, including Nate's behavior and my growing suspicions. Vivienne listened without interruption, her expression unreadable as I finished.

"That's something, at least," she said at last, her tone cool and measured.

She gestured toward Savannah. "We've managed to contain Miss Chase for now. Apparently, she was at Hocus Mochas, making a spectacle of herself. She'd posted something vague on social media about a 'big reveal.' Thankfully, Reggie intercepted her before she could do any more damage."

I jumped to the obvious conclusion. "She was going to announce Garrett's disappearance and possible kidnapping?" I asked, frowning. "How did she even know if she was at Hocus Mochas?"

"Officer Reggie," Isadora said, rolling her eyes.

I could empathize with the sentiment. It would be just like him. Too open, too eager to fill the silence with helpful chatter. He probably thought she already knew, or maybe he'd assumed someone else had filled her in. If she was behind Garrett's disappearance, the helpful police officer had made it more difficult to catch her in a lie.

Vivienne let out a soft sigh of exasperation. "Given her reach on social media, if she had publicly announced his disappearance, it could have jeopardized our plans. Even though Reggie spoke out of turn, at least he had the good sense to take her cell phone. The kidnappers haven't contacted anyone yet, which means we still have the chance to turn the situation to our advantage. We can't afford a rogue influencer muddying the waters."

Isadora glanced at Savannah, who sat hunched and sullen. "Do you think she knows anything else of use?" she asked, her words barely audible.

Vivienne's gaze narrowed, a calculating expression on her face. "That remains to be seen. But I suspect she might talk if we approach her the right way."

Isadora quirked an eyebrow. "What are you thinking? Charm her into spilling what she knows?"

Vivienne's lips thinned. "Charm, perhaps. Or just enough *persuasion* to remind her of the gravity of the situation."

I hesitated before speaking, but the words slipped out anyway. "She looks scared enough already. Maybe she doesn't need more pressure, just a reason to trust us."

Vivienne's gaze snapped to me, sharp as a blade. I resisted the urge to shrink under the weight of her scrutiny. Speaking so candidly in front of her felt like walking a tightrope over a pit of snapping crocodiles. But her expression shifted, just slightly, and I realized I wasn't immediately being dismissed.

Vivienne considered my idea for a moment, then nodded briskly. "Fine. Do what you must, but don't waste time."

Isadora smiled faintly. "We'll do our best. I agree with Harper. Sometimes a softer touch works better than being heavy-handed."

Vivienne sighed, exasperated. "Just make it quick."

Isadora leaned toward me as Vivienne strode over to the sheriff. "She's not wrong about time," she murmured. "Let's get Savannah away from the police before they scare her into clamming up completely."

"Are you thinking of more of Jacques' treats?" I asked.

"Not exactly. Know thy audience," Isadora said with a wink as she headed towards the influencer.

Savannah looked up as we approached, her eyes flicking between us and the police officers nearby. I plastered on a friendly smile and Isadora spoke up. "Savannah, would you like to come with us for a bit? Maybe get something to eat and talk?"

Her eyes lit up at the idea of leaving. "Anything to get out of here," she said, rising quickly from her chair. Then, with a flip of her hair, she leveled a haughty stare at Officer Reggie. "But I need my phone back. My fans are expecting me to go live, and I have to stay connected." She thrust out a hand and beckoned for the device demandingly.

Officer Reggie frowned and glanced at Sheriff Jackson, who shook his head firmly. "That won't be possible," the sheriff said. "Your phone is necessary in an ongoing investigation of a missing person. Until we can get the tracking software uploaded in case the kidnapper calls, we need it to remain here."

Savannah groaned dramatically. "How long does it take to upload some software? I can't function without my phone! It's my life. Don't you people get that?"

I barely held back a frustrated sigh. Was she seriously whining about social media while Garrett might be in real danger? It wasn't like she was locked in a room with no food or water.

My initial irritation softened just a little as I considered the influencer. Her phone wasn't just some status symbol—it was her work and perhaps her crutch. A security blanket wrapped in a glowing screen. She was as stressed as the rest of us, just in a different way.

Or was she?

A prickle of unease ran down my spine. Was she panicking because she felt out of control, or because she had something to lose? Did she need her phone for something far more pressing than posting selfies?

Isadora cut in to my thoughts and the conversation smoothly, her voice warm and encouraging. "Don't worry, the police will take great care of it. And we'll make sure you're okay. Why don't we focus on getting something to eat and talking? I've been looking forward to meeting you all day."

Savannah's pout shifted into a preening smile. "Well, I suppose I do bring a lot of joy to people's lives." She tossed her blonde hair again and strode toward the door.

Isadora flashed me a knowing look as she trailed after Savannah, whispering, "Oh, I can't wait to hear all about it."

I suppressed a laugh, knowing how much Isadora was laying it on thick to keep Savannah placated. Despite her theatrics, Savannah might hold the key to unlocking the mystery of Garrett Grimshaw's disappearance. Whatever she knew, we had to draw it out.

Adjusting my mental detective hat, I followed Isadora and Savannah, ready to uncover whatever secrets the influencer might be keeping.

Threads of Suspicion

Isadora led the way through the halls, putting on what I recognized as her "in front of company" face. She was polite, poised, and just engaging enough to keep the mood light. Savannah trailed behind, complaining about everything.

"I can't believe how this day has gone," she huffed. "I didn't even want to come, you know, but Garrett insisted. Now that we're engaged, I have to be at all these dull book signings. Can you believe it? And none of these bookworms have even heard of me. But honestly, I can't expect much. They barely know a thing about the fashion world, and that's where I'm really well-known."

"Speaking of fashion," Isadora said smoothly, as she opened the door to her suite with a theatrical flourish, "I thought this might take your mind off things for a while."

Savannah's eyes lit up, and her jaw dropped as Isadora dramatically gestured toward the massive walk-in wardrobe. Soft, recessed lighting illuminated rows upon rows of neatly organized clothes.

"Oh. My. Gosh," Savannah gasped, stepping inside as though she'd just entered a holy shrine to couture. "This is...it's beautiful. I think I've died and gone to heaven."

I could empathize. I'd had a similar reaction at Christmas when I'd come here to get ready for the Silverthorne Ball. Although they didn't flaunt it, the Silverthorne family wasn't just rich. They were in a different league altogether. The manor was not only massive, but opulent. Along with the walk-in wardrobe filled with designer clothes, there was also an entire closet devoted to shoes. And that was just scratching the surface.

The moment Savannah stepped into the wardrobe, it was like a switch flipped. The complaints vanished, replaced by squeals of delight and a stream of questions and comments as she flitted from one rack to another.

Isadora played the part of the gracious hostess perfectly, chatting about designers, styles, and events where she'd worn particular outfits. I lingered in the background, a bit out of place among the talk of haute couture but knowing I needed to steer the conversation back to the situation at hand soon.

When there was a lull, I seized the opportunity. "Savannah," I started casually, "you and Isadora seem really into this fashion stuff."

Savannah nodded, smoothing the sequined skirt of a cranberry-colored dress as she turned toward me. "I've loved fashion ever since I was little. Now I'm finally breaking into the industry. I'm still getting my feet wet, you know, but give me some time. I plan on developing my very own brand."

I exchanged a quick look with Isadora, who jumped in enthusiastically. "Oh! Don't tell me you're designing things! Are you? That's so exciting!"

Savannah beamed at the praise, clearly eating it up. "I am! Nothing haute couture—yet—but I'm definitely dabbling," she said with a conspiratorial wink. "I even tried to design something for Garrett to wear today, but his ex, I mean, his *publicist* insisted on his usual 'meet-and-greet' look. You know, so his fans don't feel less important just because they're from a small town or whatever."

My spine stiffened instinctively at the dismissive tone when she mentioned Havenwood. Small town or not, this was my home, and her condescension rubbed me the wrong way. But Savannah, oblivious to my reaction, steamed ahead.

"Of course, stuffy old Valerie wouldn't let me design for Garrett, but at least I got to put together a look for the drivers. I should've gotten more credit for it," she added, her chest puffing up with pride. "I designed everything—spent ages picking out the fabric, the lining, the buttons. I even made it as literary as possible, you know, as an homage to Garrett on his big day."

She rolled her eyes dramatically. "But did anyone notice? Nope. Not a word of recognition." Savannah returned to inspecting the row of dresses, oblivious to the tension she left in her wake.

I swallowed, trying to keep my thoughts under control as I decided how best to phrase my next question. "You designed for the drivers? Anyone else? I mean, I saw those jackets. A talent like yours shouldn't be suppressed."

Savannah glanced over at me, preening a little under the attention. "It's nice to see when my designs are appreciated. Yes, I also designed a jacket for Nate, not that the ungrateful jerk deigned to wear it."

"Wait, you designed a jacket for *Nate*?" Isadora asked with surprised emphasis on the name. I shot her a confused look. She knew that already. But Savannah answered before I could.

"Yeah, as a peace offering," she said casually, turning back to the rows of clothes.

"Peace offering?" I echoed, a little too sharply.

Savannah nodded. "It's no secret Nate doesn't like me. I think it bothers him that I'm practically his age but about to become his stepmother." She let out a small, bitter laugh. "Look, I'm not oblivious. I know what people say about me. That I'm a gold digger, just after Garrett for the money. But it's not like that. Garrett and I have a connection. Something special. Something I've never experienced with guys my age. They're all so vain, always seeking attention."

I exchanged a glance with Isadora. For someone who claimed to dislike attention-seekers, Savannah sure had a knack for pursuing the spotlight herself.

I cleared my throat, trying to steer the conversation. "Relationships are personal. People should be with whoever makes them happy."

Savannah tilted her head, preening slightly. "Exactly. We're happy, despite what those gossip rags write."

There was a fire in her eyes that surprised me. Either she was sincere or a fantastic actress.

But as I watched her, a memory surfaced. At the beginning of the day, Garrett took Isadora's hand, and kissed her knuckles in a dramatic, old-world gesture. Had he been flirting? Or just theatrics from a celebrity playing it up in front of the press?

I studied Savannah's expression, her fierce determination to defend their relationship. Did she ever wonder if she was more invested than he was? If Garrett enjoyed the spectacle of their engagement more than the reality of it?

For the first time, I wondered if Savannah had more to prove. To Garrett, to the world, maybe even to herself.

I decided to change tactics. "I know the police have probably asked this already, but do you have any idea why Garrett might've been targeted for a kidnapping?"

Savannah's confident facade cracked. Her bottom lip quivered, and she turned abruptly back to the clothes. "Garrett is a kind soul," she said softly. "Yes, he's a celebrity, but he's not the type who needs bodyguards everywhere he goes. Only for special events."

"Is that why he had security today?" Isadora asked gently.

Savannah sniffed. "That was mostly Valerie's idea. He'd been getting threatening fan letters. Apparently, more than usual. She convinced him to have security until things calmed down. And, well, I guess she was right."

"Do you really think a fan might've done this?" I asked.

"What else could it be?" Savannah turned to face me, her eyes wide. "Someone obsessed enough to know his schedule, following him to a small town that wasn't even on the tour until recently? Whoever it is has to be a die-hard fan."

I hesitated, but there wasn't anything to be gained by waiting around. "What if it was someone closer to him?"

Savannah's eyes went wide, and she spun to face me. "What are you insinuating?"

I held up my hands. "Not you. But you did say that it seemed like Nate and his father didn't get along and that he didn't support your relationship. Maybe he had something to do with Garrett's disappearance."

Savannah snorted, shaking her head. "Nate? He can be fun when he's not wrapped up in his own jealousy or his mother's snide influence, but he's not capable of planning something like this."

"What do you mean?" Isadora asked, glancing at me.

Savannah shifted uncomfortably. "I don't like to speak badly about people, but Nate's never learned to be independent. He's Garrett's only child, and Garrett spoils him. I don't hold it against either of them, but I think it would do Nate a world of good to stand on his own two feet. Really learn to be independent. You know, like I've had to do."

"It sounds like you know him well," I observed. "Are you two close?"

"Not anymore," Savannah said, picking up another dress and turning towards the mirror.

"Anymore?" Isadora glanced at me and raised an eyebrow. "You were once?"

Savannah studied her reflection before setting the dress aside and shaking her head. She selected another one as she said, "Not many people know this, but I actually knew Nate first. I think he thought there might've been something between us, but there never was. At least, not on my end. We just hung out with the same group of people. Then I met Garrett and...I just knew, you know?"

I exchanged another glance with Isadora. "That must've been awkward," I said carefully, hoping to encourage her to keep talking.

Savannah gave a small, breathy laugh, setting the dress down and selecting a hat. "Yeah, a little. I don't think Nate ever really got over it. He acts like he hates me. It could be that I'm just a few years older than he is, but I wonder sometimes if it's more about his dad remarrying period than it is about me."

I tried to keep my tone neutral. "And that's why you designed something for him, to smooth things over?"

She perched the feathered hat on her head, inspecting her reflection critically. "Yeah. Nate's never worked a day in his life, but he's happy to spend his dad's money while criticizing Garrett for writing books he thinks are trashy. Honestly, if I were in his shoes, I'd be grateful for everything I had. But just because he's acting like a spoiled brat doesn't mean I'm going to jeopardize my future with Garrett."

"That must make things...strained when you're all together," I said, keeping my tone sympathetic.

Savannah sighed, flopping into a chair and twisting the diamond engagement ring on her finger. "It can be. Nate can be really nasty when he puts his mind to it. I get why people judge me. They think I just lucked into all of this because of Garrett, but that's not true. I worked for everything I have."

She hesitated, then squared her shoulders, as if steeling herself for the inevitable doubt, and met our eyes. "I know being an influencer isn't exactly a respected position, but it can be lucrative, and I've built what I have with my own sweat and tears. I might not fit everybody's idea of 'normal,' but I'm proud of what I've done."

Isadora nodded encouragingly. "And so you should be. It sounds like you've worked hard."

I pressed gently. "Why do you think Nate won't change?"

Savannah shrugged. "Why would he? His life's comfortable and growth only comes from discomfort." She snorted softly. "Trust me, I know that all too well. Nate always has had everything he could ever want or need. What would possibly motivate him to change?"

I leaned back, considering her words. "What if something happened to Garrett's money? Or Nate had to get a job?"

She let out a short laugh. "Don't get me wrong, it would probably do him good. But it's never going to happen. Garrett dotes on him, even though he's an adult. Nate has enough money coming his way that he'll never have to lift a finger for the rest of his life."

I frowned. Something about the way she said it sounded so certain. Did she not know about the changes Garrett was making to his will?

Because if she did, she wouldn't be talking about Nate's financial security like it was set in stone. The will was in the process of being changed. Nate wasn't inheriting anything once it was signed.

I kept my face neutral, but my mind was racing. I studied her carefully, but her expression was open, guileless. Either she was an incredibly good actress, or she genuinely believed what she was saying.

A knock at the door drew our attention. Isadora opened it to reveal a member of the Silverthorne staff pushing in a tray of food. Despite having just eaten, Isadora and I settled around the tray with Savannah, eager to keep her talking.

Isadora, ever the natural conversationalist, steered the discussion toward Savannah's early relationship with Garrett, her influencer career, and her new ventures into fashion and perfume. I let her take the lead, my mind drifting as the conversation turned to the nuances of scent-making. But something nagged at me. There was a loose thread I needed to pull.

I waited for a lull in the conversation before leaning forward. "Savannah, I meant to ask you something. There was a perfume bottle found broken in the car. Do you know anything about that?"

Savannah blinked, surprised, then shrugged. "Oh, that. It was probably one of mine. I always carry a few samples around. Just in case I need a quick gift for someone important."

"Any idea how it broke?" I pressed.

She hesitated, then waved a dismissive hand. "Honestly? I'd forgotten about it, but Nate tossed it. He was in a mood today, and it wouldn't surprise me if it broke underfoot or when the seat got moved."

I frowned. "He threw it?"

"Not at me," she clarified quickly, her tone light, as if she found the idea ridiculous. "He was mad and tends to act out. He was in a foul mood today."

"Weren't you and Garrett riding in the car together? What was Nate doing in your car?" I asked.

Savannah sighed, brushing a hand down the front of her dress. "When I gave Nate his jacket earlier, I never dreamed he'd react the way he did."

"And he threw a perfume bottle?" Isadora asked, shocked. "No wonder you wanted to ride in a separate car."

Savannah lifted a shoulder, but she didn't seem particularly bothered. "Honestly? He's been such a jerk lately that it barely registered. I figured he'd throw his little temper tantrum and get over it."

She gestured at her outfit with a self-deprecating flick of her wrist. "Anyway, I tried to grab the bottle when it rolled under the seat, but have you seen this dress? It looks great, but it's not exactly made for easy movement."

Savannah's casual attitude about the bottle left me unsettled. Isadora shot me a look, her brow furrowed slightly, and I could almost read her mind.

"You said the seat was moved?" Isadora asked. "Why was that?"

Savannah waved a hand. "Some sort of mix up with the drivers. The short guy got into our car first, but apparently, he was meant to drive Nate's car. The guy that drove us was about twice his size and needed to move the seat back. There may have been a crunch when that happened, but it's not like it's a big deal. I have more samples. I can get you both one if you're interested." She reached for her bag as Isadora responded with appropriate levels of enthusiasm.

Savannah's story distracted me much more than the prospect of a free sample. How likely was it that a perfume bottle would break just from being dropped inside a car even if a seat had been moved? The chances had to be small. And why not just ask Garrett to retrieve it? What had really happened? And why was Savannah hiding the truth?

Before I could press further, Savannah flicked her fingers as if dismissing the whole situation. "But enough about me," she said breezily. "Have you seen some of the new designers hitting the scene lately? There's this lady I've been obsessed with who is doing the most incredible things for a woman's silhouette and—"

The shift in conversation was so quick it nearly gave me whiplash, but Isadora took the bait instantly, her eyes lighting up. "Oh! You must mean Clara Delaine. Her work is stunning. I saw her latest collection in Milan—she has this way of layering fabrics that feels almost ethereal."

Savannah nodded enthusiastically. "Yes! That's exactly what I love about her designs. I was actually thinking of reaching out to her for some custom pieces—"

As they launched into a discussion about emerging designers, my mind drifted, my thoughts swirling with uncertainty. I took the moment of distraction to step back and reevaluate everything I knew so far.

I mentally ran through the key elements of the case, searching for the three pillars of any crime: motive, means, and opportunity.

The pieces shifted in my mind, rearranging themselves like a puzzle that refused to snap into place. Was Savannah behind this? I exhaled slowly. After talking to her, I found the idea of her masterminding the kidnapping of her fiancé hard to imagine. She wasn't exactly subtle, and she had more to lose than gain. No clear motive, no real means—unless I was missing something. But there were several unanswered questions about her and her story, so I wasn't taking her off my suspect list yet.

What about Dirk, the security guard? My brow furrowed. He had the means and the opportunity since he was out of the shop when Garrett disappeared. But what was his motive?

No, I needed someone with all three.

What about a fan? The idea sent a shiver down my spine. Garrett wrote thrillers. He had an diehard fan base. Some had sent him disturbing letters. Apparently, more than normal recently. Maybe an obsessed fan had finally snapped? Maybe someone thought they were part of the next great Garrett Grimshaw mystery. After all, no one had been screening the fans today. One could have motive, means, and opportunity. It wasn't impossible.

But it didn't feel right.

I exhaled sharply. No, it had to be someone close. Someone who had access. Someone who knew not only where Garrett would be, but also how to get the driver's keys. But what would someone like that want?

And then my mind snapped back to the note I'd seen in Mindy's possession. Why hadn't I told anyone about the note? I'd been distracted, but that wasn't an excuse.

The question clawed at me, unsettling and sharp. That was a mistake. One I needed to fix. Had it really been a ransom demand? Or had I just assumed?

My breath hitched as I remembered the note and the smudged, slanted handwriting.

Handwriting.

Who in their right mind *handwrites* a ransom note these days? With fingerprinting, trace DNA, and handwriting analysis, it was practically signing your name at the scene of the crime. Why risk it? A ransom demand could have been texted. Printed. Emailed. Even handwritten and then scanned to remove any traceable physical evidence. So why write it by hand?

Unless they had no other option.

The realization hit me like a punch to the gut.

The only reason someone would have to write a note was if they couldn't use electronics.

And I knew of several people in this manor who didn't have their devices because Sheriff Jackson had confiscated them all.

My pulse quickened. Savannah. Dirk. Mindy. Valerie. Tiffany. Nate. *Nate. Again.*

Nate had been without his phone since the police took them. If someone needed to communicate without electronics, a handwritten note made sense. I quickly ran through motive, means, and opportunity for Nate.

The resentment. The bitterness. The inheritance. And he'd stormed out of the shop just before Garrett disappeared. It all lined up too neatly to ignore.

But was he capable? And if he was, could he be acting alone?

My stomach clenched. What about Tiffany? His mother. She was always nearby, always protecting him. If Nate had done this, she could be involved. Ensuring her precious son's future wasn't threatened by Garrett's latest fiancée. She certainly hadn't done much to clear herself.

A wave of nausea rolled through me. So much for my resolve to be the calm and collected business owner today. I was spiraling.

Everywhere I looked, I saw suspects. I saw deception. And the worst part? I still didn't have a clear answer. Just lots of theories. And if I didn't find out who was responsible, Garrett might never be found. The thought was too horrible to contemplate.

A cold sweat broke out across my back. The walls of the room felt too tight, the air too thick. I needed to get out.

I pushed abruptly to my feet, but I moved too fast. The room spun, and I nearly fell, having to throw out a hand to keep my balance. Isadora and Savannah both turned toward me, their expressions startled.

I pressed my sweaty palms against the fabric of my pants, forcing myself to sound casual. Calm. Cool. Collected. I recited the words like a mantra in my mind until the room stopped spinning.

"Harper? Are you okay?" Isadora asked, concern in her voice.

"I—I need a minute. I think I ate something that didn't agree with me," I muttered.

Isadora's brow lifted slightly, but ever the gracious hostess, she didn't push further. "There's a guest bathroom down the hall, three doors to the left. Do you need me to come with you?"

"Thanks," I mumbled, already moving. "I'll be fine. Just...give me a minute."

I stepped into the hallway and shut the door behind me, inhaling the cool, still air like I'd just surfaced from drowning. My pulse hammered in my ears.

I needed to breathe. I needed to think.

But most of all, I needed to find Garrett Grimshaw.

The Masquerade Plan

As I struggled to catch my breath and quiet my racing thoughts, my phone buzzed in my pocket. I pulled it out. Gabriel's name lit up the screen, and I answered immediately.

"Hey, Harper. Are you free? I want to show you something," he said, excitement bubbling in his tone.

"Sure," I said, forcing the trembles from my voice and glancing around the unfamiliar hall. "I'm near Isadora's room, but I have no idea how to get to you."

"I'll find you. Be there in a sec."

He hung up, and I slumped against the wall, my eyes drifting shut as I forced myself to breathe. *In. Out. Keep it together.* My pulse still thrummed too fast, my thoughts a tangled mess of suspects, motives, and worst-case scenarios.

True to his word, I heard Gabriel's footsteps hurrying down the hall. Time to pull it together. I straightened, smoothing a hand over my hair, adjusting my expression like a mask I knew by heart. Easy smile. Steady hands. Nothing to see here.

Gabriel was a Silverthorne. He'd grown up steeped in strategy, surrounded by people who played chess while I was still figuring out the rules.

He handled crises like they were puzzles. Me? I was duct-taping myself together and pretending it counted as composure. I didn't want to be the weak link in the plan or in his eyes.

He arrived with a grin, but it faltered as soon as he saw me. "Are you okay?" he asked, voice light but laced with quiet concern.

I hesitated, my instincts screaming at me to deflect, to not let him see any weakness. But the weight of everything pressed too hard against my ribs. It felt like a stone on my chest, making each breath a mission. I opened my mouth, but no words came. I closed it and shook my head, unable to do anything else.

His gaze swept over my face, reading too much, too fast. He didn't say anything at first. Just stepped close and reached out, fingers brushing lightly against my arm. A silent invitation.

"You don't have to pretend," he said quietly. "Not with me."

I tried to smile. Really tried. But it crumbled before it even formed. I looked away, blinked hard, swallowed the lump that had been rising in my throat all day.

"I'm fine," I started, the words automatically tumbling out of my mouth.

Gabriel tilted his head, waiting.

My resolve buckled. "Okay, I'm not fine. Not really," I whispered.

That was all it took. He folded me into a warm hug, and I let myself lean into him. My fingers curled into his shirt as the tension finally started to loosen its grip.

"What do you need?" he asked, voice steady against my hair.

I shook my head. "I don't know. Time. You. To find Garrett Grimshaw," I said, and the last part cracked right down the middle, raw and helpless.

"You've got the first two," he said, "and we'll figure out the third. Together. You're not alone in this."

His words settled something in me. Not fixing it exactly but quieting the storm just enough to breathe. I inhaled, catching the spicy warmth of his cologne and trying to match the steady rhythm of his breathing.

I exhaled, long and slow, and when I pulled back, he searched my face, waiting. He wasn't pushing, wasn't demanding that I snap back to normal, just offering space for me to be.

I swallowed past the lingering tightness in my throat. "Okay," I said, my voice rough but steady. "You're right. We can do this. Together."

He smiled, his eyes warm as he lifted my hand to his lips and brushed a kiss against my knuckles. "Absolutely. One step at a time. Fill me in on what you've found out so far as we walk."

As he led me through the sprawling manor, I told him everything I'd learned so far. The information Savannah shared, Nate's hostility, and my suspicions. By the time I finished, Gabriel's expression had shifted from curious to focused.

I sighed, weighing my words carefully. "Savannah doesn't strike me as the type to orchestrate something like this. She's too caught up in her own world. But Nate?" I shook my head. "He's bitter, entitled, and angry enough to lash out. Whether he's capable of masterminding a kidnapping? I don't know. That feels like a stretch."

Gabriel frowned. "Then maybe he's not the mastermind. Could he have a partner?"

I bobbed my head. "I thought the same thing. It's possible. I was thinking perhaps he and his mother were working together to stop Garrett cutting Nate out of the will. You should've seen Tiffany earlier. She kept blocking my questions about the jackets. She's super protective of him. I don't know if it's jealousy or self-righteousness, but she was doing everything she could to shield Nate."

Gabriel glanced at me. "If she thought Garrett was jeopardizing Nate's future, could she have done something drastic?"

I hesitated my pulse ticking faster. "That's the part I can't figure out. If one or both of them kidnapped Garrett to stop him from changing the will, what's to stop him from doing it anyway once he's free?"

Gabriel didn't answer right away. His expression shifted, subtle but telling.

When he finally did speak, his voice was quieter than before. "That's exactly what I would do. Tell them whatever they wanted to hear. Make promises. Play the part." He paused, gaze distant now. "And then I'd do everything I could to make sure they never benefited from it. Not one bit."

The silence that followed felt heavier than it should have.

"You've thought about this before," I said softly, not quite a question.

He gave a small, almost apologetic shrug. "Growing up in my family...you think about things like wills and power plays earlier than you should. We've all had those talks. Mother made sure of it." A flicker of something—maybe weariness, maybe grief—crossed his face. "It's not exactly the kind of thing you bring up over breakfast, but it's part of the Silverthorne life."

I studied him, caught off guard by the quiet pain beneath his words. There was so much he carried, so much he had learned to live with. I wanted to say something comforting and kind, but the words tangled on my tongue. Instead, I just reached out and gave his hand a gentle squeeze.

Gabriel offered a faint smile, one that didn't quite reach his eyes. Then he shook his head, refocusing his attention on the present rather than the past.

"This isn't about me," he said. "It's about Garrett. Do you really think Nate or Tiffany would kidnap him?"

I exhaled slowly, the question sinking in. "My gut says no," I said, "but logic keeps whispering maybe. If this is about the will, and Garrett really planned to cut them off, then leaving him alive becomes a gamble." My stomach twisted. "Which means their only real option would be..." I trailed off, unwilling to say the words aloud.

Gabriel, however, didn't need me to. "Murder," he finished grimly. "Do you think one or both might be capable of murder?" he asked.

I lifted a shoulder helplessly, rubbing my arms against the sudden chill creeping up my spine. "Again...maybe? But if they are behind this, letting Garrett go is a risk they can't afford."

Gabriel was quiet for a long moment, his gaze assessing. "And if it's not them? What about Savannah?"

I shook my head before he even finished the question. "No. She's still got some questions to answer, but I don't think she'd kidnap her fiancé. If money's the motive, she stands to inherit a massive chunk once Garrett signs the new will. There's no reason for her to do anything but wait."

I hesitated, thinking back to how shaken she'd seemed. "Their relationship might not be conventional, but I think she really does care about him."

Gabriel nodded slowly. "She's not exactly the type to get her hands dirty either."

"Exactly," I agreed. "She might be calculating when it comes to her brand, but she's not ruthless. And even if she were involved, why risk it? That would do more harm than good for her."

Gabriel exhaled. "So that leaves us with the fan theory or Tiffany and Nate."

"Pretty much," I admitted. "The crazy fan theory makes sense. Maybe someone obsessed enough to follow Garrett here snatched him. Maybe they're trying to force a rewrite or get close to him." My mind raced back to the book signing, to the fans who had lined up for hours. "People are going to lose it when they find out Rhett Ryder dies at the end of his latest book. I can imagine that would make some people pretty angry."

Gabriel shot me a surprised look. "Wait. He dies? Spoiler alert!" He crossed his arms with an exaggerated pout. "I was going to read that."

I rolled my eyes. "You have a pile of books waiting to be read that could classify as a small mountain. I think you'll survive."

He gasped dramatically. "Still. It's the principle."

A smile stole across my face at his antics, but I waved him off. "A literary death is *so* not the point today. Not when we might have a real one to deal with."

"Agreed," Gabriel said. "If it's not a fan or Savannah, then the only ones who stand to gain from Garrett disappearing are Tiffany and Nate."

I crossed my arms, almost as if I was trying to hold myself together. "That's the part I keep circling back to. If this was just about stopping the will from changing, they'd have to keep him alive until it was official. But then...if Garrett is already..." I swallowed, the word refusing to form. "Then Nate stands to inherit most of his estate, assuming the new will isn't finalized."

Gabriel frowned. "What about his other ex-wife? Valerie? You haven't mentioned her yet."

I shook my head. "It's not her. She's too calculated to risk something this reckless. She thrives on control, and a stunt like this would throw everything into chaos. Besides, her career is tied to his. Sure, a high-profile kidnapping might bring media attention, but not the kind a publicist like her would want. It would tank his reputation, and by extension, hers."

I hesitated, thinking it through. "And if this is about money, from what I understand, she and Tiffany would only inherit a small amount, but not enough to be life-changing. The bulk goes to Nate or Savannah, assuming the will still stands. Valerie would make far more staying on as his agent, reaping the long-term benefits of his career."

Gabriel considered this. "Right. There is such a thing as bad press. If anything, she'd be the one trying to keep him writing or, at the very least, clean up this mess rather than create it."

"Exactly. I think she'd micromanage her way out of a crisis, not burn everything down to start over," I agreed.

Gabriel nodded. "So that leaves us with the entitled son and the furious ex-wife, or an obsessive fan."

I exhaled slowly. "I don't know which is worse."

Gabriel reached for a doorknob and swung it open. "Well, either way, looks like the plan for the masquerade is moving forward."

I nodded, preceding him into the room.

The study was just as I remembered. Dark wood paneling, heavy bookshelves, and the faint scent of old paper and polished leather lingering in the air. But the memories here weren't comforting. The last time I'd been in this room was Christmas Eve, with the lights cut out and shadows stretching long as jewel thieves crept through while Gabriel and I hid, barely daring to breathe.

The ghost of that night settled over me, wrapping around my ribs like a too-tight corset. My pulse ticked up, my heart racing faster at the memory.

Then I glanced at Gabriel.

He wasn't watching the shadows, wasn't bracing for another threat to emerge. Instead, he smiled at me, a quiet warmth behind his eyes that settled something inside me. The fear and unease didn't disappear, but they loosened their grip on my gut.

For him, I was willing to take the time to overwrite the bad memories with better ones.

My gaze flicked to the far corner of the room, where a tall, sheet-covered object stood, nearly as tall as I was. I arched a brow. "Is this part of what you wanted to show me? Is it part of your illusion for the masquerade?"

He smiled softly and shook his head. "Not exactly, but now that you mention it, I could use some feedback." He waved his hand, and his form shimmered, transforming into Garrett Grimshaw right before my eyes.

"What do you think?" he asked, though his voice was still Gabriel's. Seeing Garrett's image paired with my boyfriend's voice sent a jarring wave of dissonance through me.

I stuttered, struggling to process. "Oh...sorry. It's just...well, it's weird hearing your voice come out of Garrett's mouth."

Gabriel gave me a thumbs up. "Good point. How's this?" When he spoke again, it wasn't his voice coming out of his mouth. It was Garrett's.

Gabriel twirled and posed, nailing the author's signature look: the long sweep of hair, the intelligent gleam in his eyes, and that carefully curated "meet-the-fans" outfit of the black silk shirt and dark jeans. He had it all down, right to the subtle flair of Garrett's movements.

I nodded, shooting him a thumbs-up. "It's uncanny. Seriously, it's good. A little too good, actually."

Gabriel paced back and forth across the room. He paused at the far end, flicked his hair back, and ran a hand through it in an unmistakable Garrett Grimshaw move.

I laughed, pointing. "That's it! That's so Garrett. I remember him doing exactly that when he came to Spellbooks."

Gabriel grinned, breaking character. "I've spent what feels like ages watching videos of him online. I think I've got the hair flick and walk pretty much down. I'm still working on the vocal inflections, though."

"It's impressive," I admitted. "What you've done already would probably fool anyone who doesn't know him well."

Gabriel nodded. "That's the goal. If the masquerade goes ahead, this keeps up the illusion that everything is fine. If the kidnapper is an outsider, someone after ransom or attention, they might panic when they think Garrett is here and they've mistakenly kidnapped a double. This could force their hand."

I chewed on my lip. "But the family already knows about this plan." I hesitated, glancing at him. "If it *is* one of them, this won't do anything. And if they pretend to be fooled..." My stomach knotted at the thought. "That could put *you* in danger."

Gabriel's expression flickered, but then he smiled. I envied how he was so calm, steady, and reassuring, even in the face of all that was happening. "If it's a family member, they already have Garrett. They don't need to come after me. And if they try something, we're in my home, at my event, surrounded by people I trust." His fingers brushed over mine, and he squeezed my hand gently. "I'll be on guard. It'll be fine."

I wanted to believe him. *Needed* to believe him. But my stomach churned, a sickly knot of unease winding tighter with every breath. Gabriel might not think he was a target, but that didn't mean he was safe. If the kidnapper thought he was getting too close, asking too many questions, pressing too hard...what would they do?

My pulse thudded in my ears. They had Garrett. They held all the power. If they decided Gabriel was a problem, what was stopping them from making sure he disappeared, too?

I exhaled slowly, forcing my shoulders to relax even though tension still prickled at the back of my neck.

Not now. Don't spiral. Stay focused.

"Well," I said, forcing my voice into something that sounded normal. "In the meantime, it looks like the masquerade is still happening. What can I do to help?"

I did *not* look at the conspicuously draped large object in the room.

For all of three seconds.

Gabriel chuckled, his fingers grazing the small of my back as he gently steered me toward it. "You always want to solve the mystery in front of you, don't you?"

He moved behind me, wrapping his arms gently around my waist. His breath warmed the shell of my ear, sending a tingle down my spine as he spoke.

"Look, I know this isn't the way you wanted things to go today." Gabriel's voice was low, steady. It was an anchor against the chaos swirling around us. "This was supposed to be a big night. Not just for Garrett or his family, but for you and Spellbooks. And I'm sorry that's been overshadowed by all of this. I just wanted you to know I was thinking about you."

My heart squeezed.

Gabriel still thought of today as my victory. The night Havenwood's literary scene expanded, the night my bookshop earned a place among publishing elites. He saw me as part of that success. But all I could see was the barely contained wreckage I was standing in and the truth I was desperately holding back, stitched together with forced smiles and careful words.

I should tell him. Tell him everything.

The thought rose, then curled back in on itself. Gabriel had enough to worry about without me adding to it. Besides, if I said it out loud, if I admitted that Spellbooks wasn't thriving, that *I* wasn't thriving—what would happen then?

I swallowed down the guilt, fixing my mask in place before he could catch another crack in it. His fingers brushed against mine, pulling me back from the edge before I spiraled too far. "I reached out to Elliot Ashford. Remember him? He designed your gown for the Christmas Eve Ball."

I blinked. "Elliot? Of course I remember him. Getting to wear one of his creations was incredible! Why do you ask?"

Gabriel's lips tilted in a small smile. "We worked on something special. I thought you might like to wear it tonight."

He stepped around me as he reached for the sheet. In one smooth motion, he pulled it away to reveal an exquisite gown.

My jaw dropped open as I took in the dress before me. The fabric shimmered softly as the light caught every delicate detail. I stepped closer, my fingers itching to touch it. The bodice was a soft cream, perfectly fitted, with cape sleeves that draped elegantly off the shoulders like the petals of a flower. The satin-like fabric glowed faintly, as though lit from within, exuding quiet, elegant sophistication.

My gaze traveled downward, and the skirt stole my breath. Voluminous yet impossibly light, layers of soft, asymmetrical overskirts cascaded gracefully over the main fabric. Each layer seemed to dance as I moved around the dress. Details were embroidered with delicate, flowing gold thread. I leaned in, mesmerized, and then froze as I recognized the intricate designs.

"These...these are words," I gasped, my voice barely above a whisper.

Gabriel stepped closer, his expression soft with nervous anticipation. "They are," he said. "Over the last few months, whenever you mentioned loving a book, I made a note of it. At first, I wasn't sure what I'd do with that information. I was thinking maybe a journal or something, but when this event came up, it felt like the perfect opportunity."

I blinked, stunned. "You're saying...you took all my favorite books and had a dress made, embroidered with their words?"

Gabriel nodded, a hint of uncertainty flickering in his eyes. "Is it too much? I mean, I know we're still getting to know each other, but I wanted you to have something special on this momentous day, something that reflected what's important to you."

I stared at him, then back at the dress, completely overwhelmed. The layers of the skirt felt like the chapters of my favorite novels, woven together into a single, breathtaking masterpiece. The overskirts, embroidered with phrases from books I cherished, were arranged with care. Once I put it on, it would create a sense of stories wrapping around me. Beneath them, the main skirt flowed in soft pleats, sweeping the floor with a quiet grace that hinted at movement even when still. The hemline, slightly uneven, shimmered with extra embroidery, but it felt as though the dress itself held a secret magic. It wasn't just a gown. It was a reflection of me and of every story that had shaped who I was.

Gabriel moved behind me, wrapping his arms gently around my waist once more. His voice was low and uncertain, but his warmth radiated through every word. "Is it too much?" he asked again, his breath tickling the shell of my ear. "I didn't want to overstep, but I also wanted you to know how much I see you. How much I pay attention to the things you care about."

I turned in his embrace, my hands sliding up to rest against the nape of his neck. When I met his eyes, the world around us seemed to still. His steady gaze held a quiet strength that melted something deep inside me.

"It's perfect," I whispered, my voice trembling with emotion. Tears welled in my eyes before I could stop them. "Gabriel, thank you. Truly."

His smile softened, and he raised a hand to gently brush away a tear that had slipped down my cheek. "I'm glad you like it," he murmured, his voice soothing and filled with a quiet tenderness.

Then, leaning in close, he pressed a featherlight kiss to my cheek. It lingered there for a moment, long enough to send a gentle warmth through me. His breath brushed my ear as he whispered, "For the record, it's not perfect. *You* are."

As the words settled between us, my breath caught. The world around us fell away, and, for a moment, there was nothing but the two of us in that quiet, magical space. My knees weakened, and I leaned into him, his steady embrace the only thing keeping me grounded.

Gabriel tilted my chin upward with a gentle finger, his eyes locking with mine. He paused, as if waiting for permission, before lowering his lips to mine. The kiss was unhurried and tender. It felt like the culmination of every whispered word, every unspoken feeling between us. A soft shiver ran through me, tingling all the way to my toes. My mind went blissfully blank, leaving only the press of his lips and the quiet magic that hung between us.

On Borrowed Time

A KNOCK ON THE door startled me, snapping me back to reality. I wasn't sure how much time had passed. All I knew was that it had been enjoyable, and I was sad it had ended so abruptly. I took a step back as the door creaked open, and Vivienne's perfectly coiffed head appeared in the room.

"There you two are," she said, her sharp gaze flicking between us before settling on Gabriel. "How's the illusion coming along?"

I took another step away from him, my face flushing. Self-consciously, I ran a hand through my hair. Being interrupted while kissing Gabriel wasn't exactly how I'd planned to end the moment, and being interrupted by his formidable mother was mortifying on so many levels.

Gabriel, of course, didn't seem remotely as flustered as I felt. "It's coming along well, Mother," he said easily. "Just need to refine some mannerisms, but I've got the surface level down."

"Good. Just in time," Vivienne said. "We need to strategize. Come with me." She spun on her heel and strode purposefully down the hall.

He glanced at me with a small shrug and a sad little smile. "Duty calls."

Before I could say anything, he wove his fingers through mine and gave a gentle tug, leading me toward the door.

"Are you sure this isn't something for your family and the police?" I whispered as we hurried after her. The thought of being pulled further into Vivienne's tightly controlled plans wasn't exactly comforting.

Gabriel leaned in, his voice low and reassuring. "If it concerns me, it concerns you. Besides," he added with a playful glint in his eye, "if I remember right, we couldn't have solved the jewel theft at the Christmas Eve Ball without your help. I'm sure Mother and Sheriff Jackson won't turn away another set of helping hands. Especially with Havenwood's reputation on the line."

I opened my mouth to protest, then shut it again. What could I say? It was nice to feel appreciated, that my gifts and abilities were valued. However, I wasn't sure how much I could help. And, irrationally, a part of me wanted to be back in the study with Gabriel. Only Gabriel. Perhaps with a lock on the door.

Vivienne led us into the temporary police headquarters set up inside the manor. Sheriff Jackson paced in front of an elaborate array of technological devices while Officer Reggie stood near the doorway, shifting from foot to foot like he didn't know where to be or how to help.

Sheriff Jackson looked up as we entered. "There you are," he said, nodding in acknowledgment.

Gabriel firmly shut the door behind us, ensuring that no eavesdropper could overhear our plans.

I glanced around the room, the mansion's lavish interior clashing with the seriousness of the police setup. The whole situation felt surreal. Never in a million years would I have imagined that moving to Havenwood would result in me being at the center of a kidnapping investigation, but here we were.

Vivienne clapped her hands, commanding the room's attention. "Alright, now that we're all here, we need to finalize the masquerade plan and prepare for any potential reactions from the kidnapper. What happens if we get a call? What happens if they show up? If they don't call? I want contingencies for every possibility."

Gabriel's illusion was discussed, and though I'd already made peace—well, an uneasy truce—with the plan, my stomach still twisted at the thought of what could go wrong. We'd talked about the risks, and Gabriel had assured me he'd be careful. But assurances didn't change the fact that he was stepping into the unknown, and, for all our planning, we had no real way of knowing how the kidnapper would react.

I clenched my hands behind my back, forcing myself to breathe evenly. Gabriel was a Silverthorne. He knew how to handle himself. And, as much as I hated it, this was our best shot. I could either let the fear take over, or I could make sure I was ready to act if something went wrong. After the close call just before Valentine's Day with the incident at the heartwood tree, I wasn't about to let him get hurt. Not again.

The room buzzed with Vivienne's sharp voice and the sheriff's gruff responses, but I found it hard to focus on their words. My gaze darted to Gabriel, who was calmly discussing the finer details of his illusion as if he didn't have a care in the world. How could he be so at ease when I could barely breathe?

Vivienne's voice cut through my dark thoughts. "I think this is the best way forward," she said, her tone leaving no room for argument. "We proceed as if everything is normal, and Gabriel plays Garrett at the masquerade until we get a lead."

I shot a worried glance at Gabriel. He gave me a subtle nod of reassurance. He believed in this plan but doubts still churned in my gut. I wasn't sure if it was the right move, but Vivienne and the sheriff clearly had the final say.

"You look concerned. Any thoughts, Miss Sullivan?" Sheriff Jackson asked unexpectedly, turning to me.

The question caught me off guard, but I quickly recovered. "I think it's a solid plan to draw them out as long as Gabriel stays in public spaces. We wouldn't want him to get kidnapped as well," I said carefully. "However, I wonder if there's a way to put additional pressure on them to act. Something subtle that they wouldn't see coming."

The sheriff nodded thoughtfully, stroking his chin. "Could work, and I'm always a fan of teaming up to take out the bad guy. Maybe we can leak something indirectly...a hint that Garrett's here but not quite himself. Maybe even insinuate that someone close to him has gone missing. It might be too much if we blatantly say it's a double or something like that. Might spook them. Still, it's a good thought."

Vivienne gave me an approving look, and I felt a small burst of pride. It wasn't much, but it felt good to contribute.

Another thought occurred to me, and I spoke up before I could think better of it. "Have you examined those papers we found in the trunk?" I asked.

Sheriff Jackson nodded. "I had Nathaniel Ravenscroft go over them just to be sure, but the changes haven't been signed yet, which means they aren't legally binding."

I frowned, an idea forming. "So maybe someone didn't want those changes to happen. That puts Nate and Tiffany right at the top of the suspect list."

Sheriff Jackson made a noise somewhere between a scoff and a sigh. "I wouldn't be so sure about that."

I blinked. "Why not?"

He crossed his arms. "Tiffany doesn't need Garrett's money. The Moncriefs are an old-money family. Wealthy. Well-connected. If Tiffany wanted something, she wouldn't need to stage a kidnapping to get it. And Nate?" He shook his head. "That kid's got an ego, but I don't see it. He strikes me as the type that does a whole lot of complaining and not much action. Even if his daddy cut him off, he's still got his mama's money."

I could almost feel the ground under me shift as my best theory crumbled around me. I swallowed hard, heat creeping up the back of my neck. This was exactly the kind of thing that made me feel like an amateur. I wasn't a detective. I was a bookseller who happened to stumble into mysteries far too often. Maybe I was wrong. Maybe I was wasting everyone's time by chasing theories that didn't hold water. But Garrett had disappeared, and I needed to explore every angle before I just gave up.

"Maybe Tiffany doesn't need Garrett's money," I conceded. "But what if this isn't about needing it? What if it's about control? She was blocking every question about those jackets earlier. And Nate—maybe he's not a mastermind, but that doesn't mean he's not involved. If he's working with someone else, someone pulling the strings—"

Vivienne cleared her throat, looking unimpressed. "And who exactly would that be?"

I faltered. "I—I don't know."

The words tasted bitter. My mind was spinning, but every thread of theory I followed seemed to unravel before I could make sense of it. I clenched my jaw, frustration prickling beneath my skin. I hated feeling like I was grasping at straws while everyone else seemed so steady, so sure.

The sheriff exhaled, his expression hard. "Unfortunately, we need to approach this situation with the utmost care. Even though they are a mundane family, upsetting the Moncriefs would not go over well."

Vivienne nodded. "Not only are they well-connected, but they're vengeful people. I'd prefer not to get on the wrong side of them if I'm being honest."

The sheriff grunted in agreement. "I heard they've been known to destroy a town before by cutting off trade. Don't want that happening here in Havenwood."

His words sent a fresh wave of unease through me. If both the sheriff and Vivienne were wary of them, they must wield incredible power. Before I could dwell further on it, Vivienne and the sheriff turned away, pulling Gabriel into their discussion. I looked around, noticing Officer Reggie fidgeting by the door. He clearly wanted to say something but looked hesitant to interrupt. I stepped closer, hoping to help.

"Everything okay, Officer Reggie?" I asked gently.

He jumped, nearly knocking over a side table. "Oh, uh, no...well, yes! I mean..." He fumbled with his notepad, flipping through it nervously. "I saw something earlier, but I didn't think it was important. Now, though..."

I stepped closer, craning my neck to get a look at the pad. "What's going on?"

Reggie blushed furiously, his words tumbling out in a rush. "Oh, yes. Here it is," he said, reading from his notepad. "Savannah Chase mentioned getting a text message from an unknown number claiming to be Garrett Grimshaw. It said he'd snuck a phone from his kidnappers and wanted her to mobilize her followers for kelp. Wait." He scratched the back of his head and looked up at me, confusion in his eyes. "That doesn't make sense. Why would he want them to bring kelp?"

My breath caught. The world seemed to tilt for a fraction of a second as his words hit me. The kidnapping wasn't just a theory anymore, but a fact.

"You're sure that's what the message said?" I asked, my voice a shade too high.

Across the room, Gabriel stiffened, and the sheriff's head snapped up like he'd been struck.

"What's going on?" the sheriff demanded.

Officer Reggie squinted down at his notes. "Well..." He shifted nervously from foot to foot. "Oh. Wait. That might be a mistake. My handwriting can get a bit messy."

I exhaled, heart still pounding. "Do you think you maybe wrote 'help'?"

Reggie's face lit up. "Ah, yes. That makes way more sense than kelp. I couldn't figure out why a famous author would want fancy seaweed, but I thought it was maybe one of those celebrity fads."

"Reggie! For the love of—" Sheriff Jackson groaned, pinching the bridge of his nose. "You didn't think to mention this sooner?"

Reggie flinched. "Well," he hedged, a blush creeping up his cheeks, "the message didn't make much sense. Like, why would Garrett text Savannah and not call the police?"

My brow furrowed. "You're right," I muttered.

"See?" Officer Reggie said, snapping his fingers. "It's not like 911 is hard to remember."

"That is...surprisingly astute," Sheriff Jackson murmured.

"I know, right?" Reggie said. "It only took me about a week after I started at the police academy."

"And there it is," the sheriff muttered under his breath.

Gabriel chimed in. "You've got a point, Reggie. Why would Grimshaw message Savannah first? Why would he message her at all? Surely a phone call is faster and easier."

"That's what I thought!" Reggie said, clearly thrilled to have some validation. "It was suspicious, so I wrote it down."

"Next time, bring your suspicions to me right away," Sheriff Jackson said.

"Um..." Officer Reggie cleared his throat uncomfortably.

Sheriff Jackson took a deep breath and looked like he was mentally counting to ten. "What is it now, Reggie?"

"Well, after that thing with the tuna sandwiches, you told me to keep my suspicions to myself," Officer Reggie said.

Sheriff Jackson closed his eyes and shook his head. "If it has anything to do with deli sandwiches and alien conspiracies, I don't want to hear it. If it's kidnapping related, tell me everything."

Officer Reggie perked up. "Oh, that clears things up. Thanks, boss."

The sheriff waited expectantly. When Reggie didn't say anything, he prompted the officer. "Well? Is there anything else you wanted to tell me?"

Reggie looked confused. "Never eat three day old tuna sandwiches?"

The sheriff pinched his nose again. "About the *case*."

"Oh." Reggie paused to consider. "Well...no."

Vivienne sighed audibly, and Gabriel stifled a laugh with a cough so as not to hurt Officer Reggie's feelings.

"It doesn't add up," I said, refocusing. "Why reach out to Savannah unless the goal was exposure? She was about to go live before we picked her up, right? Maybe the kidnapper wanted Garrett's disappearance to go viral."

The sheriff nodded grimly. "That tracks. If she'd gone live, this story would've exploded. Reggie must've found and stopped her just in time."

Officer Reggie straightened, puffing out his chest. "Gee, thanks, boss! Didn't even know I was saving the day, but I'll take my hero medal whenever you're ready."

Sheriff Jackson shot him a flat look. "Your medal is the continued privilege of having a job, Reggie."

Reggie nodded solemnly. "I accept. Does it come with a plaque?"

The sheriff looked at the ceiling and shook his head. "I swear, one of these days—"

I zoned them out as my mind raced through the implications. I shuddered, imagining the chaos a viral announcement could cause. Not just for Havenwood, but for Garrett. I spoke up without thinking. "Why would the kidnapper want that kind of attention, though? What's their endgame? This is definitely pointing towards a crazy fan grabbing him, isn't it?"

"Don't jump to conclusions," the sheriff warned. "That's the surest way to miss something in an investigation."

Officer Reggie spoke up. "Speaking of investigations, I had Bill trace the phone. Turns out it was a burner, used once and shut off immediately. No way to track it."

The sheriff shot Reggie an impressed look, but before he could comment, Gabriel spoke up. "Aren't kidnappers supposed to want money? Why attract attention unless their goal isn't ransom?"

A silence settled over the room as that idea sank in.

"I hate to bring this up, but could Savannah really be behind it?" I asked hesitantly. "If she went live with a kidnapping, she'd make a fortune in views and engagement. Perhaps she never knew about the will and was looking to capitalize on her relationship in another way."

The sheriff tipped his head to the side, considering my words. "It's a possibility, I suppose, and we can't rule anything out at this point. However, I'll give her this: if she's acting, she's incredible at it."

I agreed with him, but she wasn't the only suspect on my list. "If it's not her, then what about a crazy Savannah fan?" I asked. "Someone obsessed, maybe. They might want publicity or think they're helping her somehow by boosting her profile with a scandal."

"Or," Gabriel said, tapping a finger thoughtfully, "what if they pretended to be Garrett and contacted her because they want her too? Like, they're fans of them as a couple."

"That's creepy," Officer Reggie said.

"But not impossible," the sheriff added.

"What if it's a ransom after all?" Reggie piped up. "Only, instead of getting the money from Garrett's family, they're trying to crowdsource it. You know, 'Help us save Garrett Grimshaw, donate now!'"

We all stared at him.

The sheriff blinked. "Reggie, that's—"

"A surprisingly decent theory?" Reggie grinned. "Yeah, I have those sometimes."

The sheriff sighed. "Disturbing, is what I was going to say."

I shivered. "If that's the case, then the masquerade isn't just about disrupting their plans. It's about making sure people don't fall for whatever scheme they're running."

"Which means," Gabriel said, his expression tightening, "we need to act fast."

Vivienne exhaled sharply, frustration etched into her features. "If we knew their motive, we'd have a better chance of stopping them. If they wanted attention for Garrett's disappearance, then having Gabriel take his place at the masquerade seems like the logical counter to their plans."

The sheriff nodded. "I agree. And it might force them to make a mistake. It's a gamble, but one I think we need to take at this point." He turned to Gabriel, his expression grave. "We'll be around, but you need to be ready for anything that might happen. And I do mean anything."

Nervous butterflies fluttered to life in my stomach. I wasn't sure I fully agreed with their plan. In fact, I thought it might lead to a worse outcome for Garrett—or Gabriel—but I didn't have any better alternatives at the moment.

Vivienne's gaze flicked briefly toward the window, then back to me. "Gabriel, Harper, a discreet sweep of the manor might be useful. Subtle, of course."

Her words were smooth, almost casual, but her gaze held mine and I caught the unspoken meaning. She wasn't just suggesting a stroll. She was asking for magic without directly mentioning the heartwood tree.

I nodded once, understanding passing between us. "We'll see what we can find."

Gabriel gave my hand a reassuring squeeze as we headed toward the door, but it didn't steady me the way I'd hoped. The nerves still danced under my skin, impossible to shake. The masquerade, Gabriel's illusion, and the unanswered questions all felt like we were rushing headlong into something far more dangerous than we realized.

As the door closed behind us, Gabriel leaned in. "Are you okay?"

I hesitated, glancing toward the window where the sun was starting to set, and dusk was creeping in. The sky was painted in bruised shades of orange and purple, and the first hints of night were beginning to press against the glass. The world felt too still, like it was holding its breath, waiting for something terrible to happen.

I clenched my hands into fists, willing myself to think, to be worthy of the trust Vivienne and the others had placed in me. They were counting on me to help find Garrett, and here I was, empty-handed. Useless.

I shoved the doubt down, forcing myself to breathe. I couldn't afford to second-guess myself now. I had to keep reaching, even if I didn't feel ready. Even if I didn't feel like I was enough.

There was something...right there, brushing the edges of my mind, a thread I hadn't quite caught yet. Savannah and Nate. Both standing to gain. Both restless, reckless in their own ways. Money. Fame. Independence. Was it possible they'd teamed up? Was I too slow to see it?

"Harper?" Gabriel asked softly. "What's going on?"

"I don't know," I admitted finally. "It just...feels like we're running out of time."

Gabriel nodded, his expression grim. "Then we'd better find him before the clock runs out."

His words sent a chill down my spine. I turned toward the window, watching as darkness swallowed the last of the daylight, and I couldn't shake the feeling that Garrett wasn't the only one in danger tonight.

A Tree-mendous Secret

ALTHOUGH VIVIENNE'S SUGGESTION MADE sense, I wasn't sure how well it would work in practice. The sapling heartwood trees Jeremiah and I had planted deep in the forest around Havenwood were still too young to fully grasp the nuances of a conversation. Communicating with them felt like trying to talk to toddlers. The only heartwood I could effectively connect with was the sapling near the original heartwood tree. That one felt ancient, wise, and far more equipped for verbal exchanges.

Still, being away from the heartwood made things more difficult, and I'd already pushed myself too hard while searching the forest for Garrett. But if this was how I could help, I'd give it my all.

Gabriel grabbed my coat from the closet near the front door and led me through the house to the back garden, which bordered the forest. I was grateful for the coat as soon as we walked outside, pulling it tighter around me. March in Connecticut was still crisp, and the air bit at my skin as the sun kissed the horizon line.

I closed my eyes, reaching for the connection to the heartwood tree. The bond wasn't just a faint thread; it pulsed within me, vibrant and alive. Its energy thrummed through my veins as I focused, sending out a silent call to its ancient presence.

"Harper," the heartwood greeted, its voice resonant in my mind. *"Checking in again?"*

"Yes." I replied mentally. *"Any updates? Have any of the saplings sensed the missing author?"*

A pause. I could almost feel the roots shifting beneath Havenwood, the vast network of trees stretching their awareness outward, listening. Finally, the heartwood responded.

"No alarms have been raised. If he passed through, it wasn't recently. Although he would have had to wander deep into the woods to reach one of the saplings planted beyond town."

My chest tightened. Not the worst news, but far from reassuring. *"If you or one of the saplings sees him, will you let me know right away?"*

"Absolutely."

The presence of the heartwood faded, and I opened my eyes to find Gabriel watching me, waiting.

"Anything?" he asked quietly.

I shook my head. "Not yet. The saplings haven't sensed him, but the heartwood is reaching out again now. If he's passed by one of them, we should know soon."

Gabriel nodded. "Especially with a ring of them surrounding Havenwood."

I scrubbed a hand over my face. "Yeah, but I'm not sure how much good that will do. We planted them deep in the forest so they wouldn't accidentally be discovered. He'd have to make it pretty far into the woods to walk past a sapling."

Gabriel nodded. "Between them and the wards Lucas is reinforcing around town and the property, hopefully we'll get something soon."

That made me pause. "He's reinforcing the wards?"

Gabriel sighed. "Yeah. Between tracking the phones and all the magic he put into those spells earlier, he's been stretched pretty thin. But he wanted to make sure nothing was slipping past us, so he's reinforcing everything he can."

I exhaled slowly. "That's a good call."

Gabriel nodded. "I agree. He's due to check in soon. If anything's tripped the magic around town, we'll know."

A door slammed behind us, making me jump. We turned to see Valerie and Vivienne walking onto the patio. They didn't see us hidden behind the evergreen shrubs, but their conversation carried clearly to us.

"Why are you forcing this event to continue?" Valerie exclaimed, her voice sharp with frustration.

Vivienne's tone remained calm. "I believe the best way to proceed is to hold the masquerade as planned. We need to force the kidnapper to act so we can counter."

"I don't agree," Valerie snapped, her voice rising. "The masquerade should be canceled! We should be out searching for Garrett, not playing dress-up! And why the gag order? Why can't we talk about this? The more eyes looking for him, the better."

Vivienne inclined her head slightly, the picture of composure. "I understand your concerns, Valerie. But these situations can spiral out of control quickly. Until we know what the kidnapper wants, keeping this quiet is the safest course of action. The sheriff and I agree: public attention is exactly what they're hoping for."

Valerie scoffed. "Right. Let's gamble on optics while he could be tied up in a basement somewhere. Brilliant plan."

"Why else hasn't there been a ransom demand?" Vivienne said coolly. "Let's just say... someone tried to stir things up online. We're not giving them the spotlight they want. By denying them what they want, we keep control."

Valerie crossed her arms, glaring. "And when someone notices Garrett isn't at his own masquerade? What then?"

"We've accounted for that with our plan to use a body double," Vivienne said coolly. "Our focus is on maintaining order, both for Garrett's sake and for Havenwood's reputation. Acting rashly could jeopardize both."

"You're more worried about the town than about him!" Valerie's voice cracked, her composure unraveling. "I know him better than anyone, and you didn't even ask my opinion. I can't—" Her words dissolved into a choked sob as she turned away, pressing a hand to her mouth.

Vivienne stepped forward, her hand outstretched. "It might be—"

"Don't!" Valerie jerked away, her shoulders shaking. "I can't do this."

Gabriel squeezed my hand briefly. "I'll be right back," he said softly.

I nodded, watching as he climbed the steps two at a time. He placed a gentle hand on Valerie's shoulder, murmuring something I couldn't hear. Together, he and Vivienne guided her back inside.

As the door closed behind them, the patio fell silent. The tension lingered in the cool evening air, and I wrapped my arms around myself, trying to shake the unease that had settled over me.

A resonant voice, like the whisper of wind through leaves mingled with the steady strength of roots, echoed softly through my mind, pulling me away from the tense exchange between Vivienne and Valerie.

"Harper?" the heartwood asked in my mind.

I closed my eyes, retreating into the quiet connection. *"I'm here. Did you find anything?"*

"I've spoken with the saplings just to confirm," it replied. *"None of them have seen anyone pass by today."*

A flicker of hope dimmed. *"Are you sure? We need to be absolutely certain."*

The heartwood hesitated. *"It doesn't rule out the forest completely, but..."*

"But it makes it unlikely, right?" I finished, my chest tightening. *"If he's not in the forest, then where could he be?"*

The heartwood seemed to shift in thought, its voice steady but unsure. *"Perhaps he took a road out of town that bypassed the saplings. Or maybe he's somewhere they couldn't see. Inside a building, perhaps? The saplings are still young, Harper. Their reach is limited."*

I bit my lip, thinking of the ley lines crisscrossing Havenwood, their power channeled and balanced by the heartwood trees. The saplings formed a protective circle around the town, acting as both guardians and conduits. They were vital to Havenwood's magical defenses, but I'd been hoping they could do more.

The heartwood seemed to sense my disappointment. *"I wish I could be more help,"* it said gently. *"But this kind of search isn't within our abilities. We can only sense what comes close or what touches our magic. Beyond that, it's difficult. Especially for the young trees."*

I let out a quiet sigh, my shoulders sagging. *"I understand. Thank you for trying. If you do see or hear anything—anything at all—please let me know right away."*

"Of course," it replied, a thread of warmth and reassurance weaving through its tone.

Just as I was about to end the connection, I heard voices—low and urgent—coming from the patio. I pressed my back against the shrubs, peeking through the branches. My heart skipped a beat.

It was Nate and Tiffany.

"Harper?" the heartwood asked, a note of concern in its voice. *"What's happening? I can feel your agitation."*

Instinctively, I kept my mental voice low. *"Two of my suspects just stepped outside, but I can't hear them. They're whispering. They're too quiet."* I hesitated, frustration mounting. *"I need to hear them, but—"*

Before I could finish, the heartwood's voice returned, tinged with a hint of mischief. *"Let me help."*

Suddenly, it was as if someone had placed a microphone next to Nate and Tiffany. Their words came through crystal clear, each hissed syllable carrying directly to me.

My jaw dropped. "Was that...you?" I whispered aloud.

"You're welcome," the heartwood said smugly.

A small smile tugged at my lips, despite the situation. *"Thank you,"* I thought, focusing on their conversation as Tiffany's sharp voice cut through my conversation with the heartwood.

"...messing everything up!" Tiffany snapped, wagging a finger under Nate's nose. Her tone was sharp, her ire barely concealed beneath the bitterness in her voice.

Nate huffed, crossing his arms. "You're one to talk."

Tiffany stiffened. "Don't give me that! You know what your father was planning. You need my money now, so don't act all high and mighty."

Their argument spilled out into the garden, the polished mother-son facade unraveling in front of me as Nate stormed away from his mother. The hostility between them was palpable, and it was becoming clearer with every word that there was far more going on than either of them had let on earlier. I cautiously peeked out from my hiding spot as the conversation continued.

Tiffany threw her hands in the air, exasperated. "You're impossible, Nate! I've done everything for you, and you still manage to screw it all up."

"Everything for me? That's a joke," Nate spat back, wheeling on her. "You've never done anything except try to control me. Maybe you should focus on your own mess for once."

She let out a sharp laugh, but it carried no humor. "Fine. Stay here and sulk. That's what you're good at, anyway."

Tiffany spun on her heel and stormed back inside, her movements sharp and deliberate. Nate, his jaw tight, watched her go before muttering something under his breath I couldn't quite catch and heading deeper into the garden, disappearing around a row of bushes.

I shifted behind the shrubs, my breath shallow as I processed what I'd just heard. Their words echoed in my mind, the bitterness and blame laced in every syllable. This wasn't just a heated family disagreement. It sounded like something had gone seriously wrong, and they were unraveling under the pressure.

Could they have Garrett hidden somewhere?

The thought buzzed in my head, relentless and unwelcome. If they were working together, it made sense. But their argument hinted at fractures in their relationship—fractures that might just give us the edge we needed to find Garrett.

But something about all this money talk wasn't sitting right.

Savannah had implied Nate wasn't hurting financially, so where was the desperation coming from? From being cut out of the will? And what about Tiffany? The Moncriefs were supposed to be old-money, powerful enough to crush a town's economy just by pulling their business. Why would she care about Garrett's will at all? Was this really about money, or was there something else I was missing?

The pieces weren't fitting the way they should. And that meant I was looking at the puzzle all wrong.

The heartwood's voice broke through my swirling thoughts. *"Harper, are you alright?"*

I blinked, pulling myself back to the mental connection. *"I'm fine, but I think I need more information."*

"Is there anything I can do?" the heartwood offered, its tone warm and reassuring.

"Nothing else at the moment unless you've got a spare espresso tree somewhere. I could really use some energy right about now. It's been a day, and it's nowhere near done yet."

The moment I thought it, a pulse of energy surged through me. My senses sharpened, my fatigue evaporated, and I felt like I could run a marathon without breaking a sweat.

"What was that?" I whispered, stunned.

"A little magical boost," the heartwood replied smugly. *"It's the least I can do to help."*

I grinned. *"This is better than coffee, and that's saying something coming from me. You should go into business."*

"I'd consider it, but I hear coffee shops are delightful, and I wouldn't want to compete."

I stifled a laugh. *"You're right. They are. Once this is over, I'll owe you a coffee picnic."*

"I'll hold you to that," the heartwood said, warmth radiating through our bond. *"But for now, focus on what's in front of you. You've got energy now. Use it wisely."*

With a renewed sense of purpose, I glanced around the garden, ensuring it was clear before slipping out of my hiding spot. I crept back toward the manor, replaying Tiffany's and Nate's argument in my mind.

If they had Garrett, it explained why they'd been sticking so close to each other. But if they didn't, what were they fighting about? Was it possible they were working together, but their plan had hit a snag? Or was one of them acting alone, and the other was starting to figure it out?

I chewed my lip, contemplating my next move. A part of me wanted to charge after Nate, demand answers, and shake loose whatever was lurking beneath the surface. But my dad had drilled two lessons into me growing up. The first was self-defense, and the second was common sense. Chasing down an angry man who might also be a kidnapper, or worse, wasn't smart. I needed backup. I needed Gabriel.

And time was running out.

The masquerade was looming, and if we were going to pull this off, I needed to be ready. I needed answers. I needed—

I nearly ran straight into Gabriel as I stepped inside. He steadied me instantly, his grip warm and familiar, but his expression sharpened with concern.

"Everything okay?" he asked, his gaze searching mine. "You look like you've seen a ghost."

I shook my head, though my mind was still racing. "No ghosts. Tiffany and Nate were arguing outside. It was...intense. I think they might be involved with what happened today, Gabriel. I can't shake the feeling they're hiding something."

His expression darkened, his jaw tightening. "What did they say?"

I relayed the conversation as best I could, watching as Gabriel's frown deepened.

"If they're holding Garrett, they'd need food, water, and a guard or someone watching him. Now that I think about it, there has to be someone else helping them. They've been here for hours," he said thoughtfully. "We need to watch them like hawks. If they're trying to contact someone, that could give us the break we need."

I nodded, my determination hardening. "We should start with their phones. Is there a way we can see what they're doing through Lucas' spell?"

"I'm not sure," Gabriel said, pulling out his phone and flicking through his messages. "But the sheriff still has them. He said he'd send a text when he released them."

"Well, what if they have a burner? Didn't Officer Reggie say that someone contacted Savannah using a burner? Did the sheriff pat them all down?"

Gabriel scrubbed a hand through his hair. "For phones? I don't know. But it's a possibility we can't ignore."

"If either of them tries to reach out to an accomplice holding Garrett, we need to stop them! If we don't, then this could turn out badly. So very badly. What if they..." I trailed off, the thought too horrible to voice.

Gabriel squeezed my hand, his touch grounding me. "Don't worry. We'll figure this out, Harper. Together."

I managed a small smile, but the knot of unease in my stomach didn't loosen. I just hoped his confidence wasn't misplaced.

Can You Hear Me Now?

GABRIEL AND I SPLIT up, each with a target in mind. He went to track down Nate, while I set off to find Tiffany. If they were behind this, they'd either try to escape or contact an accomplice who might be guarding Garrett. Either way, we had to stop them.

Instinctively, I headed toward the drawing room. If I were in their shoes and about to flee or make a desperate call, I'd want to gather my things first. Anything important, like a phone, a coat, a purse. It's a human instinct to make sure you don't leave anything behind.

I moved quickly, breaking into a jog as I scanned the halls, my ears straining for any hint of movement. Suddenly, Tiffany's sharp voice rang out from behind the drawing-room door.

"Well, I don't care what you say," she snapped. "I'm calling them now. Someone needs to do something about Garrett's disappearance, and if the sheriff won't, I will."

Valerie's calmer tone followed, though there was an edge of uncertainty. "But the sheriff said we weren't supposed to call anyone. He wouldn't even let me contact the publishers in New York. Everything here is on lockdown."

Tiffany sniffed loudly, her tone dripping with disdain. "That gruff old sheriff can't intimidate me. This is absurd. He's a small-town cop in a Podunk town. I'll fix this myself, even if I have to call the governor."

"Do you know the governor?" Valerie asked excitedly.

"That's not the point!" Tiffany snapped.

"It's exactly the point," Valerie replied.

I knew I had to intervene before either woman did something reckless. Taking a deep breath, I pushed the door open and stepped inside. "Excuse me, ladies," I said, summoning my best Isadora-inspired blend of politeness and authority. "I couldn't help but overhear. Valerie's right. Spreading the news isn't the sheriff's plan, and for good reason. We're trying to handle this carefully to protect Garrett."

Tiffany turned on me, her eyes blazing. "How dare you say that when you're doing nothing to find him?" She waved a phone at me.

I stiffened. That wasn't the phone the sheriff had taken, I was sure of it.

A chill swept over me. So, we were right. She had a second phone. And if it wasn't shielded by Lucas' spell, then whoever was out there holding Garrett might've already heard from her.

My pulse spiked. I opened my mouth, then closed it again, scrambling for the right response as dread sank like a stone in my stomach. I needed to shut this down before she made everything worse.

Maybe she'd brought a backup herself, or maybe she'd found someone careless enough to loan her one. Either way, she was seconds away from causing the exact kind of chaos we'd been trying to avoid.

"There's no way you could possibly have Garrett's best interests at heart if you refuse to let us use the public," Tiffany snapped, stepping closer, thumb hovering over the screen. "The world deserves to know he's missing! This is insane!"

Panic flared in my chest. If she hit send, there'd be no way to contain the story or the fallout. I took a small step back, hands raised in an effort to keep the situation from escalating. "No one is saying we don't want to find Garrett—"

"But you're stopping us!" she snapped, closing the distance between us. "Every second wasted is a second we could be gathering people to help.

The entire world could be looking for him, but instead, you're all just standing here—"

I forced my expression into something neutral. "Where did you get that?" I said carefully, pointing at the phone before meeting hers again.

Her grip tightened, and her lips thinned. "It doesn't matter."

"Did someone contact you?" I pressed, my mind flashing back to what Officer Reggie said about someone with a burner contacting Savannah. "Is that why you want to go public so badly?"

For a fraction of a second, something flickered across her face. Maybe guilt? Hesitation? Or perhaps just a flash of calculation? But it was gone as quickly as it appeared.

She lifted her chin, and her expression darkened. "All I care about is finding Garrett. Who is still missing! Possibly hurt! Or worse! And you're all standing around doing nothing!" Her voice rose with every word, her frustration boiling over. "You're acting like this is some stupid game while he's out there. Alone, terrified, maybe even dying! All because you're too scared to make waves!"

Her phone slashed through the air as she gestured wildly. She stepped closer, her breath short and ragged. She was furious now, her emotions teetering on the edge of control. I stood my ground, though her anger was making my pulse race. She was so close, I feared she might accidentally hit me with her phone.

I forced myself to hold my ground, though every instinct screamed at me to back away. "We're not scared. We're being careful."

"Careful?" she spat. "Is that what you call sitting on your hands while my son's father is missing?" Her grip on her phone was white knuckled now, and I half-expected her to throw it at my head. "Do you even care, or is this just a fun little puzzle for you to solve?"

I swallowed back my own frustration, forcing my voice to stay even. "You know that's not fair."

"Oh, but *this* is fair?" she shot back. "Locking me out? Keeping me from doing the one thing that might actually help? You don't get to make that call!"

Her fury burned hot, threatening to consume everything in its path. But through the rage, something clicked in my brain.

Rather than flinch or step back, I took a small step forward. As expected, Tiffany's wild gesturing knocked into my shoulder, but I braced myself for the collision. The shock on her face was immediate; she hadn't expected me to step into her motion. Her grip on her phone wasn't tight enough and, as I'd hoped, it flew out of her hand.

"Oh, my goodness!" I exclaimed, crouching quickly to scoop it up.

Tiffany stared at me, caught off guard. "Watch what you're doing! You should be more careful," she snapped.

"I really hope it's not broken," I said, feigning concern as I turned the phone over in my hands. "The screen looks fine. Thank goodness. These falls can be so unpredictable, though. Sometimes even a tiny bump can mess up the internal hardware."

I babbled on, my nervous chatter serving as cover while I pulled on my magic. The phone warmed in my hands as I worked, redirecting its circuits to render it completely inert.

"Is it a newer model?" I asked, pretending to examine it. "I hope so. Some of the older ones don't handle drops well at all. They just...poof." I mimed an explosion with my hands, flashing an apologetic smile. "Technology these days, am I right?"

Tiffany snatched the phone back. "Yes, well, it's fine. Thank you for picking it up," she added grudgingly.

I nodded politely. "Of course. If you need anything else, just let me know."

"No, just privacy," Tiffany said pointedly, dismissing me with a wave.

"Of course," I repeated, backing out of the room. I lingered just outside, leaving the door slightly ajar so I could eavesdrop.

Inside, Tiffany's voice rose again. "I'm calling to report a crime. I want every local news network to know about Garrett's kidnapping. Now all I need to do is—" She paused.

"What is it?" Valerie asked.

"The only phone I had left won't turn on," Tiffany grumbled, her confusion quickly giving way to irritation. "It wasn't even that far of a fall! I've dropped this thing a hundred times before, and it always worked. I swear, they don't make phones like they used to."

"Well, you said it was important," Valerie reminded her. "Why don't you just call from mine? The sheriff finally returned it to me after I pressured him with threats of bad publicity for this town if he kept me from contacting my work any longer."

"Why do you get your phone back and I don't?" Tiffany gave a very unladylike snort. "Besides, it's not as if I memorize people's phone numbers anymore. Really, Valerie, we aren't living in the stone age."

"Well, how are you going to reach out then?" Valerie asked.

"I don't know!" Tiffany exclaimed, but her frustration was tinged with helplessness.

I smiled to myself. As I slipped away, satisfaction curled in my chest. Her phone was now a very expensive paperweight, thanks to a bit of creative spellwork with my metal magic.

Part of me felt a pang of guilt, but another, larger part, the part that cared about Garrett's safety, felt justified.

One down, one to go.

I was already dialing Gabriel as I slipped into the hall. If Tiffany had a secret phone, odds were Nate did too, and I was done giving anyone the benefit of the doubt.

Round Two Goes To...

I KNEW SABOTAGING TIFFANY's phone wasn't a long-term solution, but it would hopefully buy us enough time to figure out what was really going on. Now, I just needed to find Nate and either take my suspicions to the sheriff or cross him off my suspect list. Time was flying by, and I needed to start whittling the list down.

As I rounded the corner, I crashed directly into Mindy.

"Oh!" she gasped, papers flying everywhere. "I'm so sorry! I wasn't watching where I was going."

"No, it's my fault," I said, already crouching to gather the scattered papers. "I wasn't paying attention either. We really need to stop meeting like this."

Mindy shot me a small smile. "I swear, I'm not usually this clumsy. This whole situation has got me on edge."

"Understandably so," I sympathized, gathering a handful of pages. "I can't even imagine what this day has been like for you."

Mindy sighed, her movements hurried as she scrambled to collect the mess. "It's been...a lot," she admitted, shoving some loose pages into a file folder.

I crouched closer to her, picking up more loose pages. "Speaking of a lot, do you really think one of Garrett's fans could be behind this?"

She let out a small, humorless laugh. "Oh, I compiled a list of the more intense ones, and I sent it over to the sheriff. But, honestly, between you and me, I don't think anyone on that list did it."

"Why not?" I asked, curious.

Mindy shifted, biting her lip. "You start to get a feel for the fan mail after a while. The weird stuff—the handwritten poems, the love letters, even the occasional marriage proposal—that's all par for the course. But this?" She shook her head firmly. "This feels calculated. Like someone with a lot more to lose than a fan upset about a plot twist."

I frowned, reaching for another sheet. "But if that's a stretch and it's not a fan lashing out, who else would care enough to send threats?"

Mindy hesitated. "That's the part that's bothering me."

A chill prickled at the back of my neck. "Okay," I said slowly. "What about Albus? Garrett's editor? Do you think he could shed any light on this?"

She snorted softly, her tone dismissive. "Albus? Not likely. He's on a two-week holiday in Italy with his wife. The man hates being anywhere near New York during a launch. Claims it interferes with his process or something." She gave a small shrug. "He doesn't even do follow-up calls after the back and forth over the edits once a book has been sent to print."

"I didn't realize," I murmured, filing the information away.

We both reached for the last few papers, and that's when I saw a large manila envelope on the floor. My stomach flipped when I spotted Garrett Grimshaw's name scrawled across the front, along with the title of his book. Beneath it, someone had written, in sharp, urgent letters, *Contingency Plan???* The three question marks were written with such ferocity that I could see tears on the envelope.

Before I could fully process what I was looking at, Mindy snatched the envelope from my hands. "I'll take that," she said quickly, pressing it tightly to her chest.

"Right...of course," I murmured, still trying to make sense of what I'd just seen.

Mindy stood and hastily straightened the pile of papers she'd gathered. Her too-bright smile did little to hide the tension radiating off her. "Thanks for helping with the papers, Harper. I should get these back to

Valerie before she sends out a search party for me," she said, laughing awkwardly. "You know how it is. So much to do, running around..."

Her rushed words made my instincts flare. "Do you need help with anything?" I asked. "If there's something I can do—"

"Oh, no," she interrupted, her voice unnaturally high-pitched. "No, I've got it handled. Just lots going on. Valerie is really depending on me to come through in this time of crisis and I...well, I should get to it. Thanks, though." She backed away, giving me a small, awkward finger wave from under her pile of papers before hurrying off, leaving me standing there with more questions than answers.

I watched her retreat, my gut twisting. *She's lying,* I thought. *Badly.* Whatever was in that envelope, Mindy clearly didn't want me to see it. And that, more than anything she'd said, sent a chill down my spine.

What had I just glimpsed? Did she know more about Garrett's disappearance than she was letting on? Or was I reading too much into an innocent situation? Perhaps that note had been about his book launch, not his kidnapping.

My heart thudded as I made a split-second decision. Garrett's life might depend on what Mindy was hiding, and we couldn't afford to waste time. I set off after her, determined to find out what she knew.

A loud noise interrupted my thoughts. Angry shouts reverberated down the hall. My feet moved that direction before my brain could catch up. By the time I tracked the source of the noise through the echoing expanse of the manor's hallways to the open foyer at the front of the house, Nate and Gabriel were squared off, glaring at each other.

Nate stepped forward, nearly nose-to-nose with Gabriel. "You don't know what you're talking about," he growled. "Calling me pampered? You're just a spoiled little rich boy living in his mama's house with no idea what real stakes look like."

Gabriel's tone remained calm but firm. "This isn't about me or you, Nate. It's about doing the right thing. We're all under a lot of pressure, but losing control isn't going to help anyone. Least of all your father."

Nate's eyes narrowed, his face flushing with anger. "Losing control?" he spat. "You think I'm out of control? You have no idea what I'm dealing with!"

"Nate," Gabriel said, his voice steady but quiet. "I get it. You're frustrated. But throwing blame around isn't going to help bring your father home safely."

The words barely left Gabriel's mouth before Nate lunged forward, his fist flying. "You don't know a thing about it!" he roared. Gabriel ducked under the swing, sidestepping with practiced ease, but Nate didn't back down. He swung again, this time connecting with Gabriel's shoulder hard enough to make him stumble.

My breath caught in my throat as the room exploded into full-blown chaos. Gabriel retaliated with a sharp shove to Nate's chest, forcing him back a step. Nate growled, charging forward like a bull, his arms swinging wildly. Gabriel blocked one punch and barely dodged another as it grazed by his cheek, but the movement sent them crashing into a side table. The sound of breaking glass filled the room as a decorative vase toppled to the floor, shattering into pieces.

"Stop this!" Gabriel barked, his tone sharp, but Nate wasn't listening. He lunged again, his anger boiling over as he grabbed Gabriel by the collar, trying to throw him off balance.

This was getting out of hand, but what could I do? Stepping between two men throwing punches wasn't just reckless—it was asking for trouble. Still, I had to do something. My father's voice echoed in my mind: *Wait for your moment, Harper. Don't act until you see your opening.*

That's when I saw it. The edge of Nate's phone glinted in his pocket as Gabriel twisted out of his grip.

Wait a second...

He'd been outside, throwing a tantrum. He hadn't been inside long enough to grab anything, and I knew for a fact that he hadn't gotten his phone back from the sheriff yet. So where had Nate gotten one?

A sick feeling curled in my gut. It seemed like this confirmed my worst-case scenario suspicions. I'd gotten a good look at Tiffany's burner and if they matched...

Gabriel had the fight handled. Nate was too caught up in his rage to notice anything else.

This was my opening.

I pulled on my magic, yanking the phone free just as Nate lunged at Gabriel again. It slid out of his pocket and hit the floor, skidding a few feet away. I focused on the small device, reaching out with my magic. The metallic components hummed in my mind as I gave a sharp tug, pulling the phone back towards the fight.

It slid just in time. Gabriel shifted his weight, and his heel came down hard on the phone with a satisfying crunch. The sound echoed through the tense room.

"Stop!" I shouted, waving my arms and stepping forward. "What are you doing? This isn't helping anyone!"

Both men pulled back, but Nate's glare never wavered. His shoulders heaved with the effort of controlling his temper, his fists still clenched tight at his sides. Gabriel, to his credit, didn't break eye contact. His stance was ready but calm, even as his chest rose and fell with exertion. The tension in the air crackled like electricity. Then Nate's gaze dropped to the shattered remains of his phone under Gabriel's boot, and his expression darkened.

"You broke my phone," Nate spat, his voice dripping with indignation.

Gabriel straightened, adjusting the cuffs of his shirt with deliberate calm. "Consider it collateral damage. Maybe now you'll actually focus on finding your father instead of picking fights."

Nate let out a bitter laugh, bending down to scoop up the broken phone. He turned it over in his hands, his face twisting with frustration at the shattered screen. "Unbelievable," he muttered. "You think you're so much better than me, don't you?" With a disgusted noise, he tossed it toward Gabriel, who caught it easily. "You owe me a new phone," Nate sneered.

"That's enough," I cut in, channeling every ounce of my father's command voice into my tone. Both men looked at me in surprise as I leveled them with a steely stare I learned from my mother. My voice was low and firm, the kind that demanded attention without needing to be loud. "I don't know how you handle things in New York, Nate, but here in Havenwood, we don't settle disagreements with fists. Everyone's under pressure, but that doesn't give you an excuse to act like this."

Nate's jaw clenched, but he didn't back down. "Tell that to *him*," he shot back, pointing at Gabriel. "He's the one who—"

"You threw the first punch," I interrupted sharply. "So don't try to shift the blame. Take a walk, Grimshaw. Now."

Nate narrowed his eyes at me, his jaw working as if he were biting back a response. Finally, he let out a huff, running a hand through his touseled hair. "Whatever. Do whatever you want. It's not like I expected any of you to actually figure this out or even care about my dad." His tone was dripping with sarcasm, but there was no fight left in his stance.

He turned toward the door, muttering something under his breath that I couldn't quite catch, and shoved it open with more force than necessary. The sound of the door slamming echoed through the foyer as he stormed out.

I exhaled, turning to Gabriel. "Are you okay?" My eyes scanned him for any signs of injury.

Gabriel touched his cheek, wincing slightly. "I'm fine. He grazed me with one lucky punch, but clearly no one ever taught him how to box."

"Where did you learn to?" I shook my head. "Wait. Not the point. Where do you think he's going?" I asked quietly, jerking a thumb towards where Nate had disappeared.

Gabriel shook his head. "He's not going anywhere. The drivers have the car keys, and on top of Lucas' spell, his phone is broken. If he wants to leave, he'll have to do it on foot, and that's not exactly practical."

"At least we don't have to worry about his phone anymore," I muttered.

Gabriel's lips quirked into a smile. "Yeah, kind of a strange coincidence that it slid under my foot at precisely the right time."

I shrugged, fighting to keep my face completely innocent. "The universe has a perverse sense of justice." I held the expression for a beat longer and then winked. "Or maybe it was just magic."

Gabriel threw an arm around my shoulders and squeezed me to his side. "That's my girl. Did you find Tiffany?"

I nodded. "Unfortunately, her phone met a similar fate," I said before catching him up on my encounter with Tiffany. His expression darkened as I explained her attempt to call the media.

"She was going to announce the kidnapping?" he asked, his tone incredulous. "The sheriff's been clear. There's supposed to be no outside contact. She could've blown this whole thing wide open."

"Exactly. But I was more focused on how she planned to do it. You said the sheriff hadn't released anyone's phone."

"He didn't. So how did she have one? And for that matter, how did Nate?" Gabriel shook his head. "Having two phones is shady enough, but not turning them over to the police when asked? Now that makes them both look really suspicious."

"Exactly my point. I think both she and Nate had alternate phones this entire time. I said, exhaling heavily. "That's why I had to destroy her phone's hardware. But now I'm worried we could be running out of time until Sheriff Jackson is forced to give their devices back. I have a feeling the first call she's making will announce to the world that Garrett Grimshaw is missing. We need to locate him before that happens. Does the sheriff have any new leads?"

Gabriel exhaled sharply, running a hand through his hair. "We've bought ourselves a little time, but we need to act fast if we want to find Garrett before Tiffany and Nate make their move."

I nodded, but hesitation flickered in my mind. "If they're even behind it. We don't know for sure. I don't want to accuse an innocent person even if he did just throw a punch at you."

"Fair enough." Gabriel dropped his hand, his expression tightening. "So, what do we do now?"

Determination flared in my chest. "We snoop," I said simply. "We find out what they're hiding, whatever it takes. If they are behind Garrett's kidnapping, then we're one step closer to finding him. If they aren't, we can redirect our efforts to the real culprits."

Gabriel nodded, his expression determined. "Let's do it."

I opened my mouth to agree but paused when I caught a glimpse of movement outside the window. Nate, his shoulders tense, was pacing back and forth near the tree line, a dark scowl etched into his face. He stopped, tugged something from his pocket, and took a long drag from what I could only assume was a vape. His head tilted as though he were lost in thought, or maybe trying to pull himself together.

"There he is," I said quietly, tipping my chin toward the window.

Gabriel followed my gaze, his frown deepening. "Still fuming. This won't end well if we push too hard."

"Maybe not," I replied, my mind already spinning with a plan. "But it's also our best chance to get him talking."

Gabriel turned to me, incredulous. "Harper, you're not seriously thinking—"

I cut him off with a small, placating gesture. "I'll go talk to him. He's angry, but if I approach him calmly, maybe I can get him to open up. You, on the other hand, are the last person he wants to see right now."

Gabriel's expression darkened as he followed my gaze to where Nate paced angrily near the tree line. "Harper, if you're about to suggest going out there alone, the answer is no."

I sighed, already anticipating his resistance. "I'm not going out there to fight him, Gabriel. I'm going to talk to him. Right now, he's angry enough to spit nails, but if I approach him calmly—"

"No," Gabriel interrupted, his tone sharper than usual. "He took a swing at me, and now you're volunteering for round two?"

I crossed my arms, holding his gaze. "If we don't get him talking, we'll miss an opportunity to figure out if he knows anything. You said it yourself—this might not end well if we push too hard but doing nothing isn't an option either."

He scrubbed a hand through his hair, frustration radiating off him. "If he's hiding something, he's not just going to spill it because you show up with a smile."

"Not a smile," I said, already moving toward the door. "Cookies."

"Cookies?" he repeated, incredulous, trailing after me.

"Or whatever Jacques has ready. He made enough snacks to feed an army," I said, quickening my pace toward the kitchen. "If there's one thing I've learned since moving to Havenwood, it's that people usually underestimate the power of food to disarm a situation."

Gabriel followed me into the kitchen. I made my request and Jacques, ever efficient, handed me a neatly arranged plate of cookies within minutes. I murmured my thanks, marveling at how much easier it already was becoming to navigate the sprawling manor.

Gabriel leaned against the counter, arms crossed, his frown firmly in place. "Harper, this is still a terrible idea."

"It's not," I replied, adjusting the plate in my hands. "But you're coming with me."

His eyebrows shot up. "I can't go out there. He'll clam up the second he sees me."

"Yes," I said with a pointed look. "That's why he won't see you."

The realization hit, but his shoulders didn't relax like I expected. "You want me to cast an illusion."

"Exactly," I said. "You stay close, invisible, and listen to everything. If he's hiding something, this might be our best chance to find out."

Gabriel hesitated, glancing toward the window. "And you're absolutely sure about this?"

I stepped closer, lowering my voice. "I can handle Nate, but I'll feel a lot better knowing you're there."

He exhaled slowly, his jaw tightening. "Fine. But if this goes south—"

"You'll step in," I finished, smiling softly. "I know."

He muttered something under his breath, but the air shimmered faintly as he cast his illusion. His form blurred, then disappeared entirely, though I could just barely make out the distortion when he moved. His disembodied voice was low and resigned. "Let's get this over with."

I took a steadying breath, balancing the plate of cookies in front of me like a shield, and pushed open the door. Gabriel's unseen presence was both comforting and unnerving as I stepped onto the porch.

Gabriel was right. This wasn't just a conversation—it was round two. Nate had already thrown one punch, but with a little luck, maybe I'd land the knockout blow this time.

With my heart pounding, I rounded the corner of the house and spotted him pacing near the tree line. His scowl deepened as he saw me approach, and I tightened my grip on the plate. Time to step into the ring.

Seams Suspicious

I MADE EXTRA NOISE as I approached so Nate wouldn't be startled. He glanced over, his brows furrowing in irritation the moment he saw me. "What are you doing here? Coming to finish what your boyfriend started?"

I kept my voice calm. "No, just bringing a peace offering." I held out the plate of cookies. "I know tensions are high, and we could all use something to take the edge off."

Nate snorted. "Yeah, sure. Like cookies will fix everything."

"Maybe not everything," I said lightly. "But they might help. Look, we're all on the same team here. You might not like the sheriff's playbook, but he has experience with situations like this. We need to let him call the shots."

He glanced at the cookies, then back at me. "And you've handled kidnappings before?"

I raised an eyebrow. "Not exactly. Have you?"

He huffed, taking a cookie. "No."

Before I could work on building a bridge between us, Tiffany's sharp voice cut through the air behind us. "Nate! I need you! Where are you?"

Nate closed his eyes, letting his head fall back in exasperation. By the time Tiffany rounded the corner, though, his expression transformed into one of forced patience. "Yes, Mother, what is it?"

"My phone isn't working," she snapped, visibly flustered. "I need to use yours."

"Sorry," Nate said, his tone clipped. "There was an...altercation, and my phone didn't survive. If you need to make a call, you can use one of the landlines. Or, um..." he shot a nervous look at me. "Ask the sheriff for, well, you know."

Tiffany's gaze darted to me as well. "Hmph," she snorted, her composure slipping. I resisted the urge to smirk. She clearly didn't want to admit she'd been planning to undermine the sheriff's orders by using her son's extra phone. Score one for me. But how to turn the situation to my advantage?

"Would you mind telling me a little about Garrett? Maybe understanding his relationships or habits could help us figure out the kidnapper's motive," I suggested.

Nate shook his head, staring off into the distance again as he sucked on his vape. "I don't know why anybody would want to kidnap my dad. He's an author. Not only that, he's a *fiction* author. It's not like he would have gotten anybody hurt. He wrote about imaginary characters doing unbelievable things. Some people found his books entertaining."

"A fairly large number of people," I said. "But I've heard his last few books weren't as well received. Did that bother him?"

Tiffany waved a manicured hand. "You own a bookshop, you must read. If not the books, at least the reviews. The ones for this book were nowhere near as good as his previous novels. And he even went so far as to kill off Rhett Ryder, his main character, in *Masks of Deception*. Why would he ruin the one thing keeping him relevant?"

I turned to Nate, tilting my head. "That must've been frustrating for you, losing a steady source of income."

Nate opened his mouth, but Tiffany cut in with a scoff. "Oh, please. Garrett married me for my money, not the other way around. Nate doesn't need Garrett's royalties. He has full access to the Moncrief trust fund. I was the one who supported Garrett in the beginning, the one who kept him afloat so he could write." She lifted her chin. "We'll be fine, no matter what Garrett writes or doesn't write."

I looked at Tiffany, frowning. "Then why are you here?" I asked, the words slipping out before I could think better of it. "If it's not about money, and you don't care about his writing anymore...why come at all? Why bring Nate?"

Tiffany inhaled sharply, like she was about to snap, but then something in her expression shifted. The anger didn't fade, but it morphed into something raw.

"Because," she said, her voice quieter now, "no matter how much of a mess Garrett and I were, no matter how much I've moved on, he's still Nate's father. And Nate...despite how he acts, despite what he says, he still wants his father to care about him."

Her gaze flicked toward Nate, something unspoken passing between them. "Garrett made a promise. He told Nate he'd spend real time with him this week. Not a public event, not an interview, just them. No distractions, no books, no fiancée. Just father and son. But in my heart, I knew better than to believe it."

She let out a sharp breath, her composure wobbling. "This isn't my first book launch. I know exactly how Garrett operates. He gets swept up in the moment and forgets everything but smiling for his adoring fans. I knew that if I didn't come, if I didn't force Garrett to keep his word, Nate would be let down all over again. And once Garrett marries that *influencer*, things are just going to get worse. So, I came to make sure my son didn't get hurt. Again."

She swallowed hard, shaking her head. "And then Garrett disappeared. And now, instead of some half-hearted attempt at fatherhood, Nate is caught up in all of this, the police are eyeing us suspiciously, as if we'd have anything to do with this, and Garrett...Garrett is still gone."

Her voice faltered, and for the first time, her icy exterior cracked. "I just...I don't know where he is, and it's terrifying." Her eyes darted away, as if she was embarrassed to admit it. "If something's happened to him..." she trailed off, blinking fast, and then took a deep breath, steadying herself.

Nate hesitated only a second before wrapping an arm around her shoulders, his irritation giving way to something softer. "It's okay, Mom," he murmured.

She gave a small, tight nod, swallowing hard before straightening. "I can't afford to fall apart. We need to keep looking. All of us," she said to me, her voice brittle but sincere. "Please." The whispered word came out almost as a half-broken sob. She wiped her tears away quickly and excused herself, hurrying off toward the house.

That was the first real crack in her armor I'd seen—something raw and vulnerable breaking through the disdain and arrogance. As I watched her retreating figure, unease stirred in my gut. Either she was an Oscar-worthy actress, or she genuinely wasn't involved in Garrett's disappearance. My instincts told me it was the latter.

"She doesn't know anything," Nate said suddenly, as if reading my mind. His tone was quiet, but there was an edge of defensiveness. "She's really torn up about him being missing. You shouldn't have pushed her like that."

I exhaled, watching the tension in Nate's shoulders as he stared out over the grounds. He wasn't giving anything away, but I could feel the anger rolling off him in waves.

"I'm sorry," I said softly. "But I had to ask. This is about your father."

Nate's jaw tightened, his gaze fixed on the horizon. "You're barking up the wrong tree if you think my mother had anything to do with this."

I wasn't convinced. "Then help me figure out where to look," I pressed. "The sheriff found documents in the car that indicated significant changes to your father's will. Savannah is set to inherit the lion's share of his estate. Did you know anything about that?"

His head snapped toward me, his scowl deepening. "What?"

I studied his face carefully. That wasn't a faked reaction. He was genuinely caught off guard.

"You didn't know?" I asked.

"No," he muttered after a moment. "But it doesn't surprise me. Dad changed his will every six months. It was his favorite form of control. His version of the carrot and the stick, depending on his mood." He looked away, jaw tightening. "If he cut me out again, fine. That's not news. But Savannah? As the primary?" He let out a low, disbelieving laugh. "Guess I should've seen that one coming."

"There's a lot of animosity between you and Savannah. What happened?" I asked, letting the question hang between us.

Nate scoffed. "Who knows? Ever since she got her claws in my dad, things haven't been the same. Maybe I didn't smile right for the photos. Perhaps he figured I'd be fine with the Moncrief trust fund. Maybe Savannah convinced him she deserved it. I don't know and I don't care."

His words said one thing, but the tension in his jaw, the way his hands curled into fists, told another story.

"Your mother is still in there too," I pointed out. "And she didn't seem particularly interested in his money." I took a slow breath. "Savannah, though... she had something to gain. A lot, actually. Maybe she knows more than she's letting on."

Nate didn't respond. I watched him closely, waiting for...something. There. His jaw ticked to the side. He knew it too.

Tiffany might not be part of this. But Savannah? She was climbing my suspect list fast.

"You think she's behind this, don't you?" I asked, my voice quiet.

Nate let out a sharp laugh, dripping with disdain. "Trust me, she's not behind this. She doesn't have the brains. She's just some dumb blonde. Same kind he always goes for. But if I know my dad, Savannah won't be around for long."

"Oh?" I prompted, hoping he'd elaborate.

Nate nodded emphatically. "Trust me, I know the man. Fiancées come and go. They always have since he split with my mother. This thing with Savannah? It's just history repeating itself. She's a flash in the pan, nothing more."

I took a breath, then looked back at Nate. "You know what doesn't add up for me, though?" I asked, keeping my tone light. "I got a look at the person driving the car when Garrett vanished. That person was wearing a dark jacket. We found a missing button in the car that matched the drivers' jackets, but it didn't come from any of theirs."

Nate froze. His eyes snapped to mine, sharp with sudden focus. "What are you implying?"

"I'm not implying anything. I'm saying outright the button matches the jacket Savannah made for you. Those buttons are distinctive and easy to match," I replied evenly. "So where is it?"

His jaw tightened, and a flash of irritation crossed his face. "I haven't even worn it. It's in my garment bag with my costume for the masquerade."

"Then you won't mind if I take a look."

Nate's lips pressed into a thin line. "Why should I let you? You're not with the police. You don't even have the authority to ask me that."

My stomach flipped, but I forced my expression to remain neutral. "You're right. I'm not a cop." I met his gaze evenly, then pulled out my phone. "So, let's call Sheriff Jackson. We can bring in the Silverthornes too. And Savannah. I bet she'd recognize your jacket on sight."

His jaw ticked again. Bingo.

I tilted my head, keeping my tone light. "Unless, of course, you'd rather just show me now?"

He scowled, and for a moment, I thought he was going to dig his heels in. But then he muttered something under his breath and turned toward the house. "Fine. Follow me. But don't touch anything."

Relief mixed with a flicker of triumph as I followed him inside. As we walked, I caught a shimmer out of the corner of my eye. It was the faint outline of Gabriel's illusion trailing us. Knowing he was close by eased some of the tension coiled in my chest.

When we reached the room the Silverthornes had set aside for him to dress for the masquerade, Nate moved to the closet and unzipped a hanging garment bag. "See?" he said, pulling back the flaps to reveal his costume. It was a ridiculous, over-the-top ensemble complete with a mask, boots, and a feathered hat.

He pushed the costume aside, his movements growing sharper, more frantic. "The other bag! It's gone," he muttered, voice tight with disbelief. He rifled through the closet again, then stopped cold. His shoulders stiffened.

"Oh. Wait. No. I—I threw it back at her."

I narrowed my eyes. "What?"

"Savannah," he said, already defensive. A flush crept up his neck. "She brought me this stupid coat that looked just like the drivers' uniforms. I told her I wasn't staff. That I wasn't wearing it. Said she could find someone else for her deranged bellhop cosplay."

He swallowed hard, realization crashing down. "My dad took it. He shoved it in the back of his car when we were packing up."

I stared at him. "The same car he was taken in?"

Nate's eyes met mine. They were wide and too full of something I couldn't quite read. Was it guilt? Or shock?

Or a carefully rehearsed performance?

My pulse kicked up. If he was telling the truth, then the kidnappers hadn't stolen a disguise. They'd been handed a perfect one. No questions asked.

Supposedly.

My heart thudded harder. Coincidences like that didn't just happen. Not when every piece of the puzzle was lining up too perfectly. Did they?

Maybe the kidnappers had just gotten lucky.

Or maybe someone made sure they had exactly what they needed.

Someone who knew Garrett's schedule. Someone who had access to his things and who could hand over a disguise without anyone batting an eye. Someone like his son.

I studied Nate again, this time not as someone worried about his father, but as someone at the center of a very convenient series of events.

The jacket. The route. The timing.

Occam's razor said that the simplest explanation is often the right one. And right now, every breadcrumb on the trail was pointing straight at Nate.

Draped in Doubt

THE SHERIFF MET US just as we stepped back into the manor. That was fast. Especially since I hadn't called him.

A faint brush against my fingers made me pause, the barest whisper of warmth and air. *Gabriel.*

The sheriff barely spared me a glance as he crossed the threshold, his tone brisk and no-nonsense.

"Harper," he said. "Gabriel said you needed me. You've done your part. I'll take it from here."

I hesitated, glancing at Nate.

The sheriff looked between us. "Unless you've changed your mind—"

"No," I said quickly. "I haven't."

"In that case," he said, shifting his attention. "I'd like to have a word with the younger Mr. Grimshaw."

He held my gaze for half a second—just long enough to send a silent message.

Don't blow Gabriel's cover.

I hesitated only a moment before following his directive. As the sheriff led Nate away, I paused in the hallway, The mansion buzzed with activity. Trays of food glimmered in the warm light, and the hum of preparation filled the space with Vivienne's signature meticulous style. Yet, even as life carried on around me, my thoughts remained tethered to that closed door. Sheriff Jackson questioning Nate, the missing jacket, and all the unanswered questions of the night.

"Harper!" A familiar voice broke through the noise, and I turned to see Bella weaving her way toward me, her smile as radiant as ever.

"Bella!" I exclaimed. I hurried to meet her, pulling her into a hug. Her presence was like a lifeline, steady and comforting.

"You're always here when I need you," I murmured, the weight of the past few hours momentarily lifting.

Bella gave me a reassuring squeeze before pulling back to study my face. "How are you holding up? I haven't heard a peep from you, and I was starting to worry."

I sighed, the exhaustion settling deeper in my bones. "I'm sorry, Bella. It's just...it's been a lot."

Her brows knitted with concern. "I can imagine. Have they found Garrett yet?"

I shook my head. "No. We're no closer to answers than we were earlier. What about Spellbooks? Was everything okay at the shop?"

Bella's eyes sparkled. "Oh, there wasn't much to be done after Reggie wrapped up his questions. But Harper, you should've heard the buzz around town. People at the Oasis couldn't stop talking. The masquerade, the drawing, the drama with Garrett...it's all anyone can focus on. And everyone's curious about Spellbooks being involved. I heard ten different people say they were planning to stop by tomorrow just to see the place. If this is what business is always like, you might need to hire extra help!"

A laugh caught in my throat, unexpected but welcome. For a heartbeat, I let myself believe it. That things might be turning around. I shook my head, still smiling, but something warm had taken root in my chest. That maybe—just maybe—Spellbooks had a future.

Bella must've seen something shift in my expression, because her smile softened. "Hey. It really was good today. People love that place. They love *you*. You know that, right?"

The flicker of hope dimmed as guilt curled low in my stomach.

She didn't know. How could she? That days like this were the exception, not the rule. I'd purposely kept my troubles from her. I wasn't about to admit that a day like today was an anomaly, that most of my business wasn't nearly as booming as it seemed.

"That's... great," I said, pasting on a smile I didn't quite feel. "Thank you. For everything."

Bella beamed, oblivious to the storm quietly unraveling in my head. "That's what friends are for! To remind you you're amazing! I mean, come on! Running a book launch and raking in customers while solving a mystery? Multi-tasking *queen*."

I laughed lightly, but it didn't quite reach my eyes. If only she knew.

Bella raised a finger in the air. "Oh, before I forget. I stashed some of the leftovers in your fridge. I took the rest of the extras back to the Oasis, or you would've had crab cakes coming out of your ears. Mama roped me into a few last-minute things, or I would've been here sooner." She wrinkled her nose playfully. "You'd think the entire Oasis was preparing for the masquerade, not just me."

Before I could respond, Gabriel stepped into view, obviously having ditched his illusion spell. His expression was serious, and I wondered if he'd stayed in the room while the sheriff had been questioning Nate.

"Hey, Bella," he said in greeting.

"Hi, Gabriel," Bella said. "The town is all abuzz with the people who've been drawn to attend the masquerade. If the rumors swirling around are true, but from what I've heard, there are more than I ever imagined!" Bella exclaimed.

I raised an eyebrow in Gabriel's direction, and he shrugged. "It was Mother's idea. When Mindy told her about Garrett's impromptu drawing, Mother invited everyone. Well, nearly everyone," he said, winking at me. "I can think of at least two that didn't make the cut. Mother still hasn't forgiven the Puddletons for what they did at the Christmas Eve Ball. They will just have to find another way to spend their evening."

I exhaled. I was relieved, but still feeling slightly off-kilter. "Good. That's one thing we don't have to worry about." Then I hesitated, lowering my voice. "Did you hear anything more? You know...from the sheriff?"

Gabriel glanced around the ballroom, taking in the glimmering chandeliers, the shifting crowd, and the far too many curious eyes and ears. He met my gaze and gave a small nod. "Yes. But let's not talk here."

Without another word, he turned, leading the way out of the ballroom. Bella arched an eyebrow, but I just shrugged and followed him, Bella falling in alongside me. Gabriel ushered us into the deserted library, shutting the door firmly behind us.

Bella perched on a chair, turning her entire attention on me. "All right, spill. What's going on?"

Gabriel and I took turns filling her in on everything that had happened since we left Spellbooks. Her eyes widened with each detail, but she didn't interrupt until we'd finished.

"And while the sheriff was questioning Nate," Gabriel added, "I overheard a few things."

Bella leaned forward eagerly. "Like what?"

"For one, Nate's sticking to his story. He doesn't know anything, and if he does, he's not talking. But when the sheriff pushed about the missing jacket, Nate seemed genuinely thrown. He expected it to be there."

"Either someone took it before we got there or Nate's a better actor than we thought." I pressed my lips together, brow furrowed as I tried to sort through the pieces. Something still wasn't adding up.

Gabriel nodded. "That, or someone else is playing a game we haven't figured out yet."

Bella exhaled sharply. "Great. More questions, fewer answers. My favorite."

We sat in silence for a moment, the weight of everything settling over us like a thick fog. Then Bella straightened, brushing invisible crumbs off her skirt with brisk energy. The gesture was classic Bella when she was about to put the world to rights.

"Okay," she said, holding up a hand like a game show host prepping a recap. "Garrett gets kidnapped." She folded down one finger. "You suspected the drivers, but nothing sketchy turned up." Another finger down. "You looked at the fiancée, Savannah. She's possibly shady, but there's nothing concrete on her."

She ticked off another finger. "Then came the ex-wife, Tiffany who is wealthy and upset, but doesn't have a motive so far as we can tell. What about Valerie?"

"She needs Garrett working," I said. "No motive there. In fact, she probably has the opposite of a motive for kidnapping. It'd make more sense for her to do whatever it takes to make sure something like this *didn't* happen."

"Which leaves Nate." Bella's final finger hovered before she snapped it down. "Weird, angry, possibly hiding something." She paused. "So, basically, the only person still waving red flags is Nate."

"And Savannah, if we think she's not just a clueless influencer," Gabriel chimed in.

Bella shrugged. "Don't discount any possibility. Who knows? Maybe there's a ghost out there and he or she is behind all of this."

I shot her a look, but a small grin tugged at my lips. "This is Havenwood, so I suppose anything's possible."

Gabriel shook his head. "Ghosts don't make sense. Kidnapping isn't exactly their MO."

Bella nodded thoughtfully. "Okay, I'll give you that one. So, what are we left with? Hunting down Savannah?"

I exhaled. "We go back to motive and opportunity. Build a new suspect list. Someone's lying. We just have to figure out who."

Gabriel spoke up. "Good idea. Garrett was taken from a book signing, so maybe it was someone who knew where he was going to be. Or even when he might be alone."

I shook my head. "Maybe the former, but definitely not the latter. I don't think he even realized he'd be alone in that moment. Remember? Powdered sugar from the beignets went all over his shirt. When he went to change, someone took advantage of it."

"So possibly planned or potentially a spur-of-the-moment adaptation?" Gabriel suggested.

I nodded. "Maybe. I was leaning towards this obsessive fan theory, but I ran into Mindy, and she gave me the impression she didn't think that was likely. Besides, what about the missing jacket? Whoever took Garrett had to have access to Nate Grimshaw's jacket. Would a fan really be able to get their hands on that?"

"Perhaps not," Bella mused. "It does seem like a bit of a stretch. I'd say that definitely points to insider knowledge."

Gabriel drummed his fingers on the back of an armchair. "Maybe that the jacket existed in the first place, but anyone who had access to the cars could've gotten Nate's garment bag."

"That's a good point," I said. "Who had access to the cars?"

"It's gotta be a short list. The security, the drivers, the entourage," Bella said. "Hey! Wasn't there something about an editor?"

"He's out of the country." I chewed on my lip.

"How about this security guy? Dirk?" Gabriel asked.

I shook my head. "I don't see it. He said he was pushing for more security at this event. Why would he do that if he wanted to kidnap Garrett?"

"Maybe he just told you that to throw you off his trail?" Bella suggested.

"Maybe," I said slowly. "But I'm still not convinced. We should probably check him out though."

Bella snapped her fingers. "Wait! What about the assistant lady?"

Gabriel snorted. "Mindy? She's afraid of her own shadow. She'd faint at the thought of staging something like this."

"I wouldn't go that far," I countered, but then relented. "However, I see your point. I don't think Mindy would sabotage her boss, the golden goose of an author, or her future career like this."

Bella's shoulders slumped. "Then we're back to the crazed fan theory? Someone kidnaps him so he can read them bedtime stories? Or to change the ending to fit their fantasy of how the series should end? That sounds a bit extreme."

I hesitated. "I know we already tossed the idea around earlier, but I keep coming back to it. Maybe it's not about Garrett at all. Maybe it's about Savannah. Someone obsessed with her, jealous, maybe even delusional enough to think taking him out of the picture would earn her attention."

"That's really disturbing," Gabriel said, his brow furrowing.

I pounded a fist against my thigh. "There must be something we're missing. But what?"

Gabriel glanced at his watch, his expression sharpening. "I'm going to see if the sheriff has any updates. You two should start getting ready."

Bella and I exchanged a look. "We've still got some time," I said, raising an eyebrow.

He smirked. "Do you? I've been around my sister long enough to know that it takes her twice as long to get ready as it does me. Hair, makeup, and all the accessories aren't exactly my problem. I just need five minutes to throw on my outfit, and I'm good to go. Besides, don't you want to show Bella the dress?"

"Yes well..." I started.

He moved towards me and gave me a quick kiss on the cheek. "What can I say? Even with everything going on, I'd like you to enjoy this as much as possible. This might be stressful, but it's still a night to remember. I have plenty of time to check in with the sheriff and get dressed. You ladies enjoy yourselves. I'll touch base as soon as I have something new to share."

I tilted my head, watching him carefully. "You sure you don't want backup?"

Gabriel's expression softened slightly, a hint of amusement flickering in his eyes. "I think I can handle a quick conversation without getting into trouble again. But thanks for the offer."

Bella perked up immediately. "Again? What kind of trouble are we talking about?"

I grinned innocently. "Oh, you know. Just one punch."

"And a smashed phone," Gabriel added dryly, shooting me a look.

I nodded. "Right. One punch, one smashed phone. Totally normal evening."

Bella's eyebrows shot up. "Wait—what?"

I shrugged, biting back a smile. "Long story. I'll tell you later."

Gabriel gave Bella a quick wave. "Nice seeing you again. Try not to let her overthink herself into a spiral, okay?"

"Got it," Bella said brightly, but the second the door clicked shut, she rounded on me. "One punch and a smashed phone?" she repeated, hands on her hips. "You cannot just drop that and expect me to pretend it's normal."

I gave her my best innocent look. "It's not as dramatic as it sounds."

Bella snorted. "Uh-huh. Somehow, I doubt that."

Knowing I wasn't getting out of this without giving Bella something, I told her an abbreviated version of the scuffle between Nate and Gabriel. Her expression morphed from alarmed to exasperated and then to reluctantly impressed.

She narrowed her eyes, clearly not buying how casually I brushed it off, but after a moment, her face softened into a grin.

"Fine. But don't think I didn't notice you were rushing. When this is all over, you owe me details. And in the meantime, let's focus on the real drama of the night," she said, her eyes twinkling.

"Real drama?" I asked, confused. Wasn't Garrett Grimshaw disappearing and everything that followed afterwards drama enough?

"The *dress*, Harper," Bella said, curiosity sparking in her eyes. "What's going on with the dress situation?"

"Oh. Right." I couldn't help the grin spreading across my face. "You're not going to believe this."

Bella crossed her arms, her teasing smile widening. "Try me."

I opened my mouth to answer, but then paused. My gaze drifted toward the closed door, my mind still tangled in everything we'd uncovered.

Garrett Grimshaw had been a mystery, even to the people closest to him. To Valerie, he was a brand. To Nate, a ghost of a father. To Tiffany, a regret she'd once invested in. To Savannah, a headline. To the public, a celebrity. To Mindy, a ticket to credibility. Everyone had known a different version of him. And now, with him gone, all those fragments felt hollow and disconnected.

And maybe that was what finally cracked something open in me.

"What is it, Harper?" Bella asked softly.

I glanced back at her. Bella was my best friend. The kind of friend who showed up, no questions asked. Who ran my shop for the day without complaint, who cheered me on when I couldn't do it myself. She didn't owe me that. She just did it because that's who she was.

And I hadn't even told her the truth about how much I'd been struggling. She'd once trusted me enough to admit how hard things had been with her boyfriend Alex. She'd been honest—raw, even. Maybe it was time I stopped pretending everything was fine.

I took a deep breath, squaring my shoulders. "Actually...before I show you the dress, there's something I need to tell you."

Bella's brow furrowed slightly, the teasing slipping from her face. "Okay..."

"I've been holding everything in," I said, the words tumbling out faster now. "I've been trying to be what everyone thinks I should be. A confident bookshop owner, a magical guardian, a savvy businesswoman. Somehow, I'm supposed to be good at all of it and...I'm just not." My voice caught on a lump rising in my throat, and I had to force myself to continue. "I think I've just been pretending so hard I forgot I could ask for help."

Bella took a step closer, laying a hand on my arm. "Harper..."

I rushed on. "I mean, the shop's barely staying afloat most weeks, and I'm still figuring out how to be a good guardian. I keep thinking Vivienne's going to take one look at me and decide I'm not good enough for Gabriel and get him to dump me. And now, during all of that, there's a missing author that's only here in Havenwood because I won some stupid contest. Then there's the masquerade and this gorgeous custom dress Gabriel somehow pulled off in the middle of everything..." A hiccupping sob cut me off as my voice spiraled upwards and I dropped my head into my hands.

A heartbeat later, Bella was at my side, wrapping me in a tight embrace. "Gabriel was right. I didn't see it, but he did. You *have* been spiraling."

"Maybe a little," I admitted with a shaky laugh. "And I didn't tell you or Gabriel. I should've. You deserve more than curated updates and pretending everything's fine."

She didn't hesitate. She squeezed me tighter and laid her head against mine. "Then start now," she said simply. "You don't have to do any of it alone. I've got you, Harper. Always."

My throat tightened, my suppressed emotions rising like a tsunami inside of me.

"I don't care if the shop's booming or quiet, if you're the world's most powerful guardian or still figuring it all out one weird day at a time," she continued softly. "You're enough. For Gabriel, for Havenwood and especially for me."

I closed my eyes, letting the words settle like a balm over all the cracks I'd tried to hide. Maybe everyone only knew parts of Garrett, whether it was the celebrity, the author, the fiancé, the father. But Bella? She knew *all* of me. And she stayed anyway. That was more precious than all the writing royalty checks in the world.

"There is absolutely nothing," she added, pulling back just enough to look me in the eye, "that's going to make me love you less. Not magical weirdness. Not overthinking. Not even hiding in a book fort for nearly three days when you were thirteen."

"That was one time," I muttered, laughing through a sniffle.

"And I was proud of you," she said seriously. "That fort had structural integrity. If it hadn't been for the Donovan twins, it would've lasted for months."

I let out a soft laugh, brushing away the last of my tears. "You always know how to pull me back, you know that?"

"Obviously," she said, bumping my shoulder gently. "It's in the best friend job description. Right next to 'drag you to brunch when you're wallowing' and 'hold your earrings if things get dramatic.'"

I smiled, my chest finally loosening. "I should've confided in you sooner. I'm sorry."

"You have now, and don't you feel better for it?" Bella teased. "Good thing we've got a ball to conquer together. Nothing brings friends together like a ball. Speaking of..." Her eyes lit up, and she leaned in like we were sharing a secret. "Can I ask what's up with the dress situation yet? I'm *dying* over here."

"This is definitely a show, not tell type of thing." I pulled back just enough to give her a look. "You're not going to believe this."

Bella crossed her arms, grinning widely. "Try me."

I looped my arm through hers, feeling a flicker of warmth despite everything. With Bella by my side, even a masquerade full of suspects felt a little more manageable.

All Dressed Up with No Clues to Go

As I led Bella into the study, excitement bubbled inside me. For a moment, everything about Garrett's disappearance, the suspects, and the missing jacket faded into the background. It was just me and my best friend, about to marvel at a gorgeous dress and maybe at the guy who made it happen.

Bella oooed and ahhed over the dress, her fingers brushing over the intricate folds of fabric. "He really pulled this off all by himself?" she asked, awe coloring her tone. "I need to send Alex over to take some notes."

"Well, Elliot Ashford did the sewing," I admitted with a grin. "But it was Gabriel's idea. He's been jotting down my favorite quotes, apparently. Besides, you're already dating a guy who makes you gourmet dinners on a whim. Let's not get greedy."

"Fair point," Bella said, shooting me a playful look over her shoulder. "But still, Gabriel deserves credit. A lot of it. Did he seriously remember all those book references you've mentioned?"

I nodded, letting my fingers trail over the soft fabric. "Yeah. Every detail. It's like he's been quietly cataloging everything I love."

Bella sighed dreamily. "Okay, I'm impressed. This is fairytale-level romance."

I laughed. "Sure. All I'm missing is a castle with a giant library and dishes that wash themselves."

Bella made a show of looking around. "If there was anywhere in Havenwood with a giant library and magical dishes it would be this place."

"Do you think the Silverthornes have self-washing dishes?" I asked incredulously.

Bella nodded seriously. "I do. It's the magical new contraption called a dishwasher." I rolled my eyes, and Bella threw an arm around me. "But seriously, why are we talking about dishes instead of this amazing dress? Are you just going to stare at it all night? Have you tried it on yet?"

I glanced around the study, flustered. "Here? I don't think—"

Bella grabbed my hand, her eyes gleaming. "No, but lucky for you, I know exactly the right place. Come on."

We found Isadora's suite with her inside, bustling about with her usual infectious energy. The door hadn't even finished swinging open before she clapped her hands in excitement.

"Tell me everything!" she exclaimed. "You love it, don't you? Of course you do. Who wouldn't? It's incredible. And the fact that my brother managed to think of it? Miracle of miracles!"

"It's gorgeous," I said as I craned my neck, scanning the room. "Is Savannah still here?"

Isadora rolled her eyes. "She left a while ago to get ready for the masquerade. Not that I'm complaining. If I had to hear one more word about hashtags and algorithms, I'd have thrown myself out the window."

"You're good with that stuff, though, aren't you?" I asked as Bella and I laid the gown over the plush sofa.

"Social media, sure. Business strategy, no thank you." Isadora wrinkled her nose. "I'll stick to cat videos and posting about fashion week. That influencer life isn't for me."

"Honestly," Bella said, gesturing to the luxurious space, "if I had a walk-in closet like this, I wouldn't care about anything else."

"Okay, the closet's a keeper," Isadora admitted with a grin. "But you know what's better? This." She flung her arms around both of us, pulling us close. "Good girlfriends. You know how hard it is to find other women who just think you're amazing? No competition, no drama, just love. 'I'm here for you,' 'I believe in you,' 'You've got this.' That kind of energy."

Bella and I smiled back. Isadora's warmth was contagious. We wrapped our arms around each other, forming a tight circle.

"We really are lucky," I said softly.

"Amen," Bella added.

Isadora grinned mischievously. "Now, one of us is a little luckier than the rest. Because—" She paused for effect. "You have a dress to try on!"

I gave her a mock glare. "Is that a little jealousy I hear?"

"Absolutely not," she replied. "I'm amazing. You're amazing. Both of you. And I love you, but that dress is *incredible*. And if you don't try it on in five seconds, I'm putting it on you myself. Mostly because Gabriel picked out the dress, but he let me have a say in the shoes and accessories, and I am *dying* to see the entire outfit on you."

"Okay, okay, okay," I laughed, scooping up the gown and heading toward Isadora's walk-in wardrobe.

I shucked out of my clothes quickly, eager to try on the dress Gabriel had chosen for me. The cool fabric slid over my arms, and I couldn't help but marvel at how perfectly it fit. Elliot Ashford really was a whiz. He must have saved my measurements for my gown from the Christmas Eve Ball because the dress fit like a glove.

When I came out and gave a little twirl, Bella and Isadora broke into applause. "Oh, it's perfect," Bella declared, pretending to wipe away a tear. "But you're not done yet. Hair, makeup, shoes, accessories! We're going all in. Oh honey, we're gonna be your fairy godmothers."

Before I could protest, Isadora had me seated at her vanity while Bella passed me the jewelry Isadora was letting me borrow for the night. Working together, they did my hair and make-up, even helping me slide on heels that looked fabulous but that I could also walk in. Score! By the time they finished, I barely recognized myself. The reflection staring back at me looked confident and poised. Everything I didn't feel at the moment.

"You're stunning," Bella said.

Isadora handed me a narrow box. "But what's a masquerade without a mask?" she asked.

I slid a finger under the embossed sticker and carefully opened the lid. Inside was a cream-and-gold Venetian-style mask, intricate and delicate. I ran my fingers over the edge, speechless.

"It's gorgeous, Isa. Thank you," I said, my voice soft.

Isadora winked. "I know. I worked with Elliot to match it perfectly to your gown. Speaking of perfection, we've spent all this time on you, and we're still not ready. Go grab us some snacks from Jacques while Bella and I get ourselves sorted."

"Now *that* I can do," I said with a laugh.

"Just don't get anything with purple frosting on your dress," Bella called after me.

"Ha ha," I said sarcastically, but I made a mental note to avoid the cupcakes. She was right. I wasn't about to eat anything that might mess up this dress. I'd stick to hard foods or anything that wouldn't stain. Tonight, red wine, strawberry jam, and chocolate ice cream were staying far away from me. At least, as long as I was in this gown.

The halls were quiet, and I moved quickly despite the heels, marveling at how the dress seemed to float around me. For a brief moment, I felt like I was part of a different world—a glittering masquerade where nothing could go wrong.

But then a voice broke through my thoughts.

"Yes, I know what's at stake," the female voice hissed. "No, I can't leave right now. Just wait for me."

I froze mid-step, my pulse quickening. The voice was coming from around the corner, muffled but tense.

"...Don't do anything rash. I'll handle it."

I crept forward, careful not to make a sound, and peeked around the corner. Mindy Hart stood with her back to me, clutching her phone tightly. Her posture was rigid, her voice low but frantic.

"...Yes, I'll be there as soon as I can. Just trust me."

I leaned back, my heart racing. Who was she talking to? Had the sheriff given her phone back when he returned Valerie's or was this another burner like Nate and Tiffany had? And, most importantly, what couldn't wait?

A misstep betrayed me as my heel clicked on the tile, and Mindy's head snapped up. She saw me and quickly ended the call.

"Harper!" she exclaimed, her voice too bright. "Hi! Oh, I didn't see you there."

"Sorry," I said, raising my hand. "I didn't mean to interrupt. Everything okay?"

Her gaze darted down the hall as she fumbled with her phone. "Oh, yes. Just, uh, New York stuff. You know how it is."

"Sure," I said, watching her carefully.

Mindy toyed with the edge of her jacket. "Beautiful dress, by the way. I should really…um, find my shoes. And my dress. Lots to do, you know!"

Before I could say another word, she turned and practically fled.

I stared after her, suspicion prickling at the edges of my mind. That wasn't a casual phone call. She'd dropped her voice, angled her body like she didn't want to be overheard. Like she'd done this before.

Something clicked like the soft *snick* of a door unlocking in the back of my mind. To make this work, the kidnappers needed access to the cars, the keys, and Garrett's schedule. Someone no one would question having that information. Someone who moved in and out of rooms unnoticed. A helper. An assistant.

Mindy.

My breath caught in my chest. She was the one who'd given him the beignets. Had she orchestrated the dessert disaster that led to Garrett Grimshaw going to change his shirt? Was she the mastermind behind the kidnapping? There was only one way to find out.

I turned sharply, ready to confront her, but my heel caught on the edge of my skirt, nearly sending me sprawling. By the time I regained my balance and rounded the corner, she was gone, swallowed by the glittering chaos of the masquerade set-up.

Frustration bubbled inside me like a pot about to boil over. I'd been so close.

I scanned the crowd one last time, desperate for a glimpse of the mousey assistant, but the masquerade had swallowed her whole. Music swelled. Laughter danced. And somewhere in the shadows, the answers I needed were slipping further away.

For a heartbeat, I stood frozen. The old Harper, the one who masked every doubt, who followed every thread alone, would've pushed forward, chasing shadows through the chaos until she either found the truth or collapsed trying.

But not tonight.

Not anymore.

I'd just poured my heart out to Bella, admitted how hard I'd been pretending. She'd promised I didn't have to do it alone. And she was right.

I'd followed enough trails by myself. It was time to choose something better.

I drew in a breath, gathered my skirts, and turned on my heel back towards Isadora's suite.

masquerade of Lies

THE GRAND BALLROOM SHIMMERED with opulence, a masterpiece of elegance. Chandeliers sparkled like constellations, casting a warm golden light that danced across the polished marble floor. Velvet drapes pooled in lush folds by the windows, and gilded accents adorned every corner. The air was heavy with the intoxicating scent of rich foods—sweet pastries, roasted meats, and delicate herbs mingling with a soft undertone of something floral, perhaps lavender or rose.

Guests glided across the floor, their masks glittering in shades of emerald, gold, and amethyst, their laughter bubbling like champagne.

At one of the long tables, beneath a cascade of gold fabric, lay an array of dazzling masquerade-themed treats. The hors d'oeuvres, arranged with an artist's care, were as decadent as they were beautiful. Tiny tarts filled with colorful fruits were arranged to match the color scheme of the evening perfectly. Velvety pâtés sat in small, ornate silver dishes, flanked by crusty bread, their deep, earthy flavors balanced by a hint of tart cranberry chutney. There were dark chocolate truffles shaped like masquerade masks, their glossy surfaces catching the light with a nearly surreal shine.

The food looked incredible. Had this been a normal night, I would've been marveling at the golden éclairs dusted with edible glitter, or the tiny quiches filled with smoky cheese and roasted vegetables. I should've been enjoying the scent of fresh roses and warm amber that perfumed the air like a luxurious spell.

But I wasn't marveling. I was watching. Scanning. Searching.

Okay, I might have also been panicking. Where was Mindy?

Bella and Isadora flanked me, both dressed to perfection. Bella's emerald gown shimmered like a forest caught in sunlight, her mask a dramatic swirl of gold and black. Isadora's silver gown sparkled like starlight, every bead catching the flicker of the shimmering glow from the crystal chandeliers. They looked like the epitome of magic and mystery, and normally, I would've soaked it in.

But not tonight.

Not with my stomach knotted and no sign of Mindy.

"She's been in the background the whole time," I said, scanning the ballroom. "Giving Garrett the beignets that pulled him away from the signing, managing his schedule, slipping through unnoticed—"

The words caught in my throat as a thought sharpened into certainty. "She's the kind of person no one sees coming."

Isadora tilted her head skeptically. "You really think the assistant did it?"

"Maybe?" I said slowly, pulse kicking up, "but maybe we've all underestimated her. That's exactly what could make her dangerous."

Bella straightened, her expression hardening. "Then we don't underestimate her again."

"Divide and conquer," Isadora said. "We'll cover more ground that way."

"Agreed," Bella nodded. "I'll take the dance floor."

"I've got the east side of the ballroom," Isadora added. "Harper, you cover the west."

They slipped into the crowd, and I forced myself to keep moving. My heels clicked against marble as I scanned the masked faces. But each second dragged, the glamour of the masquerade turning claustrophobic. The opulence that had seemed so magical now pressed in on me. The velvet drapes were like walls, chandeliers glared down like spotlights. The glitter and gold didn't sparkle anymore. They smothered. Every masked figure was a potential suspect. Every glance felt too long. Every shadow stretched too far.

Was Mindy the key to this whole twisted puzzle? Could she really be involved in Garrett's disappearance?

I took a step toward the windows, hoping for air and clarity. But before I could move, a masked figure in green velvet stepped directly into my path. For one fleeting, foolish second, my heart jumped.

Garrett Grimshaw.

Then reality snapped back. Garrett wasn't here. We hadn't found him yet.

This was Gabriel behind the mask, his illusion magic cloaking him in Garrett's image. Relief and frustration tangled inside me as he leaned in, Garrett's eyes staring out at me with Gabriel's concern.

"Harper," he said, his voice low and measured, still carrying the uncanny cadence of Garrett's tone. "You look beaut—are you okay? You're pale."

He reached for my hand but stopped himself mid-gesture. We weren't supposed to know each other well. Any familiarity would be suspicious and might draw the wrong kind of attention.

"What's wrong?" he asked quietly, so only I could hear.

"I saw her," I whispered. "Mindy. I think she's involved. I overheard her making a very suspicious phone call. She was here a moment ago and then disappeared again."

His expression sharpened. "We need to tell the sheriff."

"But she—"

"I know you want to go after her yourself, but finding the police is the better option," he said, already scanning the ballroom. "Especially because my mother's about to call me on stage."

"What? Why?" I asked, surprised.

"She thought a grand reveal would be more effective than just mingling. We didn't tell the others. The hope is that seeing Garrett 'alive and well' might rattle the guilty party enough to slip up."

I blinked. "Okay, but how do we catch them?"

He nodded. "The police are present, watching the exits, but the more eyes the better. If Mindy knows about the double but thinks she's seeing the real Garrett, she'll act differently from the rest of the crowd."

My heart thudded. "You want me to watch the room?"

"Yes. But carefully," he said, his voice growing more serious. "And promise me something. If you see anything suspicious—anything at all—find Officer Johanna or the sheriff. Don't go after her alone. Don't take risks."

"Officer Johanna's here?" I asked. I liked and respected the capable vampiric officer.

"She arrived just after sundown," he said. "And she's already watching the exits with some help from Reggie and Garrett's security guard, Dirk. The sheriff cleared him earlier, and he refused to sit on his hands when there was work to be done."

I nodded slowly, letting that sink in. The sheriff wouldn't have cleared Dirk without good reason, and I trusted Sheriff Jackson. One more name I could take off my mental list. That helped. And knowing that Johanna was here, backed up by Reggie and Dirk, eased my nerves more than I cared to admit.

"I'll be careful," I promised. "I'll keep my eyes open."

His lips curved in a faint smile, the mask tilting ever so slightly as he stepped back. "Good. And I'd better not linger. Wouldn't want Garrett Grimshaw looking overly interested in a certain bookshop owner." He winked, then melted back into the crowd.

A gentle hand touched my shoulder.

I turned, startled, to find Bella beside me again, her brow furrowed.

"Anything?" I asked.

"Nothing," she said. "No Mindy. Either she's better at hiding than I thought, or she's slipped out."

"Maybe, but Gabriel has a plan to flush her out," I said quickly. "Vivienne's about to 'reveal' Garrett on stage. The real twist is, they didn't tell his team. It's bait. Hopefully, they think we've found the real Garrett because there's no way a double could be as good as Gabriel's illusion. So, we need to watch the crowd for anyone that's acting differently, for anything that doesn't fit."

Bella's expression sharpened. "Smart."

"Yeah. It is." I glanced toward the stage. "He asked me to scan the room for anyone acting off. And to tell Johanna or the sheriff if we see anything."

"Well," Bella said, adjusting her mask, "then let's keep watching. I'll see if I can find Isadora and update her. Don't worry, Harper. We'll be on the lookout for any suspicious activity."

She squeezed my arm, her steady presence anchoring me again before she disappeared once more into the crowd.

I stayed near the long buffet table, scanning every guest, every flicker of movement, every shift in shadow. I wasn't even sure what I was looking for anymore. The crowd swirled and glittered beneath the chandeliers, but my instincts prickled.

Something was coming. I could feel it.

But with so many masks on display, would I even recognize it?

Secrets Behind the mask

I drifted through the crowd, searching for Mindy. When I couldn't find her, I tucked myself into a shadowed alcove near the edge of the ballroom, where I could see both the stage and a wide swath of masked faces. Music drifted into silence. Conversations faded to a gentle hum on the edges of my awareness. The crowd's attention shifted toward the center of the room, drawn like moths to a flame.

Vivienne Silverthorne appeared at the top of the staircase leading down to the ballroom in a dramatic sweep. Her velvet black gown seemed to absorb all the light, while her gold and diamond jewelry sparkled in the light of the chandeliers. She raised her hand and the effect was immediate. The room hushed as people turned her way. I was in awe. Vivienne didn't even need a microphone to command attention. Just her presence.

My gaze swept the crowd. I couldn't afford to get distracted by Vivienne. Not when I had a job to do. I scanned the ballroom, but the faces blurred into a kaleidoscope of masks and gowns. No sign of Mindy. Either I'd missed her or she was deliberately keeping out of sight.

The game had started. I just had to stay one move ahead.

My gaze landed on Savannah, standing in a halo of light beside the tower of sparkling juice mimicking champagne. Her dress was influencer-perfect. It was a tight pink mermaid gown, the same color as her perfume bottle. Twinkling rhinestones cascaded down the corseted top, catching the light from the chandeliers. Obviously, she'd chosen it for maximum impact in photos, but she wasn't posing. Her hands fidgeted with the strap of her clutch, her eyes flicking toward the staircase with a pinched expression that looked more anxious than guilty.

If she were involved, wouldn't she be smug? Relaxed? Pleased with herself? Instead, she looked like someone bracing for a scandal, not orchestrating one.

Just behind her, another familiar figure caught my eye. Nate lingered near a column, arms crossed, jaw clenched. His scowl could have curdled milk. But it wasn't a scheming expression. It was the face of a man counting the minutes until he could leave. And honestly, that had been his default mode all day, except during our earlier confrontation.

Neither of them moved. Neither flinched. No glances toward the exits. No guilty tells.

I let out a breath. Despite all the suspicion and speculation, my gut was telling me it wasn't either of them. They'd had chances to crack, to slip, to say the wrong thing. But they hadn't.

Normal nerves. Normal annoyance. Nothing more.

Which left one person still tangled in every thread of this mystery.

Where was Mindy?

Vivienne's voice sliced through the air, crisp and commanding. "Friends," she called, smiling as she surveyed the crowd. "Thank you all for joining us tonight."

Her voice alone could've summoned silence, but the graceful raise of her arms sealed it. All remaining eyes in the ballroom snapped to her.

"It is always a joy to welcome such an extraordinary group to our home," she continued, gesturing to the chandeliers, the banquet tables, the guests in glittering masks. "But tonight is especially meaningful."

I tried to refocus, but my eyes darted again around the crowded ballroom. However, there was no sign of Mindy. Wherever she was, Mindy was slipping away, possibly to start the next step of her plan.

Vivienne paused just long enough to make the audience in the room lean forward, hanging on her every word. "Of course, we are here to honor someone very special. An author whose words have captivated us, whose stories have enchanted us. Ladies and gentlemen, it is my absolute pleasure to celebrate Garrett Grimshaw tonight!"

The room erupted in cheers, but I barely heard them. My eyes were locked on the edges of the crowd, searching for anyone turning away, slipping out, or moving too quickly. But all I saw were expectant, smiling faces turned towards the staircase.

"Without further ado," Vivienne continued with a radiant smile, "please welcome him. The one, the only, Garrett Grimshaw!"

Gabriel, perfectly disguised with his illusion magic, strode up the staircase, mirroring Garrett's signature swagger right down to the distinctive hair flick as he faced the audience. The cheers turned thunderous.

He removed his mask with a dramatic flourish, tossing it aside like the showman Garrett was.

"Well," he said, his voice deep and perfectly measured, "if that's the kind of greeting I get in Havenwood, I may never leave!"

Laughter rolled through the ballroom.

He continued, "Before we dive in, I want to apologize for my sudden disappearance earlier. I assure you, it wasn't some elaborate plot twist. Although maybe I should take notes for my next book!" He flashed a grin, drawing another round of laughter. "Thank you all for your patience. Havenwood has been the warmest welcome I could ask for, and I feel very privileged to start my book tour here—especially with a launch at a place as special as Sullivan's Spellbooks."

He caught my eye for the briefest second, a glimmer of something more, something meant just for me, in his smile.

Warmth bloomed in my chest, pushing back the last lingering shadows of doubt that had taken up residence in the past few weeks. Maybe I didn't have to be perfect to be part of something good. Maybe it was enough just to be here, doing my best, with people who saw the magic in me even when I couldn't always see it myself.

I smiled back at Gabriel, and this time, it wasn't brittle or forced. It was real.

His smile widened as he gestured toward a nearby table laden with small, shimmering treasures. "And because I can't leave without giving you something to remember this night by, we've arranged a little surprise. On your way out, be sure to grab an exclusive *Masks of Deception* pin and some chocolate coins. As readers, we already know every story is its own treasure, but if I believe the women in my life—and I do—chocolate makes everything better."

The crowd cheered again, charmed by the gesture.

Another round of applause rippled through the room as Gabriel, perfectly in character, paused to take it all in. I couldn't help but marvel at how well he was pulling it off, how Garrett seemed to come to life in front of me.

Vivienne, ever the gracious hostess, gave a little cough and passed her glass to a nearby server. "Well, Mr. Grimshaw," she said, "perhaps you would do us the honor of reading a passage from your latest novel? Something dramatic, something to make the evening truly memorable."

The crowd buzzed with excitement when Gabriel nodded with feigned reluctance. "Of course, if you insist," he said, "It would be my pleasure." He flipped through the pages of the book with dramatic flair, choosing a scene which had clearly been marked in advance. The words spilled out smoothly, every line flowing as though he knew them intimately.

All eyes were on him, hanging on every word, but I couldn't focus. I scanned the ballroom frantically, the opulent decorations and swirling colors only adding to my disorientation.

Where was Mindy?

"Harper," a low voice murmured at my side, pulling me back to the moment.

I jumped slightly and turned to see Sheriff Jackson standing beside me, his eyes scanning the crowd.

"Any updates?" I asked under my breath.

He shook his head. "Nothing yet. But we've been quietly floating the idea that Garrett isn't quite himself. It might rattle the right cages without tipping our hand."

I gave a small, relieved nod. At least we weren't just waiting and hoping. We were setting the bait and now all we had to do was wait for someone to take it.

"You look like you're about to bolt," he said quietly, his tone equal parts observation and warning.

I swallowed hard, my pulse still racing. "I'm looking for someone."

His gaze sharpened. "Mindy?"

I froze. "How did you—"

"Bella," he interrupted, his lips twitching under his large moustache. "I'm on the lookout for her too. But why are you so certain she's wrapped up in this?" he asked.

I hesitated, unsure how much to say. My suspicion felt like a tangled web of half-truths and gut feelings based on a snippet of an overheard conversation. I wasn't sure how much the sheriff would take seriously. However, under his unrelenting stare, I felt compelled to share my suspicions.

The words spilled out of me. "She gave Garrett the beignets. She knew his schedule. She could've planted that jacket or passed it to someone else. But it's more than that. Earlier tonight, I overheard her on the phone. She said something about time running out, like she was on a deadline," I said, my voice steadying as I replayed the moment in my mind. "And she froze when she saw me, like I'd caught her doing something she shouldn't. It could be nothing...but it didn't feel like nothing."

Sheriff Jackson's expression hardened, his voice as sharp as steel. "Desperation makes people sloppy. If she's involved, she might do something reckless. If you see her again, you keep your distance and call me. Got it?"

"Got it," I said, grateful that he didn't brush me off. But I couldn't help adding, "You really think your people can cover every exit in a place this big?"

His mouth twitched again. This time, his expression was grim. "We're trying. Reggie's patrolling the halls and Bill is outside. Johanna is on site as well and she doesn't miss much. Besides, now that we cleared Grimshaw's security man, Mr. Steele is lending a hand as well."

That helped. A little.

I shifted, then added, "For what it's worth, I don't think it's Savannah or Nate. I know they've both been on your radar, but they've just been...off in regular ways. Not criminal ones. In my opinion at least."

The sheriff gave a short nod. "I came to the same conclusion."

My pulse ticked up. "Which leaves Mindy."

He gave me a grudging look of approval. "Agreed. But I can't pick her out in a sea of masks. If she's planning something, we'll be ready. Just do me a favor and no heroics tonight. We don't need a repeat of the Silverthorne Christmas Ball."

"Agreed," I said with a shiver.

One last nod, and he disappeared into the crowd. I stayed where I was, my thoughts spinning like leaves in a storm. Had I just set the sheriff on the wrong woman? Or were we finally closing in?

Either way—I was about to find out.

The Sweetest Deception

GABRIEL CONTINUED HIS DRAMATIC reading of Garrett Grimshaw's novel, his voice rich and magnetic as he narrated the tense scene. He brought to life a chase through New Orleans, Rhett leaping from one river boat to the next as he pursued his nemesis. Gabriel's performance was flawless, his mannerisms and delivery so perfectly Garrett that even I had to remind myself it wasn't really him.

If I hadn't been so distracted by everything else, I would have thoroughly enjoyed losing myself in Gabriel's rendition of the story. He would've made an excellent audiobook narrator or actor. If he ever decided to pursue a career on stage, I had no doubt he'd steal the show.

The ridiculous image of Gabriel in full costume, singing dramatic ballads and pirouetting across a stage hit me out of nowhere, and an involuntary laugh bubbled up in my throat.

I slapped a hand over my mouth, horrified at the sound.

A few guests turned toward me, blinking curiously, and I forced my expression into something more appropriately solemn.

Okay. Focus, Harper. This wasn't the time for mental musicals.

Tonight wasn't about Gabriel's burgeoning acting career. It was about finding Garrett Grimshaw, preferably before Havenwood ended up in the headlines for all the wrong reasons.

The crowd held its breath, hushed and still as Gabriel spoke. Gilded masks gleamed in the soft light and heads tilted toward the staircase in polite attention. For the first time all evening, the swirl of music and motion paused. But instead of easing my nerves, the stillness only sharpened them. Garrett was still missing, and Mindy's suspicious behavior loomed in my mind like a dark cloud over the glittering evening.

My thoughts circled back to Mindy. Where was she? What was she doing? Was she even still in the ballroom? She had apparently vanished into the night like smoke. My eyes swept the room, not for elegance or sparkle, but for any flicker of movement that seemed out of place. A turn of the head. A quick step away. Anything that didn't match the expectant hush.

I nearly jumped as Valerie appeared at my side, her sharp black gown cutting through the sea of color like a knife. Her bobbed hair was perfectly sleek, but the faint worry lines on her face betrayed her otherwise composed demeanor.

"I saw you talking to the sheriff," she whispered, her tone clipped but laced with a hint of desperation. "Has this ridiculous charade of yours borne any fruit? I don't know how long people will buy this double," she said, gesturing at Gabriel. "They barely look anything alike. Are we any closer to finding the real Garrett?"

"It's not my plan," I said, keeping my voice calm. "And if the sheriff knows something, he hasn't shared it with me yet."

Valerie huffed, the sound jagged and frustrated. "I cannot wait to be out of this small-town dump," she muttered, the bitterness dripping from her words like poison. "As soon as I get back to New York, I'm staging a full-scale search for Garrett. I'm calling the mayor, the governor, FBI. I'm even willing to take it all the way to the White House. I've got contacts. Anyone I can get on the phone will be helping me. It will be all hands on deck, and no more of this playing in the shadows nonsense."

Hostility filled her words and, while I had agreed to the plan, I hadn't expected to be the lightning rod for all the fallout. I'd backed Vivienne's idea, but right now, it felt like I was the one paying the price for it.

I attempted to reassure her, though it felt like walking on glass. "If I know Vivienne and the sheriff, they'll have at least three, if not more, contingency plans in place as to what the next steps are. I think it's probably best to trust the professionals."

Valerie bit her lip, then ran her tongue along her teeth, removing any stain of scarlet lipstick that had transferred. "Oh, I don't know. We might have been separated, but he was my first love," she said, her voice softer now, vulnerable. "We never should have gotten married, but we were always partners, you know? I just couldn't bear it if anything happened to him." She tapped a small beaded clutch anxiously against her hand, one just big enough to hold a tube of lipstick and a phone.

Gabriel's voice rose from across the room as he snapped the book closed with a flourish, throwing himself into a deep bow for the applauding crowd.

Vivienne stepped forward, her elegant figure commanding the attention of the room. She raised her hands in a graceful motion, signaling for quiet. "And now, my friends, a toast," she began, her voice smooth as velvet and effortlessly cutting through the low hum of conversation.

The crowd broke into polite applause, and Vivienne gestured toward the servers, who stepped forward with trays of beignets. The dusting of powdered sugar on the pillowy dough looked like fresh snow under the chandelier lights. "Since Mr. Grimshaw doesn't indulge in wine, I thought it only fitting that we toast him with something sweeter—his favorite pastry."

The room chuckled appreciatively as guests reached for the pillowy treats. Beside me, Valerie demurred with a wave of her gloved hand as a server offered her a beignet. "Not for me, thank you," she said, her tone smooth but tight. "Powdered sugar and black silk do not mix." She turned and glided away.

I started to take one, then caught myself, shaking my head with a polite smile. My stomach was already in knots, and my dress didn't need a powdered sugar mishap.

Vivienne cleared her throat, drawing my attention back to the stage. Her lips curved into a knowing smile. "For those of you who have read his latest masterpiece, I think you'll remember that one scene..." She paused, her gaze sweeping the room as if daring anyone not to get the reference. "Well, if you know, you know. Now, to our illustrious author. May your career be long, your stories be entertaining, and your bookshelves ever multiplying," she said, her voice lifting. "To Garrett Grimshaw! Our honored guest, a man whose unparalleled talent and wit have captivated us all."

"To Garrett," the crowd echoed, raising their beignets.

Gabriel, still cloaked in the illusion of Garrett, grinned and plucked a pastry from a nearby tray, holding it aloft with dramatic flair. "Cheers!" he declared before taking a theatrical bite. Powdered sugar dusted the front of his gold ascot, and he made a show of brushing it off with an exaggerated flourish.

I moved along the edge of the room, scanning for any sign of Mindy. The crowd swirled and shifted, a dizzying sea of vibrant masks and glittering gowns. My pulse quickened with every step, but she was nowhere to be seen. Where was she? Was she making her move now, while everyone's attention was fixed on Gabriel?

I tried to steady my breathing as I wove among clusters of guests. My thoughts spun like carousel horses gone rogue with Mindy slipping away, Garrett still missing, and the whole plan unraveling right in front of us.

A server appeared at my side, offering a tray of pastries. "Beignet, miss?" he asked, his voice smooth and polite.

I started to shake my head, but the tray shimmered under the light, each pastry dusted with an enticing layer of powdered sugar.

"They're the specialty tonight from Pixie Pastries," the server added. "Salted caramel filling with a hint of cinnamon. Truly decadent, if you ask me."

I reached out almost reflexively, taking one. He handed me a napkin, and I accepted it. "Thank you," I murmured, my mind still elsewhere as I bit into the warm, soft pastry. For a moment, I was distracted by its sweetness. The caramel oozed out, warm and delicious, dripping onto the napkin. I froze, staring down at the sticky mess in my hand. It was like the server had known the beignet would make a mess. Valerie's words rang in my memory. Maybe I should've followed her lead and not taken one. Messy treats and a fancy gown really weren't a good mix.

The thought clung to me like a whisper, echoing in the back of my mind, but it wasn't until I glanced down at the powdered sugar on my fingers that the pieces slammed into place.

My breath hitched, and a sick feeling coiled in my stomach as my mind flashed back to the moments before Garrett Grimshaw had been kidnapped.

The powdered sugar...the ruined clothes...Mindy handing Garrett the pastry, at a time perfectly orchestrated to send him back to the car. Straight into a trap.

But it hadn't been Mindy's idea.

It had been *Valerie's*.

A chill rippled down my spine as I replayed every moment, every carefully chosen word, the veil of distress she'd worn so convincingly. Valerie hadn't just stumbled into this chaos. She'd orchestrated it. From Garrett's beignet to the distraction to her own performance, she'd played us all like pawns in her game.

My stomach churned. This wasn't just about finding Garrett. Valerie had manipulated everyone. And for what? Fame? Control? A bigger stage for her ambitions? A way to get back at her ex as he started a new life with a younger woman? Or was it because of Garrett killing off his main character? Was this a replica of *Misery* by Stephen King where an author was kidnapped to force him to change an ending? Not with a crazed fan, but with a relentless publicist as the villain? Maybe it wasn't about love or legacy at all. Maybe it was about a storyline Garrett refused to change...and the lengths someone would go to rewrite it?

I swallowed hard, my throat dry. I might not know why she was involved. Not yet. But I didn't need the full picture to know something was very, very wrong with Valerie's actions today.

I dropped the napkin on the tray, my fingers trembling. The server gave me a confused look, but I didn't have time to explain. I bolted for the exit, my heart hammering in my chest.

If Valerie was still here, her plan wasn't finished yet.

And I was running out of time to stop her.

Unmasked

I rushed out of the ballroom, my heels sliding on the polished marble floor. My breath caught in my throat as I saw Sheriff Jackson snap a pair of handcuffs onto a sobbing Mindy.

"I didn't do it!" she hiccupped, tears streaking her face. "I swear, I would never hurt Garrett. Never!"

The sheriff's jaw tightened as he growled, "We'll talk about it down at the precinct." His voice was clipped, and his grip was firm as he began to lead her away.

Officer Johanna flanked him, her gaze cold and calculating, while Reggie stood to the side, awkwardly fidgeting with his badge. Despite the sheriff's clear control of the situation, tension rippled through the air, heavy and oppressive.

"Wait!" I called, my voice ringing out in the hall as I rushed forward, my heels clicking a sharp staccato on the marble.

All four of them turned toward me. Mindy's tearful face was a mix of confusion and desperation. The sheriff, however, fixed me with a piercing glare that froze me in place.

"What are you doing, Miss Sullivan?" His tone was low, like a warning growl.

I swallowed hard, but my voice was firm. "You can't arrest her. She's innocent."

The sheriff's eyes narrowed, his stance solid as a boulder. "Innocent?" he repeated, his voice dripping with disbelief. "A few minutes ago, you were convinced she was the mastermind here. You've got five seconds to explain before I walk out that door with my suspect."

"She didn't do it," I insisted, stepping forward. "The evidence doesn't add up."

His expression darkened, and his voice dropped further. "We found the driver's jacket—missing button and all—among her belongings. There's an incriminating text on her phone from a burner number about moving Garrett tonight. Not to mention a massive deposit that landed in her account earlier today. You call that 'not adding up'?"

Mindy whimpered. "It's not what it looks like, I swear! I didn't—"

"Enough." The sheriff's sharp command cut through her protests like a knife. He turned back to me, his eyes glinting with warning. "Do not waste my time, Miss Sullivan. I'm not in the mood for half-baked theories after the day I've had."

My pulse raced as I struggled to find the words I needed. "Just give me five minutes," I pleaded. "I know you, Sheriff. You're a good man. You wouldn't want to arrest the wrong person. I think I know who's really behind this. If I'm wrong, you can take Mindy down to the precinct immediately."

He snorted. "You *think* you know? That's not exactly reassuring."

Despite the disbelief on his face, I pushed ahead. "Five minutes, that's all I'm asking for. Five minutes to make sure you've got the right person."

The sheriff's eyes narrowed to slits, and his stance was unyielding. He didn't speak immediately, but the low rumble of his growl reverberated in the air like distant thunder signaling a coming storm. It wasn't a conscious sound. It felt animalistic, instinctive, a warning that I'd clearly wandered into dangerous territory.

I fought the urge to backpedal, standing my ground despite the chill racing up my spine. "It's Valerie," I said, forcing the words out before I could second-guess myself. "She set this up. Mindy's just a pawn."

His growl cut off, but his brows furrowed as he tilted his head, the motion eerily lupine for a human. "Valerie? As in Valerie St. James, the publicist?" he said, the skepticism clear in his tone. "Do you have any actual evidence? Or are we just throwing names around now?"

I sucked in a breath, my mind racing. There had been so many possibilities. Mindy with the beignets, Savannah and the will, Nate's anger, Tiffany's distance, but none of them had quite fit. Valerie had flown under the radar. Just enough emotion to seem genuine, just enough control to keep from drawing the wrong kind of attention. It hadn't struck me as odd before. But now...now I wasn't so sure.

Who stood to gain the most? Not personally, like I'd originally assumed, but professionally? Who had motive, not for revenge, but for reach?

It wasn't about money. It wasn't about family. It was about headlines.

Garrett's last book tour tanked. Early reviews of this book were brutal. Buzz was dying. But a high-profile kidnapping? That would grab attention. Reignite interest. Sell books.

And who would be just ruthless enough to engineer that kind of stunt?

I met the sheriff's eyes, confidence welling in my gut, telling me I was on the right trail. "The beignets. The powdered sugar. It was all part of her plan to get Garrett out of the public eye long enough to stage this whole thing," I said, my voice stronger now.

Officer Johanna snorted softly, her arms crossed over her chest. "That's a stretch, don't you think?" she said, her tone dry. "Pastries as evidence? Even beats the excuse of 'there was a cat.' No offense, Harper, but you're going to need more than powdered sugar to build a solid case."

I turned toward her, trying not to lose my footing in the conversation. "It's not just the sugar. It's the whole setup. Mindy didn't have anything to gain, but Valerie does. Think about it, Sheriff. The publicity of a kidnapping would skyrocket book sales, especially after the reviews have been...less than kind."

The sheriff scratched the stubble darkening his jaw. "I don't know."

I pressed on. "I bet Havenwood was chosen on purpose. It's small, remote, and perfect for a staged kidnapping. Valerie could've manipulated every detail to make this work, even framing Mindy to take the fall if things went sideways. I bet that the 'evidence' against her will start to fall apart if you dig into it. Valerie's been playing all of us from the start."

The sheriff's expression didn't waver, but something shifted in his eyes. Was that a flicker of doubt? "So, your entire theory hinges on a dessert and some conjecture." He sounded doubtful.

"No!" I said, my voice sharp enough to make Mindy flinch. "It hinges on the motive. Valerie stands to gain everything. If this book flops, Garrett's career is done. Valerie's career is done. She *needed* this." I pointed at Mindy, her shoulders slumping as she hugged herself. "Her assistant doesn't. Mindy's just a scapegoat."

The sheriff's jaw ticked to the side as he considered my words. The silence stretched and my nerves stretched with it until I thought they would snap. Finally, the sheriff said. "Interesting hypothesis, but we don't work solely on theories. We need evidence. Can you prove any of this?"

"Yes," I said firmly, though my hands trembled. "Give me five minutes with her. Just five. I'll get her to confess."

He didn't respond immediately, his sharp gaze boring into mine as if searching for any sign of weakness. Finally, he exhaled through his nose. "You've got five minutes, not a second more," he said, his voice low and dangerous.

I swallowed hard, nodding. "Understood."

He turned and barked orders, "Johanna, bring Ms. St. James to the side room. Reggie, keep an eye on the crowd. Don't let anything else escalate."

Johanna straightened. With a quick nod, she strode off toward the ballroom. Reggie perked up at the sound of his name, fumbling for a moment before hurrying after Johanna.

The sheriff fixed me with one last look before jerking his chin toward the far room. "You have five minutes, Miss Sullivan. Don't waste them."

Relief and fear surged in equal measure. Mindy glanced at me, her tear-streaked face crumpling further, but I managed a reassuring nod. "Stay strong," I whispered, my voice steadier than I felt.

My palms were damp as I followed the sheriff toward the side room. Each step felt heavier than the last, but I drew in a deep breath, channeling every ounce of resolve Granny Bea had ever instilled in me.

Five minutes. I could do this.

The sheriff stood next to Mindy as she fought to regain composure. I'm not sure I could've, if I'd been in her place. Not with an angry werewolf beside me. The silence was suffocating, and I found myself pacing to keep my nerves in check. My hands twisted together as I turned the events over and over in my mind, desperate to piece everything together before Valerie arrived.

It wasn't long before footsteps echoed in the hallway. Officer Johanna strode in first, her expression sharp and unreadable. Behind her, Valerie swept into the room like a storm, her heels clicking sharply against the tile.

She was immaculate, as always, her sleek hair shining under the fluorescent lights and her dark eyes blazing with fury.

"What is the meaning of this?" she snapped, her gaze sweeping the room before landing on the sheriff. "I sincerely hope you have a good reason for dragging me out of an important business event. Do you have any idea what kind of rumors this will spread? Police officers interrupting a high-profile launch? If this gets out, I'll have my agency file lawsuits so fast, Havenwood won't know what hit it."

Before anyone could respond, Vivienne stepped into the room. Her icy composure shifted the dynamic instantly, her presence as sharp and unyielding as winter frost. She took one measured glance at Valerie, her lips tightening ever so slightly before turning to the sheriff.

"What is this all about, Sheriff?" Vivienne's tone was calm, but it carried a gravitas that stilled the room.

The sheriff jerked his head toward me. "This is Miss Sullivan's doing." His eyes flicked to his watch. "You've got four minutes and fifty-three seconds."

I swallowed hard and turned to Valerie, whose arms were crossed tightly. Her mouth was a thin line of disdain as she glared at me, but I forced myself to hold her gaze.

Taking a steadying breath, I began. "This whole thing started long before today, didn't it?"

My voice was calm and measured, just like my mother had taught me. She wasn't as forceful as my dad, but she had a gift all her own. She had the kind of quiet presence that could settle storms and draw secrets without force. People leaned into her calm without even realizing it. And I'd spent years watching her wield that gentle magic like a master.

So now, I channeled her by softening my edges, slowing my breath, grounding my words. I needed Valerie to hear me. To really hear me. And I knew the only way through her defenses wasn't command. It was control.

I kept my voice calm as I leveled the accusation. "I believe this entire kidnapping was a setup. A publicity stunt meant to revive Garrett's failing career."

"What?" Valerie's voice cracked through the room, sharp and incredulous.

I continued, focusing on the sheriff. He was the one I needed to convince. "Knowing what I know now, I believe Valerie orchestrated everything starting with the social media contest Spellbooks won. I think she chose Havenwood specifically because it's small, isolated, and she thought she could use her big city contacts to control the narrative. She set up the kidnapping and even framed Mindy as the fall guy, or rather, fall woman, if things went wrong."

Valerie laughed, a sharp, brittle sound. "This is preposterous," she scoffed. "Do you even hear yourself? A publicity stunt? Based on what evidence, exactly?"

The sheriff held up a hand to cut her off. "She's right, Miss Sullivan. Where's the evidence? Four minutes, ten seconds."

I took another breath and launched into a quick recap, trying to organize the scattered pieces of my theory into something coherent and convincing. "Valerie gave Mindy the beignets to give to Garrett, knowing they'd ruin his outfit. It's the same reason she didn't take one herself at the masquerade. Powdered sugar on black silk is a nightmare, right Valerie? The mess forced Garrett to step away from the crowd to change. The security and the drivers were conveniently distracted precisely at that moment, allowing the kidnapper a small window to snatch Garrett without impediments."

Valerie sneered, her eyes narrowing as she paced the length of the room. "You've got to be kidding me. Powdered sugar? This is what you're basing your absurd accusations on? Clearly, your imagination has gotten the best of you." She gestured derisively at me. She turned to the sheriff, her tone dripping with venom. "This is slander, plain and simple. When this ridiculous charade is over, I'll make sure Havenwood pays dearly." Then she wheeled on me, waving a finger as she marched into my personal space. "And your little bookshop? It'll be shut down within a week. Your reputation? Gone. I'll see to it personally."

Her words hit me like a slap, but I forced myself to stay calm, to meet her gaze evenly.

"Sit down, Ms. St. James," the sheriff growled. You didn't need to know he was a werewolf to hear the warning growl in his tone. Valerie froze, glancing between us before sinking slowly into the nearest chair.

I took a deep breath, refusing to back down. "Threaten me all you want, Valerie," I said, my voice steady despite the knot tightening in my chest. "We both know the truth. And soon, everyone else will too."

She scoffed, tossing her hair. "Please. Even if your little theory had any merit, which it doesn't, I was in public view the entire time. How exactly was I supposed to have kidnapped my own author? The thought is preposterous!"

My throat closed. I hadn't thought through that part. The facts didn't lie, but they didn't line up, either.

Valerie saw my hesitation and pounced. Her smile sharpened. "That's what I thought. You've been playing detective with fairytales and feelings. I'm sure that's fun in a small town, but this? This is real. You're in over your head, darling."

My panic surged upward, buzzing in my ears.

"You had help," I said quickly, grasping at the thread and pulling for all I was worth. "Someone waiting outside to do the dirty work while you kept yourself above suspicion. I think that person might've even been lurking around the manor. I saw someone watching me, but when I called out, they disappeared."

Her lips curled into a smirk. "Oh, so now I have a secret accomplice?" she said, faux concern dripping from every word. "Let me guess. You don't have a name or a face, just a feeling, right?"

The sheriff cut in before I could respond. "Three minutes, Miss Sullivan."

My pulse spiked. I was losing them. I was losing everything. They didn't believe me. Valerie's confidence only grew as she watched me falter, the smugness radiating off her like heat.

And then we heard it.

There was some sort of commotion outside. Shouts, muffled cries, and the unmistakable scuffle of a struggle drifted in through the narrow crack of a window. Someone must've left it ajar to air out the room earlier, despite the chill.

My head snapped toward the sound as it grew louder, the tangle of voices cutting through the heavy quiet like a knife.

Valerie stiffened. Just for a second. But it was enough. Her expression faltered, a flicker of something raw flashing in her eyes.

She knew something.

The sheriff jerked his head, his hand instinctively going to his holster. "Johanna—"

"On it," she said, already sprinting for the door. She was just a blur in my vision as she tapped into her vampiric speed.

The sheriff didn't follow. He stayed rooted by Valerie and Mindy, keeping one ear cocked toward the chaos outside and his eyes on the two women who might still hold answers. Containment. That was his priority now.

But that meant Johanna was on her own.

Without a second thought, I kicked off my heels, hitching up my skirt as I raced after her, chasing the truth. My pulse thundered in my ears. Valerie's reaction told me everything I needed to know. Whatever was happening outside was the key to this whole tangled mess.

"Stop!" Sheriff Jackson's voice rang out behind me, but I kept running.

By the time I reached the hall, Johanna was already a blur at the end of it, moving with supernatural speed toward the source of the commotion. I put my head down and ran faster, ignoring the sting of the cold marble under my bare feet.

The March air hit me like a slap as I burst through the doors, my breath misting in the frigid night. But I barely noticed the cold. My focus zeroed in on the struggle unfolding near the line of parked cars. Three men fought to shove a masked figure wearing an ornate black and silver velvet costume into the back of a black sedan.

The man in the middle shouted, thrashing against their grip. His mask was knocked from his face and dangled from his neck. In the glow of the outdoor lights, I saw his features. My stomach twisted.

Garrett Grimshaw. Wait! Was that Garrett? Or Gabriel?

My heart plummeted, and I forgot how to breathe. It took me a beat to realize the victim wore a completely different outfit to the one Gabriel had donned this evening and another to recognize the three assailants as the drivers I'd met earlier: Vic, Lenny, and Frankie. Johanna, on the other hand, hadn't hesitated in the slightest and was sprinting towards them at top speed.

Vic, the largest of the three, barked orders while fending off Garrett's wild kicks. "Hold him still, Frankie! Lenny, open the door already!"

I didn't have time to process it. My feet carried me forward without thought, but Johanna was already there.

She was a blur of determination, her smaller frame slicing through the chaos like a knife. She went straight for Vic, the largest of the group. He swung a massive arm at her, but she ducked effortlessly, her movements precise and practiced. She landed a quick strike to his ribs, and though he staggered, he recovered fast, snarling as he lunged again.

I watched, stunned. With vampire strength, she could've flattened him. Launched him through a wall if she wanted. So why was she holding back?

Then it clicked.

Johanna was an officer of the law. She was here to detain, not destroy. Especially not in front of human witnesses. That was rule one in Havenwood. Don't let the humans know magic exists.

I watched in fascination as Officer Johanna dodged, sidestepping Vic's grasp and sweeping a leg out to knock him off balance. He stumbled but didn't fall, his sheer size giving him an advantage. She didn't falter, using her speed to dart around him, landing calculated strikes that kept him off-kilter.

To my surprise, Reggie rounded the corner of the manor, his breath visible in the cold air. He barreled towards the would-be kidnappers like an unstoppable freight train. Reggie might not have been graceful, but he was determined. He collided with Frankie, and in a tangle of limbs, somehow managed to knock the man off his feet. They hit the ground with a thud, and to everyone's surprise—Reggie included—he came out on top, scrambling to pin Frankie's arms behind his back.

"Stay down!" Reggie panted, fumbling for his cuffs. "Or, uh...I'll make you wish you did!"

Lenny bolted around the car, keys in hand, clearly intending to make his escape. But I wasn't about to let him go. I pulled on my magic, and it hummed to life, responding to my touch instantly. Immediately, I could tell it was bolstered by my connection to the heartwood tree without me having to even ask. I focused on the car door, visualizing the latch, the handle, the weight of it. With a flick of my wrist, the door yanked open just as Lenny reached for it. The heavy metal swung wide, catching him square in the chest and sending him sprawling to the ground.

Johanna delivered a sharp strike to Vic's knee, sending him crashing to the ground. She loomed over him, baton in hand, her stance a picture of control. "Try that again," she said, her voice low and steady, "and I'll make sure you regret it."

By the time the dust settled, the drivers were subdued. Lenny groaned, clutching his chest where the car door had caught him, while Vic glared daggers at Johanna from the ground as she cuffed him and then moved to do the same to Lenny. Frankie, red-faced and sputtering, was being dragged to his feet by Reggie, who looked simultaneously triumphant and amazed at his own success.

My gaze flicked to Garrett.

He stood a few feet away, brushing dirt off his ornate velvet jacket with exaggerated care, as though he'd merely tripped rather than been dragged into an attempted kidnapping. Without his mask to hide behind, his unmistakably smug expression was on full display. Honestly, it was the sincerest I'd seen him look since I met him.

"Well," he said, his voice carrying an air of theatrical flair, "thank goodness you arrived in time. These men! They ambushed me! I escaped my kidnappers and didn't know where to go until I remembered the Silverthorne manor. But as soon as I got here, these men tried to force me into their car! It was terrifying, truly. But thanks to your swift action, Officers, I'm safe. I might even work your heroics into a future book," he said with a charming wink.

Officer Johanna folded her arms across her chest. I could tell she didn't buy his story for a second. She jerked her chin at him. "Nice outfit. Where'd you get it?" she asked.

"Wha—sorry, isn't this a masquerade?" Garrett asked with a quick, confused smile.

"Yes, but I find it awfully convenient that your kidnappers had a costume ready for you. Or did you stop by your hotel to change first? In my experience, having a costume available is a rather unique priority for either the kidnappers or the victim."

Garrett's face went white. "I—um—"

Johanna tapped a finger against her lips. "See, if it were me, I would've called the police as soon as I got my hands on a phone. How about you, Reggie?"

"Yep! I'd call 911 right away," the cheerful officer said with a proud smile.

"Exactly," said Johanna, pointing at her colleague.

"It's not like the number is hard to remember," Reggie said seriously.

"I agree," Johanna said. "So, why didn't you call the police for help, Mr. Grimshaw?"

"I, um, have an image to maintain," he said, striking a pose that was a dull reflection of his former confidence.

A furrow formed between Johanna's brows. "Your *image* is more important than your *life*?"

"Yes! I mean, no! I mean, you don't understand the pressure I'm under," Garrett stammered.

Johanna nodded, reaching for her belt. "You're right. I don't understand." She strode over to him, her expression flat and unimpressed. "Turn around," she said, pulling out zip tie handcuffs.

Garrett blinked. "Excuse me?"

"You're coming with us," she said, her tone leaving no room for argument. "Until we sort this out, I'm detaining you. We can do this the easy way, or the hard way. Personally, I'm rooting for hard."

"You can't be serious!" Garrett exclaimed. His bravado faltered under her unflinching gaze. With a resigned sigh, he turned and held out his wrists. "This is completely unnecessary," he muttered as she cuffed him.

"Sure, it is," Johanna said, securing his wrists. "If I'm wrong, I'll give you an apology. But just in case I'm not, I like to be thorough."

As the officers herded the suspects back inside, I felt a hand on my shoulder. It was Vivienne, her sharp gaze softer than I'd ever seen it.

"Well done, Miss Sullivan," she said quietly. "Your Granny Bea would've been proud."

The words struck deep, catching me off guard. Pride and emotion swelled in my chest, leaving me momentarily speechless. By the time I gathered myself enough to respond, Vivienne was already walking away. I hurried after her, not about to let the answers I'd searched for slip through my fingers.

The Missing Piece

The tension in the room was suffocating. The small, starkly lit side room of the manor had been hastily transformed from a police command center into a makeshift interrogation room. Sheriff Jackson stood near the door, his broad frame blocking most of it, his arms crossed like an immovable barrier. Valerie sat at the head of the small conference table, her posture rigid, her perfectly manicured nails drumming an impatient rhythm against the polished wood. Garrett sat at the opposite end, his sullen expression a poor imitation of his usual charm.

Along one side of the room, the three drivers, with their hands cuffed behind their backs, fidgeted nervously. Vic looked ready to snap the chair beneath him, while Frankie avoided eye contact with everyone, his knee bouncing erratically. Lenny glanced at the door and seemed to be measuring the odds of a successful escape.

Officer Johanna leaned casually against the wall near the drivers, her baton in hand, ready for any sudden moves. Reggie stood closer to Mindy, visibly uncomfortable, his weight shifting from foot to foot. Vivienne, ever composed, perched on the edge of a chair, her sharp gaze taking in every detail without a word.

I stood near the side of the table, the last of my adrenaline from the earlier scuffle still buzzing through me. The atmosphere was charged, like the air before a thunderstorm.

Sheriff Jackson cleared his throat, his voice cutting through the silence. "Let's make one thing clear. I'm not interested in games or excuses. You've all got one chance to talk." His steely gaze swept across the room, lingering on Valerie. "Whoever tells me the truth first might get a deal. The rest? Not so much."

Valerie let out a sharp laugh, her lips curling into a derisive smile. "Spare me the theatrics, Sheriff. I'm not saying another word without my lawyer."

The sheriff tilted his head slightly, the motion deliberate and lupine. "That's your right, of course," he said evenly. "But given the time of night, it might be a while before we can get in touch with them. Until then, my offer of leniency stands for whoever decides to speak first."

He jerked his head toward Johanna, then the drivers. "Take these three out of the room. Let me know the second one of them talks."

Officer Johanna nodded and motioned for the drivers to stand. Vic rose reluctantly, muttering under his breath, while Frankie and Lenny exchanged uneasy glances before following her directions. Johanna and Reggie guided them out, the door clicking shut behind them.

The room shrank in their absence and the tension coiled tighter. Valerie sat straighter, her smirk faltering for the briefest moment. Garrett shifted uncomfortably in his chair, fidgeting with the lacey cuff of his sleeve.

"Well," Valerie said, breaking the silence. "Isn't this cozy? What now? Are you going to accuse me of ruining your quaint little town? Or perhaps you'll get creative and blame me for global warming, too." Her tone was biting and sarcastic.

Sheriff Jackson ignored her bait, stepping forward to loom over the table. His voice dropped into a low, dangerous growl. "Let me spell it out for you, Ms. St. James. We have three men outside who are very motivated to save their own necks. And I'm guessing one of them will pin this entire mess on you. My offer of leniency won't last forever."

Valerie's eyes flickered, doubt flashing briefly before she masked it with icy defiance. "You're wasting your time. I've done nothing wrong. This entire thing is a circus, and you're the clowns leading the parade."

Garrett cleared his throat, flicking his hair back as he drew attention to himself. "Now, let's not get carried away," he said, his voice oozing with false charm. "This whole situation is a misunderstanding, I'm sure."

Something in his tone made my stomach twist. It was too smooth, too measured. And then it hit me. It wasn't just what he was saying, but *how* he said it. This wasn't panic. It wasn't fear.

Why not?

Because he wasn't nervous because he was in full scale damage control.

I turned to him sharply, everything sliding into place at once. The desserts. The missing jacket. The timing. The costume. Garrett wasn't just a victim. He was a willing participant.

But he hadn't acted alone.

My gaze darted to Valerie, and for a flicker of a second, I saw it. The slip in her perfect posture, the tightness behind her practiced smile. Not fear, but anticipation. She wasn't scrambling. She was waiting. Waiting for her partner to speak his lines so she could play her role.

It was her and him. They were *both* behind this.

"Misunderstanding?" I said, stepping closer to Garrett, letting the word curl like smoke off my tongue. "That's an interesting way to describe a staged kidnapping."

Garrett's confident smile faltered for a heartbeat before returning, weaker this time. "I don't know what you're implying, but—"

"Oh, I think you do," I said, cutting him off. "You've been lying to everyone here. You were never kidnapped, were you? Johanna saw it the second you arrived here in costume. This whole kidnapping thing? It was staged, wasn't it? A publicity stunt to boost sales for your failing book."

His composure cracked, just a little, but Valerie's didn't. "You have no idea what you're talking about," she snapped, her voice cold. "This is ridiculous."

"No," I said, leveling my gaze at her. "What's ridiculous is how far you went for a bump in sales."

She gave a tight, mocking laugh. "Sales? You think this is about selling a few books?"

"Not a few books. Thousands. Hundreds of thousands," I said. "The publicity of Garrett's disappearance would've driven sales through the roof even though his last book tour tanked, and he killed off his main character in his newest book."

"You have no proof," Garrett snarled.

I ignored him, keeping my eyes on Valerie. "You did this on purpose. Havenwood. Spellbooks. Even the beignets. Everything was selected so you could stage your little drama. A sleepy little town with just enough charm to attract attention but still remote enough to stage a disappearance without anyone noticing until it was too late."

"You're spinning fairy tales," she sneered. "You run a bookshop, not an investigation."

I glanced over just as Garrett flinched. It was small, but it was there. *Gotcha.*

I leaned in towards him, my tone sharpening. "But this one's real, isn't it? A fake kidnapping. A big, splashy stunt to save a failing book launch. It would've made you a victim and a hero. Headlines. Sympathy. Skyrocketing orders."

"Because the reviews were catastrophic," I said, my voice rising. "His career was slipping. Valerie's entire job relies on his success. So, they created a perfect story. One that made Garrett the center of attention. And if things had gone to plan, he would've miraculously reappeared just in time. An escaped hero who overcame insurmountable odds. People would've eaten up *that* story, I have no doubt."

Garrett scoffed, but it sounded hollow. "That's absurd. I was kidnapped."

"Yet you turned up at your own party," I said. "No restraints. No bruises. In full costume. How do you explain that?"

His mouth opened, then closed again.

"Then it started to fall apart, didn't it? Savannah didn't announce your disappearance to her millions of followers. When no announcement was made, when your phones were taken, you decided to frame Mindy," I continued. "Maybe that was the plan from the beginning to throw off suspicion, or maybe it was a knee-jerk reaction to the spiraling situation."

"I—" Garrett said.

"Stop." Valerie's voice was colder now, quieter. A warning.

Garrett's mouth snapped closed, but I didn't stop. "You had motive. Opportunity. And a publicist with a knack for controlling the narrative. But here's the thing—tonight, you aren't in charge of the story anymore."

"What on earth are you talking about? You're crazy! I'm the victim here," Garrett said, his voice taking on a petulant whine. "Didn't you see those men try to force me into the car?" His eyes darted toward Valerie.

"Yes, but maybe that was the plan all along," I said, moving closer to Garrett, sensing that he was the weak link. "One or all of them were supposed to kidnap you from the shop, but they got distracted or held up. You saw an opportunity, didn't you? You took Nate's jacket from the garment bag in the trunk. It was you we saw running to the driver's door. You staged your own kidnapping."

Garrett's eyes rolled around, searching for an escape. "Valerie?" he said, his voice coming out as a nasal whine.

Her jaw tightened as she coldly stared me down. "You don't have proof."

"Don't I?" I stepped closer. "Are you one hundred percent sure about that?" I crossed my fingers behind my back and hoped my ploy would work.

Garrett's face paled.

Valerie said nothing.

The silence stretched.

If one or the other didn't crack under the pressure, I wasn't sure we had the evidence to back up my theory. Perhaps Johanna had gotten a confession from one of the drivers, but if she hadn't, what was the next step?

I narrowed my eyes, refusing to give into the spiral of emotions tornadoing through me. I needed to stay calm, in control, to convince them I held the winning hand.

Don't break, Harper, I thought to myself.

I took a slow breath, my eyes burning as I refused to blink, staring Garrett down. He squirmed, his gaze sliding away from mine. Another beat passed. He wasn't going to say anything. I'd failed. I knew it.

And then—

"Don't pin this all on me!" Garrett burst out, his voice cracking. "It was her idea!"

Valerie spun on him, eyes blazing. "Shut up!" she hissed.

But Garrett wasn't done. "She said it was flawless. Those were her words! Savannah was supposed to go public and post some weepy video, beg her followers for help finding me. Poof! Instant sympathy and it kept both of us clean."

Valerie's laugh was short and sharp. "Please. Like you had the brains to pull this off. You were the one who came crawling to me, *begging* for help with your tanking book sales after you turned in that disaster of a manuscript. Maybe if you'd spent less time fawning over your new fiancée and more time writing, you wouldn't be in this mess."

Garrett turned, fury igniting. "Then why didn't you post it when she didn't?"

"I couldn't! Not without dragging myself into it!" Valerie's voice cracked with rage. "That's why I messaged you. I told you to send it from the burner I bought for you."

He gaped at her. "Are you kidding me right now? You're really blaming me?"

"I sent it!" Valerie shrilled.

"Well, I never got it!" he snapped.

The pieces all fell into place. To my surprise, I felt a flicker of unexpected gratitude for Savannah's chronic need for attention. If she hadn't left Spellbooks to snap selfies with that perfume bottle, she might've been in the shop when everything went sideways. Between her absence, Lucas' spell, and my inconvenient habit of asking too many questions, their plan might've gone off without a hitch.

Garrett looked around the room, his eyes wild. "This was all Valerie! The drivers. She hired them. They were supposed to grab me, but they weren't by the cars. However, they'd left the keys inside. I saw an opening, and I took it. I grabbed the jacket from the back of the car, hoping that everyone thought it was a driver behind the kidnapping. I even ripped one of the custom buttons off and left it in the car. You know, as a clue? Then I ditched the car where we'd stashed the backup and went to the hotel where Mindy made a reservation. We told her it was for the drivers, but really it was for me to lay low—"

Valerie cut in, voice shrill. "Exactly! You were supposed to wait for me there!"

"I did wait! I sat in that rat trap, glued to the news for hours! But when nobody reported anything, I knew you botched it!"

Valerie sneered. "You botched it when you went off-script. I should've known you couldn't do this. Patience has never been your strong suit."

"Patience?" Garrett barked. "No one was answering my texts! I had to do something! I thought you'd abandoned me—"

"And so, you decided to show up at the masquerade? What were you going to claim? That you fought off your kidnappers single-handedly? You? The grown man who still calls me to kill the spiders in the hotel showers?" Valerie threw up her hands. "Brilliant. Truly inspired." Sarcasm dripped from every syllable.

Garrett's face flushed beet-red. "Hey! This was all *your* plan! You promised it would work!"

"And *you* promised not to be an idiot," Valerie snapped. "But that didn't work out because Garrett Grimshaw *always* knows best!"

"Why you little—" Garrett moved as if to lunge towards her.

"Enough!" Sheriff Jackson's voice cut through the room like a whip crack, silencing the two instantly.

The air seemed to hum with tension as he fixed his hard gaze on Valerie. "No one was supposed to get hurt? Tell that to Mindy, who you framed. Or to this town, whose reputation you dragged into your mess."

Valerie waved a dismissive hand, though her confidence had clearly taken a hit. "But did anyone *actually* get hurt? No. Mindy's just fine. And your precious little town will survive this...misunderstanding."

"Yeah! No harm, no foul," Garrett chimed in.

"Exactly," Valerie agreed, a hint of triumph creeping into her voice. "It's not a crime. Nothing you can hold us on."

"That's not true," Sheriff Jackson said, his tone steely. "We've got you on conspiracy to commit fraud, conspiracy to commit kidnapping, obstruction of justice, and that's just for starters. I have no doubt we'll find more when we really start digging."

A tap sounded at the door and Officer Johanna stuck her head in. "Boss? You're going to want to hear this. Those three drivers are singing like canaries, and you won't believe the tale their telling."

Sheriff Jackson jerked a thumb at Valerie and Garrett. "Let me guess. These two hired them to make the kidnapping look real."

Officer Johanna's eyes widened in surprise, but she nodded. "Yep. Exactly that."

The sheriff turned back to Valerie. "Any comment for the record, Ms. St. James?" he asked, his tone low and carrying a hint of warning. "I should warn you that anything you say can and will be used against you in a court of law."

Valerie opened her mouth, but no words came out. Her perfect veneer crumbled entirely, leaving only fury and panic.

I looked between the two of them. Valerie's face was a mask of rage, twisting her features into something ugly and unrecognizable. Garrett, in stark contrast, looked smug and disturbingly calm, despite his earlier outburst. It was as if he thought his involvement in all of this was nothing more than an amusing footnote.

"I swear, I thought the whole thing was all just a PR stunt," he said with an easy shrug, his words dripping with casual indifference. "It was just a story. The same sort of fictional entertainment I write. PR is about telling the public what they want to hear to get the best reaction. In this case, book sales. Everything else came from Valerie. The three goons she hired to masquerade as drivers, the kidnapping. It was all her. I just did what she told me to do. I had no idea she planned to take it this far."

"You..." Valerie sputtered, her voice trembling with disbelief. "You, you, you..."

"I think I've heard enough," Sheriff Jackson said, stepping forward with steel in his voice. His hand hovered near his holster as he turned toward Officer Johanna. "Get the drivers. I want them taken to the precinct immediately."

Johanna gave a sharp nod and pivoted on her heel, already pulling out her radio as she strode toward the hallway.

"As for you two," the sheriff said, turning back to Valerie and Garrett, "you're coming with me."

Valerie's jaw dropped. Garrett didn't move.

"You can't be serious!" the author exclaimed. "I'm the victim here!"

The only problem for him was that no one was listening anymore. Footsteps echoed behind me. I turned to see Lucas Silverthorne approaching. He looked as impeccable as ever, but I noticed the strain around his eyes, the tension in the set of his jaw. He'd always appeared in complete control, but the constant spells must've really taken it out of him today.

Still, he managed a faint smile as he read the situation at a glance. "Sheriff, please allow me to escort you and your...guests...to somewhere less conspicuous until we can transport them to the precinct," he said, voice low and composed. "I think you might be running low on seats in the cruisers, and there's no reason to disturb the rest of the party."

The sheriff grunted. "Good plan. We don't need this turning into a circus."

I couldn't help but smile, a sense of relief washing all of my doubts from the day away.

If this was a circus, at least now the ringleaders were in cuffs.

A Quiet Resolution

MINDY GRABBED MY HAND as Lucas led the sheriff and the others away. "Oh, Harper, how can I ever thank you?" she said, her voice trembling with gratitude.

I patted her hand, offering a small smile. "There's no need. I'm just glad we figured it out in time before your reputation was tarnished by this mess."

She exhaled sharply, her shoulders relaxing. "I need to call New York straight away. This kind of publicity..." She hesitated, biting her lip. "You know how they say all publicity is good publicity? Not this time."

"Yeah, I've heard something to that effect," I said.

Mindy sighed. "Well, this is going to be a disaster. They need to know what's happening. I need to get my phone back and start doing damage control."

I nodded sympathetically. "With the sheriff taking care of business, maybe check in with Lucas? I bet he knows where your phone ended up." And, with any luck, he'd quietly lift the shielding spell too.

She paused for half a second, then gave a small nod and hurried off.

As Mindy walked off to make her call, I turned and headed back to the ballroom. Relief settled over me, but it was tempered by the knowledge that tonight's events would leave ripples. I'd done what I could to preserve Havenwood's reputation—and Spellbooks'—but the consequences were far from over.

The ballroom, still shimmering with glittering lights and polished marble, had lost some of its magic. I moved through the crowd, finding Bella, Gabriel, and Isadora one by one to update them on what had happened. After some discussion, we agreed Gabriel would continue playing Garrett for the public until we could give the "author" a more convincing exit.

At midnight, Gabriel, still in disguise, gave a grand farewell from the staircase. He waved to the crowd with a flourish, his gold ascot and mask catching the light as the guests cheered and applauded. He bounded up the stairs two at a time, flashing a confident smile. A few minutes later, he reappeared as himself, having swapped the costume for a simpler ensemble. No one seemed to notice the switch, their attention already waning as the night stretched on.

Soon after, the guests began filtering out, the late hour catching up with them. I joined Bella, Gabriel, Isadora, and an exhausted-looking Lucas by the door to see them off. Vivienne emerged from the shadows, her expression as serene as ever.

"So, what happened?" Gabriel asked his mother, his tone curious but cautious.

She raised a finger to her lips, shaking her head slightly. "Now's not the time, son," she murmured, tipping her head towards the remaining guests.

Gabriel nodded, though he didn't look happy about it.

When the last masked guest disappeared into the night and the music faded into memory, exhaustion settled in. Glitter still clung to the marble floors, but the illusions were gone and there were still things to resolve.

As Lucas returned their phones with a quiet efficiency, the fallout began. Savannah stood in the foyer, arms crossed. Her gaze flicked to the room where the sheriff still detained Garrett and Valerie. Savannah snatched the phone from Lucas, pressing it to her chest.

"I could turn this into a media storm," she said aloud, though no one had asked. Her voice was too calm, too measured. "Play the betrayed fiancée, milk it for sympathy and reach."

Vivienne tilted her head, expression unreadable. "But you won't."

Savannah exhaled. "No. I'm not giving him the satisfaction. Or the attention."

She smoothed her gown, slipped her phone into her clutch, and walked out without another word. The sharp click of her heels faded as she strode into a future she hadn't planned.

"She's not going public?" I murmured.

Gabriel leaned in. "I think Mother might've made her a deal, and, knowing my mother, I'll bet Savannah took it."

Tiffany glided forward, flanked by Nate. Her face was drawn, lips pressed into a thin line. "Same old Garrett," she muttered, voice tight as she accepted her phone from Lucas. "Still only thinking about himself and not caring who he hurts as long as he gets what he wants."

She turned to Nate, brushing invisible dust from his sleeve. "I swear, if you ever pull something half as idiotic—"

"I won't," he blurted out, then looked at Gabriel. "For what it's worth...I was wrong. I got defensive. But I wasn't trying to cover for him. I just was scared for my dad. I didn't think he'd do something so stupid."

Gabriel gave him a quick nod. "Don't worry about it. Stress can get the better of all of us." He paused and then lowered his voice. "You don't have to be your dad, you know. You can choose to do better, to *be* better. And that choice counts for everything."

Nate looked taken aback, pausing for a moment as Gabriel's words sunk in. Then, the other man gave a small nod, a faint but genuine smile lifting the corners of his mouth. "I like that."

Gabriel returned the smile and offered his hand. Nate hesitated and then took it, shaking it firmly. As he turned to escort his mother out of the Silverthorne manor, I noticed he stood taller, as if something had relieved him of a burden.

Dirk strode up, holding his security badge like it had personally betrayed him. "I quit," he said simply, handing it to Mindy. "Body guarding a guy who fakes a kidnapping? No thanks." He accepted his phone from Lucas and marched out of the manor without a backward glance.

Mindy looked at the badge in her hand, appearing to be slightly stunned.

"Are you okay?" I asked.

She shook herself as if waking from a nightmare. "Yeah. Better than okay. My company wants me to head the rest of Valerie's projects until they can hire her replacement," she said quietly. "The big boss thinks I've earned it. Apparently, being loyal, organized, and not involved in felonies goes a long way. I can't believe that I'm getting my big break!"

I squeezed her arm. "From what I've seen you absolutely deserve it. Congratulations!"

She beamed. "Thanks! It still feels like a dream, though. But this time, I'm waking up in charge. Oh, I've got so much to do!"

I waved goodbye as she hurried towards the door, phone already pressed to her ear. As I watched her go, a sudden realization struck me. We'd all worn masks tonight. Some were literal, and some weren't, but when the glamor of the masquerade faded and the guests disappeared, what lingered wasn't the sparkle or spectacle.

It was the truth. Who we were underneath the polish. The loyalty that held strong. The courage that rose when it mattered. The quiet, steady magic of becoming.

Because in the end, the real strength, the real transformation, didn't come from donning a mask.

It came from daring to take it off.

Zeroes and Wings

Once everyone had left, Vivienne turned to the five of us. "We have a few matters to wrap up, and I think you all deserve to see how justice is served in Havenwood."

I wasn't about to argue. Curiosity nearly had me bouncing with excitement. Then again, maybe it was the sugar rush from the éclairs that had gotten to me. I'd been nervously cramming treat after treat into my mouth in an effort to distract myself as I wondered what was happening.

We followed Vivienne as she led us to the drawing room, where a tray of tea and snacks had been set out. A moment later, and, much to my surprise, the sheriff ushered an uncuffed Valerie and Garrett past the open door of the drawing room and out of the manor. Valerie and Garrett refused to make eye contact with anyone, including each other as the sheriff loaded them into the back of his police cruiser. I nearly choked when I recognized the fourth person trailing behind them.

It was Nathaniel Ravenscroft, Granny Bea's lawyer.

He moved with quiet efficiency, handing Vivienne a folder before offering her a formal bow and leaving without a word, shutting the door to the drawing room behind him.

As soon as we were alone, Vivienne addressed the room. "What I'm about to say must stay within these four walls," she said, her tone carrying a gravity that silenced any protests.

I nodded, as did Bella, Gabriel, Isadora, and Lucas. Satisfied, Vivienne continued. "Valerie St. James and Garrett Grimshaw are not being imprisoned. No one is to comment on this publicly."

My jaw dropped, but Isadora beat me to demanding an explanation. "What? But why? Harper said they were guilty, that they staged the kidnapping, and the sheriff charged them with a bunch of things!"

"They did," Vivienne replied, her tone measured. "But I convinced everyone that there was a better option for all involved."

"Does this include the drivers?" Gabriel asked, his calm tone a stark contrast to the outraged indignation in his sister's voice.

Vivienne grimaced, a rare crack in her composure. "Unfortunately, yes. They were discovered prowling around the grounds, likely attempting to finish the job Valerie hired them to do. However, charging them would have exposed the entire conspiracy and compromised what I believe to be the best step for Havenwood."

I blinked, a piece of the puzzle sliding into place. So that shadow I'd seen lurking in the hall hadn't been my imagination after all. It had likely been one of the drivers, poking around the manor, hoping to salvage the job.

Lucas interjected. "Best step? What are you talking about, Mother?"

Vivienne held up the folder Nathaniel had given her. "We entered into what's called a quiet plea deal. Valerie and Garrett have admitted their involvement in staging the kidnapping, but, on behalf of Havenwood, we have agreed to avoid full prosecution and prison time. They are both thankful to avoid the public scandal, as am I. I do not want Havenwood's name dragged through the mud in the press."

"That's not fair!" Isadora exclaimed. "They committed the crime; they should have to do the time. Isn't that how it works?"

"There's more than one way to punish someone," Vivienne said, her eyes glittering with calculated intent.

"Mother," Gabriel said, his voice a little more cautious, "what did you do?"

Vivienne smiled. "The best I could. As part of the plea deal, Valerie will resign, effective immediately, and will pay a substantial settlement fee to Miss Sullivan for the emotional distress her little stunt caused." She handed me a thin legal envelope, and I hesitated before opening it. "I'm sure you'll find the amount quite satisfactory," she said. "If so, Mr. Ravenscroft will be over in the morning with a conditional NDA for you to sign."

My hands trembled as I opened it, revealing a legal document with a number so large it didn't seem real. "That's a lot of zeros," I said, glancing up at Vivienne.

"Yes, well," she replied coolly, "it's the price one must pay to stay out of prison. And trust me, Valerie was happy to pay it in the end when I explained the other consequences available to her."

Bella wrapped her arm around me, staring at the settlement amount. "This is going to make such a difference for Spellbooks," she whispered.

I nodded, still too stunned to fully process the implications.

"And Grimshaw?" Lucas asked, his tone laced with suspicion.

Vivienne smiled slightly. "Mr. Grimshaw has agreed to pay his restitution in a different manner. He will fund an annual scholarship for Havenwood High School students interested in literature. Additionally, he will donate to the town's library, including a new wing."

"He's funding an entire new wing?" Gabriel asked. "Really?"

Vivienne nodded, a sly smirk playing on her lips. "Let's just say he much preferred the positive publicity option to the negative of being arrested and Martha Morningstar has been hinting for a new wing for years."

Isadora folded her arms, looking unconvinced. "How can we be sure they'll follow through?"

Vivienne held up the folder again. "The sheriff and I both have a copy of their signed confessions. Should they so much as breathe in the wrong direction, these documents will be released to the public. And as we've learned tonight, not all publicity is good publicity."

Gabriel exhaled with a wry smile. "You've thought of everything, haven't you?"

Vivienne returned his smile, her composure unshaken. "I always do."

As the night wound down, I felt a surprising sense of peace. The deal wasn't perfect, but it protected Havenwood's reputation and ensured justice, however unconventional. Spellbooks would thrive, and the truth had its own quiet victory. For now, that was enough.

Turning the Page

DESPITE THE LATE NIGHT, I found myself awake early, the soft light of dawn creeping through the curtains. The shop was silent, the kind of stillness that only came with the early hours of an untouched morning. Mr. Wigglesworth was curled up on the armchair by the window, his tail flicking in slow, dreamy movements. Luna, ever vigilant even in sleep, was snuggled in her hutch, her ears twitching towards the street as if standing sentinel in her dreams.

I tiptoed around the shop, laying out food for the animals and basking in the calm that blanketed Havenwood. It was a rare moment of quiet after the whirlwind of the past week. I brewed a fresh pot of coffee, letting its warmth and aroma seep into the corners of Spellbooks as I wrapped myself in a cozy blanket. Armed with my laptop and mug, I headed out to the sunroom overlooking the garden, where the morning was crisp but not too chilly. Spring might finally be on the way.

Settling into my favorite spot, I ran my fingers across the weathered wall and felt the familiar hum of the shop beneath my fingertips. Spellbooks was alive in its own quiet way, a comforting presence that had seen me through more than I could have imagined. Once comfortable, I began filling Spellbooks in on everything that had happened last night.

I had promised Vivienne I wouldn't share the details with anyone, but Spellbooks could hardly be considered a person. Besides, who was the shop going to tell?

I ended by explaining the quiet plea deal Vivienne had arranged and the substantial settlement she negotiated on my behalf.

"We're going to be okay," I told Spellbooks. "This money will see us through so we can keep the business afloat."

The shop responded with a warm, gentle vibration that rippled through the wall. I smiled, sipping my coffee as I pulled up my accounting software. For the first time in months, the numbers didn't feel like an insurmountable mountain. The settlement from Valerie would allow me to make overdue improvements to the shop's security system, expand our collection, and maybe even hire some help. I could finally see the light at the end of the tunnel.

The settlement couldn't have come at a better time, and I was grateful that Vivienne had thought of both me and Spellbooks. I wondered if it was her way of giving tacit approval of my relationship with Gabriel, but I wasn't going to ask. It felt like looking a gift horse in the mouth, and, despite everything, Vivienne still intimidated me.

I lost myself in the numbers, enjoying the quiet of the morning, until a sharp knock sounded on the walls behind me. Surprised, I looked around, wondering who was knocking on the walls of my shop. Then I realized it was likely Spellbooks alerting me to someone at the door. I placed a hand on the wall, feeling the warm vibration ripple under my palm.

"Okay, I'm coming," I said to the shop, gathering my things.

To my surprise, a bespectacled face stared in through the front window.

"Mindy?" I said, unlocking the door and opening it wide.

She stepped inside, pushing her hair out of her face and looking more put-together than I'd expected. "Oh, thank goodness. I was hoping you were up. I didn't wake you, did I?"

"Not at all," I said, gesturing toward the counter. "Come in. Can I get you a cup of coffee?"

"That'd be lovely, thank you," she said, her voice still tinged with lingering exhaustion from the night before.

I poured her a cup and handed it to her. "How are you holding up after, well, everything?" I asked.

She wrapped her hands around the cup, inhaling deeply. "I'll admit, it all came as a bit of a shock, but I am so grateful for what you did. You've made such a massive impact on my life, Harper. I can't thank you enough." A faint smile tugged at her lips. "That's actually why I came by, to try to express my gratitude. For everything."

"I'm just glad you're okay," I said, leaning against the counter. "But what's going to happen to you now?"

Mindy's eyes lit up with a mix of excitement and disbelief. "Well, after everything that happened, my firm called me this morning. They wanted me to take over her projects in the interim because of her sudden resignation, but they've just hired her replacement." Without pausing to let me respond, she rushed ahead. "It's me! Can you believe that? They offered me her position. Effective immediately, with a substantial raise and a bonus."

"That's amazing! Congratulations!" I said, genuinely thrilled for her. "How do you feel?"

She nodded, her smile growing. "Honestly? It's all a little surreal. I've been working toward this for years, and now it's finally happening. I couldn't have done it without you."

"You deserve it," I said firmly. "All I did was make sure the truth came out."

Mindy hesitated, then leaned forward slightly. "I was thinking...maybe we could work together? I mean, with my new position, I'll have a lot of say in where we send our authors. And after everything, I think Spellbooks deserves to be on that list. Permanently."

My breath caught. "What?"

"I mean, let's make this place a literary hub," she said with a grin. "Havenwood is special, Harper. And Spellbooks? It's one of a kind."

I blinked, overwhelmed for a moment, before a smile broke across my face. "Mindy, that's...incredible. Thank you. It means more than you know."

She reached across the counter, giving my hand a squeeze. "Consider it my way of saying 'thank-you'. This is a fresh start for both of us. And this time, I want to enjoy working with people who love books, not just making money."

As Mindy left, a quiet sense of fulfillment settled over me. Spellbooks wasn't just secure. Together, we were stepping into something bigger, something I hadn't even dared to imagine.

Later that morning, Bella, Gabriel, and Isadora stopped by. Each of them was eager to dissect the chaos of last night and, maybe more importantly, to make sure I was okay. We gathered around the small table, the scent of cinnamon scones and rich coffee in the air. The warmth of the shop wrapped around us like a familiar quilt, and for once, I didn't feel the need to fill the silence with reassurances or pretend I had everything handled.

Because the truth was—I didn't. Not always. And maybe that was okay.

"I have a confession," I said, fingers wrapped around my mug. "Things haven't exactly been going smoothly with the shop. I've been pretending everything's fine, but...it hasn't been. Not until recently."

No one flinched. No one looked disappointed.

Bella reached across the table and squeezed my hand. "You don't have to pretend with us, Harper. Not ever."

Gabriel nodded, his voice gentle. "We're in this with you. You don't have to carry your burdens alone."

Isadora lifted her coffee with a grin. "We're like the musketeers. Always there for one another." She tilted her head, considering. "But with fewer swords," she finished.

"Speak for yourself!" Luna called from her hutch.

"Luna with a sword?" Bella whispered. "Now, *that's* a terrifying thought."

Her words elicited a round of chuckles as we clinked our mugs together.

"What's going on over there?" Luna demanded.

"Nothing!" we chorused in unison, which brought on another round of laughter.

"It doesn't sound like nothing," Luna grumbled. "It sounds like the start of a radish ruckus and it's too early in the morning for that nonsense."

Something in my chest loosened. I hadn't realized how tightly I'd been gripping the belief that I had to *earn* this. That I had to be perfect to deserve the shop, the people, the magic.

I wasn't perfect. But I was still standing. Still trying. And that had to count for something.

"So," Bella said, nudging me playfully. "What's next for Spellbooks?"

I looked around at the mismatched mugs and the friends who had become a second family since I moved to Havenwood.

"We keep going," I said. "We keep growing. And we keep being exactly what we are."

Not flawless.

But enough.

And maybe even a little magical.

Thank you!

Dear Wonderful Reader,

Thank you for making it this far. I hope you enjoyed the story. Now, I'd like to share another, albeit much shorter one with you, along with a piece of my heart.

Once upon a time, I was a kid with mountains of notebooks, each one bursting with stories and dreams. Writing was my sanctuary, my escape from the world. But as I grew older, reality knocked on my door and whispered, "Writing won't pay the bills." So, I did the "sensible" thing and focused on the real world. For a while, at least.

Then came 2020, a year that turned many of our lives upside down. As an athlete and musician, I suddenly found myself unable to do the things I loved most. In a desperate bid to fight against depression, I turned back to writing. It was like finding a long-lost friend. The stories poured out of me, and I started to feel alive again.

Not that it has been without struggle. Trying to fit writing in around work, kids, and life is like juggling flaming torches while riding a unicycle. But I've kept at it. Since then, I've written and published over 20 books, each one a labor of love and infused with a piece of my heart. I'm not an overnight sensation or a best-selling author, nor do I have a stack of rejection letters from traditional publishers. Instead, I've taken a different path, connecting with incredible readers like you who cherish a good story and a touch of magic. These small victories, and the connections I make with readers like you, are what keep me going.

This is where you come in. Your review is more than just words on a screen—it's a lifeline, a beacon that helps me reach new readers and continue this incredible journey. If you could take just a few minutes to share your thoughts, I would be deeply grateful. I read every single review, and they touch my heart in ways you can't imagine.

So, if my stories have made you smile, laugh, or brought a little magic into your life, please let me know. Your support and feedback mean everything to me, and they help keep this writing dream alive for me.

Thank you for being a part of my story, for believing in my characters, and for sharing this journey with me.

With all my gratitude and a heart full of hope,

L.L. Gray

Your FREE novella is waiting

Want a free book?

Of course you do, what madness could possess someone to **not** want free books?
There's no catch - you do sign-up for my mailing list but you can unsubscribe at any time.
There's also no spam.
Ever.
Sign up here to get your free book!
https://www.subscribepage.io/havenwood

About the Author

L.L. Gray writes captivating, fast-paced fantasy full of wit, warmth, and magic. Her books transport readers to charming, cozy worlds brimming with lovable characters and whimsical adventures. A lifelong enthusiast of fantasy and myths, L.L. Gray blends humor and heart, inviting readers to escape into her spellbinding stories that feel like home—cozy, magical, and impossible to put down.

Psst, it's me—L.L. Gray!

I love connecting with fellow story lovers and adventure seekers. If that sounds like your cup of tea (or coffee, or whatever magical potion you prefer), come say hello! Visit my website www.llgray.com to join my newsletter, where you'll find exclusive goodies, or join us in my Facebook readers group. And if email is more your style, feel free to drop me a line anytime at info@llgray.com.

I hope you stay in touch!

Also By

Havenwood Paranormal Cozy Mysteries

The Mystery in the Margins
The Chaos in the Chronicles (exclusive novella)
The Puzzle in the Pumpkin Patch
The Secret of the Silver Serpent
The Riddle at the Revelry
The Manuscript in the Moonlight (exclusive novella)
The Heist of the Hidden Heart
The Mayhem in the Masquerade
The Legend of the Leaf
The Conspiracy on the Cruise (coming soon!)
The Curse at the Carnival (coming soon!)

Smoke and Shadows Series

Shadows and Relics
Pixie Pranks (exclusive novella)
Felons and Fangs
Bones and Blades
Tempest and Treason
Daggers and Deception
Sleuths and Scoundrels
Legacy and Lies
Crossroads and Curses

Children's Books

The Secret About Mistakes
Corner of the Sky
To Mom. Love, Me
To Dad. Love, Me
To Grandma. Love, Me
To Grandpa. Love, Me

Acknowledgments

To you, the reader: thank you for stepping into this world with me. I hope you felt the magic, warmth, and wonder woven into these pages. If you'd like to stay up to date with new releases and special content, head over to my website. And if you're looking to connect with a welcoming, book-loving community, join us on Facebook—there's always room for another story lover.

To my fabulous ARC and Street teams: you've become like a second family to me, cheering me on through every twist, turn, and chapter. Your unwavering support, encouragement, and excitement fuel my creative fire—I truly couldn't do this without each of you. Thank you for believing in these stories as much as I do.

Lastly, to my wonderful husband: your support is the foundation of every story I write. Thank you for believing in me, for being my rock, and for making all of this possible. I'm endlessly grateful to have you by my side.

Legendary Acknowledgments

Some readers visit a story.
Legends step into it.

This space is to thank those whose support rises above the ordinary. These are the readers that are quietly extraordinary, steadfast, and full of heart. Their encouragement helps carry the magic forward, even when no one is watching. They aren't just readers, but companions in the cozy, bookish adventure.

Thank you, dear Legends, for standing with these stories. Not behind the scenes, but beside them. Steady, present, and deeply appreciated for all you do to support Havenwood (and me!).

With heartfelt gratitude to:

Linda Woestendiek

From the bottom of my writerly heart (and Spellbooks' slightly chaotic shelves):

Thank you for being part of the story.

Curious about becoming a Legend?

Unlock early access to secret stories, cozy chats, exclusive content, and a magical seat at the table.